MOTOR DYNASTY

A Conner Pennington Novel

To Janice,
my loyal Conner
Pennington fan,
Rich

R.N. ECHOLS

outskirts
press

Outskirts Press, Inc.
http://www.outskirtspress.com

ISBN: 978-1-4787-9763-0

Cover Image by R.N. Echols

Outskirts Press and the "OP" logo are trademarks belonging to Outskirts Press, Inc.

PRINTED IN THE UNITED STATES OF AMERICA

To Mimi,
My chief editor,
My soul mate,
My life companion.
I love you.

Prologue

Automotive franchise dealerships are primarily controlled by the automotive manufactures. Granting a franchise may be based on a number of factors, including location and potential sales. Competition among the producers of automobiles is cut throat, for a market share. Positioning is critical to the success of a dealership.

In 1954 Ford Motor Company began producing the Interceptor, designed to be used by law enforcement agencies in the United States. For over fifty years the Police Interceptor was one of the primary vehicles used by most agencies.

Chrysler Corporation also wanted a piece of the pie and introduced a high-powered car for police use, although as used by the Missouri Highway Patrol this was a two-door hardtop. Not particularly suited for normal police operations, but certainly a striking vehicle. General Motors also became involved in producing specialized vehicles for law enforcement use.

Dealerships that won state bids for providing vehicles to the Missouri State Highway Patrol quickly saw their profits soar, as many of the local enforcement agencies relied on the wisdom of the Highway Patrol and purchased the very same vehicles that were being used by the state agency. Often, those vehicles were purchased from the same dealership, as the city fathers did not have to solicit bids for those purchases. If a dealership was fortunate enough to garner the bid from the state, they reaped huge profits from the sale of thousands of vehicles.

The probability of getting a state bid can be enhanced when a senior state senator on the appropriations committee is a silent partner in dealerships that are in a position to provide vehicles for law enforcement agencies. The financial benefits are tremendous, with greed and avarice fueling the automotive industry.

Such was the case when a well-known dealer, having obtained franchises from Ford, Chrysler, and General Motors, was found dead in his home. An accidental death from carbon monoxide poisoning. The investigation by the local police concluded that the dealer had accidentally left his automobile running when he returned home with his wife from a New Year's Eve celebration at the local country club. An unfortunate and tragic incident.

Years later, the granddaughter, while sifting through documents left by her grandfather, felt that the deaths may not have been accidental, as originally determined by the local police investigation. Having learned of an earlier case involving Conner Pennington, Private Investigator, she contacted him to explore the old case of an "accidental death." There were issues that led her to believe this incident was not an accident.

The intricate involvement of the auto industry, the franchised dealerships, and the political arena becomes entwined in a mystery of deceit, greed, passions and revenge as the case of the Motor Dynasty unfolds.

As in all cases, Conner Pennington searches for the truth.

Part One

Chapter 1

"Mr. Pennington, do you have a copy of your DD 214?" Sandra Williams was an administrator at the VA Hospital in St. Louis, Missouri. She wanted documentation of service periods and a record of service locations.

"I do have a copy of my DD 214, discharging me from my enlisted rank at OCS, showing an honorable discharge." I had worked for the State of Missouri and had earned enough years to retire, which I did. My retirement also ended my medical insurance. I knew that as a combat veteran I was eligible for Veterans Administration health benefits.

"We can accept that DD 214 into our records, but at the present time we are only taking combat veterans into the health care program. Let's see, you served in the Marine Corps, and you received a discharge from the Marine Corps to accept a commission, correct?"

"Yes, that is correct, on both questions. Unfortunately, I do not have a DD 214 for my time as an officer."

"Excuse me? Did you lose your DD 214? You know you can get a copy of that through the records center here in St. Louis. We will need that to show that you have been in a combat zone."

"Okay, Ms. Williams, I understand. Let me explain. I have my original orders assigning me to FMF/WESTPAC Ground Forces. In non-military jargon that simply translates to Fleet Marine

Forces/Western Pacific. On the back side of those orders there is a stamp, signed by a Marine commanding officer, indicating the time and date when I arrived in South Vietnam. Those orders specify that I was to report as commanding officer of Company A, 5th Tank Battalion, attached to the 26th Regimental Landing Team (RLT 26), 9th Marine Amphibious Brigade (9th MAB). I also have a copy of my orders when I returned to the United States thirteen months later."

"Well, Mr. Pennington, I will certainly need to make copies of those orders, but you will also need to contact the St. Louis record center to get a copy of your DD 214, which will show your time as an officer. When you get that information together, come back and see me." This was delivered with what I perceived to be a condescending smile.

"I'll put this as simply as I can. I cannot get a copy of my DD 214 showing my time as an officer, nor can you. That record is sealed, and has been ever since I left the Corps. I can't even discuss what is in that record." I thought about my often-accused role of being a smart ass and thought of adding to that comment that if I tell you about the closed record I will have to shoot you. Ms. Williams didn't seem to be the sort of person that would appreciate the unwarranted humor I sometimes displayed.

You need to curb your smartass humor, Conner.

"Mr. Pennington, this is very unusual. I'll have to get my supervisor to review this."

"I understand your position and I know you don't make the rules. I do have a letter from the Commandant of the Marine Corps thanking me for my honorable service, verifying the years I spent in the Marines as an officer. But, there is no available DD 214 for my time as an officer. I'll give you a copy of the letter from the Commandant and you can make copies of my original orders. Will that suffice for now?" Having worked in state government for over 26 years I understood the levels of bureaucracy and the limits extended to any employee in the system. Ms. Williams made copies of the information I had and indicated she would get back with me after a review by her supervisor.

Back in the parking lot of the VA John Cochran Hospital in downtown St. Louis I turned my cell back on and proceeded to my vehicle. I had one message on my phone, but didn't recognize the number. Or the female voice. "Mr. Pennington, this is Mandy Barrows. You probably won't recognize the name, as I'm sure you would remember me as Mandy Klienknect. It has been many years since I was one of your students in the Jefferson City Park Board ice skating program. I read in the paper that you recently solved a cold case in Jefferson City and that you are now a private investigator. I would like to hire you to investigate a possible crime. Please call as soon as you can. Thank you." I don't drive and talk on my cell. I thought this would be as good a time as any to call Mandy Barrows. I was in no hurry to get caught in the downtown St. Louis traffic again. Let's see what Ms. Barrows has in mind. She answered on the third ring.

"Hello, this is Mrs. Barrows." Well, that answers one question in my mind about Mandy's marriage status. Divorcees seldom use the title of "Mrs." As they move beyond the bonds of marriage, that title goes by the wayside.

"Hello. This is Conner Pennington. I had a message indicating that it was urgent I call you. And yes, Mandy, of course I remember you. As I recall, you were one of my son's first skating partners. I am a bit curious, though, about how you got my cell phone number and why you selected me for an investigation."

"Mr. Pennington. Thank you for returning my call so quickly. You were always punctual and detail oriented when you gave me skating lessons. I believe I mentioned that I saw an article in the paper recently that you had worked on a cold case in Jefferson City. The Valenti suicide case. I found Bobby Joe Valenti's number in the phone book and he gave me your cell number. He does like to talk, doesn't he? He emphasized that when you're on a case your mission is to arrive at the truth. That's exactly what I want. I live in St. Louis now and have for almost twenty years. So, are you available to work another cold case?"

"Well, Mandy, I'm between cases, at the moment, so I may be available. Tell me briefly what this is about. The urgency of your message gave me a sense that you felt you may be in danger."

"Oh, I'm sorry. No, I don't think I'm in any danger. Maybe all of this is just my creeping paranoia, suspicions, or whatever. This situation goes back to 1958 and relates to the deaths of my grandparents. My grandfather started an automobile dealership in Jefferson City over eighty years ago, and died over forty years ago. I was going through some of his old papers and came across some documents that leads me to believe he and my grandmother did not die accidentally, as was reported by the Jefferson City police. If you are available, I would like for you to examine these documents and let me know if this is something you would be interested in investigating."

"Okay, Mandy. I don't charge for a consultation, but if I decide to investigate this case my fee is $175 an hour, plus expenses. Is that okay with you?"

"Mr. Pennington, I've done some research and your reputation is such that I trust both your discretion and your investigative skills. So, yes, I'm okay with your fee and I understand there may be nothing to my suspicions about the untimely deaths of my grandparents." Mandy Barrows must have been anxious to share her findings with someone that would reveal to her the truth about the deaths of her grandparents.

"Very good. Where and when can we meet to review the documents you mentioned?"

"My schedule is open tomorrow. All day. Does that work for you?" Mandy obviously wanted to get this investigation moving.

I haven't entirely progressed into the current century. I'll use technology when necessary, but my pocket size electronic calendar serves my needs and I quickly reviewed my appointment schedule. Sure, I could put all of that information in my computerized phone data bank, but old habits die hard.

"Okay. How about early afternoon, say around one thirty? Depending on where we meet. I live on the Illinois side of St. Louis. I will need to plan travel time to your location. Where do you have the documents?"

"I have the paperwork at my late parent's home in Creve Coeur. We could meet there. One thirty would work for me. Do you know where Creve Coeur is?"

"Yes, I do. Give me an address and I'll be there." I knew where Creve Coeur was. Anyone familiar with St. Louis knew where Creve Coeur was located and the reputation it had. A suburb of St. Louis. The City of St. Louis is unique in the state of Missouri. It is the only city in the entire state that is not located in a county. St. Louis City is restricted in land growth, as it is surrounded by St. Louis county. I also knew St. Louis was the only city in the state to have a Sheriff's Department and St. Louis county was the only county in the state to have a police department. Creve Coeur is in St. Louis county. Old money. Big homes. McMansions. Wrought iron fences and imposing gates. Yeah. Creve Coeur. I was sure Mandy Barrows could afford my fees. She gave me an address on Ladue Road, the heart of Creve Coeur. St. Louis area residents knew the French translation of Creve Coeur. Broken Heart. The city's emblem portrayed that image. A red heart with a jagged split down the middle.

Late the next morning I left Belleville, Illinois at 11:15 am, making allowances for road construction, particularly on the Poplar Street bridge, and whatever other traffic snarls there might be. I drove my red Maserati, thinking I might be less obtrusive in the old money neighborhood of Creve Coeur. Traffic was light, until I took the on ramp for Interstate 64 west. The Gateway to the West arch loomed on the horizon as I approached the Mississippi River bridge, always referred to as the Poplar Street bridge by the locals, and always under repair. Today was a continuation of the ongoing construction. Four lanes of traffic were being funneled into one lane. We've all been there. I don't need to tell you what that's like. I dropped the six-speed transmission from sixth gear down to first gear and spent the next 45 minutes exercising patience and resisting the urge to tap the steering wheel mounted paddle shift, shifting to a higher gear and moving around the traffic. I wasn't worried about distracted drivers. Hell, they had nowhere to go. Should have brought a novel with me. Instead, I tuned in my radio to a St. Louis oldies station.

Relax, Conner. You have plenty of time. Sister Mary Margaret Theresa once said, "Patience is a virtue, possess it if you can. Seldom found in a woman, and never in a man." Accept it, Conner. You've been in the military. You've been in state government, and now you're a private investigator. Patience is supposed to be one of your attributes.

The engineers in Modina, Italy, at the Maserati/Ferrari plant, were up to speed, so to speak. My Maserati Gran Sport had a navigation system, operated by inserting a disc into a slot under the center console arm rest. There was a minor problem with the system, unless you were touring Europe. Specifically, Italy. The disc contained maps of Italy and parts of surrounding countries. None of it current and the voice indicating locations was delivered in Italian. I was multi-lingual, but not so much in Italian. My multi-lingual abilities extended as far as saying in four different languages that I didn't speak that language.

Leaving the bridge behind, I was able to up-shift to fifth gear as the new Busch stadium, situated to my right, blatantly displayed the Cardinal's World Series wins, and traffic returned to the normal hectic race to some unknown destination. The sultry voice beside me told me I should continue driving on Interstate 64 for seven miles, then turn north on Lindbergh Boulevard. I originally called her Shirley, but it somehow seemed more fitting to give her an Italian name. Gina replaced Shirley with the snap of a finger and a change in mindset. She was my replacement for the basically nonexistent Italian navigation system. She wasn't always entirely reliable, but at least she spoke English. Although I was familiar with the St. Louis area, I relied on Gina to give me precise directions to the location of my meeting with Mandy Barrows. I talk to Gina often, but she never replies. She is the GPS voice on my cell phone.

Road construction at Kingshighway presented another snarl of traffic. Gina hadn't mentioned this delay. Off ramp construction on my right and an accident on my left. Red and blue lights flashing, vehicles moving at a snail's pace and a St. Louis cop standing in the roadway waving trucks, SUVs, and high-rise pickups through a chicane that challenged even the most skilled drivers. As Gina and I crawled past the St. Louis police officer my memory banks reverted to my past experiences with the St. Louis Police Department. Based on my conversations with older officers, I knew that in the past they all carried .38 caliber revolvers in holsters with a flap over the butt of the weapon. No quick draws and very cumbersome to access your weapon when you needed it most. This type of holster was referred to in the old days as a "Widow Maker." I rendered a half salute as I passed the officer and noted that the .38 revolver and Widow Maker holster had been replaced by what appeared to be a tactical holster and a Glock .9mm semi-auto. Progress, no doubt.

My retention of useless information and old jokes surfaces when I least expect it. The traffic cop I had just passed resembled an old friend that spent years with the St. Louis PD. He also had a strong connection with the St. Louis Mafia, but that's another story. Over a cup of coffee, Crazy Joe told me his slanted version of a traffic stop.

"A man was driving with his wife in the northern district on I-70, westbound. Crazy Joe was partially hidden, parked on the side of the on

ramp at Jefferson Boulevard and I-70, working radar. His radar locked on a vehicle that he clocked at a speed registering on his radar unit as being 20 miles per hour above the posted limit. Crazy Joe flipped on his lights and hit the switch for his wailing siren. The offender was quickly overtaken. Pulling to the side of the highway the driver waited for the marked police unit. Joe approached the offending driver, keeping his hand on the Widow Maker, and asks the driver for his license and insurance, while also noting the presence of a female passenger in the right front seat. The driver asks, "What's the problem, officer?" Joe replies with his officious stern look and voice, "Sir, I clocked you at twenty miles per hour over the posted speed limit. I'm issuing you a citation for excessive speed." The driver then comes back with an innocence and a condescending remark that he never, ever goes over the speed limit. His passenger responds with, "John, you know you always drive over the speed limit." Looking at his wife he replies, "Would you be quiet?" Crazy Joe doesn't stop there. "Sir, I also noticed that you didn't have your seat belt on. That's an additional offense I'm adding to your citation."

"Oh no, sir. I always wear my seat belt. I just took it off to get my driver license out of my wallet." Wifey interjects again, "John, you know you never wear your seat belt." This results in another reprimand from John. "Will you shut the hell up?" By this time Crazy Joe is having fun with John and his wife. "Sir, I also noticed you have a broken tail light lens, which doesn't pass our vehicle inspection regulations. I'm adding that violation to your citation." John just won't acknowledge he has ever done anything wrong. "That must have just happened today. I sure didn't know about that." His wife doesn't let him off the hook. "John, you know that has been broken for at least six months." His face is red as a beet as he turns to her. "Damn it, for the last time, shut your mouth!" Crazy Joe leans down to look through the open window and addresses the innocent, demure wife. "Ma'am, does he always treat you like that?" Her reply ends the story. "No sir, only when he's been drinking!"

There is absolutely no relevance in this long-winded joke to my upcoming meeting with Mandy. Just more useless information and part of entertaining myself. Gina interrupts my thoughts and tells me to take the exit ramp to Lindbergh Boulevard one quarter mile from now. I really didn't need to hear that from Gina. I was quite familiar with this area. The only thing I didn't know for sure was the exact location of the address given to me by Mandy Barrows. A few miles north on Lindbergh, then west on Ladue. I was early for my appointment with Mandy when Gina told me my destination was 500 yards on my right. Gina then succinctly informed me that I had arrived at my destination. Grandiose life size lions stood regally on elevated pillars located on both sides of a driveway that snaked to the north through mature trees. A wrought iron fence was partially obstructed by overgrown hedges that were no longer simply hedges. More like untended trees. I try to be punctual with my appointments. Not too early. Not too late. To kill some time, I drove further west on Ladue to the entrance of a country club a quarter of a mile from the address Barrows had given me as the residence of her late father.

The world has gone casual. Very few men wore ties, even in an office environment. I parked near the palatial country club, turned off my cell phone and stepped out of my vehicle to make sure I was presentable. A potential new client and I truly believed first impressions were important. It seemed the latest in-thing for men was some level of facial hair. I had grown a beard, which I kept neatly trimmed. My friends and associates assured me that I looked more academic. Like a college professor. I wasn't sure that was the image I really wanted to present, but it seemed to work to my benefit so far. My dark brown silk shirt was mostly covered by a light cashmere sport coat. It was late May and warm, so the jacket wasn't necessary for keeping out any chill. Mostly worn to conceal my shoulder holster, providing quick access to the Walther PPK semi-auto that was nestled under my left arm. Under my right arm was a leather pouch that secured two extra magazines in an upside-down position. Tan slacks and a light brown leather belt complimented my polished brown Italian leather driving shoes. Ah, the shoes. Very comfortable for driving, or even running, but only if running is absolutely necessary. I had purchased them at an exclusive store while visiting Key Largo, Florida. Checking my wrist mounted time keeping device, as the millennials referred to my Timex watch, I noted that I had five minutes before my scheduled appointment at the Barrows address.

Returning to Ladue Road I drove slowly to the twin lions and turned onto the cracked blacktop driveway. An eight-foot tall wrought iron gate, hinged on both sides, had been left open. Perhaps in anticipation of my arrival. The lush green trees encroached on the narrow drive, obscuring what lay ahead and almost brushing the sides of my Maserati as I negotiated the undulating curves leading to what I guessed would be an older estate.

Approximately 800 yards from the front gate a fountain sat in the center of a circular drive. At least it appeared to be a fountain. Cascading water was absent from the center figure of a bigger than life Neptune, clutching the traditional trident. Now that I could identify with. The Trident is the recognized symbol of the Maserati. At the apex of the drive was a three-story home. Four white fluted columns, adorned with Tuscan caps, supported a second level balcony. Substantial carved wooden double doors artfully displayed stained glass inserts. Snarling heads of the twin lions at the front gate were repeated in heavy brass on each door. They appeared to be replicas of the brass door knockers at One Downing Street in London. I parked at the top of the circle and walked up six broad granite steps to the front doors. The thud of the brass knocker on the right-side door received a quick response.

It must have been quite similar to opening a heavy bank vault door. The doors were at least nine feet tall, culminating on the top at the bottom of an ornate marble center piece. As the door swung open I was greeted by the lady of the house.

"Mr. Pennington. You are precisely on time. I like that. I see you appreciate finely engineered automobiles. I like that, too. A Maserati Gran Sport, right? Please come in."

"Mrs. Barrows. A pleasure to see you again after all these years."

"Please, please. Call me Mandy, as you did many years ago."

Barrows was five six or seven and slender. Difficult to tell age with some women, but my guess would be a well cultured and elegantly mature forty-something. Her hair was highlighted in what I had observed to be the current trend among classy ladies. Very little makeup and minimal jewelry. An ivory pendant hung from a gold braided chain around her neck. The ivory appeared to have been carved to resemble perhaps a family crest. Her attire consisted of a causal jogging suit, the color and texture of gardenia pedals. My olfactory senses may have been affected by the color of the jogging suit, but I thought I caught the subtle scent of gardenias. Pleasant and not overpowering, as some scents can be.

I stepped into an entryway that was dimly lit by a crystal chandelier, fifteen feet above my head. The floor was polished marble, partially covered with a muted oriental rug.

"I lived in Jefferson City for many years before moving to St. Louis as an adult, but St. Louis is now my home. When you gave me figure skating lessons I thought, as many girls did at the time, that I would be skating in the Olympics. Of course, that didn't happen. I still skate some, but not often enough. Just too many other things that occupy my time."

I remember voices, which don't change that much over the years. "Mandy, it's really good to see you again. I dare say, you were one of my best students. I guess I lost track of you over the years and hadn't even realized you had moved to St. Louis. Please, call me Conner. I didn't associate the name Barrows with the four dealerships your father had in Jefferson City. I seem to recall that he expanded his operations into the St. Louis area with "Royal Motors" and franchises for Rolls Royce and Bentley automobiles. Quite a success."

"Yes, he was very successful, which is relative to my request for your investigative skills. This home belonged to my parents. They both died eight years ago. They were involved in a high-speed police chase on Lindbergh Boulevard. Such a horrible tragedy. It happened at one of those crossover intersections when a fleeing stolen vehicler veered into the oncoming lane, resulting in a head-on collision, killing both of my parents. I'm now married to a surgeon, who spends a lot of time at the hospital and I volunteer my time with a number of charity organizations. Sorry, I'm sure that's more than you wanted to know."

"No, no. That's fine, Mandy. It helps me to know more about the people I'm working with, especially if I decide to investigate the deaths of your grandparents."

"Okay. Anyway, we live in Ladue, but I wanted to meet here, as this is where my father's records were kept. Documents from my grandfather were gathered by my father and they are here also. We have caretakers coming in once a month to maintain and clean the home, but it has not been occupied since the death of my parents. I inherited the estate, but just haven't been able to bring myself to sell. A month ago, I convinced myself it was time to think of selling. There are still a lot of memories, keepsakes, and records that need to be gone over before I can bring in a crew to rehab the home. I was intent on shredding old records handed down from my grandfather, until I came across a journal, a couple of scrapbooks and some old dealership records."

Mandy led me down a broad hallway with hardwood parquet floors, past a huge sitting room. Furniture was still in place but covered with white sheets. The hallway was decorated with what appeared to be original paintings, depicting sailing ships, stormy seas, and random paintings of classic automobiles. One prominent painting caught my attention. A deep maroon 1938 Mercedes Benz Type 500K roadster. In my opinion, one of the most beautiful automobiles ever built. The "K" designation was for the German word, Kompressor, meaning supercharged. The long hood was necessary to cover the straight 8-cylinder engine, equipped with a Roots supercharger. The huge chrome headlights on each side of the signature Mercedes grill were complimented by matching spot lights mounted near the split windshield, which crossed the graceful cowl. Sweeping fenders descended to functional running boards, extending to the rear of the suicide doors. Chrome instruments were strategically located in a polished Spanish walnut dash. An original 500K, formerly owned by Baroness Gisela von Krieger recently sold for close to 12 million dollars. Very impressive.

I paused to admire the 500K just as Mandy reached an intricately carved mahogany door. With her hand on the brass door lever she turned toward me. "Beautiful car, isn't she? I love those hand-built coaches, the elegance and fine leather, wire wheels, and throaty engines."

"You echo my sentiments exactly. You piqued my interest when you mentioned this investigation would involve automobiles. Let's see what you have, Mandy."

When she opened the door, I stepped into my dream room. A multi-shelved library, with a ladder on rollers to reach the top layer of leather bound books. Hundreds of books. A large mahogany desk sat to one side, with an overstuffed worn leather chair. The leather was beginning to crack and showed signs of frequent use. Piled on the floor and desk were 15 to 20 white cardboard records boxes, of the variety I had often seen in the office of the lawyer I worked for in Belleville.

"Well, Conner, here it is. I haven't gone through all of this yet, but there are records here you might find interesting."

Mandy first picked up a scrapbook that was on top of the desk, centered on a leather desk blotter. "I won't prejudice your judgement with what I think is important. Just peruse the contents and let me know what you think. My father compiled this scrapbook. If you believe I'm being paranoid about what I think is there, I'll accept that. I have some things to take care of in other parts of the house, so make yourself comfortable. Would you like something to drink? A glass or wine, water, soda?"

"No, thank you. I'm fine." Mandy left the library and I settled into the big leather chair facing the desk and opened the scrapbook. On the first page was an aging news article.

Jefferson City News Tribune
January 1, 1958
LOCAL CAR DEALER AND WIFE FOUND ASPHYZIATED

Gerard Klienknect and his wife Marilda were found at 10:45 this morning in their bedroom at 2642 Hobbs Lane by a close friend and associate, Senator Antonio Giocomolli of St. Louis. Senator Giocomolli stated that he had been with the Klienknects the previous evening and he was scheduled to meet them for brunch at the Jefferson City Country Club at 9:00 a.m. to celebrate the new year. The senator also stated that he had been friends with the Klienknects for many years and had always known them to be punctual. When the Klienknects had not arrived at the club by 9:30 a.m., the senator called their home, but did not receive an answer. Not able to reach his friends by telephone, he then drove to their nearby home. After repeated ringing of the doorbell and knocking loudly, the senator stated that he tried the front door and found it be unlocked. Entering the home, he called out their names, but again received no response.

Moving toward the master bedroom he noted with alarm that the door in the kitchen that led to the garage was open and the automobile parked there was running. Exhaust fumes from the automobile permeated the home. While still calling loudly for the Klienknects he rushed into the garage, opened the garage door and shut off the engine.

Arriving in the master bedroom he found his friends in bed, apparently asleep. He quickly determined they were not asleep. Rushing to the bedside he used the phone to call for medical assistance. An ambulance and Jefferson City Police arrived within minutes.

Mr. and Mrs. Kleinknect were pronounced dead at the scene. Preliminary findings indicate carbon monoxide poisoning. Investigations by the Jefferson City Police Department are ongoing.

An unusual article to be found at the front of a family scrapbook. Typically, a family scrapbook begins with the start of a family and progresses to their later years in life. I turned to the next page, which contained another news article.

Jefferson City News Tribune
January 12, 1958
ACCIDENTAL DEATHS OF MR. AND MRS. KLIENKNECT

The Jefferson City Police Department has concluded their investigation into the recent deaths of a local car dealer and his wife. Witnesses at the Jefferson City Country Club have stated that the Klienknects were at the Country Club late on New Year's Eve, celebrating the incoming year. Friends indicated the Kienknects left the club around 1:00 a.m. and were seemingly in control of their faculties.

The JCPD investigating officer has concluded, based on the available evidence, that the Klienknects arrived home within ten minutes, as they lived only one mile from the club. Having celebrated with Champaign during the evening, it was the conclusion of the investigators that when the couple arrived home Mr. Klienknect drove into the garage, parked his vehicle, and forgot to turn off the ignition. An additional error was made when the door from the garage to the kitchen area was left open.

An autopsy confirmed carbon monoxide poisoning and high levels of alcoholic content in the systems of both victims. The county coroner, Seth Overstreet, has ruled the two deaths an unfortunate accident. Time of death was estimated to be between 3:30 and 5:00 a.m. on New Year's Day.

Mr. Kleinknect was a well-known automobile dealer in this region, owning and operating five dealerships in Jefferson City and Columbia. A close friend and associate, Senator Antonio Giocomelli of St. Louis, had discovered the Klienknects after they did not arrive at the Country Club for a prearranged brunch.

Senator Giocomelli stated, "This is such a tragedy. I have known the Klienknects for many years and they were such delightful people. They will be terribly missed."

The following pages in the scrapbook were what I expected. Photos. Lots of photos. A photo of Gerard had been included with the initial notice of the accidental deaths. The first photo I saw that followed the news articles was a posed shot of a younger Gerard Klienknect and a gentleman with his arm across the shoulder of Gerard. A hand-written note below the photo identified the pair as Gerard and Senator Antonio Giocomelli. Additional photos portrayed a younger Gerard and more photos of the senator.

I found it interesting that the album had been compiled beginning in the more recent years, then reaching back in time. Subsequent photos were of an older Gerard, many of them showing him in front of various dealerships that he apparently owned. Standing in front of a 1956 Dodge was a middle-age Gerard, with a Chrysler sign on the building showing ROYAL MOTORS. Almost cut off in the black and white photo was a 1956 Dodge, with Missouri Highway Patrol markings. An earlier photo on the next page of the album showed an even younger Gerard at another dealership. The Ford dealership simply had the KLIENKNECT FORD sign prominently displayed. I knew from experience that most dealers wanted their name on the marque. Whether it was vanity, ego, or name recognition I couldn't say. I suspected a combination of all of those. An accompanying photo showed Gerard proudly standing in front of a new 1954 Ford Interceptor, with distinctive Missouri Highway Patrol emblems and the old-style bubble light mounted on the roof.

The next photo made it obvious to me that the album had not been compiled in a chronological order of ascending or descending years. Gerard had posed with Senator Giocomelli in front of a 1958 Chevrolet sedan, adorned with Missouri Highway Patrol markings. A sign in the distance proudly proclaimed this to be the KLIENKNECT CHEVROLET dealership. Although the photos were a bit grainy, it appeared there were similar models lined up on the parking lot, all with STATE TROOPER on the front fender and across the trunk lid. All of them with the shield of the Missouri State Highway Patrol on the doors. Interesting. I glanced back at some photos showing Dodge autos with Patrol markings and noticed something unusual. Almost all law enforcement vehicles today are four door sedans. The Dodges in the photos were two-tone light blue and white and were two door hardtops.

I quickly understood this was not a family photo album. No Kleinknect family members were shown in any of the photos. Dealerships, automobiles, Gerard and Senator Giocomelli. I wasn't sure what relevance this would have in an investigation, or even why Mandy would have me peruse the album, although it was interesting to see the progression of a successful man expanding his operations in the auto industry. Good for him. And it seemed to me, at the time, that it was such a tragedy his life ended with such a mishap. In a later photo Gerard stood proudly in front of a shiny Cadillac. Perhaps this was the motor car he owned at the time of his death. Killed by one of his own vehicles that he apparently loved. A new limited-edition Cadillac Eldorado Brougham.

Further into the album there were more photos of the senator, one of them showed the senator with a young man I assumed to be his son. They were both casually dressed in what appeared to be golfing attire. Although the golf course at the Jefferson City Country Club had been totally redesigned several years ago, I saw a resemblance to the course that had been in use for over fifty years. There wasn't what I would call a family resemblance, as the senator was olive skinned and the young man with him was not. Still, the senator probably had a wife with a light complexion. The senator's right arm was loosely draped over the shoulder of the young man.

Before I could entertain any deep thoughts about why Mandy wanted me to look through the album, she returned to the library.

"Mr. Pennington, a lot of history there. Sorry, I know you asked me to call you Conner. When you were instructing me at the ice rink I always called you Mr. Pennington. I was taught to respect my elders, no offense. I guess I still think of you as Mr. Pennington."

"No offense taken, Mandy. I always appreciated your respect. It seems these are less formal times now, so I'm quite okay with you calling me Conner."

"Yes, I understand. A lot of things have changed over the years. You've aged well, and I like the beard. Again, no offense about the age comment. You still have the steely blue eyes I remember, but something has changed. I can't put my finger on what that is. Just an observation."

"Just age, Mandy. Just age."

"I suppose we're all getting there. Are you still married Conner?"

"I'm currently in a relationship with a lovely lady, but no, I'm not married."

"Anyway, before I ask for your thoughts concerning the album, I would like for you to look though this journal. My grandfather kept a record of every dime he spent. It's all here. More than thirty years of record keeping. I'm not a detective, but there are some things in there you might find interesting. I did." With that, Mandy left me with a large ledger book, bound in dark green leather. A quick glance in the book revealed line after line of hand written entries and dollar amounts. The lettering was precise and listed each item for payment. Okay, I'm a private investigator, not an accountant. Why am I researching accounting records?

What did Mandy see that I had not yet found? I had been in the library for almost two hours and thought about how bad the St. Louis rush hour and the Poplar Street Bridge traffic would be when I left this old home and drove back to my residence in Belleville on the east side of the Mississippi. I rose from the old leather chair and went in a search for Mandy. After calling her name and getting a distant response, I found her in the dining room. Piles of sterling silver serving ware, goblets and flatware covered an ornate dining table that could seat at least sixteen guests. Two chandeliers were centered above each end of the long, heavy mahogany table.

"Sorry, Conner. I got caught up in an inventory of all this silver. Probably the only value is in the silver content, and even the value of that has gone down in the past few years. I've heard that younger generations don't set a dining table the way my mother did, and I don't either, so the market value for ornate silverware is off quite a lot. Most likely they just don't want to go through the trouble of polishing this stuff. Different times. Anyway, have you found anything yet that looks interesting or suspicious?"

"It's all interesting, Mandy, but I haven't found anything yet that indicates a crime has been committed. Could I possibly take the album and the accounting journal with me for further study?"

"Sure. Does that mean you will undertake an investigation? I also have some folders and boxes of legal documents that I will send with you, if that's okay with you. There's a lot of information in those papers. I'm sure you didn't plan on staying here all afternoon, but I'll be here for some time yet. I have the folders, boxes, album and journal in the library and you can gather whatever other items you think might assist you in your investigation."

Driving my Maserati today may not have been a wise choice because of its limited trunk space. It barely accommodates a reduced size golf bag with only four or five clubs.

"I'm not going to make a commitment at this point, but I will go over these items and make a determination about the validity of a continuing investigation. I'll let you know by the middle of next week. I may need to return later and examine more of these records."

"Thank you, Conner. I've always appreciated your honesty, even when you told me you didn't think I should set my sights on an Olympic spot in figure skating. I'll help you carry out whatever items you want to take with you today."

We carried enough to my car to fill the limited trunk space. Mandy stepped forward when I turned to open the driver side door and she glanced inside the Maserati.

"I've been in a lot of very nice cars, but never a Maserati. I love exotic cars. Maybe someday you'll take me for a ride?" She gave me a hug, then turned back to the estate. I have never been opposed to a hug from a lovely lady.

Just as I was stepping into the cockpit I heard Mandy's voice. "Thank you, Conner. You know how to reach me. Bye for now."

As I pulled onto the curving driveway I saw Mandy in my rear-view mirror, standing by the Neptune fountain, watching as I drove through the overgrown trees and shrubs. Maybe it was a misread action of throwing an air kiss, but most likely just a simple wave. Perceptions can be deceiving.

I drove on.

Chapter 2

Leaving the Barrow estate, I turned left on Ladue and retraced the route Gina had provided earlier. Back on I-64 I drove east toward downtown St. Louis and reflected on my meeting with Mrs. Mandy Barrows. I'm human and not immune to attractive ladies, but I also had my own lovely lady at home.

Get your mind on the case, Conner. If, in fact, there is a case.

Traffic was not as congested as it was when I earlier drove to the Barrows estate. Arriving home, I pulled into the garage and began unloading the items I had gathered from the estate in Creve Coeur.

Margo heard the garage door opening and came through the connecting door to the garage, looking sensual and ravishing as usual. Any thoughts of Mandy quickly dissipated.

"Welcome back, handsome. How did your meeting go?"

"Interesting, but I'm not sure yet that there is even a case to investigate at this point. I've brought some items that Mrs. Barrows thought had some relevance to an investigation in what may be some level of misdeeds. I just don't know yet."

"So, what was it like to reconnect with one of your past ice skating students? What's she like?"

I knew from experience that you never pit one woman against another. The only loser will be **you.** "Well, she's certainly older than when I gave her ice skating lessons. She's an attractive lady, married to a surgeon. Lives in Ladue and finally getting around to selling her parent's estate. For some reason, she seems to think the deaths of her grandparents was not accidental, as was determined by an investigation at the time. Not to worry, my dear, you are still the loveliest lady and you're stuck with me. How about we plan on an early dinner at the Main Street Bar and Grill? I'll put this stuff in the office and then we can have a glass of wine."

"Sounds like a plan." Margo always likes to have a plan. Sometimes Plan A, Plan B, or even Plan C. Just in case.

Over a glass of wine, I confided in Margo that I had not seen anything in the items Mandy gave me that would indicate foul play or a reason for an investigation.

The Main Street Bar and Grill was busy. There were tables on the sidewalk and it was quite nice outside. Late May in southern Illinois can be very pleasant…at times. We opted for an outdoor seating arrangement. As we sat under a colorful umbrella a couple of motorcycles roared by. Harleys, no doubt. Harley Davidson even had a patent on the sound of a Harley. It reminded me of the rides Margo and I had taken in the past and I looked forward to more such rides through the countryside. Margo was not one of the ladies that rode "up", as the bikers say. She was not one to cling onto the operator of a motorcycle. She'll ride her own damn bike, if you please. Private pilot's license, expert pistol shot, and a trim five-foot two-inch lady who rides her own Harley Fat Boy. Many people have asked her how a lady her size could handle such a big bike, to which her response was usually the same, "It's not about size, it's about skill."

It was an enjoyable evening, as it always is with my lady.

Early the next morning I retreated to the office and opened the photo album Mandy had given me the day before. What had Mrs. Barrows seen in this album, or the other records, that had aroused her suspicions about the deaths of her grandparents? What role did Giocomelli play in this scenario? Page by page I scanned the album.

I brought out my magnifying glass to take a closer look at the photos. One photo in particular caught my attention. It was the photo of Giocomelli with his assumed son at the golf course. I called my friend, Crazy Joe. He knows the important Italians in St. Louis. Mostly those in low places, but I thought he may know something about Senator Antonio Giocomelli.

I first met Crazy Joe after I met Marie. Marie and Joe's wife were friends and worked together at Bell Telephone. Mind you, I wasn't the only one that called Joe "Crazy Joe." Marie was a certified nymphomaniac, and that was okay with me, at the time. Joe was also most likely certifiable at some level. When Marie was transferred to San Antonio, Joe's wife was also transferred to Texas. My career had ended with the Missouri Department of Public Safety and I moved to Texas, too. What the hell? Joe and I met frequently, over coffee, or a beer, or two. Joe liked to talk. I learned a lot about Joe. He was Italian. Joe Ferranti. His mother was from Sicily, but Joe had never been out of the United States. Didn't speak Italian either. Not much, anyway.

Back in St. Louis, Joe had been the driver and close friend of the Chief of Police for St. Louis. I was sure when Joe told me about this connection that there had been some background surrounding this that he hadn't shared with me. He had told me about his father who had driven a beer truck, even during prohibition. Unfortunately, he had been caught and did some time downstate for running alcohol. The proceeds from his illegal deliveries of beer went into the coffers of the "family." Joe's father never revealed who he was working for, served his time and the "family" looked after him and his wife for as long as he lived. It was an honor thing and a matter of loyalty. The "family" took care of family.

When I called, Joe answered on the third ring. "Joe, this is Conner. Let's do lunch." Not the usual euphemism. I really did mean "Let's do lunch." Joe knew that.

"Yeah, Conner, I can do that. When and where?"

"How about the Steak and Shake on Manchester Road?" I knew Joe lived close to that location after having moved back to St. Louis from San Antonio. "We can beat the lunch crowd if we meet there at 11:15."

"Right. I'll be there."

Sure. Joe was never on time. At 11:25 he walked in the door.

"Order what you want, buddy. Today it's on me." It was not my usual policy to let someone know I was paying for the meal before they ordered. On the other hand, I wanted some information from Joe and I was willing to at least pay for a lunch to get what I wanted.

"Joe, you told me a long time ago, when I questioned you about your long fingernail on your left pinky, that it was a family thing. Sort of an identification. You grow your fingernail long on the little finger of your left hand and the "family" knows you are connected. Is that right?"

"Okay, you're my buddy, but you don't want to get too much into this stuff. You know I keep this fingernail long and you know why. Where are you going with this?"

We were interrupted at this point by the waitress. "Good morning gentlemen. What can I get for you today?"

Joe always ordered coffee, regardless of the time of day. I ordered a Coke and we both ordered the patty melt and fries. I knew that was what Joe liked. Not necessarily a healthy diet, but I'll go along with the program.

"Okay, Joe, here's the deal. I know you are about 84.7 percent bullshit, but I need some straight stuff now. It's been at least twenty or twenty-five years, but I had a friend in the St. Louis PD that I went to lunch with. He was a captain in Internal Affairs. You may have known him. James Morelli. Anyway, we went to lunch on the Hill. I don't remember which restaurant and that part isn't really important. What I do remember is when we were seated in a back room there were four men that came up to the captain and each of them kissed him on each cheek. Some sort of Italian greeting? I didn't think so. I asked the captain what that was all about. His reply was that he did his job and they did their business. A mutual respect thing. I then asked, in a low voice, if these guys were Mafia. His short response was I shouldn't go there. Now, my question to you, Joe, are these types still around? Just maybe not so obvious?"

"Yeah, I knew Captain Morelli. Nice guy, even though he was Internal Affairs. He gave you good advice. You don't want to be asking too many questions about the family. You didn't hear it from me, but they're still around." Joe had scanned nearby booths before he gave me this last bit of information. His voice was so low I barely heard him, even though he had leaned halfway across the table. "Conner, you have any more questions about these guys we'll relax here, talk about traffic, sports, the weather, eat, then take a ride. Capisce?"

"Okay, Joe. I get it. So, tell me about your family. How's everybody doing?"

"I guess I don't have your current address. We sent out invitations and yours came back last week. Little Joe is getting married next month. June 24. That's a Saturday. The wedding and reception will be at the Laumeier Sculpture Park. You and your lady are going to be there, right?"

"Little Joe is getting married? Congratulations. Is he marrying the girl he's been living with for a while? I won't even check my calendar. We'll be there."

Our food had arrived, and Joe asked the waitress for a fresh cup of coffee, as his had gotten cold. Joe did that a lot. When he talked he didn't drink his coffee. He would typically go through three or four cups during a meal, but rarely drank more than one actual cup of coffee.

"Yeah, that's the one. Her name is Morgan. Now what kind of a name is that for a girl? I dunno, Conner. They broke up at least five times, but maybe it'll work. My daughter's doing great. Got a big job downtown with a law firm. Sarah is doing fine and looking forward to retirement in September." As Joe attacked the patty melt and French fries, with a healthy splash of ketchup, I knew that would be the extent of an update on his family. It's a guy thing. If they don't tell, you don't ask.

Joe had devoured the patty melt and all of his fries, then glanced at me with a questioning look when the waitress picked up our plates and left the check on the table in the space between us.

"Don't worry, Joe. My treat." I left a tip on the table, paid with cash at the register, then turned to Joe. "Let's go for a drive."

Joe didn't often drive his new Corvette, but he did today. He had parked in a handicapped spot, using his mother's handicapped placard. Driving a red Corvette with a handicapped placard, in my opinion was like riding a motorcycle with handicapped license plates. Some people wondered why I called him Crazy Joe. Really?

When we were settled in the red leather bucket seats, Joe started the engine, revving it three or four times, then pulled into the traffic on Manchester Road, heading west. I didn't ask where we were going, and it didn't matter. Six miles down the road he pulled into an area called a scenic overlook. It didn't look like much of a scenic overlook. Mostly rolling hills covered with a forest of trees. Much like most of the rest of Missouri.

We left the comfort of the car and sat on a nearby park bench. Joe lit a cigarette, then asked what I wanted to know about the "family."

"I've been hired to investigate an incident that happened in 1958. It involves auto dealerships and possibly individuals that may have had connections to the St. Louis mafia. I value the wealth of information you have about people around the St. Louis underworld. I'm never sure where you get your information, or how you get it. I just know you travel in circles that I know nothing about. The first question I have for you is do you know the name Giocomelli?"

"Sure. A bunch of them. We had at least four of 'em in the police department. A couple of 'em pretty high up and a couple on patrol. What's your interest in the Giocomelli's?"

"I'm just starting on this investigation and I don't want to unnecessarily ruffle any feathers, but in reviewing a photo album from my client I noticed a photo of a state senator named Antonio Giocomelli. He was apparently in the Missouri legislature during the fifties. When I looked closely at his photo in the album I had to use a magnifying glass to make sure of what I thought I saw. On his left hand, the fingernail on his pinky finger was considerably longer that the other fingernails. What do you make of that?"

"Conner, I've told you about that. Okay, the Giocomelli's were tight with the "family" and were involved in a lot of activities. The Senator had a lot of pull, but there were basically four families that ran St. Louis back then. William Comisano, also known as "Willie the Rat" was around for a long time, then left to go to Kansas City. He got pushed out. Too much heat. He got his nickname from stuffing his hits in sewers, where the rats ate them. Then there was the Gomecci family. Luciano Gomecci had three or four sons that carried on after he died almost twenty-five years ago. The Calabrese family had connections back east in the New York mob, as did the Genovese family. It was generally accepted that one of your guys in Jefferson City was connected too, but that was after the families here in St. Louis were getting hammered by the Feds. You probably heard of Carmine Vignolla. He started a couple of legitimate businesses out your way. Still, the Feds kept an eye on him. Conner, you never heard any of this from me. Capisce?"

"I understand, Joe, but I'm not through yet. Tell me about Senator Giocomelli's connections. Based on the little bit of research I've done so far, the Senator was in the legislature for about eighteen years. He must have had some pull after being there that long."

"I know a little bit about him from my father. My father drove a beer truck for Tommaso Genovese before and during prohibition. Got caught and did some time. Never talked to the Feds about Genovese or anyone else. I think I told you this before. Anyway, Tommy, that's Tommaso, was the Senator's cousin. The Senator's dad and Tommy's mother were brother and sister. I'm going way beyond what I should be telling you. I gotta' warn you, my friend, these are not folks you want to fuck around with." Then Joe changed the subject.

"Remember when we lived in San Antonio and we took a drive down to Mexico, just for the fun of it? You bought one of those fake Gucci watches and I bought a fake Rolex. Well, my friend, the people you're asking about don't wear the fake stuff. What I'm saying is, they still got things going that bring in some big bucks and they sure as hell don't want a PI nosing around in their business. You know what I'm telling you, right?"

"I got it, Joe. By the way, I met 'Willie the Rat' when I was with DPS. I was evaluating the Platte County Sheriff's Department, north of Kansas City, riding with a deputy. We were working radar and stopped an old pickup for a speeding violation. The driver looked like a farmer, bib overalls, sort of scruffy, probably mid-sixties, graying hair. Anyway, he contended he was not going as fast as the deputy said he was, so we put him in the back seat of the patrol car and showed him the radar unit and the recorded speed. When the deputy ran a check on his driver license the sheriff came back on the radio and told us to come to the station and report to his office, and don't issue a citation. When we got back to the sheriff's office we were informed that the "farmer" was being followed by the FBI and the guy we had in the car was none other than William Comisano, a.k.a. Willie the Rat. I went up north to Maryville and the next day came back through Kansas City. I had my radio on and heard that William Comisano was being indicted in federal court. So, my guess is he is out of the picture for a while."

"Lucky you. You probably know that the Giocomelli family is in the car business, and has been for a long time. You probably won't tell me who your client is and maybe it's better I don't know."

"You're right, Joe. I can't tell you who the client is, but I may have more questions for you if I get involved in an investigation. I haven't really decided yet, but what you have told me does interest me. I never talked to you about any of this."

"Right, Conner. Let's head back to your car. I've got some errands to do anyway. The next time let's just do lunch and not get into the lives of my friends over on the Hill."

"I can't promise that, Joe. But I understand what you're talking about and I appreciate all the information you have provided. I didn't get it from you."

We went back east on Manchester Road, which is also Highway 100. It also happens to be the busiest highway in the St. Louis area for automobile dealerships. After leaving the Missouri Department of Public Safety I worked for the Missouri Auto Dealers Association, the St. Louis Auto Dealers Association, The Kansas City Auto Dealers Association, and the National Auto Dealers Association for over seven years. I had visited more than thirty of the dealerships on Manchester Road. Now I would be visiting most of them in a different capacity. I needed to know if there were still connections with what was left of the St. Louis underworld.

I drove east on Manchester Road, making a mental note of the many dealerships along the way. When I reached Kingshighway Boulevard I turned north to get on I-64. From the village of Ellisville, where Joe had returned me to my car at Steak and Shake, to the intersection of Manchester and Kingshighway I had counted forty-six auto dealerships.

Driving east on I-64 takes me home to Margo. The Poplar Street bridge across the Mississippi was still under repair and traffic was backed up, as usual. On the Illinois side of the river the traffic flow gets much better, as more than sixty percent of the vehicles turn off on I-55 and I-70, either going to Chicago or Indianapolis. Who knows? As I exit onto Green Mount Road I give Margo the heads-up call, for clearance and landing permission. Having a private pilot's license, Margo understands the coded communication this message reveals. *I'm on my way home and I have just exited I-64 at Green Mount Road. I'll be there shortly.*

When I hit the remote for the garage door Margo was standing on the other side, awaiting my arrival.

"Welcome home, handsome." That was Margo's typical greeting, sometimes matched by sensual and sexy outfits that brought thoughts of afternoon delights. Today it was obvious she had been in therapy. That was her term for working in the back yard, with flowers, trees, shrubs, plants, and her koi pond. "I hope you had a productive day with Crazy Joe."

"Yes, my lovely lady, I did. Joe knows a lot about the Italian families, but he warned me not to be poking around too much, especially concerning Senator Giocomelli. I'm not sure it's as dangerous as he has lead me to believe. Anyway, I think we should have dinner on the Hill tonight. How does that sound to you?"

"I'm up for Italian food. It's been quite some time since we have been to the Hill for dinner. What time are you thinking about going?"

"Will 6:30 give you enough time to get ready after your therapy session today?"

"That will work for me, my dear."

The Hill is a small area in St. Louis that has a large concentration of Italians, and therefore, Italian restaurants, as well as little, quaint Italian specialty grocery stores. Having visited some of those stores in the past, I came to realize that there must be fifty varieties of olives and more than one hundred varieties of olive oil and probably that many varieties of pasta. Fascinating stuff and always a fun visit.

Margo can be depended on to be punctual. At precisely 6:30 she was ready to depart for an evening on the Hill.

Such a selection of restaurants on the Hill. I thought we might start with a cocktail and tapas at Guido's Pizzeria and Tapas on Shaw Avenue. Sort of an eclectic place, serving pizza, Italian dishes, American cuisine, and Spanish tapas. It had been my experience, while skiing the slopes in New Mexico at Ski Apache, that American Indian establishments employed Native Americans near the rate of ninety percent. As it is with the restaurants on the Hill. Approximately ninety percent of the employees were of Italian descent. And what would you expect of an establishment named Guido's? More Italians.

There is limited available parking on the narrow streets of the Hill, but I was able to find a small opening around the corner from Guido's, which nicely accommodated the smaller size of my Maserati. The air was scented with the spices of Italian cooking. Evening diners had not yet arrived. Being a Tuesday evening, there may not be the crowds we had experienced during the past visits to the Hill on weekends. Although Guido's does not have a dress code, I wore a sport coat as I anticipated dining later in the evening at Giovanni's, which did have a more restrictive dress code. Another reason for the jacket was to provide concealment for the shoulder holster carrying my Walther PPK.

Margo and I were seated almost immediately, and I ordered a Manhattan Up, with Maker's Mark, for each of us. Our waiter was an older gentleman and appeared to be Italian. His accent was merely a confirmation of my initial observation. He was well built and taller than most Italians I have known, including Crazy Joe. The name tag on his uniform read Vito. When he returned with our cocktails I told him that we would order our food shortly. Vito returned five minutes later.

"Vito, we're celebrating our anniversary and will probably take a little tour of the Hill. I understand this is a very good place to start. Maybe tapas as an appetizer. Do you have any suggestions for a nice, white table cloth restaurant nearby?"

"Senor, all restaurants on the Hill are so very good. You are wanting upscale Italian restaurant, no?"

"Yes, Vito. An upscale restaurant would be nice. I understand the culture on the Hill is totally Italian. Have you been around this area very long?"

"Yes, senor. Not this restaurant so long. Two years. Thisa' new on the Hill. Momma and Papa come from Sicily when I was'a boy. Papa had restaurant near here, but big highway come through and they buy his place and tear it down. Its'a shame."

"I'm sorry to hear that, Vito. I have one more question for you. I'm looking for an old friend of my father's. He was a state senator from St. Louis. Senator Antonio Giocomelli. Have you heard of him?"

"Ah, Tony. He'sa not so young anymore, but still come in soma' time."

"So, he's a well-known personality? Do you know how I can contact him?"

"No, no, senor. You dona' contact the Senator. He want to talk to you, he will find you. You give me contact information, I will give to him when he come by. Capisce?" Apparently, a favorite word used by Italians, or even pseudo Italians. "Capisce."

"Thank you, Vito. My cell phone number and my e-mail address are on the card." I handed him my business card, boldly imprinted with **E. Conner Pennington**. I rarely used my first name. Elijah. A bit antiquated. A family name from my great-great-great grandfather, who fought in the Civil War for the Lone Star State of Texas. My card also gave the name *Condor Consulting Group*. No indication that my business was Private Investigator. Vito glanced at the card and put it in his vest pocket.

"Mr. Pennington, I will give card to Senator Tony when he comes in. Would you like to order now, senor?"

"Thank you. Yes, we will have the variety plate of tapas. The one with the beef tartar."

"Very good, senor." With that, Vito returned to the kitchen. By the time we had finished with the Manhattans Vito returned with the tapas. To accompany our appetizers, we ordered a nice Italian red table wine. Moments later Vito left the check on the table. I tucked three twenties into the little tray holding the check. It was enough to cover the bill and provide a nice tip for Vito. The tapas were good.

We left Guido's and walked two blocks west on Shaw Avenue to Giovanni's. The wait here was much longer. A popular place. No reservation, but we were seated twenty minutes later in the main dining room. I noticed before being seated that there were private dining rooms on the north side of the main room. All very nicely decorated. A prominent framed photo hung on the wall just inside the entry. It was an autographed photo of Senator Antonio Giocomelli. "To my good friend Giovanni. Best regards, Tony."

Shortly after being seated by the maitre' d we were approached by a lovely young lady, bringing us menus. She didn't appear to be Italian, but how can you know? Northern Italians had blonde hair and fair complexions. "Welcome to Giovanni's. May I take your order for drinks this evening?"

I usually like to address people by their names, and her name tag read "Gina." Now that I could remember. That was the name I had given my cell phone GPS voice. Maybe she was Italian after all. Or maybe that was simply the name she used while working at Giovanni's. An attractive girl may not want every patron to know her real name. Not really my concern. To Margo and me she was Gina.

"Just water for now. We'll look at the menu and decide which wine will go best with our selection."

The back of the menu gave a brief history of Giovanni's. Giovanni Gabriele was the owner and the restaurant had opened in 1973. When Gina returned with the water, I asked her if Giovanni was in this evening. He wasn't. Not having had time to peruse the menu, we again put off ordering. So many choices and most selections were in Italian, although there was a description in English of the fare. I'm not what you would call multilingual, as the extent of my Italian is to say I don't speak Italian. When Gina returned to our table again, we were ready.

"Gina, I believe we are ready to order. My lady will have a glass of Pinot Grigio and I will have a glass of the Montepulciano d'Abruzza. For dinner, my lady will have the antipasta salad with bocconcini and green olive tapenade, followed by her selection of the linguine piccolo with grilled swordfish and parsley anchovy sauce."

"Yes, sir. And for you?"

"I'll have the warm seafood salad with pistachio and capers. The menu says that's a shrimp and squid salad with a piquant dressing of capers, olive oil and ground pistachios. Is that right?"

"Yes, sir. One of my favorites."

"Very good. For the main dish, I'll have the penne rigate with spicy braised swordfish. It isn't on the menu, but I noticed a photo of Senator Antonio Giocomelli as we came in. Tony is an old friend of mine and I would like to look him up. I haven't seen him for years. Apparently, he's a friend of Giovanni's. Perhaps Giovanni would know how I can contact the Senator. I can give you my card and I would really appreciate it if you give it to Mr. Gabriele when he comes in and have either Giovanni or Tony contact me."

"Yes sir, I can do that. I'll put your orders in and will be right back with your wine."

The dinner was excellent and we each had another glass of wine with our entrée. When we completed our meal and Gina brought the check I left a sizeable tip for her, hoping she would remember my request for Giovanni or Tony to contact me. Returning to the Maserati, I noticed four young boys admiring my vehicle. Not an unusual event, especially in an Italian neighborhood.

Back on the interstate, we arrived home by eleven. It was a good evening and I hoped productive.

Rising early Wednesday morning I went to my upstairs office to review the materials Mandy had given me. At 8:15 a.m. my cell phone buzzed. The caller's number was unlisted.

"Good morning. This is Conner Pennington."

"Mr. Conner Pennington. Some advise. It's not in the best interest of your health to be asking around about the Senator. Capisce?" Before I could respond the call ended. No number given. Anonymous. Not the first time I had been threatened, but it does tend to get my attention. Five minutes later my cell buzzed again.

"Hello, this is Conner Pennington."

"Mr. Pennington, this is Sandra Williams at the John Cochran VA Medical Center. I'm calling to let you know you have been accepted in the VA health care system. We will be sending a letter of confirmation and you will need to come in to have a photo identification card made. Instructions will be included with the letter."

"Thank you, Ms. Williams. I appreciate your letting me know."

"Have a good day, Mr. Pennington, and thank you for your service."

Good news and bad news. Some days are like that. Some days you're the pigeon; some days you're the statue.

When serving with the Missouri Department of Public Safety I had met the resident FBI agent assigned to Jefferson City. He had been a Marine, an officer, and a Vietnam Veteran, and we became good friends. I lost track of him after he was transferred to the St. Louis office. Gregory Taylor. It was well known among his friends that when he got in a tight situation or became excited his left hand would twitch. Forever more his nickname was Twitch Taylor. We most likely adopted the nickname from the baseball player that was left handed and always "twitched" his left arm when he came to bat. Some people speculated it was a result of Tourette's Syndrome. I never thought that was the case. Just a habit. Nevertheless, most of his fans simply called him "Twitch Morgan."

I called the FBI office in St. Louis and asked for Gregory Taylor. I was informed that Mr. Taylor was not in, but I could leave a message. I was a little surprised that I wasn't told there was no Mr. Taylor at that office. Years ago, while traveling through Denver, I had called the office of a friend from the Marine Corps and was told there was no such person in that office. I knew there was. He was a DEA agent assigned to Denver. Anyway, I left a message for Mr. Taylor to return my call, leaving my contact information, and knowing he would recognize the name. Around 1:30 I got a call from "Twitch."

"Damn, Conner. How the hell are you? I didn't know you still existed. What do you need, my friend?"

"Well, first let me thank you for calling me back so quickly. Now, what makes you think I need something? But you're right, I do. I'm a private investigator now and I'm looking into an old case. There may be something to it, because this morning I got a threating call telling me to basically stop and desist. If you have some time, I would like to come in and talk to you about any information you might have in your files about Senator Antonio Giocomelli."

"Oh, shit! Do you really know what you're getting into here? Didn't you get enough action in Vietnam to last you for a lifetime? Tell you what, my friend, come to my office about this time tomorrow. That will give me some time to pull up whatever we have on the Senator. By the way, I'm familiar with the name."

"Great. I'll see you tomorrow. Your office is in the Post Office on Market Street, right?"

"Right. I know you. Don't be bringing a weapon into the Post Office. Not allowed."

Perhaps I expected too much, too soon. Having not heard from anyone on the Hill about my search for the Senator, I decided to stir the pot a little more. The threat I had received by phone was not a deterrent. When I checked with Margo about another visit to the Hill and more Italian food, she indicated she would pass on more Italian restaurants so soon.

I began early in the afternoon, making walking forays to a number of restaurants on the Hill. At Adriana's I had a cocktail and an appetizer, asking about the Senator and leaving my card. Cocktails only at Zia's, Dominic's, Trattoria Marcella, and Rigazzi's. I told different stories at these establishments, but scattered my business card among the employees at each place. Most recipients of my card and my message indicated they knew of the Senator and would pass on the word that I would like to meet with him. Or, as they say on the Hill, have a "sit down." I had a gut feeling that the Senator played a central role in this investigation.

No discernable progress as a result of my visit among the Italians that inhabited the Hill community. I probably shouldn't have been driving back to Belleville that evening. Too many cocktails and glasses of wine. Driving home on I-64 my mind whirled around the possibility that I just might be driving into a world of shit. Figuratively and literally.

It was just past 10:30 and Margo was waiting up for me. Her awareness of my more than slightly impaired condition was evident when her welcoming home remark was, "I think you're pushing this investigation a bit too much, especially when you come home smelling like a winery and looking like you're not really sure how you got home. Why don't you go take a shower and get yourself into bed?" Good advice, which I accepted and subsequently shut down for the evening.

After three cups of coffee my head was clear by late morning. I'm an early riser and now it seemed that half the day was already past. It was nine thirty and I was reviewing more of the documents I had gathered at the Klienknect estate. Mandy Barrows had not yet revealed to me what had prompted her to request my services in an investigation of her grandparent's deaths.

Never sure what the traffic would be when I crossed the Poplar Street Bridge I left home at eleven to meet Twitch Taylor at one thirty. Parking could also be a problem in the downtown St. Louis metro area, especially on Market Street. I left my every day driver, a Jaguar S-Type, for Margo, and drove my Maserati. Repairs were still being made on the bridge, but that was expected. Taking an exit off I-64 west for Market Street, I quickly discovered limited parking available on Market Street. The closest and most secure place seemed to be west of the Post Office in the vast parking lot of Union Station. It was my habit to park just about as far as I could from clusters of vehicles already parked, so I found a space on the south side of Union Station, where train tracks had delivered thousands of travelers every day when the station was at its peak. The tracks were no longer there, and no trains came into Union Station. Hotels, restaurants, and multiple retail stores were now the main attraction. I locked my Walther PPK and shoulder holster in the trunk and walked toward the Post Office for my meeting with Twitch.

Entering the main part of the Post Office wasn't a problem, but going up the stairs to offices located above the first floor required security checks and passage through a metal detector. On the second floor, I was directed to the FBI offices, where I was met by an efficient gate keeper that wanted to know who I was and why I was visiting the FBI office. Upon approval of my two forms of government issued photo ID cards and confirmation that I did indeed have an appointment with Mr. Gregory Taylor, I was escorted to a remote office down a narrow hallway, which was appropriately adorned with photos of past FBI directors, beginning with Mr. J. Edgar Hoover. My escort, I had noticed from his desk name plate, was Mario Carmellini. Mario rapped twice on the solid wood door that displayed the name of my friend, Resident Agent in Charge, Gregory Taylor.

Mario didn't wait for a response. He opened the door and announced, "Mr. Taylor, Mr. Pennington to see you, sir."

Behind a massive desk sat my old friend. He had aged well, but had also put on a few pounds. Rising from a government issue office chair, he met me halfway and extended his hand. His handshake was firm, and I noted that he still wore his Marine Corps ring. "Conner, it's been a long time." Pointing to a small round conference table, piled with paperwork, he said, "Join me over here."

"Greg, I'm impressed. I'm impressed that the FBI hasn't found a reason to boot you out and I'm very impressed that you are the RAIC. I'm sure you have a lot of things going on and I know the way you operate, cutting to the chase and eliminating the bullshit. So, what do you have for me?"

We sat at the table and Twitch picked up a folder that was an inch thick, handing it to me, but with what I perceived to be some reluctance and concern.

"There's some information in here that is confidential, and I want this folder back when you have read and digested the material. Three days, then deliver all of it back to this office. Sounds pretty harsh, huh? I'm only putting this in your hands because I trust you. Now, I have to apologize. I got a call from the Eastern District Federal Prosecutor just minutes before you got here. He wants me in his office immediately, if not sooner."

"No need to apologize, Greg. I understand. Everybody, somewhere along the way has a boss. I appreciate your getting this info together and it's good to see you again. I'll let myself out and promise to return this folder very soon."

"I'll walk you out, Conner. I hope we will have some time to catch up when you bring the folder back."

Back on Market Street Taylor turned to the east. The recently constructed federal courthouse was three blocks from the Post Office. It might be the only exercise Greg would be able to fit into his schedule. I headed west to my car parked at Union Station. I could use the exercise too, but I wasn't in a big hurry to get anywhere at the moment. I entered through the huge doors at the front of the station, passing through the old lobby, then into the covered area that housed the retail businesses.

The smell of fresh, hot fudge was enticing as I passed a couple of guys that were massaging gobs of hot chocolate on marble slabs, their paddles rolling and stirring the dark brown confection. No fudge today, Conner. The exercise I probably needed. The fudge I didn't.

I exited the back of Union Station, but didn't spot my car immediately, as there were now three or four vehicles parked near where I had left my Maserati. A newer model black Cadillac was very close to my vehicle and I noticed two men inside, the passenger talking on a cell phone. I approached my car from the opposite side of the parked Cadillac, circling to the back in anticipation of releasing the trunk latch and retrieving my weapon. Hitting the proper remote button on my key fob, the trunk latch released, and I raised the lid, tossing in the folder Taylor had given me. Just as I reached for the concealed side panel where I had placed my handgun I heard a car door open.

"Mr. Conner Pennington?"

"Yes. What can I do for you?"

Based on my combat experience I knew I wasn't dead, simply because I distinctly heard the shot. But I was down. I felt like I had been hit with a baseball bat. The sky was getting darker and there was a perception of a whistling wind. Then there didn't seem to be enough air to fill my lungs. I rolled to my left side, not realizing why or how. My shirt was soaking wet, and that didn't make sense either. The sound of squealing tires was the last thing I remembered.

Then the lights went out.

Chapter 3

"Margo Webster? I'm Doctor Nathan Barrows. You're here with Mr. Pennington?"

"Yes. How is he? Can I see him?"

"He's out of surgery. He has lost a lot of blood and is in intensive care. We removed the bullet that was lodged in his right lung and he is sedated. We repaired as much as we could, but it will take some time to heal. He's stable and we'll be closely watching him. You can look in on him, but only for a minute or two. He needs to rest."

"Thank you, doctor."

It felt like mid-morning, somewhere on a busy sidewalk. Could have been New York, or it could have been St. Louis. Hell, it could have been any big city, but it didn't seem like anything on the west coast, or even Texas. The air was chilly, and the wind was sharp. Maybe Chicago? What would I be doing in Chicago? I wore a long, dark blue cashmere coat and a gray cashmere neck scarf that was whipping wildly in the turbulent wind. Pedestrians passed me from behind and even more walked briskly toward me. Young and old, they all looked at me as though they thought they recognized me, then moved on. It seemed the air was filled with a fog from the warm breath of each individual. I could see it. I could sense it. I could feel it. It reminded me of a horse snorting out clouds of moisture on a very cold day as it pulled a one-horse sleigh through a raging snow storm.

Why was I here? Where was I going? My sense of direction and purpose was fraught with wonder and indecision.

I saw him at a distance of maybe twenty yards. He was tall and handsome, in a chiseled way. With so many people on the sidewalk why did I notice him? A three-piece suit, but no overcoat. An intricate gold chain looped from one side of his vest, through the buttonhole and disappeared into the pocket that was most likely designed for a pocket watch. He seemed unaware of the cold and moved with an ease that belied his muscular stature. Besides being seemingly oblivious to the cold, there had to be something else that caught my attention. There was no evidence of a fog of breath. As with everyone else that passed me, his piercing eyes focused on me from the moment I noticed him. Ah, the suit. Was this what they called a "zoot suit" back in the thirties or forties? I'm not a fashion authority, but this was not a recent model from any haberdashery I was familiar with or had ever visited.

His gaze was more of a stare and was very penetrating. When the distance had closed to two or three feet he tipped his fanciful fedora with his left hand, nodded and said one word. "Conner." Then he moved on with the flow of the mass of humanity moving quickly in both directions. I had never seen him before. I turned to catch a last glimpse of him, in hopes I could possibly place him somewhere in my memory. There were only two or three pedestrians remaining on the sidewalk, as though the wind may have whisked away the ephemeral beings I had seen earlier. The stranger was not there! When I turned around, there were no pedestrians on the sidewalk in front of me. Empty! This couldn't be real. It seemed as though the fog from the warm breathing of passersby had filled the air. Everything was closing in. I felt a crushing sense of claustrophobia. Through the enveloping mist I heard the sound of a throaty engine. A large oval grill surrounded by flaming red appeared and stopped by the curb. In the center of the grill was an emblem I recognized. A large Trident. The vehicle stopped at the curb, two feet from where I stood. My enthusiasm for rare cars helped me identify this one as a Maserati A6 GCS by Paninfarina. I had only seen one of these in my lifetime. I wasn't even sure it was street legal. It had been built and designed primarily for racing. But then was any of this real? This was the 1947 model that had debuted at the International Motor Show in Geneva. The driver? The stranger with the fedora.

"Get in, Conner." It wasn't a command, nor was it a request. I felt as though I had no choice.

When I opened the passenger door and slid into the contoured bucket seat, the interior of the car smelled of rum soaked pipe tobacco. The stranger never looked at me after I entered, but quickly engaged the clutch and propelled the Maserati to an amazing speed. My head was spinning, the mist and fog was swirling as we approached an expansive bridge crossing what seemed to me to be an ocean. The bridge supports zipped by at what must have been at least 150 miles-per-hour. What's happening? Why am I here? Who is this stranger with the fedora? Then there was total silence.

I had a sense of being home. My apartment. Still, I had never had an apartment like this. It was large, and it was comfortable, but as I glanced into the living room I saw a disarray that led me to believe my "home" had been vandalized. The Marine officer's sword with the Mameluke hilt was on the floor, snapped in two just below my engraved name and the scrollwork on the blade. I was crestfallen. This sword had been with me for more than 45 years. Not a fighting sword. A well-crafted ceremonial sword. I knelt and picked up the pieces. The hilt in my left hand. The pointed end with the blood groove, in my right hand. As I rose to my feet I heard and felt a movement behind me. My immediate perception was a threatening aggressor was charging me. Black pajamas, a maniacal grin, and barefoot. Vietnamese? No doubt in my mind. As he lunged I held the point of the broken sword, then pushed it easily into his body, between his ribs and into his chest cavity.

"You sonuvabitch! You have no idea what I went through to earn that sword. I can replace it, but it's not the same, you bastard." I was stunned and bewildered. He was dead, but there was no blood.

"LT. LT." The deep baritone voice came from the open doorway. When I turned to the source, the entry door was filled by a man in a Marine green Alpha service uniform. The left chest was filled with rows of ribbons and two expert shooting medals. Crossed rifles and crossed pistols. Each sleeve of his blouse bore his rank. Three chevrons up and three rocker stripes below, with a diamond in the middle. I knew the rank. First Sergeant. Why was he here? TOP? What the hell? How did he get here? What did he want? Fog filtered into the room from the open doorway and the figure vanished.

Thoughts and visions of an episode in South Vietnam. What's real and what isn't? It all seemed too real. Someone, some entity, some crazy bastard representing the U.S. government decided it would help in the elimination of Viet Cong if village chiefs were paid to collect ears from the VC and present them for payment. A job well done. It soon became evident that ears presented for payment were not ears from VC. A village chief of Ton Hue Lai was collecting ears from Caucasians, claiming they were VC. Eliminate the village chief and you eliminate the immediate problem. Those records are sealed. We don't selectively assassinate village chiefs. But that was my mission. Deniability. Didn't happen. The issued K-Bar fighting knife slid easily between his ribs and the night swallowed the deed.

If this is some crazy dream I wanted to wake up. I struggled, but the fog persisted. Slowly, very slowly, I sank into the depth of the murky water. Seaweed swirled around me, wrapping its tentacles around my arms and legs. Sea snakes swam easily through the debris. I hate snakes. Any snake. Poisonous or non-poisonous. It made no difference. The only good snake is a dead snake! I kick. I try to scream. When I finally surface, there is a dense mist spreading across the churning, muddy water. I'm equal distance from the shoreline. At least five hundred yards in each direction. It's a river. The banks are shrouded with a dense jungle and fog. Faintly, I hear the throbbing of a diesel engine. I turn toward the sound, keeping my nostrils above water. Moving directly toward me is a slow river boat, filled with boys, grass and seaweed entwined in their hair. All of them are armed with AK-47s. I could submerge and deal with the snakes or I could hope they had not seen me. I kicked furiously to stay above water. Waves from the bow of the boat swept over me as I exhaled and sank into the murkiness again. Had I survived? Were the snakes still there?

Wake up. Wake up. I fight it, but it doesn't happen. That voice again. The fog masks the words, but I hear a woman's voice repeating, again and again, "Conner, Conner. Wake up. It's okay. I'm here."

Blackness again. Nothing. It sounded like Margo, but I couldn't be sure. Soothing. Comforting. Can she help me escape this deep, depressing fog?

"Ms. Webster. We need to let him get some rest. We're not sure what's going on right now, but his vitals have become elevated. We're watching him closely. I think you probably need to get some rest also. We've given him some medication that will help him rest and he most likely will be out for at least five or six hours. We have your phone number and will contact you if there is any change."

"Can you tell me any more about what happened?"

"According to the police investigators he was shot by unknown assailants in the parking lot of Union Station. The trunk of his car was open. They don't know if he had anything in the trunk, but it was empty when they arrived on the scene. The car was locked, then transported to impound for possible evidence. Mr. Pennington had a sucking chest wound and he was very fortunate that there was a first responder nearby that took action and sealed the wound with a plastic shopping bag. The prognosis is that he will recover, due to fast action. As far as I know the police have no suspects. They are continuing to investigate. I'm sure they will want to talk to Mr. Pennington when he is able."

"Thank you, doctor. Is there anything else?"

"He's had a couple of other folks asking about him. One of them was from the FBI, as I recall. The other two didn't leave their names.

We have just gotten word that Mr. Pennington will be transferred to the Jefferson Barracks VA Medical Facility in the morning. He should be stable enough by then to be transported by ambulance. The hospital at Jefferson Barracks has excellent rehab facilities. If you would like, I believe we can arrange to have you ride in the ambulance with him."

"Do you have any idea what time that will be? No, that's okay. I'll be here anyway. Conner has an old friend who came to town and he can drop me here and pick me up later at Jefferson Barracks."

"If there is any change I'll let you know." With that, Dr. Nathan Barrows returned to the nurse's station and picked up a computer notebook, proceeding with his busy schedule.

Chapter 4

I awoke to the throbbing rhythmic sounds of machines, glanced around and felt like I was wired up to the Grand Coulee Dam. Wires and tubes everywhere. I lost count of how many times the nurse woke me up during the night to give me a sleeping pill. My eyelids were heavy, and I had no recollection of going back to sleep, but somewhere in my subconscious I was back in the Maserati A6GCS. The mystery man with the fedora was driving. The fog was heavy and there was a chill that permeated my entire being.

When my eyelids fluttered I heard her voice. "Conner, Conner. You're okay. You have been moved to the VA hospital at Jefferson Barracks. I was in the ambulance with you when your vitals spiked at one point and you seemed very agitated. Whatever was going on passed and they told me you are stabilized. I'm not sure you are up to having guests, but at least one of them you might want to see."

Margo sat in a chair close to my bed and on the other side stood a man I didn't know. Slightly behind the man in the suit was a man I did know. First Sergeant Ronald Meza, USMC, Retired.

"Conner, thank God you're going to be okay." Margo reached out and gently touched my right forearm, somewhere between the tube that disappeared into my right hand and the blood pressure cuff on my right bicep. "These gentlemen have been waiting to talk to you and I called them in as soon as I saw you stir."

"Wow! I've had some really weird dreams. How long have I been here?"

"You were brought in two days ago to the Barnes-Jewish hospital, and then you were transferred to the VA hospital this morning. It's now almost seven in the evening. I'm not sure why, but your friend Mr. Meza called two days ago, and I told him what happened and that you were in the hospital. His only reply was, 'I'm on my way.' He's been with you most of the time since he arrived. I'll let him explain."

I was still a bit groggy, but I certainly recognized my old first sergeant from Vietnam, who was now a retired homicide detective from Los Angeles. He had recently assisted me with a cold case investigation by locating a person of interest in that investigation.

"Top. I'm not sure why you're here, but I appreciate it."

"Well, LT, I just called a couple of days ago to see how things were going and your lovely lady gave me the lowdown on your situation. We had each other's back in Nam, where quite frankly I had to cover your sorry ass a number of times when we were there. So, here I am again, covering your sorry ass. The investigators don't know who did this, but someone was intent on doing you great bodily harm. The security at the last hospital was minimal. It's better here at the VA hospital, but what I'm telling you is I've got your back." Meza had been my company first sergeant when I was a tank company commander in Vietnam. Obviously aged since those days, but still a formidable character. Two or three inches taller than the man in the suit, he wore his graying hair in a Marine-type cut. His broad chest filled out the sport coat he was wearing, and I thought I detected a slight bulge under his left arm. This is not someone I would want to piss off, but we had been through hell together and I knew I could count on my friend and mentor.

"Mr. Pennington, I'm Detective Daniel Tanner, St. Louis P.D. I'm in charge of the investigation about the shooting. Do you feel up to answering a few questions?"

"Sure. If your questions aren't too difficult. I'll tell you what I can."

"Ms. Webster has told us that you're investigating a cold case and that you received a threatening phone call before the shooting. We have talked to witnesses at Union Station, who stated they saw a dark sedan leave the parking lot immediately after they heard a shot. There are security cameras at the exit of the lot, but there were a number of dark sedans leaving the lot that day. We have narrowed the time frame to between 2:15 and 3:00 that afternoon. Can you tell us anymore about the vehicle or the occupants?"

"Just before I was shot I saw a black Cadillac close to where my vehicle was parked. There were two men inside and the man in the passenger seat appeared to be talking on a cell phone. I did notice the car had Missouri license plates. I was bending over my open trunk, having just placed a file in the trunk and was retrieving my handgun that I had concealed in a secure compartment, when I heard a car door open and a man called my name. I turned toward the voice and BAM. I was down, but I think I heard the squeal of tires, then nothing."

"Do you think you could identify the shooter?"

"I don't think so. It all happened so fast. I really didn't get a good look at him, but my impression was that he had a stocky build. Not as big as Ron Meza over there. That's about all I remember about him."

"Okay, Mr. Pennington. You say you had put a file in the trunk just before the shooting?"

"Yes. It was related to the case I'm investigating."

"I'll need to know more about that in a minute. When the officers arrived at the scene your vehicle trunk lid was open, but the trunk was empty, except for an umbrella. Nothing else seemed to be disturbed and if you had a weapon in the trunk, there was no visual on it. There were no shell casings at the scene, so either the shooter picked up the casings or used a revolver. We don't know yet. Who or what does your investigation involve, who is your client, and what was the threat you received?"

"Detective, I'm still a bit fuzzy in the brain housing group, but I was hired to look into an incident that happened in 1958, involving the suspicious deaths of two people, specifically, the grandparents of my client. Their deaths were ruled accidental at the time, but my client, Mandy Barrows, believes there were circumstances that indicate otherwise. A friend of my client's grandparents found the bodies and gave a statement to the police that he discovered them in their home after they missed a brunch date with him. The friend was at the time a state senator and I'm still in the early stages of the investigation, but I wanted to locate the senator and gather more information about the morning of his discovery of the bodies. After checking with residents and restaurants on the Hill, asking about Senator Giocomelli, I received a threatening phone call, telling me to stop my search for the senator. I contacted a friend at the FBI office here in St. Louis and asked him if he had any information on the senator, which he did. I picked up a file from him and had returned to my car when I was shot."

Detective Tanner was not quite through with his questions. "I'm not aware of this senator you are looking for, but why would you go to the FBI to gather information on this person?"

"I had a connection with the resident agent when he was assigned to Jefferson City and I was working for the Missouri Department of Public Safety. On the off-chance the FBI might have information concerning the senator, I contacted the resident agent in charge here in St. Louis, who just happened to be my long-time friend, Gregory Taylor. He gave me a file containing information about the senator, which I took to my car and placed in the trunk."

"As I indicated earlier, Mr. Pennington, there was no file in the trunk of your car when officers arrived at the scene." Detective

Tanner gave the distinct impression he didn't much care for civilians that immersed themselves in his line of work and particularly in his city. "Okay, I understand you were retrieving a weapon you had placed in a secure area of your trunk. We'll need to talk about that also. I'm going to assume for now that you have a concealed carry permit allowing you to carry a weapon in Missouri. We'll get to that later. If you are looking into criminal activity that has gone down in my city I need to know about that. Are we clear?"

"We're clear on that, detective, but the situation I'm investigating happened in Jefferson City. Not St. Louis. I'm just trying to locate the senator, whom I believe lives in St. Louis. I'm not implying he had anything to do with the incident in Jefferson City in 1958. He seems to be quite elusive. I just wanted to get his input on the events surrounding the deaths of my client's grandparents."

Detective Tanner gave me the impression that I was somehow the villain in this situation, not a victim. I understand territorial issues, still it has never been my intent to circumvent local law enforcement authorities.

"Excuse me, Detective Tanner, I'm a retired homicide detective from Los Angeles. This man was my commanding officer in Vietnam and we go back a long way. I can assure you that Mr. Pennington has no intention of interfering in an investigation by your department. Nor do I. We looked out for each other when we were Marines and that's the only reason I am here now. That's what we do. Before you have any further questions, particularly relating to my presence here, I do have a permit to carry a concealed weapon in Missouri and I am exercising that privilege. I will be here as long as my friend needs me and as long as there is a threat."

"Mr. Meza, I appreciate your honesty and being upfront with me. I'm sure your experiences in Los Angeles have been extensive, but when it's all said and done, I'm in charge in this city. I would hope we have an understanding about that."

Meza's facial expressions and body language told me he would not be close friends with Detective Tanner. First Sergeant Meza was most comfortable when he was in charge. "Understood, Detective Tanner."

Tanner left the hospital room, with the assurance he would be in contact with me again. I could hardly wait.

"I don't know what the hell you have gotten yourself into, LT, but I'll be here for you until this situation is resolved. Yeah, I know, you picked up Captain before you got out of the Corps, but to me you will always be LT." Meza was a crusty old bastard, but I trusted him with my life. Together we had survived hell. This too would pass.

I was still groggy from the pain meds and felt my eyes closing with a burden that weighed heavily. I faintly heard Margo talking to Meza.

"Ron, let's let him rest and go grab a bite to eat."

"Okay. I noticed they have stationed a uniformed VA police officer outside the door. It's the late night here at the hospital that concerns me about security issues. I'll be back later tonight to make sure things are secure for LT."

I awoke sometime later and sensed that Margo had her hand resting on my arm. When I glanced to the side of my bed I discovered it wasn't Margo. Mandy Barrows sat primly on a chair close to my left side. Her attire was not the jogging suit she had worn when I last saw her. A double string of pearls accentuated the low neckline and an ample bosom.

"Conner, I am so sorry. If I had known this would turn into such violence I would not have asked you to become involved."

"Listen Mandy, it isn't your fault. I pushed too many buttons, but I'm not stopping. If anything, I'm even more determined to find the truth. I have a question for you, though. How did you know I was here?

"My husband told me about a surgery he had done a couple of

days ago and mentioned your name. Mr. Pennington. I don't know any other Mr. Pennington. My husband doesn't even know that I know you, or that I've hired you to look into the circumstances of my grandparent's deaths. Well, when I checked at the hospital this morning they told me you had been transferred here. Anyway, I need to tell you something, Conner. When you were my skating instructor I had a crush on you. I'm here because I care, and I'm concerned. In a strange way, I still have those feelings for you."

"I don't know what to say Mandy. You are an elegant and lovely lady, and I'm flattered that you have concerns and feelings for me. I have a lady in my life now that is my present and my future. I'm sure you will meet her one of these days and will understand my commitment to her. I'll tell you, though, when I get out of here, I'm still on the case."

"I understand. I hope what I've told you about my teenage crush doesn't have a negative impact on our relationship in this investigation."

"Well, I certainly never picked up on a teenage crush. Again, I am flattered. I know you have moved past that by now and I accept that we have a status of mutual respect. Let's go back to the original reason we have reconnected after more than twenty years. I haven't had the time to thoroughly examine all the documents I picked up at the estate. Consequently, I haven't come across what information you found that led you to believe the deaths of your grandparents was not accidental."

"Perhaps my suspicions are unfounded, but it seemed to me there are a series of things supporting my conclusion that my grandparent's deaths were not accidental. I find it hard to believe my grandfather would drive his car into his garage, close the garage door, and leave the engine running. Then, according to the reports, he left the door to the kitchen open and he and my grandmother went to bed. I just feel that one of them would have been aware enough to recognize the fact that the car was still running and the door to the kitchen was left open. It just doesn't make sense."

"You mentioned there were a series of things supporting your conclusion about their deaths. I'm not really out of my brain fog at the present time, but I recognized from the album that Senator Antonio Giocomelli was a central figure in your grandfather's life and in his auto dealerships. I guess I should have been more cautious in my approach to contact the senator, in which case I probably wouldn't be here in this hospital bed. My intent was to interview the senator about the events of the evening he spent with the Klienknects at the country club and his discovery of them the next morning.

"I feel as though I'm fading. Getting sleepy. I think we have a lot to discuss, but it will have to be another time. Thank you for coming to see me. I appreciate your concern." Mandy gently touched my arm and rose from her chair.

"Get well, Conner." As she opened the door and stepped into the hallway I noticed she also wore fashionable high heels, as though she were going to one of her charity events. Given the late hour, I doubted that was the case.

I drifted off into a fuzzy dreamland, fraught with people and images that made no sense.

Chapter 5

Hospital food is pretty much like airplane food used to be. On a flight to San Francisco, during the time when they actually served food on domestic flights, an airline attendant came down the aisle, stopped by my seat and asked me what I would like for lunch. My options were beef sandwich, ham sandwich, or chicken sandwich. When I asked for a beef sandwich, her reply was, "I'm sorry sir, but we are out of beef sandwiches. Just between us, it doesn't matter…they all taste amazingly the same." I reflected on that as my breakfast tray was wheeled into my hospital room shortly after daybreak. As the cart contents were transferred to my bedside table and the serving dishes were uncovered I could not tell with any degree of certainty what the breakfast menu actually was.

As the serving cart was wheeled out, a visitor came through the door. Crazy Joe. I certainly wouldn't have expected a visit from my old San Antonio compadre. To the right side of my bed the curtains on the window were drawn, the impending dawn seeping through the thin layer of curtains. Seated in the easy chair under a dim table lamp was Ron Meza. When Joe stepped into the room, Meza rose and placed his hand inside his sport coat. There was no doubt about the ethnic heritage of Crazy Joe. Italian. Meza was alert to the potential threat, as he knew the strong possibility that I had been shot by a person of Italian descent.

"It's okay, Ron. This is Joe. An old friend from way back. Not as far back as we go, but he's not a threat." Meza relaxed, but remained standing. "Joe, this is a Marine friend from my days in Vietnam. Retired first sergeant and retired homicide detective from the LA police department." They closed the gap between them and shook hands.

"You guys have some common ground. Joe was with the St. Louis Police Department for ten years. Lord knows what he does now, and I don't even ask." Before I could proceed with any further introductions I noticed another visitor standing in the doorway. Little Joe, Crazy Joe's son. Soon to be married. "Well, Joe and Joe. I never really knew whether you were to be addressed as Joe, Senior and Joe, Junior, or Big Joe and Little Joe. Either way, come on in. For the younger Joe I have mostly heard you addressed as Little Joe, so that's what I will go with, if that's okay?"

"I don't have a problem with that, Mr. Pennington. I've been called Little Joe as long as I can remember. I don't take offense with that. It's just the way it is."

"I told your dad I would be at your wedding in June. It's damn near June now and I seem to somehow have gotten a lot of my plans rearranged when I got in the way of someone's bullet. Still, the doctor assures me I will be out of here soon, and as long as I don't do something stupid I'll be okay to come to your wedding. Congratulations, and I look forward to being there."

"Look, I'll understand if you can't make it. Dad told me what happened to you and I just wanted to come by and see how you were doing. Dad and I haven't always agreed on everything, but when it comes to hanging together with family, I'm with him. That means I'm on board with whatever direction my old man takes in relation to your incident. You know we have some connections, and this just isn't right. You and dad have been pretty tight, and we don't condone this sort of action. Shit, you could have been killed." A grin crossed

Little Joe's face and he followed up with, "If the shooter had succeeded, I most likely wouldn't have gotten a wedding present from you."

"Point taken. Just to satisfy your curious mind, I can assure you that you aren't in my will. So, you are very right in assuming you would not have gotten a wedding present from me if some enterprising individual out there hadn't been just a bit off 'dead' center with his aim. He did get his message across, though.

"I've known you and your dad for some years now and we're all adults here. I appreciate your respect in calling me Mr. Pennington, but let's move on to calling me Conner. In addressing some of the issues you brought up in your comments about family loyalty, I don't want to involve you or your dad in issues that may not have anything to do with the shooting. I know about your family connections and I appreciate your concern. You're just weeks away from your wedding and I don't want to be responsible for your fiancé to be grieving because you got yourself tangled up in complicated 'family' issues. Capiche?"

Crazy Joe, or Big Joe, perhaps feeling left out of the conversation, interjected, "We understand. Little Joe gets a little cocky at times, but he eventually falls in line. My father, bless his soul, established ties to the family that continues to this day. That's a hand-me-down to me and my son, as long as my son listens to me. Loyalty was paid for a long time ago. I don't begrudge your friend there, Mr. Meza, for being here to cover your back. I'm sure he's good at what he does. My father grew up here, I grew up here, and Little Joe grew up here. This is our town. We don't fly a banner saying so, but that's the way it is.

"Conner, you may recall that not too long ago we had a conversation about your getting involved in 'family' business. My advice was, don't go there. That's my side of town."

"Off the current subject, momentarily. Is there still an armed security guard outside in the hallway?"

"Yes, there is, and she's pretty damn good looking. Tight uniform. I could fall in love with her."

"Good to know. So, how did you get in here. She just let you walk in here because of your Italian charm?"

"Well, well, well. I'd be willing to bet that your friend over there still has a badge from the LAPD. I still have my badge from the St. Louis PD. Special assistant to the Chief. It gets me into a lot of places. No questions asked."

"Back to the subject of family. Yeah, Joe. I recall that conversation. It just seems a bit strange, or coincidental, that I pay a couple of visits to the Hill, asking for a meeting with the Senator, then someone decides to take a shot at me. I don't believe in coincidences. I picked up a file on the Senator from the FBI and that went missing during this little incident. Let me lay it out for you. I only wanted to talk to the Senator about the morning he found a friend of his dead in the his home. I'm not accusing the Senator of being involved in that death. I just wanted to get his take on what the hell happened. They were in business together, but I haven't seen any records that would indicate the Senator would greatly benefit financially, or otherwise, by removing his partner from the scene. I have to assume you are indeed still connected, and if that is the case, then maybe you can put out the word that I only want to talk to Senator Giocomelli. I don't want any confrontations, although I would like to nail whoever the hell pulled the trigger on me."

"We don't talk about 'family' connections, Conner. Let me handle this. I'll put out the word that you want a 'sit-down' with the Senator and we'll see what happens."

"Okay, Joe. Fair enough. So, you've interrupted my delightful hospital breakfast and now it's cold. No big loss. I think it was cold when they brought it in. Next time you come by, bring me a cold beer and a hot pastrami on rye. It always gives me heartburn, but it's damn well worth it. Keep in touch and I'll see you both at the wedding, if not before." Big Joe and Little Joe took the hint, bid me farewell and best wishes for a speedy recovery as they stepped into the hallway and closed the door.

Mcza isn't normally that quiet, although listening and observing have no doubt been a part of his success as a homicide detective in LA. "Your buddy is right. I do still carry my badge. I remember the day I was presented a little black emblem…the Eagle, Globe and Anchor. I earned the title US Marine. I look at my badge from my years with the LAPD and consider that I earned that badge. Now, do you think Joe earned his badge from the St. Louis PD?"

"I doubt it, Ron. From what I know about Joe, becoming a special assistant to the Chief was through connections. Maybe 'family', maybe not. He was with the department when a lot of influences were being taken advantage of, in many ways. I can't even explain how he graduated with a master degree in education, because he can't tell you the difference between to, too, and two."

"Be that as it may, LT, I don't doubt that he has some unsavory connections with what may be left of the 'family'. If I might make a suggestion, I would let him gently put out the word that you simply want to talk with the Senator. If he can pull that off, I would also suggest you include him in a 'sit-down' meeting. Granted, he may not be the sharpest tool in the shed, but neither of us look even the slightest bit Italian, and he certainly does. It might help. Besides, being of Hispanic descent I look a lot more Italian than you do. I would also suggest a meeting in a very public place. If this meeting comes about, the Senator will no doubt have his associates included. One or two, anyway. It wouldn't be out of line for me to be there also, along with Joe."

"All very good suggestions, my friend."

Before our discussions proceeded any further the door opened and in walked Margo. "Good morning, my lovely lady. And what do you have in the sack?"

"I thought you might want something besides savory hospital food. I'm probably violating all the rules here and your doctor may evict me from the premises, but I brought you a biscuit sandwich from McDonalds. Sausage, egg and cheese. And, a senior coffee to go with it." She gave me a hello kiss on the lips.

"Fantastic. I had some early visitors. Crazy Joe and his son. Just chit chat, but they interrupted my breakfast. I'm not sure what it was, or if it was ever warm, but it soon got cold. So, your thoughtfulness is very much appreciated. It's good to see you, my dear."

"You may not think so when I tell you what's been on my mind. First, I sorta' like having Ron around while you're here in the hospital. I certainly feel more secure, even though you know I keep my loaded .357 by the bed. Secondly, when I encouraged you to pursue a new career as a private investigator I had no idea it would lead to a situation like this. I know you have been in danger before, when you were in the Marines. That was a long time ago. This has been above and beyond anything I expected. I'm not going to tell you what to do. You're hard headed enough to continue with your investigation, but I want you to know I'm not happy with the way things have gone, like getting yourself shot, because I love you and care what happens to you."

"I understand why you would feel that way. I love you and I plan to be around for quite some time. When this is all over we'll take a relaxing trip somewhere. Besides, I've got Ron here to cover my sorry ass, as he calls it."

"Just be very aware of where you are and what your surroundings are. I know you are cautious, or you wouldn't have made it this far in life. Still, I'm concerned."

"Whatever I do, I will make every effort to ensure that you are not in any danger. That's one of the reasons Ron is staying at our home until all of this blows over. Just don't get too attached to him. I'll be sending his ass back to LA when we get this investigation resolved and hopefully arrive at the truth."

"Okay. Eat your breakfast. I also brought you a couple of books. I know you like Patterson and Sanford books, so I picked up one of each. I hope you haven't already read these two novels. Who knows? Based on what I do know, you have read over a thousand books written by various authors.

"Have you talked to your doctor today? Being a typical male, you don't tell me much about your condition, so I may have to either stay until he shows up, or I'll just go on a search for him."

"Thank you for bringing me reading material. Two of my favorite authors. And, no, my doctor hasn't been in yet this morning. I did talk to him briefly late last night. He said I was healing nicely and I might be able to go home either later today or in the morning. No lifting weights in the near future. Nothing over twenty pounds and no sit-ups or push-ups. I didn't ask if there would be any restrictions on making love with my lady."

"Conner!! When the time comes I'll make that call. Don't worry about that. So, does your doctor usually come around in the morning?"

"Usually, but that's not entirely predictable. I suppose it depends on his patient's needs and any emergency that may arise. In fact, he's usually here by now."

"Fine. I'll wait right here with Ron. I know you won't ask him all the questions that I would if I were you. I'll have some questions for him when he shows up." Fifteen minutes later there was a light knock on the door, the door swung open and my attending physician came into the room.

"Good morning, Mr. Pennington. I see you have visitors. I'm Dr. Benson, and you are?"

"I'm Margo Webster, Conner's partner, and this is Ron Meza, a long-time friend of Conner's. Is it okay if we stay here while you talk to Conner?"

"Absolutely. If you hadn't been here I would have had to call you in to talk to you anyway. My patients aren't always cooperative, and I find they don't always follow my instructions. Especially my male patients. You seem to be one that can enforce the rules, so, I'm glad you're here. As to the issues at hand and the recovery period for Mr. Pennington, it will take some time. Fortunately, he is in good physical condition, which will assist in his recovery. I was an Army surgeon in Vietnam and I saw a lot of wounds very similar to this. The body is amazingly resilient, and I am confident there will be a full recovery. From what I have learned about this incident, Conner is quite fortunate that a hollow-point bullet was not used. There would have been more extensive damage to his lung, with long-term effects. It was also apparent that a large caliber weapon was not used, or there would have been deeper penetration. It was most likely a .380 caliber handgun, or something very similar.

"We did notice on his x-rays that there was previous scar tissue on his left lung. We aren't sure how long that has been there, or the cause. There was no external scar tissue, so it doesn't appear to have been the result of a penetrating wound. Can you enlighten us, Conner?"

"Based on past physical exams and chest x rays, I think I can probably fill you in reasonably well on the cause of that scar tissue. It was about the sixth week of OCS and we were running the obstacle course, which includes a ten-foot wall that you have to scale as fast as you can. My boot slipped as I was propelling myself up the wall and I crashed on the top, smacking my chest against the 4x4 on the top edge. I broke one rib and cracked two others. The broken rib did not actually penetrate my lung, but it did leave scar tissue. The crazy part was, they told me I could go home, recuperate, and come back to start the entire program over again. I had already been through hell at this point and I told them I would stick it out. It hurt for a long time, but I got my brown bars pinned on with the rest of my class."

"That explains what we saw on the x-rays."

Margo couldn't wait any longer to ask her questions. "Dr. Benson, you've indicated that you expect full recovery. What is your estimate on the time period for Conner's recovery?"

"We can never be sure about that. It would be my professional judgement that full recovery would be anywhere from four to six months. During that time there should be no strenuous activity that would challenge his lung capacity. No jogging, no excessive physical workouts, and very limited lifting."

"Okay. What medications will you prescribe when Conner is released?"

"There will be some prescribed pain medication, as well as two weeks of antibiotics. I would also recommend an over-the-counter stool softener, as the pain medication tends to promote constipation. We've already given him some stool softener, but you need to continue that for at least a week."

"When will he be released from the hospital and will there be a copay?"

"I'm thinking tomorrow for checking out. As for the copay, you'll have to check with the admin office. We try to take care of our veterans here, so if there is any copay, it shouldn't be very much. I'll check his blood pressure and heart rate and I'll be on my way. Are there any further questions?"

"Not at this time, Dr. Benson. Thank you."

Margo seemed to be satisfied with the report from Dr. Benson.

"Conner, if you're okay for a while, I'm going to do some retail therapy. The Koi supply store is just a mile or two from here and I need some fish food and a new filter for the pond. I'll see you in an hour or two." A quick kiss and she was out the door.

Meza looked as though he needed a break also. "My friend, I'm going back to your house and take a power nap. Are you okay with that?"

"By all means. I have some reading material now, and I'm getting a bit drowsy myself. Talk to you later, Top."

Chapter 6

A dry throat coughing spell woke me from another senseless dream. The mystery man with the fedora made another appearance, but I couldn't recall any details. I sipped cool water through the straw that was protruding from the plastic cup on the bedside table. I was alone in my room and had no idea of the time of day, or even what day it might have been.

Dr. Benson entered my room bearing great news. I was to be released today. Whatever today was.

"I'm giving you a list of things you need to do, and things you shouldn't do. It will take a couple of hours to process everything through admin, but you're going home."

"Thank you. I'm ready to be out of here."

I called Margo and told her the news. Pick me up, I'm coming home.

Two days later I awoke late in the morning to the smell of coffee. I slowly trudged down the steps to the kitchen and found Ron at the kitchen table with a cup of coffee in his hand. Margo was sitting on the other side of the table, also with a cup of steaming coffee.

"Good morning, my lovely lady, and top of the morning to you, Top." My attempt at Irish humor didn't appear to impress either one, but I was greeted in return with a cheerful good morning.

Margo's response, beyond the greeting, was, "You look as though you feel better this morning. What would you like for breakfast? Pancakes and sausage, eggs and sausage, or a sausage biscuit?" I surmised from those offerings that we had a decent supply of sausage, until Margo followed up with, "Just kidding about the sausage. We actually don't have any sausage. That was just a play on my bringing you a sausage and egg biscuit from McDonalds when you were at the hospital."

"I get it. Ham and a couple of eggs over easy will work for me. Ron, what would you like?"

"I'll have the same, Conner." I was surprised that Ron had changed from referring to me as 'LT', to now addressing me by my first name. Making progress, as I saw it. Perhaps my calling him by his first name brought some level of realization that our days of rank and Marine camaraderie, were easing into a friendship reaching beyond a level of mutual respect.

"Boys, it's a beautiful morning. Why don't you fill your coffee cups and enjoy the morning on the patio while I whip up some breakfast? If you aren't opposed to the idea, we can have our breakfast outside."

"Sounds great to me. I'll bring some place settings out and silverware." I had reasonable assurance that Ron would not be opposed to breakfast on the patio. When I had visited him at his home in Los Angeles, we had dined on his patio. He seemed to also enjoy being outdoors whenever possible.

Finding a tray, Ron and I loaded it with appropriate dining ware, condiments, napkins, and a carafe of hot coffee and proceeded to the patio. Placing the dishes and napkins in an arrangement for three, we settled into our chairs and raised our cups in a salute to friendship and a sunny morning. Intermittent puffy clouds scuttled across the sky and a couple of fighter jets from nearby Scott Air Force Base flew low in formation over the secluded backyard garden.

"Conner, doesn't that noise bother you?" I was a bit surprised at Ron's comment. He was no stranger to such noises, but that had been some time ago when we experienced those sounds on an hourly basis in Vietnam.

"No, Ron, it doesn't bother me. It's the sound of Freedom, my friend. We often relied on those guys years ago and I'm actually delighted to see them fly over. I've never been up with one of those guys, but I've often thought about what it would be like. Pretty awesome, I'm sure."

"No doubt, Conner. No doubt. I've really had no desire to wedge myself into one of those cramped cockpits, sitting behind a flyboy jet jockey. I respect their flying skills and their missions, but as I told you back in-country, I never even like tanks. We all do what we have to do, which brings me back to your investigation. It seems to me you've gotten yourself embroiled in a situation that you probably didn't bargain for when you embarked on this truth-finding mission. Reminds me somewhat of the case you got me involved in when we talked to a person of interest in your last foray. That one ended in a death we hadn't foreseen. I hope this doesn't go that way. It came damn close already."

"You're right, and I very glad you're here. I can't think of anyone I would rather have covering my back. Let me share one thought with you. When I was shot, I had my Walther PPK hidden in the trunk of my car. My car is still impounded at the police lot and I'm sure they have located by now my .380. That's okay, for the time being. I have three or four other weapons I could carry, and I'm thinking, based on my last experience with gunfire, that I will be carrying something a little bigger, at least until this is all over. I have a Colt .45 Defender. I'll be carrying that. It has a lot more take down power than a .380."

The Colt Defender had been introduced in the year 2000. It was a scaled down model 1911 and was promoted as a concealed carry weapon. The frame is a lighter alloy, with a stainless-steel barrel. The barrel is only three inches, compared to the longer five inches we had on our government issued .45's we carried in Nam. It also has three dot Novak sights, providing quick target acquisition. Colt had made some modifications early in the development of the Defender, including an upswept beavertail grip safety and lowered and flared ejection ports. The grips are Hogue wraparound rubber, absorbing the sharp recoil of a lighter weight .45 ACP. It's no secret that a .45 caliber bullet will knock you on your ass, regardless of the point of impact. Given my past experience in the parking lot at Union Station, I liked that aspect of the Defender.

"That's a very nice weapon, Conner. Not too great at any distance, but it gets the job done. For now, I'll carry my 9mm Glock, although I do have a 9mm Sig Sauer at home, as well as a Model 1911 .45. The Glock was my department issued gun and that's what I became most familiar with. Still, the Sig Sauer is damned accurate, but then we both know that a lot of that accuracy depends on the shooter."

Margo emerged with breakfast through the sun room near the kitchen, and placed the eggs, ham, toast, butter and preserves on the table. The deep yellow yokes were huge, and there was evidence that they were just runny enough to mix well with the thick country ham. Another masterpiece delivered by my lovely lady. I rose and pulled out her chair as she joined us for a leisurely breakfast.

Conversation was at a minimum as we consumed our morning fare. Sharing a meal with Margo and Ron didn't require conversation. I had not expected to see Meza again, at least not so soon after my last investigation that took me to LA. I sensed that he had missed being involved in investigations since he retired from the Los Angeles Police Department. As we sat at the breakfast table there seemed to be a calming drift toward the companionship we shared for thirteen months in Vietnam. Those memories never go away.

"The circumstances that brought me here were totally unexpected, especially since you made it through some tough times in

Southeast Asia without receiving a purple heart." Meza tended not to discuss details of our time in-country, nor did he now. "We knew back then that we had formed a bond that would last a lifetime. I'm quite comfortable being here and spending time with you and your lovely lady."

Margo interjected, "Ron, I can't ask you to stay around here for the duration of Conner's investigation, but your presence here is appreciated. You have probably heard about the upcoming wedding on June 24th, with a lot of Italians gathering in one place. I don't know if you can be away from LA that long, but if you are still here, it would be a comfort to me if you could attend with us. I can't imagine there will be any confrontations at such a gathering, and I don't think there will be if you are there. I'm not being overly cautious, I don't think. It's just that Conner seems to have temporarily lost his situational awareness abilities."

"I can arrange to be here as long as you can put up with me and as long as you and Conner need me. That's what Marines do."

"I think I've taken enough time off from the Barrows investigation. I still haven't found anything that led Mrs. Barrows to believe her grandparent's deaths were something other than an accident. I'll help clean up here, then I'm going to go through some of those documents in my office. Margo, I heard you mention that you needed to resupply our food staples, which I assume means you're going to the commissary on base. Ron, I have no doubt that you have your retired military ID with you, so if you need anything on base, you won't have a problem getting past the front gate…even though it is Air Force. Incidentally, since it is now a joint command, they do have a few Marines on board. You won't find platoons of Marines running in formation on the streets, but you might find it interesting anyway. I once told a friend of mine, a retired Army general, that they had an overabundance of reserved parking spaces for flag officers at Scott AFB. His comment was, "As well it should be." On the other hand, they do have reserved spaces for senior NCOs. They also have a very nice facility for working out, if you're so inclined." I didn't want to push Meza into thinking he had to accompany Margo on a shopping trip, but also felt he probably needed some space and free time.

"Now that sounds like an interesting proposal. I did bring some jogging clothes and I've missed a bunch of days in my workout schedule. I might even stop by the exchange and pick up some items I didn't have a chance to pack when I got the word you had stepped in front of a bullet." It was obvious Ron had a regular regimen for exercise. I had no doubt that he regularly pumped out at least eighty push-ups every morning and could most likely bench press a minimum of 250 pounds. Probably more. Close to seventy years old, but still intimidating. I would always want him on my side.

"Sounds like a plan," Margo said. "I think I'll join Ron at the gym, then go to the commissary. You'll be okay while we're gone?"

"Sure. I won't be violating any of the doctor's orders. I just want to review some of that material Mandy sent home with me. I promise to not even lift any of those boxes full of documents."

"Okay, Conner. Ron, I'll be ready in twenty minutes."

Always gotta' have a plan, even if that plan falls apart somewhere down the road. I went upstairs to my office and settled into my now worn leather chair sitting askew behind my cluttered desk. A few minutes later I heard the garage door opening, and knew Ron and Margo were on their way to Scott Air Force Base.

My laptop, centered on my desk, had not been powered up for at least a week. Sitting to the right of my darkened computer was the accounting ledger that I had briefly reviewed before my unscheduled visit to the emergency room. It was obvious to me when I first opened the ledger that it was a personal accounting of expenses. Not a business-related account.

Kleinknect kept meticulous records of every penny he spent, including allotments to his wife. As was typical of the era, the man in the house kept tight stings on the purse. I turned the pages back to three months before his death, searching for any entries that may have clues, possibly revealing irregularities. I saw no unusual entries, but did note a pattern. It appeared that Gerard purchased gas every Thursday, in varying amounts and always paid for with cash. So detailed was each entry that he even recorded where the gas was purchased. Only occasionally were there purchases of gas on any day other than Thursday. On days other than Thursday gas had been purchased in St. Louis or Columbia. I surmised he had made road trips to his dealerships, which required a fill up before he returned home. I would have to ask Mandy if she had any recollection of her grandfather's habits, as this may be an indication of some level of OCD. I never knew anyone that had just "some" level of OCD. Everything I had seen relating to this disorder had always been full blown. It may be worth checking into.

Flipping the pages back to the latest entries, I saw that Klienknect had indeed filled his car with gas on the previous Thursday before his death. He was found dead on January 1, 1958. A Wednesday. His last fill up was for seven and a half gallons of gasoline at a cost of 24 cents a gallon. One dollar and eighty-eight cents. Cash. I wasn't sure what significance this would have in my investigation, but it was interesting that a person would be so organized and compulsive enough to record such a seemingly insignificant amount. I never had that level of interest in record-keeping for minor expenditures. I was also never as wealthy as Mr. Kleinknect apparently was. Some relationship there, maybe. Know where your money goes.

I next did some research on the internet, feeding my curiosity about the vehicle Gerard had when he died. Based on the photos I had seen in the album, it was the latest model Cadillac, a 1958 Cadillac 60 Special. It was a hand built limited production Eldorado Brougham. Very few were made, and at a cost of $13,074, not many were sold in the later months of 1957. It was eighteen feet long and had a curb weight of 5,490 pounds. The earlier photos had shown the vehicle with sabre spoke wheels and it was painted Nassau Blue. I knew that later model Corvettes had also used that color in some of their production cars. Another sign of the times, it was a four door, hardtop sedan. The six-liter, V-8 engine would be called a gas guzzler today. Sitting atop the heavy cast iron engine were three carburetors, fed by a 20.1-gallon gas tank. My research indicated that it achieved a whopping 9.7 miles per gallon on the highway and a lesser 6.5 miles per gallon in the city. I pondered that for a moment.

My gut feeling still told me that the Senator either had information I needed, or that he was deeply involved in the overall operations of the Klienknect auto franchises and could very likely have benefitted from the untimely death of his partner. Old records had not yet revealed what that might be. I was sort of depending on Crazy Joe to make contact with either the Senator, or his people, to arrange a sit-down. I had no doubt that the Senator knew more about Gerard Klienknect than Mandy did, as she was still very young when her grandfather died.

My next step was to search his business records for any indication that his demise would benefit anyone other than the Senator.

Chapter 7

Losing track of time is not my usual habit, but when I heard the garage door open I glanced at my watch and noticed three hours had passed since the departure of Ron and Margo. Must have fallen asleep at some point. Before I could gather my thoughts and meet Margo and Ron as they came in from the garage, my phone buzzed. I didn't recognize the number, but the displayed area code was St. Louis.

"This is Conner Pennington."

"Mr. Pennington. This is Detective Daniel Tanner, St. Louis PD. I'm sure you remember that I'm the lead investigator on your case. I was probably a little brusque with you when you were in the hospital, especially given your condition at the time. Still, you need to know, as I told you at the time, this is my city and I run the investigations here."

"Sure, I remember you, Detective. You probably didn't call simply to reiterate what you told me when we first met. What can I do for you, Detective Tanner?"

"Understand, Mr. Pennington, I am not calling to apologize for my comment about St. Louis being my city, but if we work together on this, perhaps we can solve it and I can get it off my case load. I indicated to you that I would be contacting you again. I have the bullet that was removed during your surgery at the hospital. Our lab has processed that bullet through the national ballistics database and we came up with some matches. No names, but a bullet fired from the same gun was used in a shooting six months ago in south St. Louis. It was identified as a .380 caliber jacketed bullet. Lucky for you. I would guess that a hollow point round would have done much more damage to your lung than did the copper jacketed projectile. There was also another ballistic match related to a shooting about two years ago in St. Charles. That's obviously not my jurisdiction, but we're working with the St. Charles PD to get as much information as they can provide about that shooting.

"Now, Mr. Pennington, have you thought of anything else that may help us in this case?"

"No, Detective, I haven't."

"Okay. I gave you my card when you were still in the hospital. My cell number is written on the back. If you think of anything else, call me. As I recall, you had a friend visiting you at the hospital. A retired police detective from LA. Is he still with you?"

"Ronald Meza. Yes, he is still in town. He'll probably be here for another two or three weeks."

"My encounter with him was very brief, but he seemed confident and experienced. Being with the LAPD would have given him a lot of experience in dealing with shootings. On the other hand, I don't know much about your background, so I have more trust in his abilities to look after you, in case there is any follow up from the shooter. Hell, we have so many shootings in St. Louis proper that we simply cannot assign officers to check on victims that survive a shooting. We're not as bad as Chicago, yet, but we're getting there. What I'm saying, Pennington, is don't be a victim again in my city. We'll get the people that were involved in the shooting, but I'd prefer it if you stayed out of this investigation. Have a good day."

I started to respond to Detective Tanner's dialogue, but the line was already dead.

With a look of concern on her face, Margo entered the small office just as I replaced my cell phone beside the computer. "Conner, are you okay? At first, I thought you might be resting in the media room, but when you weren't there, and you didn't greet us when we came in I thought maybe you weren't feeling well and had gone back to bed."

"Oh no, I'm fine. I just had a call from Detective Tanner. He's the lead investigator on the shooting. He was just giving me an update on the case and wanted to know if I could give him any more information, which I couldn't."

"Okay. Ron found some marvelous looking steaks at the commissary that he insisted on buying. He told me you seemed to really enjoy the steaks he grilled in California when you were out there on your last cold case. He also bought some sort of marinade that he had used on his steaks. Anyway, he said he could grill those whenever you wanted them. It's almost noon, and I'm thinking around 2:30 or 3:00 for an early dinner, or late lunch. Is that okay?"

"Sounds like a plan. I'll be down in a minute and thank Ron for getting the steaks. I'll make a quick call to Crazy Joe first and ask if it's okay for Ron to attend the wedding."

Television is Joe's main source of information, second only to rumors and gossip gathered from a variety of friends. It is not within the realm of possibility that he would read news, opinions, or commentary on current events in a newspaper, magazine, or other written word. So, I was fairly confident I would catch Joe at home...in front of the TV. He answered on the second ring.

"Joe, this is Conner."

"Yeah, I know. You keep telling me that and I keep telling you your name shows up on my cell phone screen when you call. I'm watching one of my favorite shows, so, what's up?"

"My friend Ron Meza is still here, and probably will be for another three or four weeks. At least until we get some things settled in this investigation. I'm calling to ask if it's okay to bring Ron with us to your son's wedding?"

"Sure. No problem. Oh, by the way, I've been talking to some folks around town, and it looks like you may be able to get a sit-down with the Senator. I'll let you know when I find out for sure. Okay? Gotta' go, my friend."

End of conversation. Time to take a break from the office and find out what Meza and Margo are up to.

"Well, Ron, those are some savory looking steaks. Almost as nice as the ones you grilled when I was staying with you in California. Just as the two of you came back, I got a phone call from your good buddy, Detective Tanner, with the St. Louis PD."

Meza looked at me as though I had begun pushing all the wrong buttons. "Don't start that shit, Conner. I believe it was obvious we weren't going to become bosom buddies. Detective Tanner needs some work on his people skills, and maybe have a greater under-standing of reciprocal agreements and professional courtesy. So, what did the Duke of St. Louis City have to say?"

"He let me know it's still his city. He also informed me that the bullet removed from my chest during surgery has been matched through the federal ballistics database. Apparently, the same weapon was used in a couple of other shootings dating back a couple of years. The bullets were all full metal jacket, .380 caliber. That's pretty un-usual. Detective Tanner didn't say that, but I did. What respectable hit-man uses a .380? Close up, maybe a .22 caliber, but if you want some serious damage, you would more likely use a larger caliber. Probably loaded with hollow points."

"I understand your logic, Conner, but before I retired from LAPD we had a rash of shootings with at least a third of them carried out with a .380. A lot of very small handguns are hitting the streets, mostly stolen from legitimate owners that are carelessly leaving weapons in unlocked cars or they are tucked in a night stand drawer beside their bed, where they are stolen during a burglary. Happens all the time. We have found that the influx of caliber .380 handguns is flooding the market, mostly due to concealed carry laws. Mind you, I'm not by any means against concealed carry permits, but, dammit, the owners should take some responsibility in securing those weapons when they aren't carrying them."

"I didn't mean to put a burr under your saddle. Hell, I carry a .380 most of the time, as you know. At least up until now. As I told you earlier, my Colt .45 Defender is going to be my companion for the duration of this investigation. At least until someone finds the SOBs that put a round in me. Personally, I would like to be the one that nails these guys.

"This may be a unique thing about the St. Louis Police Department, as well as the Kansas City Police Department. They are both pretty much controlled by the Missouri legislature, with legislative approval of the board of commissioners and even approval of salaries. As a result of that, both departments have statewide police powers. They can make arrests anywhere in the State of Missouri. I'm sure Tanner knows that, but wants to make sure we know St. Louis City is his kingdom. A matter of turf, I suppose."

"I get it. I'm no stranger to turf battles, whether it's a gang situation or city or state government, even federal agencies, there's always someone staking out their power grid. Now, when do you want these steaks?"

"How about 3:30 or 4:00. I'll show you our outdoor kitchen, then I'm going back to the office and review more documents relating to this case."

Returning to my office, I withdrew documents from one of the white storage boxes Mandy had loaded in my car weeks ago. One of the first documents I picked had a note attached by a paperclip. No sticky notes in 1957 or 1958. Gerard Klienknect had made a note to himself about an upcoming change in the Code of Federal

Regulations that was to go into effect on January 1, 1958, pertaining to record keeping. There was no indication he knew specifically what those regulations would entail, or how it would affect his business operations. Little did he know that January 1, 1958 would come and go, but he wouldn't. An item to reflect on, for sure. We never know what the next day will bring. Live it to the fullest, and apparently, he did, even though it seemed to me that his life may well have been complicated by some level of OCD.

The following legal papers established the relationship between Gerard and the Senator. The Senator was a silent partner in Klienknect's burgeoning auto dealer franchises. Based on the photos in the album, I surmised that the Senator had a significant influence in garnering bids from the Highway Patrol for purchasing fleets of vehicles from their jointly owned franchises. No surprise there. I had often seen such collusion in state government officials when I worked in Public Safety. One case involved my boss, the director of the Department of Public Safety. He had been a silent partner in an upstart university. He had pushed bypassing the bidding process to allow his business to receive federal grants for training police officers. I was later fired because I wouldn't endorse those unscrupulous programs. Gotta' look at yourself in the mirror in the morning and face your decisions. I'm comfortable with that.

Additional legal papers defined the allocation of assets in the event one or the other should be preceded in death by the partner. The Senator would retain one third ownership in the business operations if he were the surviving partner. In the event the Senator passed first, Klienknect would inherit two thirds of the business operations, with all of those assets going to his son if he should die after the Senator had died. There was a lot of legal jargon that went on for pages. It seemed like a very strange arrangement, and not really an equal partnership. Perhaps that was the way the Senator wanted it. It appeared Senator Antonio Giocomelli had no one to pass the assets to in the event of his death. The gist of these agreements did not seem to warrant the untimely death of Kleinknect. At least not to the advantage of the Senator. I still worked for an attorney in Illinois, investigating cases on his agenda. I would present him with what I had seen and let him tell me if there were hidden agreements or financial benefits that I had not noticed. Years of schooling and indoctrination prompted attorneys to couch their legal documents in terms that practically no one else could understand, even if they had the patience to read through such voluminous writings. At least that was my take on it.

It was the fourth of June, one thirty in the afternoon when I called Mandy. Either she wasn't busy, or she was attached to her cell phone. She answered on the second ring. Apparently, she had my number recorded in her phone memory bank.

"Hello, Conner. I stopped by the Jefferson Barracks hospital and discovered you had been released. I hope that's a good sign and that you are doing better. I am a little disappointed, though, that you didn't call me and let me know. Sorry. You really don't need to check in with me, but it would have been nice to know that you are on the mend."

"Okay. I have been properly chastised. Laid up in a hospital bed, I had a lot of time to think, and I will admit that I thought a lot about what you told me when you came to visit. As I told you at the time, I had no idea you had a crush on me when I knew you many years ago. I believe I told you I was flattered, but that I was involved with a wonderful lady. Still, you are quite lovely, charming, and sensual in an elegant and desirable way. So, yes, I've thought about you a lot. I also found it interesting that your timing in visiting me at the hospital was impeccable. You arrived just after Margo and my friend Ron Meza left to get something to eat."

"That was no accident, Conner. I knew they were there, and I knew when they left. I had waited an hour before I came to your room. I didn't want anyone else to hear what I wanted to say to you, and I have no regrets about revealing my feelings to you."

My thoughts went back to a comment made by an associate of mine forty years earlier. A crusty older man, with a sense of humor that I appreciated. He had been one of the original state troopers with the Missouri Highway Patrol and had been on the scene when there was a shootout with Bonnie and Clyde in Platte City, Missouri. I was never sure if he was totally serious, but one day he told me confidentially, "The only regrets I have in life are all the temptations I have successfully resisted."

"Well, Mandy, you are not only quite lovely, but also quite clever. And how did you get into my room when there was a security person at the door, with the mission to prohibit entry for unlisted personnel?"

"It wasn't very difficult to convince her that I was your secretary, even though I know you don't have one. I don't think I appeared to be a threat, although she did look through my purse. When I showed her the business card you had given me I think she was convinced that I was indeed your secretary."

"Interesting. I didn't really call to discuss your visit to the hospital. I have been going through some of the material you gave me, and I haven't found much at this point that gives me a clue why you believe the deaths of your grandparents was anything but an accident. There are some things I did find interesting, though. Reviewing the accounting ledger, I got the impression that your grandfather possibly had some level of OCD. I don't see how that fits into the investigation, but his meticulous accounting of every dime he spent leads me to believe he was a captive of his own design, or demons, whatever the case may be."

"I didn't know my grandfather that well, but my own father affirmed your impression about obsessiveness and OCD. They never really identified such a disorder in those days, but I would agree that he was a self-imposed victim of OCD. I don't understand that disorder fully, but I think you are correct in assuming grandfather exhibited signs of OCD."

My interest in human behavior had prompted me to pursue a degree in psychology. I still subscribed to Psychology Today, the leading magazine for definitive studies in psychology, particularly for a large population having an interest in recent studies relating to mental health issues.

I had recently read that the obsessive-compulsive disorder is an anxiety disorder in which people have unwanted and repeated thoughts, feelings, images and sensations (obsessions) and engage in behavior or mental acts in response to these thoughts or obsessions. A person's level of OCD can be anywhere from mild to severe, but if left untreated, it can limit his or her ability to function at work or school or even lead to a comfortable existence at home or around others.

The article in Psychology Today further described the symptoms of people with OCD. They have repeated thoughts, images, and urges about diverse issues, including being compulsively neat and organized; fearing germs, dirt, contamination, intruders, or violence; or imagine hurting loved ones or committing sexual acts or behaving in a way that conflicts with religious beliefs. They also typically engage in repetitive behaviors or mental acts such as washing hands, locking and unlocking doors, counting, keeping unneeded items (hoarding), or repeating the same steps to any task again and again.

"You are a very perceptive person, Mandy. It seems you wanted me to arrive at a conclusion that you had already reached. Without your input that may have clouded my assessment of your grandfather's condition. Was your grandfather compulsive about locking doors?"

"I think you understand now why I was suspicious that his death was not an accident. Yes, he was very compulsive about locking doors. When I was a little girl and my mother and father took me to my grandparents for a visit, my grandfather always locked the door connecting the kitchen to the garage. I thought he was hiding something in the garage that he didn't want me to see or play with. While I was visiting, I would see him check that door three or four times before going to bed, to make sure it was indeed locked."

"Yes, I do understand. The news article about the accidental deaths indicated that Senator Giocomelli found them in their bedroom on January 1, 1958, with the front door unlocked and the door from the kitchen to the garage open, allowing fumes from the car that was still running to fill the house with carbon monoxide. I would guess that even if your grandfather had consumed a lot of alcohol on New Year's Eve he would still have compulsively locked the kitchen door leading to the garage."

"Yes, that's what I believe, Conner."

"Still, that doesn't tell us who might have planned an event that would appear to be either suicide or accidental deaths as a result of carbon monoxide poisoning. If you have any thoughts along those lines, please let me know."

"The only person that was there, had access to the house, and might have had the means, opportunity, and motive is Senator Giocomelli. He usually stayed with my grandparents when he was in town for legislative sessions, and I would guess he had a key to the front door. I'm not accusing him of involvement in the deaths, but I really can't think of anyone else."

"Thank you, Mandy. I'll keep that in mind. Take care, be careful, and we'll talk again soon. Bye for now."

Chapter 8

I began to understand Mandy's doubts about an accidental death. With the conversation ended I reflected on the news article about the discovery of Mandy's grandparents. Senator Giocomelli had stated that he found the front door unlocked, as well as the door that led from the kitchen to the garage that was open. Were his statements truthful? I felt that a conversation with the Senator might shed some light on the events of that early morning discovery. Would not the Senator have found it unusual to arrive at Kleinknect's home and immediately notice that the front door was not locked. They were friends and partners. Surely the Senator knew of Gerard's obsession concerning locked doors. Even Mandy, as a young girl, had noticed her grandfather's obsession.

I left my office and met Meza in the kitchen, where he was preparing the steaks for the grill. He was also preparing baked potatoes to go on the grill. He had just stabbed the potatoes with the tines of a narrow fork when I approached him.

"Ron, that was very thoughtful of you to pick up those steaks at the commissary. I appreciate it. When you get a minute, I would like to run some things by you. It's about the Barrows investigation."

"Sure. Let's go out to your outdoor kitchen, and I'll put these potatoes on the grill. They'll take a bit longer than the steaks."

"Based on my experience with you at your home in LA, I'm

guessing you prefer using charcoal. I'll admit that charcoal does give a better flavor to steaks than grilling with gas, but I switched to gas some time ago. I just got tired of waiting for charcoal to reach a grilling temperature, and then the maintenance that it takes to keep that temperature throughout the grilling process, especially if I'm grilling ribs, or anything else that takes a longer period of time. Anyway, I have to give credit to Margo for this outdoor cooking area. She built it herself, long before I arrived on the scene. I'm not even sure why she built it, as she confided in me that she never used the gas grill that is in the central part of the counter. I replaced the grill she had originally installed with an updated Char-Broil infrared grill.

"I'll open the valve on the gas bottle, fire up the gill, then you're on your own. Just so you know...it will get very hot in just a matter of minutes. Great for searing. I'd recommend you put the potatoes on the top rack."

"I'm a Marine, Conner. Improvise, adapt and overcome. I actually have cooked with gas before now, so I believe I can adapt to this grill."

"No offense intended, Top. I just didn't want you to have any surprises. Having spent thirteen months with you in-country, I know you are capable of many things. Some of which we don't mention. When I first met you in the jungles of Vietnam you took me aside and advised me, as a boot lieutenant, that we should operate based on your combat experience in Korea and Vietnam. That was excellent advice. I recall telling you that I was there to learn from you. Well, I believe we are in a similar situation here. You have vastly more experience in dealing with the criminal element than I do, and I would like to get some input from you concerning this investigation and what I have learned thus far."

"Don't underestimate your abilities, LT. Tell me what you've found, and we'll see where that leads us."

"Let me summarize what I think are the pertinent issues in this case."

"Stop right there. I thought I taught you better than delivering a discourse on important matters without a shot of scotch in hand. So, break out the scotch, take a seat, and we'll continue this discussion."

"Now that sounds like a plan, only this time we won't be sitting in the shade of a 52-ton tank solving all the world problems. I'll be right back with the elixir that fuels the solving of important issues."

When I returned with a bottle of Johnny Walker Blue Label scotch Ron had taken a seat at the table near the outdoor kitchen. Placing two tumblers on the table, I poured a healthy shot of scotch into each.

With a slight smile, Ron raised his glass in a salute, clicked his tumbler against mine, and said, "To the Corps, God and Country. Now, proceed with your discourse."

"I'll add one more thing to that. Let's also drink to a lasting brotherhood.

"You know I've been trying to locate and talk to this Senator Giocomelli. He was the friend and partner of the deceased car dealer and was the one that discovered the bodies on the morning of January 1, 1958. According to a statement he gave the newspaper, when he arrived at Klienknect's home the front door was not locked and the kitchen door leading to the garage was open. The car in the garage was running, the garage door was closed, and the home was filled with the fumes from the exhaust. He allegedly opened the garage door, turned off the ignition and went directly to the master bedroom, finding the Klienknects in bed. DOA.

"While studying a personal ledger that was meticulously kept by Kleinknect, I noticed patterns that led me to believe he had some level of OCD. I asked Mandy if she recalled anything about her grandfather that would confirm such a disorder. She recalled, as a young girl, that her grandfather seemed to be obsessed about locking doors, particularly the door that led from the kitchen to the garage. At the time, she just thought he didn't want her to play in the garage. Apparently, he often checked that door while she was there. Again, I'm thinking OCD.

"Where I'm headed with this, is, I can't get my mind around the issue of the two doors being unlocked when the Senator arrived. Even if Klienknect had consumed a lot of alcohol the night before his death, his compulsive-obsessive behavior regarding locked doors would have overridden any fuzzy mental state resulting from alcohol consumption. I just haven't convinced myself that he left those doors unlocked. The mystery to me is who unlocked those doors, and why.

"Legal documents indicate that the Senator may have gained financially as a result of Klienknect's death, but probably would have benefitted more had he remained alive. Seems to be an oxymoronic conundrum. Damned if you do, and damned if you don't." My focus was to have a conversation with the Senator, concerning his involvement in the deaths of the Klienknects, as well as his possible involvement in my having been shot. Having left my name in various places on the Hill, with the message that I would like to meet with the Senator, then shortly after that being warned off, and then shot, well, what was I to think? The Senator's link to these events seemed to be the bond that compressed all of this into one neat little package. Another sip of scotch as I waited for a response from my old first sergeant.

"Logical thinking, my friend. But, having a meeting with the Senator most likely will not illicit an admission from him that he was complicit in the shooting, or in the deaths of the Klienknects. Addressing those issues on a different level might be the way to proceed. Present your case to him as though you are simply seeking his knowledge on who could be involved, without expressly exposing any level of conspiracy or collusion. I don't think you want to imply that he has anything to do with illegal activity. I have no idea what his power base is, but I have a sense that at some point in the past he was a power broker, at least in St. Louis, and maybe even statewide. Tread carefully, LT."

Meza continued, "Do you believe your friend, Crazy Joe, can arrange a meeting with the Senator? I gather he still has some connections with the Italian family. I don't find it unusual that law enforcement personnel involve themselves in activities that benefit their role in dealing with organized crime. Sometimes crossing over the line becomes easier each time you step on that line and the line then becomes quite vague. Joe seems like the sort of guy that could justify to himself that the line doesn't even exist. Am I right?"

"I think that would aptly describe Joe and his relationships with the Italian family. He makes no secret of those connections and uses those ties to his advantage. To answer your question, yes, I believe he can foster an understanding with the right people that I merely want to talk to the Senator about his discovery of the bodies of his partner and his partner's wife. We're all ignorant…just on different subjects, but Joe has a knack for discerning the intentions of people. He's a survivor and to a great degree an accomplished manipulator. I hope you are still here when, and if, we get an audience with the Senator."

"Count on it. Most of the time I loved my work with the LAPD and I'm looking forward to being involved at some level in this investigation. A bit like old times. I'll take a refill on the scotch, with one ice cube, then I'll check with Margo and see where she is on the schedule for dinner. It's all in the timing, you know. I was told a story by an old Native-American friend that the success of a rain dance was all about the timing. I don't want to put the steaks on too early. Timing, my friend, timing."

Returning from the kitchen, Ron had the steaks on a platter, apparently having gotten the go-ahead from Margo. "For steaks this thick it's going to take at least fifteen minutes on each side, even though Margo warned me that her steak should still be moving and bleeding. Quite a catch, my friend. You don't want this one to get away." The smell of the meat and marinade wafted into the still air, while Ron and I sat at the table and enjoyed another two fingers of scotch. It took me back to the night on the back deck of Ron's home in the low hills of California.

Twenty-five minutes later a wonderful later lunch/early dinner was spread on the patio table. Margo opted for a red wine and Ron and I stayed with the scotch. Everything was perfect. The smaller steak for Margo had been placed on a cooler side of the grill and she informed Ron that the pink inside was perfect. It was all good.

Conversation for the next two hours never ventured near the subject of the Barrows investigation. Meza shared with us highlights of his life, but not without a lot of prodding from Margo. Although born in the US, Meza's parents had migrated from Mexico City two or three years before he was born. His father had studied to be an architect and further pursued his studies when he arrived in California. He became quite a successful man and it was with a great deal of chagrin that he watched Ron depart for MCRD (Marine Corps Recruit Depot) San Diego two weeks after high school. Fathers often have expectations for their sons that aren't matched by the whims and desires of their offspring. I listened in fascination, as Margo probed and unmasked the life of Ron Meza. Back in the jungles of Southeast Asia we had never discussed our personal lives. It just didn't seem to be a guy thing, or maybe we had too many other issues to discuss.

Although my father told me just prior to his death that he was proud of me, I had the sense that he would have liked for me to follow in his footsteps and be a preacher man, just as his father had been, as well as his grandfather. I didn't pursue that avenue, I left it up to my brother to go in that direction, which he did, to a certain extent. Oh sure, Ron and I had seen a lot of men and boys get in-stant religion when the bullets and incoming rockets were flying around during that crazy war in Nam. My prayer was, "God, give me a steady hand and a true aim."

After twenty years in the Corps, a tour in Korea, duty as a drill sergeant, and two tours in Vietnam, Ron retired as a first sergeant. He was quickly accepted by the Los Angeles Police Department, where he advanced to the level of a homicide detective before retiring. His days in uniform had long since ended, and he confided that he often missed those days. He loved the intrigue of solving mysteries, and he was looking forward to seeing where the Barrows investigation would lead. I gave him no assurances that we would eventually arrive at the truth of this case, but that was my goal. Being the son of a preacher man, I reflected on what I remembered of John 8:32, "Then you will know the truth, and the truth will set you free."

Being of Hispanic descent, Ron had experienced discrimination while a civilian, but very little while serving in the Marine Corps or the LAPD. I was dismayed to hear that my friend had gone through some of those experiences. We had both agreed many years ago that we didn't judge a person by their color, religion, or ethnicity. Our assessment of an individual was based on their actions. We operated our tank company that way, and it seemed to work…most of the time.

It was soon evident that the sun was slipping toward the tree line in the west. Margo had gone back to the kitchen, then returned with a surprise…apple pie and ice cream. It seemed like a fitting close to an early dinner and companionship. Having grilled Ron about his life, Margo was now on the pedestal.

"Now that I have divulged almost my entire life as a result of your expert questioning techniques, it's your turn, Margo. Tell me about yourself. You don't have to start with the day of your birth. Conner has already told me you were born in Louisville, Kentucky and that you host a Derby Party each year, regardless of where you are in the world. What I would like to know, is how in the world did you two meet? Not through military circles, I'm sure."

"Well, Ron, I suppose turn-about is fair play. I lost my husband some years ago. He was a career Air Force officer in charge of security at Scott Air Force Base, and after he retired we stayed here."

I had to interject at this point, "Margo was already oriented to military customs, so I didn't have to retrain her. It's been a good fit."

Continuing with her dialogue, and answering Ron's last question, Margo smiled ruefully and told Ron, "We met on-line. Match.com. We communicated by e-mail and by phone for three or four months and finally decided we needed to meet in person. So, we picked a date and met at a place in Alton, Illinois called Fast Eddies. After months of commuting between Jefferson City and Belleville, Conner packed up and moved here. We've been together since then."

"Interesting, but that doesn't tell me everything about you and your life." Ron seemed to be intent on learning more about Margo.

"That's all you're getting for now, Ron. Now enjoy your pie and ice cream. It's been a long day and I'm going to exercise my 'mother' options and send Conner off to bed. Not to be judgmental, but I doubt the doctor's recuperation recommendations would include copious amounts of Johnny Walker Blue Label. I'll clean up here, which will give you about five minutes to enjoy the sunset, then we're shutting down for the evening. It has been a wonderful afternoon and evening, but Dr. Benson gave me orders to enforce his recommendations, knowing that Conner probably wouldn't follow his orders anyway. He told me most of his male patients simply didn't exercise good judgement during the recovery stage, so it's up to me."

Ron and I responded at the same time. "Yes ma'am."

Chapter 9

S lowly removing myself from the comfort of a snug bed, I had to admit that Margo's advice to terminate my consumption of Johnny Walker's elixir the previous evening was the right and proper thing to do.

It was overcast and if it didn't rain all day, it was missing a damn good chance. Maybe do a rain dance? The timing seemed to be just right for producing results. I joined Margo and Ron downstairs at the breakfast table and discovered Margo preparing one of my favorite breakfasts that I shouldn't be eating. Biscuits and gravy. A steady drizzle was now blanketing the area. We needed it.

After breakfast I returned to my office to review more documents concerning the Barrows investigation. The photo album finally progressed in time, with twenty or thirty photos showing Klienknect with Highway Patrol vehicles in the background. His last photos with Patrol vehicles was a series of Chevrolets at his dealership in Jefferson City. It was noted that he had sold 455 Chevy sedans to the MSHP in late 1957, even though they were early productions of the 1958 models. It wasn't noted with the photos how many of these vehicles they sold to other law enforcement agencies, and maybe it never happened until after the death of Gerard Kleinknect. Evident in some of these photos was Senator Giocomelli.

Returning to legal documents and statements about sales in his various dealerships, I discovered that by the end of 1957, Kleinknect owned a total of 23 dealerships. Some in remote locations around the state. Springfield, Joplin, Kansas City, Blue Springs, Macon, Rolla, St. Louis, and St. Joseph. I found it interesting, though perhaps not relevant, that most of those dealerships were near Highway Patrol Troop Headquarters. Either strategically located to service the vehicles sold to the Patrol, or just happenstance. Later photos, after 1958, were of Gerard's son at those same dealerships. Mandy's father Alfred, had obviously taken over the reins of the business. Still, in some of those photos the Senator was standing with Alfred Kleinknect, with what appeared to me to be a close family or business relationship. Again, there were no family gatherings throughout the entire photo album. Unusual, to say the least. There may have been family albums located at the estate that Mandy had inherited when her parents were killed in a traffic crash. Were there other forces at work that Mandy had overlooked? Were the deaths of her parents a tragic accident, or was there some level of conspiracy that was intent on eliminating the Klienknects from the motor dynasties that had been created through the assistance of a state senator and the entrepreneurship of Gerard Klienknect? I began to question the overall role of the Senator, the underworld in St. Louis, and the potential for corruption and collusion in state government.

The sales of hundreds of vehicles purchased through a questionable bidding process seemed to have fed the coffers of the Klienknect kingdom to assist in spinning to the top of the heap among auto dealers. Reinvesting what may have been illegally gotten gains, Gerard sought and gained additional franchises for high end automobiles, such as Bentley and Rolls Royce. The estate I visited in Creve Coeur, when I met with Mandy, was evidence that a lot of wealth had been handed down from the senior Mr. Klienknect. My friends, there is no crime in that. It's the American dream.

Did the Senator continue to influence bids after the death

of Gerard Klienknect? I noted in my historical research that the Highway Patrol purchased Oldsmobiles in 1966, and Mercury vehicles in 1967. In 1968 more Oldsmobiles won the bid and in 1969 Buick won the bid. All were sold to the Patrol through dealerships owned by the Knienknect dynasty. Interesting.

Development of questions for a sit-down with the Senator kept flashing in my mind as part of a to-do list. Accusatory questions would most likely put the Senator in a defense mode, with no truthful information gained. It was my understanding that the Senator stayed at the Klienknect home when he was in town, but that apparently wasn't the case for that tragic New Year's Eve, the last day of 1957, and the last day for Mr. and Mrs. Klienknect. The Senator had been with the fated couple that evening at the country club and had scheduled brunch with them the next morning. It would have been logical for the Senator to have spent the night at their home. Did he not have a key to let himself in if he arrived at the home after his friends departed from the club? Were his statements to the newspaper and the police truthful?

Pondering the formation of non-accusatory questions was not even relevant to the case, unless a meeting with the Senator could be arranged. While reviewing additional documents relating to auto sales in cities spread across Missouri, my cell phone buzzed.

"Mr. Pennington, this is Detective Tanner. Our lab techs have gone over your vehicle with a fine- tooth comb and haven't found any relevant evidence that would lead us to the individuals involved your shooting. We did find your handgun in the compartment you indicated. You can come by the police impound lot and retrieve your car, as well as your Walther PPK, at your convenience. You will, of course, sign a receipt for the weapon and your vehicle. The sooner you do that, the better it will be for all of us. There is an average of twenty cars a day brought into that lot. Two more days and we will start charging for storage.

"Have you thought of anything that you may have forgotten to mention in our previous conversations?"

"No, Detective, I haven't."

"Well, Mr. Pennington, other than the match on the ballistics that I mentioned to you, we have nothing else to go on. Until we can tie those matches to a specific weapon, and then to a specific person, we are simply casting about in the dark. The case is headed no-where for now. Call the impound lot and let them know when you're coming. Have a good day, Mr. Pennington, and remember, this is my town." With that reaffirmation of his turf control, the Duke of St. Louis ended the call. Tanner was as brusque as he had been on previous occasions and Meza's tag of calling him the Duke of St. Louis was right on. I would make arrangements to retrieve my Maserati and the Walther PPK tomorrow. Until then, I would continue a review of materials provided by Mandy.

Sunrises are an awakening of the soul, as well as singing birds and life in general. I was reminded of a nonsensical poem, allegedly by Henry Gibson, of the TV series *Laugh In*.

As I awoke this morning, a bright new day was born.
A robin perched upon my sill to signal the morning dawn.
I smiled at his cheery song, then it paused a moment's lull.
And I gently closed the window and crushed his frigging skull.

What a morbid thought to start the day. Not even funny when you think about it. There are times when twisted humor remains in the recesses of my mind and then surfaces when I least expect it. Events, names, places, small details of conversations, all seem to be stored in files somewhere in my brain housing group, with a seeming inability to purge those useless files.

The rain had moved on to Indianapolis, or at least somewhere to the east of Belleville. Not eager to become entangled in rush hour traffic, particularly the slow- moving traffic on the Poplar Street Bridge, I waited until 9:30 before I shaved and dressed for my trip to the impound garage and lot. I was hoping that Tanner had instructed the keepers at the lot to keep my Maserati in the garage, not simply sitting in the open with other impounded vehicles of much lesser value. My experience with Detective Tanner doesn't give me much hope that he would exercise any authority to look after my best interests. Not much I can do about that at this point.

I had given Margo and Meza a heads up that I wanted to pick up my Maserati today. Top indicated he would relax in the botanical garden Margo had created in the back of the house, all of it surrounding the Koi pond. It was a secluded park, with tall wood fences shutting out the neighborhood. The sound of splashing water cascading into the pond was soothing and helped to drown out ambient traffic noises from nearby streets. I couldn't much blame Ron for opting out of a trip into downtown St. Louis, instead staying for a relaxing morning in what we referred to as "Hide Park." A subtle play on Hyde Park. Besides, Margo had a thing about giving places and rooms identifying names. Margo would drive 'Mr. J', our Jaguar, to shuttle me to the impound lot.

The impound lot was located five blocks from police headquarters, and eight blocks from the new Busch stadium. As expected, traffic was stop and go until we reached the off ramp for Market Street. After passing two streets that were one way, going the wrong way, we finally arrived at the lot. An old warehouse was part of the fenced compound. Razor sharp concertina wire adorned the top of the cyclone fence that was at least ten feet in height. The aura of a secure prison yard was the impression I had, but then, in this neighborhood it was probably necessary. I'm thinking there should be guard towers at each corner of the compound, but there weren't. I parked on the street and told Margo to lock the doors and wait for me.

A gray steel door, with steel mesh embedded in the small window, appeared to be the entrance to the building housing the offices. The door was locked, but a speaker next to the door allowed me to announce my arrival to the occupants barricaded inside the fortress. Having verified my legitimacy and my mission for gaining entrance, a loud buzz and a mechanical click gave me a clue that the fortress door is now unlocked. I pulled the door toward me and noticed that the hinge pins had been welded, preventing unauthorized entry by some enterprising thief.

Fluorescent lights glared on the bare concrete floor and a musty smell permeated the vast interior. Directly in front of me was a cage, surrounding a government issue metal desk, a clerk in faded gray overalls, and rows of file cabinets and what appeared to be locker room lockers. A scarred metal shelf protruded through a six by eighteen-inch opening in the enclosure.

With a bored, tired expression, the keeper looked up from whatever videos he may have been watching on his three monitors that were bolted to the desk and addressed me. "Mr. Pennington, I presume. I'll need to see some identification before I can release your property." Sunken cheeks, missing teeth, close set eyes, and a scraggly mustache. Looked to me like a meth addict.

I produced my driver license and inquired if that was satisfactory. After a perfunctory examination, the keeper pushed the photo ID back through the opening and noted that I was who I said I was. Keying a hand-held radio, he called for someone named Rodney to come to the front.

"Okay, Mr. Pennington, I'll need your signature on this receipt, showing that you have received your property."

This is no time to be a smartass, but I'm not signing a receipt until I actually do have my property. "I'll be glad to do that when I have examined and have in my possession what I can to retrieve."

"Right. The property list shows that we have a Walther PPK,

with holster and two magazines in our locker. In the lot we have a red Maserati that has been released from the crime lab. Is that the extent of your property that we are holding?"

"I'm sure it is, but I would like to see those items before I sign."

In response to my request, the keeper rolled his chair back from his desk and opened a locker using a key fastened to a chain attached to his belt. I was not able to see if there were additional items in the locker, but the keeper removed my Walther and slid it through the opening of his cage. I'm wondering at this point if the cage is to keep him inside, or to keep me out. I carry a list of my handguns in my wallet, with the serial numbers…just in case any of them are stolen I can report the number and model of weapon to law enforcement. From that list I compare the serial number with the weapon the keeper has presented. It matches. The magazines are loaded, but the Walther is not. I always keep it fully loaded, with one round in the chamber.

"Sir, were there additional rounds that were removed from the gun?"

"Let me check." Turning back to the locker, the clerk I have designated as the "keeper", fumbled inside the locker and brought out seven hollow point rounds. "Sorry, I didn't notice them. I'll make a note on the property receipt that you also took possession of seven loose rounds."

Distracted temporarily by the exchange with the "keeper", I hadn't noticed that Rodney had entered the room. Rodney also wore what must have been the uniform of the day…faded gray coveralls.

"Rodney, show Mr. Pennington where his vehicle is. It's the red Maserati."

Turning to the keeper, I asked, "Is it okay if I put on the shoulder holster and take the weapon with me when I examine my vehicle?"

"Sorry. I can't release any property until you sign the receipt. Just leave those items here, and when you came back from examining your car I'll give you the keys and the rest of your property and you can be on your way."

I followed Rodney through the cavernous building, weaving through cars, pickups, and a few delivery trucks. The delivery trucks and pickups blocked my view of the number of cars in the indoor storage area. I didn't see my Maserati. For good reason. I was led to a sliding door that opened onto the outside compound. On the back edge of the lot I spotted my Maserati. Shit. They could damned well have stored my car inside. As I got closer I could see bird shit on five or six places, not to mention the fact that it was covered in dust. Further examination of the condition revealed a dent on the edge of the driver side door. Was this an indication that Detective Tanner simply didn't give a damn what happened to my car, or did he even have anything to do with its placement in the impound lot with rows of abandoned pieces of crap?

Don't theorize about Tanner's motives, or his involvement in where your car was parked. Okay, Conner, you're pissed. File a complaint about the dent, for all the good it will do. Take your vehicle and weapon, sign the damned form and get the hell out of here.

Back inside, standing before the keeper, I couldn't ignore the condition of the Maserati. "I'll sign the property receipt, but I am also making a note on the form that there is a dent on the edge of the driver side door. I'm very unhappy that my car was stored outside, instead of inside, where I noticed you had plenty of room to do so."

"Mr. Pennington, you can do as you damn well please, but understand, I don't make the rules. We expected you to pick up your vehicle six days ago, but you didn't. So, now here you are. I was told by a plainclothes cop to leave it outside."

"I was only informed yesterday that I could pick it up."

"Again, I don't make the rules. Make whatever notes you want on the form, but as far as I know, that dent was on your car when it was brought in. Probably put there by the towing guys. Here's your keys, your weapon and your holster. Rodney will open the gate at the front of the lot."

I signed the form, noting the dent, took my keys, weapon and holster and left through the steel door that I had entered thirty some minutes earlier. Margo was waiting in the Jag, saw me coming and hit the toggle switch to unlock the doors.

"Okay, my dear, it's all settled, but I am not a happy camper. I'll tell you about it later. You can head for home and I'll be there soon. Before you leave I'll put my shoulder holster on. They're opening the gate to the lot, so I'll go over and head out. See you at home." I strapped on my holster, inserted the seven rounds in the magazine, chambering the final round, then tucked the PPK into my holster. I gave Margo a kiss and returned to the impound lot. I glanced back as she drove around the corner and out of sight.

Rodney was waiting for me at the open gate and closed it immediately as soon as the rear of my car cleared the enclosure. I turned left and headed east on Belmont. Glancing in my rearview mirror, I noticed a black Cadillac leaving the curb a block to the west. Some level of paranoia, or was this car following me? I turned north on 15th Street, then made a quick right on Clark Avenue, heading east again. The Cadillac was still back there. I knew Clark Avenue ended just before Busch Stadium, so I took a fast right onto Tucker. Detective Tanner was probably sitting at his desk at City Hall, which was on my left. Looking over his domain, no doubt. My issues with Tanner was not my primary focus at the moment. A bit of anger and animosity, yes. The Cadillac made the right turn with me. I no longer had any doubts about being followed.

Passing under I-64, I continued south on Tucker. My Maserati goes like a bat out of hell and corners like a scared cat. I doubted the Cadillac had that ability, and if it did, I was hoping the driver didn't. Soulard district takes on the flavor of New Orleans, or they say in Louisiana, Nawlens. Wonderful restaurants and night spots. Historic U.S. 66 crosses Tucker, where I took a fast left. If you don't know the area, it can be confusing. This street is also Highway 100, as well as its official city name of Chouteau Avenue. When I headed south on Broadway, the Cadillac was just turning onto Chouteau. "Social House Soulard" is on my right. Too early to be open, but I know there is a parking lot behind the restaurant, which will hide my car if I get there quickly. I don't see the Cadillac yet. The Social House is billed as a sports bar with scantily clad waitresses, which is true. I park around the back of the bar, exit my car, and thumb off the security strap holding my Walther in the shoulder holster. Watching from the corner of the building I see the black Cadillac going south on Broadway, greatly exceeding the posted speed limit.

I left the sports bar parking lot, going in the opposite direction, and found an entrance ramp to I-55/I-44, which will take me to I-64 and across the Poplar Street Bridge. Checking my review mirror frequently, I see no evidence that the Cadillac has followed me. Probably still wandering around the Soulard District, caught in the traffic around the Anheuser Busch brewery.

Coming home, Margo.

Chapter 10

L ong before I reach my turnoff from I-64 onto Green Mount Road, when I call Margo and ask for landing permission and my approach, I ponder the events of the last twenty minutes. Are the Cadillac occupants the same goombahs that shot me while I was at my car in the parking lot of Union Station? If so, how the hell did they know I would be picking up the Maserati from the police impound lot? Furthermore, how did they know I would be in the parking lot at Union Station? They either have one helluva' communication system or there are more goombahs around than I would have suspected. Granted, I have never seen another red Maserati Gran Sport around St. Louis, so maybe I'm not too difficult to find. I knew from prior research that only 480 Gran Sport models of the Maserati had been imported to the United States in 2004. Perhaps less than 100 of those were still on the road. Less than fifteen percent of that model was the Italian designated color of Rosso Mondiale. Red. My appreciation of rare automobiles may not be to my advantage since meeting Mandy again.

The off ramp for Green Mount Road reminds me to call Margo about my approach and landing.

"Hello, my lovely lady. I'm just turning onto Green Mount Road, requesting clearance for approach and landing. I'll be there in a few minutes."

"Conner, I've been home for some time now. Did you get delayed at the impound?"

"I'll tell you about it when I get home. It's okay."

Margo and Ron Meza met me at the door to the garage when they heard the garage door opening.

"It may be a bit early for problem solving liquids, but I think a shot of scotch and a gathering in Hide Park might be in order." Retrieving two tumblers from the glass cabinet, I dropped an ice cube in the tumblers and poured a couple of fingers of scotch into each. I didn't think Ron would object to a before five o'clock libation, and he didn't. When we were seated around the patio table I told them about the events when I left the impound.

"I'm more than slightly pissed about the condition of my car when I retrieved it from the impound, but that's another issue to be dealt with later. After Margo left, I pulled out of the lot and noticed a black Cadillac about a block away, to my right. It pulled away from the curb when I turned left on Belmont. I didn't think too much of it at first, but then they took the same turns I took. I made two or three turns that would not have been the normal route for anyone in the downtown area, and they were still behind me. After some evasive maneuvers, I parked behind a bar in the Soulard district. The Cadillac sailed on by and I left in the opposite direction."

There was no doubt in my mind, based on the intensity of the expression on Meza's face, that my old friend loved the intrigue and mystery of an investigation. "That's very interesting, Conner. My first question would be, how would these people know when you were going to be there at the impound lot to pick up your car? It wouldn't make sense to think they had placed a tracking device on your car. That would only tell them where the car was, not when you would be there to pick it up. I think we can discount that idea. Besides, if they had placed a tracker on your car, you would not have been able to lose them. Based on my experience, gut feeling, and instincts, I would guess that someone at the impound lot gave these people a heads-up about when you would be there. I'm thinking maybe a little cash exchanged hands."

"I have a feeling you are right, Ron. A tracking device would not have told them when I would pick up my car. Just to be on the safe side, I'll check my car for any hidden tracker. I have a scanner that I have used to debug offices, when some of my clients have felt they were being recorded surreptitiously. It picks up most frequencies that are used by tracking and bugging devices."

A later thorough scan of my Maserati revealed no discernable radio frequencies.

"Conner, I don't know how they handle things in St. Louis, but back in LA we would have a chat with the people at the impound lot. Perhaps you and I should go over there and have a Come-to-Jesus meeting."

"If you're up for that, it sounds like a plan to me. I won't be driving the Maserati back there, though. I'd suggest we take the Jag. I'm sure you have a lot of experience in gathering information from guys that may be reluctant to share what they know, or what they think they know. Having said that, I'm going to leave the questioning techniques up to you."

At 9:15 the next morning Ron and I left Belleville and drove the fifteen miles east on I-64 to downtown St. Louis. The Poplar Street Bridge was surprisingly free of congested traffic and we arrived at the impound lot forty-five minutes later. We approached the steel door to the office and I announced through the wall mounted speaker who I was and that I had some questions concerning the receipt I had signed the day before when I had retrieved my property.

There was thirty seconds of hesitation before a metallic voice came back through the speaker, "Don't know what you need, Mr. Pennington, but I guess I can buzz you in."

Ron and I were greeted by a quizzical look on the face of the 'keeper', who likely didn't expect anyone to be with me. Ron can be a very intimidating personage, as he was now. I also noticed that he had attached his gold detective badge to his belt, in a place where it was sure to be noticed.

Ron started the conversation. "I don't see a name tag on your coveralls. I'd like to know who I'm addressing."

"It's William. Everyone around here calls me Willy. What's this about? You're not really here about the receipt, are you?"

"No, we're not, William. Mr. Pennington was followed when he left here with his vehicle. We don't think those people were waiting around here for days, on the off-chance Mr. Pennington would be here on any given day. When Mr. Pennington called you, and let you know he would be picking up his car yesterday, you were the only one who knew he would be here on that day. Unless you are involved in a criminal conspiracy with the people you called to let them know Mr. Pennington would be here, it would be in your best interest to share that information. Who did you call?"

"Look, man, I don't want no trouble. Three or four days ago a guy comes in, says he's with a collection agency and a guy named Pennington has a Maserati in the impound lot. Tells me Pennington owes a lot of money and he wants to collect. He wants to know when Pennington comes in for the car. He lays a hundred-dollar bill on my desk and tells me to call a number that he writes on a piece of paper. I was just helping the guy out. Everybody's gotta make a living, you know. I didn't see anything wrong with that." Pointing at me, Willy continues, "I pay my debts. Just because he owns a Maserati doesn't mean he can't pay his debts, you know?"

I was waiting for a response from Ron, which didn't take more than five seconds. "You were duped, William. Your benefactor is a gangster. When we leave here we will be leaving with that phone number and you will not call that number again. Do we understand each other?"

"Yes, sir, we do. Like I said, man, I don't want no trouble. I got his number somewhere in my desk. You know, I thought this collection guy might want some help again. I can't tell you much about him, though. He wore a suit. He was big, dark hair, and looked like maybe he was one of those guys that go to a gym a lot. I don't know nuthin' else. I swear."

"Okay, William. Let's have the phone number and forget you ever saw it, or us. You won't be calling him again and we were never here today. You understand everything I'm telling you? I'm quite certain you don't want another visit from either of us." Willy dug in his desk and came up with the phone number.

Leaving Willy to his thoughts, we left through the steel door. Before reaching the car, Ron turned to me and said, "Dollar-to-a-doughnut, that number we just got from Willy will belong to a burner phone."

I punched in the number Willy gave us. Meza was right. That number was disconnected. No leads from that end.

Meza had another thought. "My guess is that one hundred dollars either went up Willy's nose or into a vein."

No black Cadillac today. Driving back to Belleville, my phone buzzed, and I let it go to message. Pulling into a gas station on Green Mount Road I filled up and checked my phone for messages.

Crazy Joe had called and informed me that Senator Giocomelli had agreed to a sit-down. Tomorrow at 3:30 pm. A private dining room at Giovanni's on the Hill. There was no indication how Joe had arranged the meeting, and I knew not to ask. Joe didn't always do things above board. In his message he told me to call him and confirm that I would meet the Senator at that time.

Ron agreed to accompany me, then reminded me that it might be advantageous to invite Joe, as long as he didn't get involved in the conversation with the Senator. I called Joe and became a bit worried when he didn't answer after eight rings. With nothing to do and all day to do it, Joe usually picked up on the second or third ring.

On the tenth ring Joe answered his phone.

"Joe, this is Conner."

"I've told you before. You don't have to tell me who you are. It shows up on my screen. You got my message, huh? So, will that time work for you?"

"I plan to be there, and Meza will be with me. Let your contact know, and I would like for you to be there also. Can you arrange your busy schedule to make time for that?"

"I don't know that I want to get involved in your investigation, but I guess I am already. Why don't you pick me up around 2:30 and we'll go to the Hill together. Makes it a lot easier for me." Joe was always looking for the easiest way to do anything. I agreed to pick him up and the call was ended.

Part Two

Chapter 11

At least the sit-down would be in a public place, although owned, operated, and situated among a bevy of Italians.

Heavy rain, with lots of thunder and lightning had interrupted my sleep several times during the night, as well as thoughts about the upcoming meeting with the Senator. Sometime during the night, I thought about the significance of all that commotion outside my window. *Thunder is impressive as hell, but it's lightening that gets the job done.* I wondered now if it might be some sort of omen. I hoped not.

For the thirteenth of June it was cool, which suited me, as well as Ron. I was carrying my Colt .45 Defender and Meza strapped on his 9mm Glock. Sport coats covered our weapons, both of them being in small-of-the-back holsters. It didn't appear as though we would be uncomfortable in jackets. Ominous steel-gray clouds moved quickly toward the northeast as I moved my Jaguar S-Type from the garage. Ron was riding shotgun and I had almost suggested a shotgun under the front seat might not be a bad idea. There was one overwhelming problem with that idea...I had one shotgun, a twelve gauge, and it definitely would not fit under the seat. Still, I had seen Top in action in combat and had confidence that he would have my back covered. I was also relatively confident that when he retired from the Corps his combat days were extended through his years with the Los Angeles Police Department. I had the feeling he looked forward to the adrenaline rush. As for myself, I wasn't ready to experience another episode with bullets being exchanged. On the slim chance our situation deteriorated to that point, First Sergeant Ronald Meza, USMC, (Retired), would be the first person I would want on my side.

On our way to pick up Crazy Joe I drove down Highway 100, also known as Manchester Road. My plan was to stop at four or five dealerships on Manchester, getting a feel for those that were, or might be, owned by either Mandy Barrows or the Senator.

Our first stop was at a dealership located on the north side of Manchester Road. It was simply named "The Senate." Now why would I believe this was owned by the Senator? Very few cars that were for sale were parked outside, but there was a large showroom, with floor to ceiling glass facing the highway. Upon entering the show room, we were greeted by a young gentleman wearing a black tuxedo, with tails. The floor was covered with highly polished marble and oriental area rugs. Not your run-of-the-mill dealership, for sure, but the vehicles housed inside were not your everyday automobiles. My thoughts flashed back to my one visit to Pebble Beach and the annual Concours d'Elegance held each August.

"Gentlemen, would you like coffee, or perhaps champagne? Ah, perhaps a bit early for the bubbly?" This was delivered with a distinct British accent. "May I show you our collection? We're very proud of our motor cars, all of them on consignment. They have all been serviced to the highest standards in our well-appointed service facility."

At the back of the showroom was a 1962 British Racing Green Series I Jaguar E-Type. Tan convertible top, tan upholstery, and polished wire wheels. So pristine, that in my estimation it could have been previously owned by Steve McQueen, a collector of fine automobiles. It was sensual and elegant, worthy of display at the Guggenheim Museum of Art, located in the Upper East Side neighborhood of Manhattan. For some time, an E-Type had been displayed at the Guggenheim as a masterful work of art. Velvet ropes on stanchions surrounded the silver automobile to the left of the E-Type. Another Jaguar. An open two-seater, as the British referred to such vehicles. If it was authentic, and I suspected it was, this was an original 1938 SS Jaguar 100. While attending college I had owned a 1953 Jaguar XK 120 open two-seater. It was the successor to the SS 100, and I knew Sir William Lyons, the founder of Jaguar, had an affinity for adding a number after a certain series of Jags, denoting the top speed of that model. A vintage classic, very rare, and very expensive. In 2010 at the Pebble Beach auction a perfectly restored 1937 SS Jaguar 100 sold for $1,045,000. The SS 100 was built between 1936 and 1940 by SS Cars Limited of Coventry, England. Only 49 were exported.

"Gentlemen, an exquisite motor car, isn't she? We negotiated with the estate of Alan Kenneth Mackenzie Clark to sell this vehicle. I'm Scot Mackenzie, and this was my great uncle's vehicle. Uncle Alan served in Margaret Thatcher's government as Minister for Defense Procurement. It was rumored he was a bit of a rogue, and became known for his flamboyance, wit and irreverence. We currently have a bid of $2,550,000, which we are considering, pending approval of the estate. The E-Type was previously owned by Steve McQueen. We have a buyer in Paris that has shown a delightful interest in this classic jewel. On the other side of the E-Type we have a 1953 Jaguar XK 120, perfectly restored. This is also a very rare motor car. As you can see, an open two-seater, wire wheels, dual exhaust and an aluminum body. It was set up for racing, with three oversize SU side draft carburetors, racing heads from the C-Type Jaguar and a sixteen-quart oil pan to keep the engine cool. It was previously owned by the first American-born driver to win the Formula One World Driver's Championship, Phil Hill, who was quite an accomplished race car driver throughout his career. Quite an excellent example of the XK 120." I also knew that Mario Andretti, an Italian American driver, won the World Driver's Championship in 1978, but he was not born in the United States.

Oh, my God. If this was indeed the vehicle previously owned by Phil Hill, then this may be the Jaguar I owned when going to college. I had lost track of it after selling it to a collector in Missouri.

Our host continued. "The XK 120 is being shipped to a buyer in London next week."

I couldn't just let this slide by without comment. Seemingly useless information continues to be stored in the recesses of my mind, sometimes surfacing at the least expected time. I remembered the serial number of my first Jag. I also recalled a lot of history about Phil Hill. Hill had died sometime in 2008, having retired from racing, then becoming a narrator for TV sports programs that related to racing. He also had judged the Pebble Beach Concours d'Elegance longer than any other person. His 40th judging was in 2007, shortly before he died. He was a gentleman race driver. One I always admired, and not simply due to the fact that I had owned one of his early race cars. "Mr. Mackenzie, the 120 is indeed a fine example of a revolutionary motor car. If the serial number on this car is 670138, I can provide you additional provenance for your personal edification on the history of this Jaguar. If that is indeed the number on this 120, I can tell you that I once owned this very Jaguar, back in 1963. It was my first Jaguar, but not my last. I sold it to a collector when I was going to college." Confirming the matching serial numbers, I continued my part of the history on this storied vehicle. "The aluminum body was beginning to show signs of metal fatigue and I was not in a financial position at the time to undertake a full restoration. I'm very impressed with its current condition. May I sit in it for old times sake?"

"And you are, sir?"

"I'm Conner Pennington and this is my associate, Ronald Meza, with my office in California." He really didn't need to know that much, even though a large part of it was fiction.

Scot glanced toward a large window that displayed a very comfortable office, where a white-haired gentleman sat at a desk with his back toward us. I suspected he was checking out the powers that be before he made a decision on my request.

"Well, well, Mr. Pennington. This is very unusual. We don't often receive potential customers in our show room that have previously owned one of our exotic motor cars. Since this vehicle had been sold and will soon leave for England I see no harm in your reminiscing behind the wheel of her."

It was not quite as I remembered the '53 XK 120. Perhaps age was a considering factor. Getting positioned behind the steering wheel was more of a challenge than when I was much younger. My thighs touched the bottom of the huge steering wheel and it was much too close to my chest. Either the car had shrunk, or I had gotten bigger over the years. I couldn't convince myself that the car had shrunk. Those things happen, but not to cars. It reminded me of the oft used excuse for clothes not fitting as they did in the past. Closet shrinkage.

Scot Mackenzie was obviously a car guy and was proud of the motor cars in the inventory. Partially hidden behind a huge white 1957 Rolls Royce Silver Cloud was a bright red Maserati. Before I could examine the Maserati, Scot informed us that the Rolls had been previously owned by the Duke of Wellington. The asking price was upwards of four million. I nodded my acknowledgement of the importance of this vehicle and moved on to the Maserati. It was an A6GCS, 1955. Although silver instead of red, this was the car in my crazy dreams. Driven by the stranger wearing the fedora. Scot informed us that the legendary Juan Manuel Fangio had piloted this car in the 1955 Monaco Grand Prix. I was Impressed. I'm not sure Meza was.

"Scot, I'm very impressed with your motor cars that you have on display. Quite a collection. I don't believe I would be wrong in assuming you are a person that is very interested in classic motor cars. Tell me, have you seen the collection of vehicles at Hyman LTD on Chaffee Drive? A wide variety, but not quite to the standards here."

"Oh, yes sir. The owner of this dealership also owns Hymen LTD. We're also very proud of the vehicles we have at that location."

My love of fast cars overwhelmed my need to keep a low profile. "Have you ever, in your time with the dealership, had in your inventory a 1959 Tipo 61 Maserati Birdcage?" I had never actually seen one in person, but in my mind, that is the most awesome Maserati race car ever built. I knew that the Birdcage had won the Nurburgring 1000 Kilometer in 1960 and 1961. A stunning car.

"No, Mr. Pennington, to my recollection, at least during my time with Senator Giocomelli, we have not had a Tipo 61 Maserati. I have heard there is one in a collection somewhere near Springfield, Missouri."

My curiosity was getting the best of me, but I had come to this dealership to get a sense of the operation. "Scot, you must have some amazing connections to be able to collect such motor cars in one place. I was totally unaware of the magnitude of this dealership."

"Oh, yes sir, we are very well connected throughout the rare motor car collectors in the UK, the continent, and Asia. We are often in contact with collectors such as Craig McCaw. Such collectors, for insurance and other reasons, prefer anonymity, which we honor religiously. In fact, Mr. McCaw has recently assigned one of his prominent vehicles to us for sale, which we have completed. The vehicle is now in our service area being prepared for shipment to Dubai. It's a 1962 Ferrari 250 GTO, which he allegedly purchased for $35,000,000. Clearly, McCaw had something left of the $11.5 billion AT&T paid to acquire McCaw Cellular in 1983. I'm not allowed to discuss the current purchase price, or the new owner, but I can show you the vehicle, if you would like."

Not sure if Ron was interested, but I sure as hell was. "By all means. I would love to see in person a Ferrari 250 GTO. Surely it's the famous Ferrari racing red?"

"It is, indeed, Mr. Pennington. Shall we?"

The service area appeared to have been surgically scrubbed. The floors were polished concrete, with carpet pads under the wheels of each motor car in the vast cavern. My attention was immediately drawn to the gleaming red Ferrari 250 GTO. Stunning! I could only guess the sale price, but undoubtedly somewhere beyond the $35,000,000 McCaw had paid. I dared not even ask to sit in this work of engineering art, but I circled the vehicle and admired the lines at great length.

"Thank you, Scot. I truly appreciate the fine motor cars you have in this facility. You have been very gracious in showing us this awesome collection. I'm afraid we have other appointments and have to be on our way."

"Certainly, Mr. Pennington. If you have a chance, you might stop again at our facility at Hymen LTD, where we have a revolving collection of pre-war American motor cars, as well as a very nice 1936 MGPB open two-seater. A delightful collection there, but, unfortunately, none of them have the provenance of the vehicles we have at this facility. Thank you for stopping in. Do return when you have the time."

Ron and I had spent more time at "The Senate" dealership than I had anticipated. We left the opulence of "The Senate" and drove west on Manchester to pick up our conspiratorial passenger, Crazy Joe. I didn't want to be late for our sit-down with the Senator and the traffic on Manchester Road was getting heavier as the day progressed.

Chapter 12

"I would say the Senator has a lot of connections in a lot of places, and a lot of money." I gathered from Ron's comment that he was less impressed by the vehicles than he was by the influence and connections the Senator had in various parts of the world. "Well. College boy, you never shared with me when we were in-country that you like fast cars. How the hell did you end up in tanks? They weren't sleek and they weren't fast. So, you actually owned that Jaguar that was sitting in the showroom?"

"Yup, I did. When I had it, it didn't quite look like it does now. It needed restoration, and I did some of that, but I didn't have the resources to do a complete job. Still, it was very interesting to see something that went that far back in my past. Hell, even further than we go back, Top. It's also interesting to see the influence the Senator still has in the realm of auto collectors. I was thinking while we were there that the Senator probably has multiple off-shore accounts. Given his alleged background, that wouldn't surprise me."

"Right. I don't think we need to address that when we meet with him."

"No. That's not a part of my investigation. That's up to the feds. Let's pick up Joe and head back to the Hill."

After another forty-five minutes of fighting increasing traffic on

Manchester Road we arrived at the residence of Crazy Joe. He had cleaned up reasonably well.

I had to know. "Joe, are you carrying?"

"Conner, I haven't carried since I left the department. It's okay if you guys are, but I've had enough of that. You know I'm still connected with the family, but only the soldiers carry, and we don't talk about that either."

"Okay, my friend. You don't really have to do anything in this sit-down with the Senator. Just stand by and they'll recognize you're connected, right?"

"Yeah, they know. Remember, I'm the one that set this up, through some old connections my father had. There won't be any problems. My father, God rest his soul, paid the price years ago. They know who I am. Just try not to piss anyone off. Capisce?"

"Yeah, Joe, I understand." To my knowledge, that was the only Italian word in Joe's vocabulary.

Conversation was minimal as we drove back east on Manchester Road to the Hill. Approaching from this direction we turned north to arrive at Giovanni's fifteen minutes early. We were scheduled to meet the Senator at 3:30, between lunch and start of dinner service, but then the Senator was apparently a good friend of Giovanni Gabriele.

When we approached the entry, the maître d opened the door. "You are here to see Senator Giocomelli, no?"

"Yes, we are."

"Come in, come in. The Senator waits. Please, this way."

We wound through dimly lit hallways until we reached a back-dining room, far removed from the main dining area. The door was open. Seated behind a round table that would accommodate eight, was a white-haired gentleman of approximately eighty to eighty-five. He wore an off-white three-piece suit, an expensive silk shirt, no tie, with his hands resting on the table. He was obviously of

Italian descent, with an olive complexion, and bushy white eyebrows that were neatly trimmed. Behind him, to his right and left were two gentlemen standing, with their arms by their sides, jackets unbuttoned. Dark haired Italians with noncommittal expressions. Not someone to be messed with, I'm sure.

Meza and Crazy Joe followed me into the room, but stopped just inside the doorway, as we had previously discussed. They took the same position as the two men standing behind the Senator.

"Mr. Pennington, I presume." There was no evidence of an Italian accent. Deliberate, with a deep baritone. "Sit." Not a suggestion, nor even a command. Just do it.

"Yes, sir. I am Conner Pennington. These are my associates, Ronald Meza and Joe Ferranti."

"Well, Mr. Pennington, I don't know you, but I know of you. Apparently, you have been asking around the Hill to have a meet. My associates," motioning to his left, "Vinny Tommaso," and motioning to his right, "Sal Moretti. I do know of Mr. Ferranti, and he is welcome. So, Mr. Pennington, talk."

"I am investigating the death of Gerard Klienknect. You were a good friend and associate of Gerard and discovered his and his wife's bodies shortly after their deaths, according to the news reports and the police investigation. I simply want to find out what you recall about that incident. I have no reason to believe you were complicit in those deaths. From what I have discovered, you had nothing to gain as a result your partner's early demise. I'm just trying to piece together information. As I understand it, you were with them at the country the evening before and had a brunch date with them the next morning at the club. Is that correct?"

"Such a tragic incident. Yes, I was in town for the upcoming legislative the session and frequently stayed with Gerard when in town. As you noted, we did have an arrangement to meet for brunch the next day at the club. When he didn't show up on time, I called his home and got no answer. He was always very punctual, so I went to his home and discovered them in their bedroom. They were dead."

"Senator, tell me what you remember about that morning when you discovered the bodies."

"When I arrived at the home of Klienknect I rang the doorbell and got no answer. Then I knocked very loudly on the door. Still no answer. I tried the door and it was not locked, so I went in the front door and loudly called for Gerard, letting him know I was in the house. There was still no response."

I felt this was an opportune time to ask one of the questions I had written on my notes for details only the Senator could answer. "Since you stayed with the Klienknects often when you were in town, did you have a key to the front door?"

"I did have a key but must have misplaced it. Now, let me finish. When I entered I smelled exhaust fumes in the house and also heard a car running. Passing through into the dining room and glancing toward the kitchen I noticed the kitchen door to the garage was open and Gerard's Cadillac was running. I immediately opened the garage door and went to the car to turn off the ignition. The radio was on, and to this day I remember what was playing. Pat Boone was singing "April Love". Strange, that I still remember that song. I ran back to the front door and opened it to clear the air in the house. I still called for Gerard as I moved to their bed room. They were both in bed. I couldn't wake them, so I called for medical assistance using the phone beside the bed. An ambulance and the police came. I gave my statement to the police. That's all."

"Thank you. I have another question for you, Senator. Since you were going to have brunch with them that morning, why didn't you stay with them that night?"

"Next question." His eyes told me that I was not to pursue that line of questioning. I wasn't sure why, but neither would I ask for clarification.

"During the time you knew Gerard had you ever known him to leave the kitchen door to the garage unlocked?"

"No. Never. He was, how do you say, anal about locking that door, as well as the front door. It did seem to me at the time to be very unusual. He was a man of habit and did things in a regular routine."

"Do you think he had a condition that we now call OCD?"

"I don't know that term. Tell me, Mr. Pennington, what is OCD?"

"The letters stand for obsessive-compulsive disorder. Many people who have characteristics of OCD exhibit an obsession about locking doors, checking them often."

"Yes, Gerard did that often, that's why I found it very unusual to find the front door unlocked and the kitchen door to the garage open."

"Thank you, Senator. His granddaughter also noted that he had an obsession about locking doors, particularly the door from the kitchen to the garage. When you were celebrating New Year's Eve with the Klienknects the night before, did you leave the club before or after they did?"

"Next question."

"What I'm really interested in, based on your observations, was Gerard impaired to the point that he shouldn't be driving, or that he would forget to shut his car off and then leave the door to the garage open?"

"We all had a lot of champagne that night, but Gerard was used to that. I can't tell you what impact that had on him, but the whole situation seemed unusual."

"Are you aware, Senator, that after asking around on the Hill for a connection to you and asking for a meeting that I was warned to back off and then a day or two later was I shot?"

"I've heard that."

"Well, Sir, I'm not a big believer in coincidences. What can you tell me about the shooting?"

"I can tell you I had nothing to do with that incident. Obviously, you don't understand the connections on the Hill. When you begin asking about me there are people that get anxious. Associates I may have known in the past are not happy about having their activities looked into by a private investigator. I suspect family connections may have thought you were trying to gain information related to me that may potentially expose certain investments and activities they may have been engaged in over the years. It would be wise for you not to continue searching for certain connections here in St. Louis. This, Mr. Pennington, is my town." It seems that a number of people think this is their town, including Detective Tanner.

"Have you heard who wanted me taken out of the picture?"

"Next question."

"I will assume your associates are here for the same reason my associates are here. Am I correct?"

"I dunno, Mr. Pennington. My associates are always with me. I will tell you that I have heard there was a contract on you. Your associates may be useful in that regard, but I will put out the word that you and I have talked, and you will be welcome on the Hill, but only for the fine restaurants. Capisce?"

"Yes, sir, I understand. Thank you for your time and the information."

The Senator stood and offered his hand. I stood and shook. I very strong grip for a man of his age. He looked me in the eye, and with his left hand touched me on the shoulder. With a knowing half smile, he commented, "Be careful, Mr. Pennington."

I nodded an acknowledgement, turned to the door and left the room with Meza and Ferranti bringing up the rear.

I didn't expect anyone to follow us, and they didn't. In the safety of my car I turned to Joe and asked why he didn't tell me that he knew the Senator.

"I have never met him before today. He didn't say he knew me.

He said he knew **of** me. I told you before, my father went way back with the family. There's history there, that's all. Remember what I told you when we took a ride…don't be messing around with family business. The Senator told you the same thing."

"Okay, Joe. I get it. If you don't know the Senator, then how did you arrange for me to have this sit-down with him?"

"Shit, Conner. Do I have to explain everything to you? I know people who know people. Doesn't mean I'm involved or know who contacted who to get this done. I just put out the word that you wanted to talk to the guy."

Meza injected, "So, Joe, do you think he was telling the truth about the shooting? That he had nothing to do with that incident?"

"When asked a direct question, we have an honor code. Yeah, I believe he was telling the truth."

Not believing in coincidences, I addressed Joe. "Okay, I make some contacts on the Hill and put out the word that I want to talk to Senator Giocomelli, then I get a warning to quit asking, then I get shot. What the hell would you think?"

With a note of chagrin and seeming as though he's addressing a third-grader, Joe replies, "You talked to too many people. When you shake enough trees, something is going to fall on your head. That doesn't mean the Senator had anything to do with the hit. There are a lot of goombahs out there that don't want a private dick looking into activities where they already have the rails greased. Capisce?"

"I'm not sure I do, Joe. Are you telling me that the Senator may not in fact be involved in illegal activities, but perhaps he engages in some things that may be on the shady side and those people on the edges may have wanted me to quit digging?"

"Yeah, Conner, that's pretty much what I'm telling you. When you find yourself in a hole, don't keep digging. Obviously, there are people out there that don't want you digging. Whatever it is that they think you were digging for, they most likely have their asses already covered. Could be city officials taking a little retirement package on the side, cops looking to retire in the Bahamas. Who knows? You start pulling on loose strings and things start unraveling. It's like a blanket made of yarn. When it's all unraveled, whatever was being covered up is now exposed. Stick to your investigation of this guy that died a hundred years ago. The Senator ain't going to bother you about that."

"I get your point, but it wasn't a hundred years ago. What do you all think of the Senator not answering the question about why he didn't stay with the Klienknects on New Year's Eve? I think there are a whole lot of things tied together, and I think the Senator is somehow in the middle of it. I agree that the Senator probably didn't have anything to do with the shooting, but he may have an idea who was involved. I also have no doubt that he was involved in some shady deals when he was a senator. He had a lot of influence when he was in the state legislature and I think he used it to his financial advantage. On the other hand, what politician doesn't?"

Meza had years of experience in questioning suspects and I respected his insight. I listened when he had input, like now. "There could be a number of reasons why the Senator didn't answer your question about not staying with the Klienknects that night. There is a possibility that he could have known prior to the incident that there would be two deaths that night, although I don't think that was his reason. Another scenario is that the Senator had something going on the side and either didn't want the Klienknects to know or didn't want to disturb them. Do we know if he is married, or was married at the time?"

I had not come across any documents that indicated whether he was or wasn't married at the time. I had assumed that a young man he had posed with in a photo was his son. Perhaps not. "Joe, you indicated you knew of the Senator. Can you tell us if he was married at the time of the deaths?"

"I have no fuckin' idea, Conner. Hell, I can't even remember if I was married back then."

"From what I know about you, Joe, it would not have made any difference in your sexual activities if you were married or not. Then or now."

"Careful, Conner. Careful."

"I'm not impugning your character, Joe. Just making an offhand observation. Another issue. When I asked the Senator if he had any idea as to who may have wanted me out of the picture he wouldn't answer that question either. What do you make of that?"

"Well, my friend, you still don't understand the family code, do you? My father taught me a long time ago, no matter what you know, and whether you agree with it or not, you just don't rat on any family. The Senator may or may not know, but it just ain't somethin' you talk about. He as much as told you that. So, if you really want to know, you'll have to find out on your own. The Senator won't help you and, my friend, I won't either."

The traffic was light for late afternoon on Manchester Road and we had arrived at Joe's home.

"Thanks for coming, Joe. It was important to me and to get your input on the nuances of family operations and thought processes. We'll see you on the 24th at Little Joe's wedding. Ciao."

No further discussion. Joe was closing his front door as we left the curb and headed back to Belleville.

Chapter 13

There was that to think about. Little Joe's wedding. Not counting Crazy Joe's immediate family, how many members of the "family" would be there? I knew Joe still had connections, so this may be an opportunity to do some checking on folks that may have some idea who wanted me removed. I doubted that the Senator would be there. I didn't think he had been invited, since Crazy Joe had told me he really didn't know the Senator.

Before I could ruminate further on the family connections in St. Louis my cell phone signaled an incoming call. It couldn't have come at a more appropriate time. The screen indicated the call was from Gregory Taylor, a.k.a. "Twitch", St. Louis FBI.

"Good morning, Mr. Taylor. To what do I owe the pleasure of your call."

"Even though you lost an important file, I'm going to do you a favor. And, no, you don't get any more files from me. I have information from a reliable source that you had a meeting with Antonio Giocomelli. Is that correct?"

"Yes, Greg, that is correct."

"Okay. Obviously, you haven't taken advice from those in the know. Namely, those who have told you to not be nosing around mafia connections in St. Louis. I'm going to do you a favor, though. I have one of my guys that has been undercover for eight years, working inside the organizations of organized crime in the city. He has agreed to meet with you and tell you what he knows about the current state of affairs with the Italian organizations. We have a comfy little bar and grill we use for conversations. My guy will meet you there at 2:30 this afternoon. No names on the phone. Alphonse's is located at the corner of Washington Avenue and 14th street. Identify yourself to the bartender when you get there. He will show you to a private room in the back. Are you up for this?"

"Sounds like an opportunity I can't pass up. I believe you briefly met my retired first sergeant, Ron Meza, when I was in the hospital. I'm still a little cautious about traveling around your city without a backup. That was an explanation of why I would like to bring Ron with me to the meeting. Is that okay with you and your guy?"

"Ummm, I don't usually have civilians meet with my undercover guys. I'm making a big exception to even have you meet him, but I've known you for years and I trust you to keep your mouth shut about what you hear. I know Ron was a Marine and a retired homicide detective from LA, but can you vouch for him one hundred percent?"

"I would trust him with my life and have. There aren't too many people I would call a trusted friend, but you are one, and he is the other."

"Good enough. So, you'll meet my guy at Alphonse's?"

"We'll be there. Thanks for being where you are. Semper Fi, my friend."

I had no desire to be driving in that part of town in a red Maserati. Ron and I loaded up, Ron with his 9mm Glock and I took my Colt .45 Defender. You never know.

We arrived at the bar and grill at 2:15 and parked a block from the hole-in-the-wall building that fronted Washington Avenue. I thought it prudent to park on 14th Street. No parking meters there. Alphonse's couldn't have been more than eighteen feet wide, most likely built in the 20's or 30's. As with other buildings on that strip of Washington, there was a depth of sixty or seventy feet. One window was high on the front of the building, with rusty bars covering the frosted glass. Facing north, there couldn't have been much light penetrating the interior, which I'm sure was by design and perhaps why this location had been selected for a clandestine meeting.

After surveying the area for anyone that may be taking an unwanted interest in our presence, we pulled the front door open and stepped inside. A long bar to the left had seen a lot of service. A burly bartender leaned against the worn counter, attentive and wary, but not showing any outward level of concern about our entering his domain. Given his bulk and the oversized shirt that more than adequately covered his muscular frame, my perception was that he was carrying. Considering the location of this establishment, why not?

"Gentlemen, what's your pleasure today?"

"I'm Conner Pennington and this is Ron Meza. We were instructed to be here at 2:30 today for a meeting."

"Right you are. Please follow me." Before leading us toward the back of the bar, he stepped to the door and turned a sign hanging in the reinforced window. "Closed" until sometime later. He then led us to a private room, where the scarred door was open. Seated at a small, round table was Taylor's guy. A battered dartboard hung on the wall over his left shoulder and a cold mug of beer left another wet ring on the surface of the wood tabletop.

"Gentlemen, have a seat. I'm Sal Moretti."

"Of course you are. I recognize you from our meeting with the Senator. His trusted associate. Well, now I know how your boss discovered so quickly that I had a meeting with Giocomelli. I'm sure you remember from that meeting that my 'associate' here is Ron Meza."

"Certainly. Before we launch into some more serious discussions about who runs St. Louis, would you like a beer, or perhaps something else?"

"Sure. A cold beer would be good. A pale ale works for me. Ron, what would you like?"

"I'll have the same." I hadn't noticed the bartender still in the doorway behind us, until he responded with, "I got it, Sal."

Our beers arrived in short order, in frosty mugs. A few more wet rings on the table couldn't hurt. Maybe even add to the authenticity of a well-established neighborhood hangout.

"Well, gentlemen, Taylor has told me a bit about you two. I understand you were both Marines and Vietnam vets. I was a Marine grunt during our first foray into Baghdad. We had just crossed the river on the south side and were advancing through a swampy area with tall grass when we got the command no grunt ever wants to hear. Fix bayonets. That will pucker you up fast. I'm sure you both have some pucker-factor stories to tell and that could take most of the rest of the day. I lieu of that, I propose a toast. To the Corps, gentlemen. Semper Fi." We raised our mugs, clinked them together and echoed a mutual sentiment of Semper Fi.

"Let's get on with it. First of all, this room is wired, as is the rest of the bar. For now all recording devises are off until we finish here. Everything I tell you is off the record and doesn't go beyond these walls. Now, your friend Joe is a made man. His parents were both from Sicily. He's involved in low level and mostly petty stuff. He passes information within the family. No record of any illegal activities, but we watch him. The mafia has had a presence here in St. Louis as early of 1876, when the Italians from New Orleans began their trek north shortly after the Civil War. They had some activity during Prohibition, and that's where Mr. Ferranti, Joe's father, got his foothold in the family. You probably know that Joe's father did some time when the Feds caught him running beer. He never talked, and the family has taken care of Ferranti ever since. However, the Italians didn't dominate organized crime until after the repeal of Prohibition.

"By the time Prohibition arrived, there were five gangs of importance in St. Louis. The Sicilian Green Ones, the Pillow Gang, the Egan's Rats, the Hogan Gang, and the Cuckoos. Strange names, I know. The one branch of the family we are interested in descended from the Sicilian Green Ones. The Green Ones reportedly received their name from the farming communities in Sicily where they came from. The leadership of this group, brothers John and Vito Giannola, and Alphonse Palizzola, came from the Stoppagleria faction of the Sicilian Mafia. As a bit of irony, we named this little establishment after Palizzola. Pasquale Santino, a member of a rival gang, put the finger on Alphonse Palizzola, and he became the first of the Green One's leadership to be murdered. I believe it was sometime in 1927 when four gunmen blasted away at Palizzola on Tenth Street, just a few blocks from here. Thus, the honor bestowed up on him by having his name above the door. Great, huh? Conner, I hear you almost earned a similar honor."

"Right. Close, but not there yet." Apparently, Sal knew a lot about what goes on in St. Louis.

"To continue. I love this history. When you're a part of it, as we were in the Corps, you learn the history. Now, Vito Giannola was the next to die when he was shot 37 times while hiding in the house of Augustina Cusumano sometime in late 1927. Giannola had chased away Cusumano's husband and had been living with the woman. You might start recognizing some of these names. They're still around. Cusumano is a broadcaster on local TV. Another guy I'll bring up in a minute is Bommarito. Owns a big car dealership. Actually, three of them now.

"Anyway, back to Giannola. Two men, claiming to be police officers, came to the house and, after finding Gianolla hiding in a secret compartment upstairs, murdered him. John Gianolla went into hiding after the death of his brother and was never again a factor in St. Louis. He was said to have died peacefully in his sleep sometime in 1955. During the short reign of the Ginnola/Palizzola led Green Ones, police records show 30 people were murdered and 18 wounded. Among the wounded was James Licavoli, the future boss of the Cleveland Mafia. Licavoli was shot by police as they attempted to arrest Joseph Bommarito, an associate of the Green Ones. The police killed Bommarito when he resisted arrest."

"Lot of familiar names. I'm sure most people in St. Louis have no idea about those characters of the past. I didn't know the mafia was that strong in this area." I had heard those names in the past, but certainly didn't associate them with the St. Louis Mafia. Sal was on a roll, displaying his historical knowledge and didn't appear as though he wanted to be interrupted again. So, I shut up and took another sip of my pale ale.

"This is the interesting part. After all of those murders and passing of the RICO Act in 1970 the influence of organized crime in St. Louis diminished tremendously. To maintain some level of influence, they aligned with the Kansas City Mafia, and the Chicago, and Detroit Mafia. That's pretty much their status today. Not as strong, but they're still here."

I had to interject again at this point. "That's very interesting history. It does give me a perspective of what has happened here in the past and how things have evolved. So, where does Antonio Giocomelli fit into the scene?"

"Giocomelli has some time in the mafia history. I'm sure you know he is called "Senator' because he was a state senator for many years, beginning in the fifties and ending in the seventies. It wasn't unusual for the family to have top level people in the state legislature. Giocomelli was only one of many. The Senator is currently the boss in St. Louis. That's the head of the family that runs the show. He decides who gets made and who gets whacked. The boss also gets points from all family business. I'm sure you have seen movies about the mafia, where the boss was referred to as the don, or chairman."

"You're telling me the Senator is still involved in family business?"

"Oh, sure. The guys in the family simply refer to it as 'garbage business', which is their euphemism for organized crime. A lot of the mafia guys made a chunk of money illegally, then invested that nest egg in legitimate businesses. The Senator has done well with those investments. We don't have any evidence yet that we can present for a grand jury and may never get that evidence. The Senator is involved very deeply in the auto industry. St. Louis is a union-controlled town and the family controls the unions. The union of International Association of Machinists and Aerospace Workers control the automotive technicians in the auto dealerships in St. Louis and the surrounding area. The guys that move your car into the service bay to be worked on by the union auto technicians are members of the Teamsters Union. That's all controlled by the local unions, and the family, including Teamsters Local 688 and 1187. Antonio Giocomelli is at the top of the heap. Any union that has anything to do with auto dealerships is still pretty much controlled by the Senator."

I thought at this point that I still wasn't grasping the magnitude of the Senator's influence. "It appears to me that when Giocomelli was a state senator he may have had a significant influence on awarding state bids for law enforcement vehicles. From my years in state government I don't find that unusual, unless there were some heavy-handed threats, blackmail, bribes, or intimidation. Usually, it was a quid pro quo situation. It was more like one legislator would tell another, I'll do this for you, if you vote for my bill. Hell, that still goes on, even in Congress. I don't see that it is illegal. It's just politics as usual."

Sal wasn't finished. "I don't think we'll ever change the nature of politics in America. Not that those same manipulations aren't used across the globe. It is what it is. I've seen new politicians come into the fold thinking they are going to change the world, or at least their little part of it. Within a few years, sometimes months, they realize they can't make progress with their agenda until they play the game. Absolute power corrupts absolutely. That's a quote from someone. Just don't remember who said that, but I totally embrace the truthfulness of that quote."

"Mr. Moretti, since you are on the inside, do you have any idea who was involved in putting a hit on me?"

"Hell, Conner, if I did we would have already had them behind bars. All I can say, with a high degree of confidence, is that the Senator had nothing to do with that incident. I suspect it was another faction that felt you were going to be investigating events or operations that may have an impact on them. The most likely group would be the Detroit connection. I went undercover in Detroit for six months, and I can tell you they have strong connections to the St. Louis family. I worked closely with an undercover Michigan State Police officer who filled me in on the Detroit operations. Great guy named Bob. Never knew his last name. Anyway, that's my take on what may have happened. If we get a line on that connection, we will certainly follow up."

"Mr. Sal Moretti, thank you so much for a trip through the St. Louis underworld and for your candor. It has been a very informative meeting. As for Ron and myself, we never saw you today."

"As it should be. Be careful out there, gentlemen."

With that, we all shook hands and Ron and I departed Alphonse's Bar and Grill.

Chapter 14

B ased on the information provided by Sal Moretti, the undercover FBI agent, it appeared I was potentially stirring up a
veritable hornet's nest.

When my cell phone chimed I was reluctant to connect. Lately
it had been calls bearing borderline bad news. Not this time. The
phone screen displayed the caller's name as I had entered it into my
phone database. The St. Louis Maserati dealer. I took the call and
they informed me that the replacement floor mats for my Maserati
had arrived. Must have been shipped from the factory in Modina,
Italy, as I had ordered them over seven weeks ago. I told them I
would pick the mats up tomorrow.

After a conversation with Ron, we decided to make a trip to
the dealership, then go further down the road to the west, where he
could buy a suit for the upcoming wedding. I had previously purchased a very nice suit, at a very reasonable price, at Saks OFF 5th at
the outlet mall in Chesterfield.

Not actually in the shadow of the new Busch Stadium, simply
due to the fact that the stadium is on the north side of I-64 and it
never casts a shadow on the interstate, still it looms massively on my
right when Meza gets my attention with an observation. "LT, not to
be concerned at the moment, but I do believe we have company on
our six. I noticed him a few miles after we got on the interstate. A

black Dodge Charger. Maybe he just likes this red Maserati, or he wants to challenge you to a race. On the other hand, it could be the FBI, or the St. Louis PD, but since we picked him up while we were still in Illinois, I doubt it's the latter. He's been weaving in and out of traffic and staying two or three cars back."

"Okay, Top. Keep an eye on him. We'll continue on west on I-64 until we get to what we used to call Gumbo Flats, which is west Chesterfield, about fifteen or twenty miles from here. If he is following us, we'll know for sure when we turn off the highway at Boones Crossing. The Maserati dealership is in that area, as well as the outlet mall and the Saks OFF 5th store. I'll pick up my new floor mats at the dealership and if he's still with us I'll make a command decision at that time."

"Sounds like a plan, LT."

For the next twenty miles the Charger stayed with us, weaving across multiple lanes, but never getting any closer than two or three cars back. Two or three times Meza lost sight of him, but he always reappeared. When we took the off ramp at Boones Crossing we had a green light, proceeding with a left turn onto Boones Crossing. The light turned amber as we entered the intersection and was most certainly red by the time the Charger entered the intersection. Horns blared as the Charger came through the intersection on a red light, obviously intent on not losing sight of us.

I took a right on Chesterfield Airport Road and then another right on Arnage Boulevard, with the Charger still on our tail. The dealership for Maserati also has franchises for Aston Martin, Rolls Royce, Lotus, Lamborghini, Bugatti, and of course Bentley. The dealership apparently had enough influence with the Chesterfield city fathers to have the entrance roads named after the Bentley Arnage. A cross road is appropriately named Arnage Road, which is where the Dodge turned off and parked. Meza and I had no doubt that the driver was not interested in a race challenge, nor was he interested in simply admiring the Maserati. Had that been the case, he would have proceeded on to the dealership where automotive "eye-candy" was exhibited in abundance.

We parked in front of the dealership and Meza got out to stretch his legs while I went inside to pick up my new floor mats. They must have been handcrafted by artisans in Modine. Using my Cabela credit card to pay the $480.00 I at least accumulated some points that I could use to buy ammo. About the same cost as an oil change for my Maserati.

I put the new mats in the trunk and pulled Meza away from admiring a new Bentley. It was time to develop a strategy. We could leave the dealership on a back road, or we could leave the same way we came in and pick up our tail again. I opted for the latter. We were both armed and I was ready this time, if in fact these were the goombahs that made the hit on me. I had every reason to believe they were the same, even though they were in a different vehicle.

"Top, you know when we leave here the guys in the Dodge will follow us. Are you up for a confrontation with these guys?"

"It's been a while since I've had that sort of run-in with bad guys, but I'm ready. What do you have in mind?"

"I'll let them follow me to a state highway that I know very well. We'll see if that Dodge Charger can keep up with a Maserati. Even if they can keep up, I'm betting they won't know that highway well enough to negotiate the hills and curves. Let's do it."

As we passed Arnage Road, I noticed the Dodge had turned around and now faced Arnage Boulevard, which was our exit from the dealership. When we turned west on Chesterfield Airport Road the Dodge followed us at a distance of four or five hundred yards. Just as we expected. Continuing on the airport road led us back to the interstate and across the Missouri River. Another four miles and we took the exit ramp that put us on Highway 94. I wasn't ready to ditch our shadow yet, so I took my time getting on 94, making sure our observers were still with us. They were. Surely, they knew that we knew they were back there.

Recent developments of palatial estates had been constructed in the rolling hills to our right. I drove at the posted speed limit in the interest of safety in a sprawling residential community. When cresting a hill or negotiating a sharp curve in the road the Dodge temporarily disappeared. Meza noted with the next sighting that they had closed the gap between us, most likely in an effort not to lose us.

Leaving the newly developed communities behind, we found a long straight stretch, running parallel to the Missouri River. With no traffic in sight I pushed the Maserati to 150 miles-per-hour, which didn't take long. It also didn't take long for the Dodge to match my speed. Probably had a hemi under the hood. We'll find out in another twelve miles if the hemi powered vehicle also has the suspension to match the Skyhook suspension in the Maserati. I've often said, she goes like a bat out of hell and corners like a scared cat. We'll see how this works out.

I had had some past experience racing my XK 120 on closed circuit tracks, sanctioned by SCCA, the Sport Car Club of America. The challenge would be to reach back into muscle memory and apply what I knew about racing a more primitive sports car compared to this much more technically advanced Italian vehicle. I just wasn't quite ready yet to put my plan into action. Later.

Entering the small town of Defiance, I slowed to the posted 35 mph speed limit, then down to 25 mph to negotiate the sharp turn to my left. It was somewhat more congested in Defiance, as this was a local watering hole for bikers and for bicycle riders traveling the KATY trail that wound through Missouri. Useless information surfaced again as I drove slowly out of this quaint village. Early settlers in Missouri must have had a sense of humor or were making a statement about something when they named their cities and towns. The settlers that named Defiance probably moved on west and named their next settlement Independence, or Peace Valley. Having traveled through all 114 counties in Missouri, I was aware of some unusual names; Climax Springs, Conception Junction, Romance, Success, Devils Elbow, Fair Dealing and Fair Play, Frankenstein, Novelty, Skidmore, Tightwad, and my favorite, the little town of Peculiar. Peculiar is located in western Missouri. This community of 200 souls decided it needed a post office, so they wrote to the Post Master General and asked that he locate a post office there. His reply was they would have to name their community and they should give it an unusual or peculiar name. They didn't like the name Unusual, so they chose Peculiar. It still has that name, but no post office.

Shut out extraneous thoughts, Conner. Get your mind back on the task at hand. You have some potentially badass guys on your six.

"Conner, the Dodge is just coming around the bend, but he is still there. No vehicles between us now."

"Okay, Top. This is where it gets interesting. We have a straight stretch for about two miles, then we leave the river bottoms and take a right turn up into the hills, with a lot of sharp curves along the way. Another five miles and we come to an exit that winds up a hill to the Montelle Winery. It's almost a 'Y' at that point. There's a parking lot at the base of the hill and a stand of trees and brush between the lot and this highway. If we can get far enough ahead of these guys, we can pull into that lot and be hidden by the trees before they come up the highway. You haven't forgotten your ambush tactics, have you?"

"I assume they will spot the car when they catch up to that exit, so we'll only have seconds to set up in the trees and wait for them to show up. I'm not sure that's a good tactical plan for an ambush."

"Well, you're right on one account. We will set up an ambush in the tree line, but the way that concealment area is positioned around the edge of the parking lot, they won't see the parked car as they come up the hill. I'm guessing that once they get a couple of miles further down the highway, where it is straight and flat for a mile or so, they will realize we are no longer in front of them. If they are intent on finding us, they will circle back. Coming down the hill toward our location my car will be visible. If they turn into the parking lot, we will have had time to set up our ambush."

My driving skills on these curvy, undulating hills would be critical to the success of that plan. *Now where was that town named Success?*

I accelerated hard across the last of the river bottom road, approaching the first sharp curve to my right. The yellow caution sign for the curve indicated a safe speed would be 30 miles per hour. I took it at sixty. The Skyhook suspension adjusts to road conditions forty times a second. It felt like the Maserati squatted and stuck to the highway like contact cement. Hell, it felt good! With an aluminum engine in the front, pumping out 400 horsepower, and the transmission in the rear, the distribution of weight was perfect for performance driving. The curves and hills had only just begun, and I was gaining confidence in my driving and in the capabilities of the Maserati with each new curve. A driver unfamiliar with this highway could be left dangling in midair if topping a hill at high speed without knowing that the highway might possibly take a sharp turn one way or the other, as it often did. Not being aware of those idiosyncrasies could put your vehicle off the highway in a flash, wrapped around an old oak tree. No yellow ribbons on the tree! I concentrated on those hills and curves, but I also had been on this part of Highway 94 many times and had seen the evidence beside the highway of those drivers unaware of the unpredictable hills and curves. There were no guard rails, but a lot of scarred trees. In my mind's eye I knew where the next curve and hill would be. A bit like Google Earth.

"Shit, Conner. Is this a Mario Andretti imitation, or what? I haven't seen that Dodge for at least five minutes. We might just be able to pull off this ambush after all."

Even with the challenge of the hills and curves, we often hit speeds of a hundred plus, the throaty exhaust echoing through the forested hills in the depths of Missouri wine country.

"Hold on Ron, our turn is coming up soon." No sooner said then the sign for Montelle Winery sprung up on the side of the road. The oversize disc brakes slowed us quickly and safely enough to make the right turn onto the entry to the winery, then a quick left into the parking lot. The tree line between us and the highway was approximately thirty yards long and at least ten or fifteen yards deep, with a lot of undergrowth that provided concealment. I stopped close to the tree line, but far enough forward that the red Maserati could be seen by anyone coming down the hill on Highway 94 from the west.

My retired first sergeant knew the rules and knew the difference between cover and concealment. As we left the car, he drew his Glock and headed for an area that provided both. The overgrown brush provided excellent concealment and the bulk of an old oak tree provided the necessary cover, protecting him from any incoming rounds. I gave him a hand signal that I would be taking the uphill side of the trees. I noticed a heavy metal dumpster at the edge of the lot, in front of the Maserati, and calculated that I could use that as cover after the Dodge returned, spotted my car, and turned into the lot. It would take only a few seconds to dash from my position in the trees to concealment and cover behind the dumpster. Ron and I had operated together in sphincter tight situations, but that was a long time ago. Still, we seemed to instinctively know what the other person would be doing and what our mission was.

We were in position less than two minutes when we heard and saw the Dodge Charger roar up the hill and pass by the Montelle exit. So far, so good.

A guy jumps off a forty-story building and every window he passed people heard him say, "so far, so good." Come on, Conner, get back in the game. Not able to control those wayward thoughts, are you? On the thoughts of jumping, a blonde and a brunette are sitting at a bar watching the ten o'clock news. The news alert is focused on a guy that appears to be ready to jump from a forty-story building. The brunette turns to the blonde and says I'll bet twenty dollars that he jumps. The blonde takes the bet and lays her money on the bar. At that moment, the guy jumps. The brunette reaches over to pick up the bet money, then stops. She tells the blonde, I can't do this. I saw the news at five o'clock and I knew he jumped. The blonde responds that she had also seen the five o'clock news, but she didn't think the guy would do it again.

I love it when a plan comes together. The Dodge came charging back down the hill a few minutes later and obviously spotted the Maserati sitting on the Montelle parking lot. As a testament to the efficiency of interlock braking systems, there was no screeching of tires when the driver evidently stomped on the brakes to make the turn into the drive. Before he could make the turn, I dashed from the tree line to the dumpster, using it for cover and concealment.

The dodge stopped six feet behind the Maserati. The driver and passenger bailed out, with drawn weapons. As they approached the Maserati, Meza, in his commanding voice, shouted for them to drop their weapons. They were apparently startled, but neither one obeyed.

From my position behind the dumpster I also shouted for them to drop their weapons. I wanted them to know they were being con-fronted from two different directions. The passenger turned in my direction, with weapon raised. Three shots rang out, with two of the rounds pinging off the metal dumpster. The rules of engagement had just changed. My Colt .45 was in a ready position, which I then thrust forward in a two-handed grip and fired. The recoil from a light weight .45 can throw off your aim if you aren't familiar with that weapon. I was. The passenger was down. I wasn't sure where he was hit, but a .45 caliber bullet will put you on your butt regardless of where it first makes contact. The driver laid his weapon on the ground.

Meza was certainly familiar with taking down bad guys. Twenty years in the LAPD will give you some sort of edge. "Lock your fingers behind your head and get on your fuckin' knees. NOW."

Meza moved from the tree line and I came forward from behind the dumpster. The passenger was only winged in the left arm. Damn, I was aiming for center mass. I needed to spend more time on the range. I kicked his weapon away and hauled his ass up from his prone position on the paved lot.

"Keep 'em covered, Top. I have handcuffs in the trunk. I'm sure as hell not transporting a bleeding sonofabitch in my Maserati. We'll cuff them to a damned tree or something and call for the authorities. Let's just leave the weapons where they are and let the boys in blue collect them."

I retrieved the hand cuffs and we cuffed then together around a persimmon tree on the north end of the parking lot. It was almost comical. These guys facing each other around the tree. I had a first aid kit in my trunk and opened it to apply a wraparound gauze bandage on the arm of the passenger. If he died, so what. It wouldn't be my first kill. I would like to know, though, who paid this lowlife to make the hit on me.

"God dammit, Marcus, I told you that little .380 wouldn't take down the target. Look at where the fuck we are now. Somethin' bigger and this muther' wouldn't be here now to take us down."

"Shut up, Frank. Just shut the fuck up."

It was time for me to interject my observations into this conversation. "I noticed you fellows have Michigan plates on your car. Detroit, maybe?"

Frank was the passenger I had shot, and he liked to talk. My question was addressed to him. "Yeah, we come from Detroit."

"Shut up, Frank."

"So, Frank, why would you guys come after me if you're from Detroit?"

"Uhhh, we got an assignment from the capo…"

"Shut up, Frank."

"We know who you are, but who the hell is this big mother fucker?"

"That, my friends, is a retired first sergeant from the United States Marine Corps. Someone you really don't want to fuck with. Whatever kills you may have accomplished in your incompetent way will in no way match the kills recorded by my friend here."

"Oh shit. You ain't going to kill us, huh?"

"Shut up, Frank."

"Jesus, I got two kids back in Detroit. You can't do this"

"Shut up, Frank."

I had had enough of the "Shut up, Frank." I called Detective Daniel Tanner with the St. Louis Police Department.

"Detective Tanner, this is Conner Pennington. I think I may be able to help you out with a couple of your unsolved cases."

"Just how do you think you can do that, Mr. Pennington? I hope you're not talking about some level of your investigative prowess that you might be using in my city."

"No, sir. I have in custody two men that I believe were involved in shooting me at Union Station. One of their weapons is a .380, which may match the ballistics from a couple of your old cases. One of the subjects has been shot, but it doesn't appear to be life threatening."

"Dammit, Pennington. Is this in my city?"

"No, sir. We're west of St. Louis, on Highway 94, at the entrance to the Montelle Winery. I'm calling you first because I know as a St. Louis police officer you have statewide police powers. Now, do you want these guys, or not?"

"I don't know what you've done, Mr. Private Investigator, but you're going to end this call right now and call the local sheriff and an ambulance. I'm on my way out the door. Stay where you are. One last question. Did you shoot one of those guys?"

"All I said is one of them has been shot. I'll be right here, waiting for the sheriff and your arrival."

"You damned well better be, Pennington." With that, the phone call ended.

I called 911 and was connected to a dispatcher somewhere. When asked the nature of my emergency I explained there had been a shooting, there was an injured person, and two men were in custody. I gave them my name and location and assured the dispatcher I would be there waiting for the ambulance and law enforcement.

Frank still wouldn't shut up and his partner was quite sullen. Given the circumstances, I could understand why Marcus was not a happy camper. He had failed again to take out his assigned target and probably had no confidence that Frank would honor the code of silence.

Chapter 15

I hadn't seen any law enforcement personnel in the area and wasn't sure how long it would take for a deputy to arrive. I had every confidence though that when I told the dispatcher there was a shooting someone would be on the way very soon. That little bit of information seems to get the attention of local law enforcement types.

I had the feeling that Frank was the weaker of the two and couldn't imagine how he had gotten teamed with Marcus. I also had the feeling that once he was patched up and subjected to Detective Tanner's interrogation he would spill his guts. At least that was my hope.

"Marcus. Marcus. They're gonna' let me die out here. We don't even know where the hell we are. We should have taken care of this before we got ambushed out here in this God forsaken country."

"The code, Frank. You know the code. Shut up, Frank."

At least ten minutes had passed since I made the 911 call and I could hear the wail of a siren fading in and out as the vehicle approached from the east. The surrounding trees and hills were absorbing the sounds, but it was evident that Tanner or the sheriff would be at our location shortly.

No sooner had that thought entered my mind when a tan and white sheriff's vehicle careened into the Montelle parking lot.

Typical of most sheriff's department vehicles, it was an older Crown Vic. Lights flashing and the siren winding down, the deputy came to a skidding halt and jumped out of his patrol car. His weapon was drawn, but he didn't use any part of the vehicle for cover. He was young and eager. Too much so.

"Freeze. Hands in the air. No one move!"

Not eager to be shot by an excited, young and inexperienced deputy, Ron and I complied.

"Deputy, I'm Conner Pennington. I made the 911 call. We've had an altercation here and one man has been injured. These two men were following us, then attempted to shoot us when they discovered my car parked here. The two men are handcuffed to a tree over there. Mr. Meza and I are both armed and have permits to carry."

"Very slowly, put your weapons on the ground. An ambulance is on the way. I see two handguns already on the ground. Who do those guns belong to and why are they there?"

"Mr. Meza and I disarmed these guys who were threatening us. I'm a licensed private investigator and Mr. Meza is a retired LAPD homicide detective. At least one of those weapons may be tied to homicides committed in St. Louis some years back. I've called the investigating detective in St. Louis and he's on his way here."

"Okay. Step back from your weapons, lock your fingers together and place them on your head. We'll get this sorted out when my supervisor gets here."

I heard more sirens trilling through the forested hills. I couldn't be sure if an entire posse was on the way, or if Tanner was charging up the hill foaming at the mouth, anxious to nail my ass with some charge of interfering with his investigation. As it turned out, a top-heavy ambulance careened into the parking lot. The alternating flashing lights from the ambulance and the deputy's vehicle were beginning to give the Montelle parking lot the surreal glow of a county fair. The only difference being Ron and I seemed to be the main attraction, or more appropriately, the side show. The driver and his assistant emerged from the ambulance and wanted to know where the injured person was. I pointed to the tree line and informed them two men were handcuffed together around a tree.

Carrying a bag that probably had all manner of emergency medical supplies, they both started up the slight grade to the tree line. The young deputy, not really sure what to do, stopped their progress. There were too many people and too many things going on at once for him to control the situation. Fortunately, another tan and white Crown Vic sped into the lot. More lights and added chaos. Must be the young deputy's supervisor. Three brown stripes on his tan uniform confirmed that he was most likely the supervisor. He donned his smokey bear hat, or as we say in the Corps, his cover, as he exited his vehicle. His weapon was still holstered, but the deputy had his raised, not entirely sure where he should be aiming.

I had a few questions of my own. "Sergeant, what county are we in?"

"You're in the lower part of St. Charles County. The EMT has decided to transport these guys to the county jail in St. Charles. I have some questions for you. First, what the hell went down here? I see guns all over the place. Who belongs to what? And who the hell are you two?"

I handed the sergeant my driver's license and my private investigator license, as well as my photo ID for the concealed carry permits covering Missouri and Illinois. Meza produced his photo IDs, showing permits and a retired LAPD photo ID. The sergeant glanced at Meza's identification, then took a second look at Ron when he saw the retired LAPD ID.

"Mr. Meza, all of these cards indicate you're from California. What, may I ask, are you doing in the middle of wine country in Missouri?"

"I'll try to make a long story as short as possible. Mr. Pennington and I served together in the Marine Corps in Vietnam. He was my company commander and I was his first sergeant. A month ago when I found out that he had been shot, I packed my bags and came out east. Marines take care of each other. It's just what we do."

"I get it, Mr. Meza. I was a gunnery sergeant in the Corps. Being a former LAPD detective I'm sure you know we have to follow procedures when a shooting is involved. And what is your connection to these guys you have handcuffed to the tree?"

"We believe they were involved in the shooting that almost killed Mr. Pennington. They tailed us from the Illinois side of the Mississippi. Just between you and I, Gunny, we led them to this spot and you might say we set up an ambush. They went for it and the yokel that got himself injured started the shooting."

"Hold on a minute. Deputy Johnson, don't pick up those weapons by putting your pencil in the barrel. Ballistics will be checked on those weapons and I don't want them messed up. Use your pencil inserted through the trigger guard, then put them in an evidence bag. Back to you, Top. Which weapons belong to whom?"

"The Glock 9mm belongs to me. The Colt .45 Defender belongs to Mr. Pennington. The other two weapons belong to the fellows in custody, cuffed around the tree up there. You'll probably want to take those fellows to your county jail, but there is also a St. Louis PD detective on the way here. He is heading up the investigation of the Pennington shooting. I understand that the bullet removed from Pennington matches the ballistic analysis of two other shootings in St. Louis, so he probably has an interest in those two weapons."

"We've worked with the St. Louis PD and I don't have a problem with that, but since this incident happened in St. Charles County we're going to take the primary lead until this all gets sorted out. You realize I'm bending a number of rules here, but given the circumstances and the fact that you're both former Marines, I'm going to ask that when we get everything rounded up here you can both follow me back to the Sheriff's office in St. Charles.

"Mr. Pennington, are those your handcuffs on those guys?"

"Yes, they are, sheriff. Smith & Wesson. A standard S&W key will open them."

Turning to deputy Johnson, the sergeant instructed him to remove my cuffs and replace them with his own, then place the uninjured man in the back of his patrol car. "Make sure the other one stays put and when the EMT is finished with him, place him in the backseat of my car. Got that?"

"Yes, sergeant. I can't watch both of them at the same time if I take the cuffs off. What do you want me to do first?"

"Johnson, we're not going anywhere for a while. Leave the uninjured one cuffed around the tree and stay with the injured guy until the EMT releases him, if he does. Then cuff him and lock him in my car." Turning back to Meza and me, he asked if we knew the names of these men.

Meza responded with, "The injured one is called Frank. I'd keep him separate from the other one, since he might be inclined to be more cooperative. The other one was addressed as Marcus. I haven't heard any last names."

I barely heard Frank talking to Marcus when deputy Johnson went to the tree to uncuff him. "They're going to take us to jail, Marcus. What do I tell them?"

"Nothing. Just shut up, Frank." I had to smile. Frank was not going to shut up.

I noted the sergeants name badge on his uniform. Schulte. A lot of German descendants in this area. "Sergeant Schulte, you might want to check the dumpster over there. I think you'll find two dents made by rounds fired at me by Frank. I believe that will help corroborate my story that Frank changed the rules of engagement by firing at me before I fired my weapon. The expended cartridge casings are where they were when they were ejected from my weapon, as well as his. You'll find one casing from my .45 and at least three or four casings from his weapon. Frank went down when I fired, so his shooting stopped at that point."

"I don't doubt you, Mr. Pennington, but we will check it out."

A sedan drove in from the highway and slowed at the far edge of the parking lot. I thought it might be Tanner. It wasn't. Apparently, customers were beginning to arrive to wine and dine at the restaurant that was a part of the winery. With all the red and blue lights flashing I expected cell phone cameras to appear, looking for a posting on U-tube. To my surprise the cars continued on up the hill.

Red and blue lights behind the grill, siren baring, and the engine at full throttle. Okay, this was the infamous Detective Tanner. It had only been about fifty-five minutes since I had called him, and although the traffic would most likely be fairly light at this time of day, he must've gotten a wiggle on. Why not add more to the calliope of lights flashing in the parking lot?

Tanner pulled his vehicle around the others already there and bailed out of his unmarked detective car, a new Chevy Impala. His walk toward me indicated he was either pissed or thought he was in charge in this remote area.

He stopped close enough to my face I considered for a moment that he might have been a Drill Instructor in a past life. He was talking only to me and apparently didn't want anyone else to hear the conversation.

"What the fuck is going on here, Pennington? You drag my ass all the way out in East-bum-fuck Egypt, for what?"

"To do you a favor, Detective Tanner. I believe you told me that the bullet removed from me matched two other homicides in your city and you didn't have anyone to tie to those incidents. I'll let you argue with the sergeant from the Sheriff's Department over there about the evidence. I suspect that the .380 that has been collected by the deputy will match the ballistics connected to those murders. Mr. Meza and I were going to the mall in Chesterfield to buy a suit and we noticed these guys following us. We tried to evade them for miles, but it didn't work. I got ahead of them on this highway and we pulled into the parking lot to hopefully lose them. They found us and started a gunfight. You might want to talk to the guy named Frank. With a little coaxing, I think he'll spill his guts. I do believe this will clear up a couple of your old cases." Maybe that wasn't exactly the way things happened, but I sure as hell wasn't going to tell Tanner that Meza and I had set up an ambush. He can close at least three of his cases and get these goombahs off my ass. A win-win in my book.

Detective Tanner marched off to talk to the sergeant. It was a very animated conversation, and I really didn't give a damn what was happening between them. A casual observation on my part made me think that Tanner wasn't impressing the former Gunny to the level that he thought he would.

Meza was off to one side of all the activity going on, talking on his cell phone. When I approached him, he had a hint of a smile.

"Girlfriend wanting you back home?" I didn't often see my old first sergeant smile.

"Naw. That was one of my daughters wishing me a happy birthday."

"Really? Today is your birthday?"

"Yup."

"What year, my friend?"

"Every year."

"Well, now. Aren't you the smart ass? Come on, how old are you today?"

"I'm sixty-seven."

"Damn. You must have been young when you joined the Corps."

"Yeah, I was seventeen. My mother signed for me. Seven months later I was in Korea. God awful place. The Frozen Chosin and all the shit that went with it."

"Top, we spent thirteen months together in Nam and I never knew when your birthday was. I guess we just didn't have time to celebrate birthdays, did we? Let's get settled up with the sheriff's people and Detective Tanner and see if we can get the hell out of here. We'll go someplace, and I'll buy you the best damn scotch we can find."

The sergeant with the sheriff's department told me we could meet up with him later. We're good to go. Tanner wasn't so agreeable. He wanted to keep us there and question us. He finally agreed that we could leave, but we needed to come to Police Headquarters tomorrow to finish up his investigation. He said he knew where to find me.

I didn't concern myself with the transportation of the two guys from Detroit. Not my job. Meza and I got into the Maserati and left the scene.

Chapter 16

The drive back to the St. Louis metropolitan area was less frantic than the ride out to Montelle Winery. Driving east on I-64 I crossed the Missouri River bridge and took the exit for the Chesterfield Airport Road, thinking we would stop for a drink, then go to the mall to get Meza a suit for the Ferranti wedding.

It was now 2:30 in the afternoon and the Brick House Tavern and Tap didn't appear to be busy, which meant quick seating and service. The weather was decent enough that we decided we would sit at a table on the deck, but preferably in the shade. When we were seated, we both ordered a double Johnny Walker Blue Label scotch, on the rocks, with one ice cube. The bartender obviously wasn't busy, as we expected, and our drinks arrived three minutes later, along with menus.

"A toast, my friend. I'm sure you've had many exciting birthdays, but this one has to rank right up there. I'm indebted to you, again. Happy birthday, and may you have many more, but hopefully a bit more relaxing than this one. Thank you for being here and having my back."

"It's what we do, Conner. I'm just glad things worked out the way they did. Based on the events today, I believe the threat has been removed. Just don't go around pissing off more mafia-type guys."

"Believe me, Top, I have no intention of getting involved with those types. Hell, I'm still recovering from the incident at Union Station. Now, neither of us have eaten since our early breakfast, so take a look at the menu and let's have a celebratory meal. I've had the pork chops here before and I highly recommend them."

When our waiter returned, we both ordered the pork chops and another round of Johnny Walker.

"I've been thinking about the current situation. With the threat removed, I think I'll skip getting a suit for the wedding and head back to LA. Besides, there's someone I'd like to get back to."

"Oh, really? I'm guessing you're talking about a lady in your life? You haven't mentioned that you were involved with someone. What's the story on that?"

"Involvement may be a strong word for our relationship. But, yeah, she's pretty special. I met her at the VA hospital in north LA, where she's a nurse. She hasn't asked my age, but I know she is 12 to 15 years younger than I am. A very passionate lady. Athletic and sensual. I've been seeing her for almost a year and I'm hoping for a bit longer with this one."

"Congratulations, Ron. Another toast to you and your lady." We raised our glasses, clicked them together, and drained the remaining nectar of the gods.

Conversation diminished when our food arrived. The pork chops were thick and juicy. Garlic mashed potatoes on the side, all washed down with another round of Johnny Walker. Reminded me of the old days, except back then we washed down ham and mothers with mediocre scotch. The pork chops we were now consuming were a far cry from the C-ration boxed package of pork fat and lima beans, affectionately known as ham and mothers in Indian country.

"My friend, I suppose we can get you booked on a flight back to LA, but we probably need to make some sort of written statement about our earlier activities today. I'm just not sure which agency will want a statement from us. I get the feeling the St. Charles County

Sheriff's Department would just as soon wash their hands of this and turn it all over to The Duke of St. Louis, Detective Tanner. On the other hand, my friend over at the FBI, Greg Taylor, might have an interest in those goombahs from Detroit. What do you think, Top?"

"I don't think we need to make any formal statements for Taylor, but you might want to make him aware of the incident. Give the Sheriff's Department a call and see if they want a statement from us, but I agree, they probably want to dump this thing on Tanner. I'll stick around long enough to give a written statement, if they want one from me. In the meantime, I think we should get our stories straight about what happened. Along those lines, I don't think it would be in our best interest to spell out that we plotted to ambush these guys. Tell whatever lies you want to and I'll back you up. I'll certainly corroborate your story that Frank fired the first shots, but I gotta' tell you, I'll also let anybody that wants to know that I never fired my weapon. Hell, I'd probably have my weapon confiscated and I'd be questioned for the next thirty days. I like your company, LT, but enough is enough."

"You always were a tough old fart, weren't you? You never had any problem telling people what you thought."

"Not so tough and not so old. Telling people what I think comes with the territory. No sense in sugar coating the situation. I seem to recall that even as a boot lieutenant you had no problem with kicking ass and taking names. We just do what we need to do and let the chips fall where they may."

"We should probably leave here before we have another round. Another issue we need to reach an agreement on, and that's what we tell Margo when we get home. I'm not going to lie to her, but I don't think we need to relay every detail of our adventure today. She isn't the sort of woman that worries, but she may be concerned about me getting myself into more altercations, resulting in another trip to the hospital or funeral home. So, what I'm going to tell her is we think the guys that shot me at Union Station have been apprehended by the St. Charles County Sheriff's Department. If she wants to know how or why I'll expand on that. A little."

"Okay. As I said before, say whatever works for you and I'll back you up."

"Let me make a quick call to Twitch Taylor and bring him up to date. I'll take care of the bill here and we'll hit the road." I had Greg's number saved on speed dial. He answered on the fourth ring.

"This is special agent Gregory Taylor. I am unavailable at the moment. Please leave a message stating your name, phone number and reason for your call. I will return your call as soon as possible. Have a good day."

Hell, my initial thought was that I had reached a live person. Good ole' Twitch was probably playing golf or fishing. I'm not sure why I thought FBI agents had nothing else to do, except having conversations with federal prosecutors or their bosses back at the Justice Department in DC. I left a message relating the apprehension of the guys we believed were the shooters at Union Station.

The waiter asked if we wanted another round, which I declined. Just bring the check, which he did in short order. Another round of Johnny Walker and we would most likely need assistance to reach the parking lot, much less navigate the increasing traffic on I-64 on our way back to Belleville.

Having consumed our limit of celebratory scotch, when we reached the car I pushed the button for the trunk release, moved to the open trunk and removed my weapon. Meza seemed to agree with my decision to disarm and without a word also moved to the trunk. I suppose due to the fact that the Maserati wheel and tire sizes are different for the front and back, there is no spare tire, although there is a compartment under the trunk space for an optional spare tire. I lifted the panel revealing a rather large area I used for storage of certain items and this is where we placed our weapons.

"Are you good to drive, Conner? I saw a Star Bucks down the road. We could stop and load up with some coffee."

"Come on, Ron. We both know better than that. If I'm not good to drive coffee won't do a damn thing other than to make me a wide-awake drunk. That's about as logical as taking a cold shower to sober up. That's when you end up with a wide-awake wet drunk."

"Yeah, I know all about those fallacious rumors on how to sober up. I also know that the only thing that makes an intoxicated person less intoxicated is time, and that's what I was suggesting."

"Actually, Ron, that's probably a good idea. We really don't have to be anywhere anytime soon. For now, we have nothing to do and the rest of the day to do it."

Two and a half hours later, after three cups of coffee and endless ruminations of mutual war stories, we left Star Bucks, drove to Boones Crossing and took the on ramp for I-64. Heading east the traffic wasn't as bad as I thought it would be at 5:50 in the afternoon. Workers leaving their day jobs were leaving the city headed west for their suburban homes. Not too many were traveling east. Good for us. It didn't get nasty until we neared the construction area on the Poplar Street Bridge. The other problem at this point is that the other workers headed home from downtown to Illinois were now traveling the same direction we were. Paradox happens.

Our next exit was Green Mount Road, where we had a red light, giving me the chance to call Margo and request clearance for landing. This was our humorous habit. I let her know we were on approach and would be there soon. Pulling into the garage ten minutes later the connecting door was open, and Margo was waiting.

"Welcome back. I hope you had a successful day. Now, show me the suit Ron got for the wedding."

"It's a long story, my dear. We didn't get Ron a suit, but if we had it would have been his birthday suit."

"What do you mean, his birthday suit?"

"Ron only informed me this afternoon that today is his birthday. We didn't get the suit because Ron has decided he's going back to LA before the wedding. It's been comforting to have Ron here for my backup, but the threat appears to have gone away. Today the St. Charles County Sheriff's Department apprehended the guys that were involved in shooting me at Union Station. One of the guys as much as admitted it. Ron also hadn't told me until today that he has a lady waiting for him and he would kinda' like to get back and do a little work on that relationship."

"Well, that's all good news. I think that calls for a celebration this evening."

"Incidentally, we stopped at the Brick House Tavern and Tap in Chesterfield, near the Maserati dealership, and had a late lunch, as well as a few rounds of scotch to celebrate his birthday and the arrest of the two guys that were certainly involved in my hospital stay."

"Celebrating without me, were you? I'll forgive you this time. Unfortunately, Ron, I didn't know about your birthday and I don't have a cake for you."

"Well, dear lady, there's a story I'll tell you about that. General Gray was the 29th Commandant of the Corps, from 1987 to 1991. He much preferred to be with his Marines in the field, but due to his position and obligations he occasionally had to entertain at the Marine Barracks at 8th and I Streets in Washington, with an evening soiree. On one such occasion he had a platoon of young marines, in dress blues, lined up on the perimeter of the ballroom. Politicians and blue haired ladies meandered around the facility, consuming a variety of sweets and delicacies. One of the ladies approached a young Marine and offered him one of the chocolate truffles that she had on her plate. His reply was, "Sorry, ma'am, I don't eat that shit." She was aghast! She trotted over to the commandant and told him what the Marine said to her when she offered him a chocolate truffle. His reply was, "Fuck him, then, don't give him any." My point is, I'm quite okay with your not having a cake, because I don't eat that shit."

Margo had been with me long enough to understand and appreciate Marine Corps humor.

"Well then, we'll just have to find another way to celebrate your birthday. Since you and Conner have already had your protein for today in the form of huge pork chops, how about a Greek salad, with sautéed octopus? You can have your choice of wine with that, or maybe even go all Greek and have some Ouzo."

"Great. I haven't had a Greek salad in a long while. How can I help?" Meza sounded genuinely enthusiastic about a Greek salad. When enthusiastically committed, we usually simply referred to that state of being as "Gung Ho."

"Okay, birthday boy, you can just relax here with your drink of choice and I'll send Conner to a little specialty store down the street where I've seen baby octopus that will blend wonderfully with the salad.

"Conner, you'll also need to pick up some feta cheese. Got it?"

"I'm on my way. Is there anything else?"

"No, Conner, I think that should do it for now."

I had a pretty good idea what would transpire when I left. Margo was quite good at subtle interrogations and Meza would be in for an intensive grilling about the actual events of the day. Of course Ron wasn't a novice at interrogations and we had already rehearsed what our story would be if anyone asked. Ron wouldn't really lie to her, he just wouldn't spill the beans about how we had set up an ambush for the Curly and Moe duo. There was no need to expound on the potential for a gun battle between us and the comic duo. Maybe Meza would bring me up to speed on his conversation with Margo, and maybe not. Margo would eventually learn the whole story anyway.

When I returned with a healthy supply of tiny, fresh octopus and a container of feta cheese Margo and Ron were sitting at the outdoor table on the back patio. Margo had a glass of what appeared to be her favorite Chardonnay and Ron (surprise) had what appeared to be a tumbler with one ice cube, slightly melted, and an amber colored liquid I assume to be scotch.

"Welcome back, Conner. Ron was just telling me about the lovely lady he met at the VA hospital, who he hopes is still waiting for him when he gets back. He used my computer to book a flight for the day after tomorrow. I told him you would be glad to shuttle him to the airport. Warning. It's an early flight to LA, with a connection through DFW. Ron, it has been a real pleasure having you here, and particularly comforting to me to know you were watching over Conner. He doesn't always recognize the potential danger, but he's getting better. He's also told me some of your shared war stories and I'm somewhat surprised you are both still alive to tell the tales. Get yourself a libation and join us."

I have often been asked what I do. My frequent response is, "I do whatever Margo tells me to do." Which I did this time, moving to the liquor cabinet and fixing a drink that I'm sure matched the drink Meza had.

I knew the day would come, very soon, when I would have to get back on track with the Barrows investigation. With Meza leaving the day after tomorrow, it seemed reasonable that we would need to meet with Detective Tanner and give a statement about the events of today, before Ron flew back to California.

As the evening approached, Margo left our company to prepare the salad. It was a delightful salad. Perhaps even better than the salads I had experienced when touring the Greek Island of Corfu. Margo set a bottle of Ouzo on the table, but with a look of mild disdain. She literally was appalled that anyone would drink a concoction that tasted and smelled like licorice. I had been introduced to Ouzo by Major Slovik, whom I worked for as the S-4 at Camp Lejeune when I returned from Southeast Asia. My trip to Corfu was my next extended relationship with Ouzo, perhaps contributing to an accident that damaged the motorcycle I had rented. Listen, it wasn't entirely my fault. The mountain roads on Corfu were narrow, with frequent switchbacks. Ignoring my common-sense caution, I took to the byways after having consumed way too much Ouzo. A huge tour bus was descending the mountain as I was going up. Closing the distance between us I soon realized I would either become a hood ornament on the bus or I could lay the bike down or go over the edge of the road. I laid the bike down. I thought of that mental miscalculation as I picked up my tumbler of licorice liquid and took a sip. Contrary to Margo's impression of this Greek liquor, it goes remarkably well with the delicious salad she had prepared.

We ended the evening with another toast to Ron's birthday and his devotion to a fellow Marine. Being the son of a preacher man I reflected on John 15:13. *Greater love hath no man than this, that a man lay down his life for a friend.* I had been through hell with Meza and knew we both felt that way. Back then, and now. So be it.

We retired for the evening and rose reasonably early to meet with Detective Tanner. Surprisingly, we weren't asked to give written statements about the incident of the day before. We were separated and taken to interview rooms in police headquarters, where we were videotaped as we were questioned about our interaction with the boys from Chicago. It was brief and painless, and we stuck to the story we had agreed on. No mention of setting up an ambush.

Back in Belleville Ron began packing for an early morning departure to the St. Louis airport and a trip home.

The next morning the trip to the airport was uneventful and the traffic was very light at 0420, military time. Ron had packed his weapon in check-through luggage and I left him at the departure gate.

No hugs. Just a firm handshake and a Semper Fi. I watched as his bulk moved through the revolving doors and passed out of sight. So long, my friend. I hope to see you again.

Chapter 17

I t did seem a little strange not to have my old friend Meza around, but we move on, don't we?

Something still nagged at the recesses of my brain concerning the Barrows investigation. It now seemed a given that the senior Klienknect was pretty much a full-blown victim of OCD. His handwritten account ledger still fascinated me, and I was sure it held more secrets I had yet to uncover. I returned to my office and began to look closer at his entries. If I go back 20 years in his ledger I may find something that will reveal a clue about his untimely demise. Then again, maybe not.

During the more recent years, before his death, I noted that he had "loaned" large sums of money to his son. There was no evidence that his son had ever paid him back. There must be other documents somewhere that would indicate why the "loans" were made to his son and whether or not the son repaid his father. The personal ledger only recorded expenditures, not income. Given the financial detail that Gerard was prone to recording I reasoned that he had another ledger where he recorded the income from investments, dealerships, or even payments from his son. Perhaps Mandy still had those records at the estate she had inherited from her father, Alfred, who I had gathered from scanning numerous documents was known by friends and family as Al. Hell, the senior Klienknect had even recorded the amounts of money he had given his wife. Whatever else he recorded in his accounting systems, I'm sure he never expected his wife to repay him. That was just how things were done in that era. He provided her living expenses for shopping and pocket money. As best I could tell from the history of the elder Klienknect, his wife Marilda never worked at any job. She was more of a social hostess than a career woman. Back in the day of single income families it was evident from the Klienknect lifestyle and substantial income that it was never necessary for her to be employed outside the home. Scanning through the piles of records and paperwork I had obtained from the estate on my first visit, it became obvious to me that records of income must be located back in Creve Coeur. Still, I wasn't sure what relevance an accounting of income would tell me, but I didn't feel as though I was making much headway with the information I currently had on hand. A more thorough search may yield something of importance. I called Mandy.

"Mandy, this is Conner Pennington. I must admit that I have been temporarily sidetracked on the investigation, but I'm back on it now."

"Oh, Conner, it's really good to hear from you. There is no need to apologize for any delay. You have been through quite enough. How are you feeling?"

"I'm still recovering from that little incident at Union Station, but the good news is the people involved in the shooting have been apprehended. I really didn't want to pursue this investigation as long as they were still on the loose, with the strong possibility that you may also be put in danger. I wasn't sure what the connection between the shooting and the investigation might be."

"That's very thoughtful of you, Conner. You are such a gentleman. Thank you for calling and letting me know those elements of danger have been removed."

"Admittedly, that isn't the only reason I called. I have been searching through the paperwork we gathered from the estate, but I haven't found an accounting of income that I'm sure your grandfather must have recorded. I'm assuming there is such a ledger, as he certainly recorded every penny he spent. Is there a time convenient for you when I can come by and look through more of the storage boxes?"

"Absolutely, Conner. I'm not in St. Louis today, but I can meet you at the estate at 10:00 in the morning. Does that work for you?"

"That would be excellent, Mandy. I'll see you then."

For the trip to Creve Coeur to meet Mandy I drove the Jaguar S-Type, as it had a lot more trunk space than did the Maserati. When I passed the two guarding lions at the entry gate, it was obvious no gardener had visited the property since I was here last. The overgrown trees and shrubs encroached even more on the curving drive. Neptune, with his raised trident in the middle of the imposing fountain, was still dry as a bone. It also didn't appear as though Mandy had made much progress in securing assistance to prepare the estate for sale. It was precisely 10:00 a.m. when I stopped in front of the massive front doors, one of which was open, with Mandy standing on the top marble step.

Exiting the Jag, I heard Mandy say, "Welcome back, Conner. It's good to see you, and I must say you're looking much better than the last time I saw you, which was in a hospital bed. I see your appreciation of automobiles extends to your daily driver. The S-Type if one of my favorite Jags. In fact, my father kept one in the garage, along with the rest of his collection. Would you be interested in viewing that collection before we go to the library?"

"That sounds very inviting. I do love fine automobiles and I'm sure the collection is worth my time, which only fulfills my desire to lust after beautiful motor cars, meaning that doesn't add to your billing on my hourly rate."

Mandy descended the steps and placed her hand on my arm,

leading me around the side of the McMansion to the stable of cars located to the left and rear of the home. Again, she smelled faintly of gardenias, but no running suit this time. It was warm for this time of day, although it was mid-June. A low-cut sun dress, gold bangles and bracelets and freshly applied lipstick that complimented her painted fingernails, as well as the painted toenails that peeked out of her leather Italian sandals. An alluring package to be sure.

Careful, Conner, you are not here to admire Mrs. Barrows. Admiring the collection of automobiles is quite enough, then down to the business of finding the material you came here to collect. Damn, it's difficult to ignore the sensual brush of her full breast as she guides you to the motor car stables. The first time may have been accidental, but the second, third, and fourth time, probably not.

The stables could have been originally built for horses, but only if they were on the grounds of Grants Farm, where Anheuser-Bush stables their massive Clydesdales. There were at least fifteen timber trimmed wooden doors, each ten feet wide. No windows were evident on the front of the building that was primarily constructed of quarried stone. A stone pathway led from the paved drive to a side entrance, where another impressive wood door protected the entry with a substantial brass lock, having a patina that led me to believe it had not been polished, or even used, for quite some time. The shrubbery surrounding the entry was also overgrown here, as it had been along the entry driveway. An angry squirrel chattered his warning to scampering squirrels in nearby trees that intruders were invading their self-proclaimed kingdom.

"A pesky bunch of tree rodents. They once got into the garage and ate through some wiring in one of the Mercedes. My father was furious. He bought a German air rifle and was determined to eradicate the entire bunch of them. It probably didn't help that we had pear and apple trees toward the back of the property. I'm sure the squirrels passed the word to other squirrels in the neighborhood, as there was evidence of their pirating fruit during the late summer and fall. Obviously, they are back in force."

Other things were obvious to me. Mandy had no pockets with her clinging sun dress, but she did have a huge brass key in her hand, which I had not noticed before now. Maybe my attention had been drawn to other attractions. The architecture of the garage or maybe the architecture of Mandy? She knew I loved aristocratic and classic automobiles and had planned to entice me to view the collection before I had arrived. The key to the garage had been in her hand as she stood on the step waiting for me.

The door swung easily on what appeared to be handcrafted hinges, reminiscent of old world European craftsmanship. Mandy fumbled briefly inside the door and located the overhead light switch. Stepping into the brightly lit garage, I saw at least ten vehicles, four of which had dust covers. My thought was that they should have all had dust covers. Those without covers were dull in appearance and covered with years of dust.

"Sorry, Conner, I know you appreciate fine cars and this dust and lack of care must be appalling to you. I just haven't had the time to take care of these motor cars the way they should be cared for."

"No apologies needed. I understand. Are all of these vehicles going to be on the market, or have you decided to keep a couple of your favorite cars?"

"I haven't decided anything yet. Actually, I would love to keep all of them, but there is a problem of where to store them, as well as upkeep. They need to be driven."

Indeed, the vehicle closest to the entry door was a Jaguar S-Type. Although an early model, it had changed little from the model I drove.

Mandy was familiar with each car in the stable and explained the history of this S-Type. "This Jag was probably driven more than any of the rest of the cars in the collection. It's a 1999 model, the first year they were produced. My father simply had to have the first model, as it reminded him of the classic 3.8 Jaguar. This particular one was fitted with a 4.2 liter V-8 and was quite peppy on the road. As I remember, it has less than 110,000 original miles and is still in very nice condition. As I'm sure you know, Jaguars are typically long legged. Not very impressive from the start, but you can cruise all day at well over one hundred miles per hour and arrive at your destination none the worse for wear."

The paint color was what I knew Jaguar called Platinum. I had an earlier one that same color. Jaguars can sometimes be quirky and have their own personality, but I love the lines and the speed and handling of this model.

Mandy took my hand and led me to the next vehicle. This one was covered. Much lower than the Jag, the tire size, slightly visible under the bottom of the dust cover, indicated a serious race car. I almost gasped with admiration when Mandy pulled the front of the cover up over the grill.

"This is an original Ford GT-40. I have never seen my father drive this one, but I suppose he might have. I just don't know where he would drive this vehicle and exercise it properly. He was quite proud of this car and kept it in showroom condition. He was a true car guy. Waxed it often, not allowing our in-house mechanic to touch it. It was his pride and joy. I've never been in it. How's this for a crazy idea, why don't you and I take this baby for a spin sometime?"

"Oh, Mandy, I'm human and I have weaknesses. Don't tempt me like that. We don't even know if this car will run. I suspect it's been sitting for some time, unattended. Probably has old gas, a dead battery, and low tires. But it certainly is an exciting idea."

Pulling me close to her, with her arm around my waist, she replied, "Conner, life can be full of temptations. If we pass them all up and quash the dreams and desires that we have harbored are we certain they will ever again present themselves?"

Was this a hint for more than a joy ride in an original Ford GT-40? My thoughts went back to a comment made to me by a retired Highway Patrol captain. An original himself. One of the first members of the Missouri Highway Patrol. "The only regrets I have in life are all the temptations I have successfully resisted." Watch it, Conner. This was a past ice skating student, and you're treading on thin ice. Stick to the investigation.

The gardenia scent from Mandy was becoming intoxicating. Or was it really just the perfume? She was a lovely lady and very sensual, but I had one of my own at home.

The next car was also covered. Low and sleek. Raising the cover from the front I immediately recognized a Series II Jaguar E-Type. Much like the one I had seen at The Senator dealership earlier. This one was silver and appeared to be a museum quality vehicle.

"Mandy, I will have to admit that this is, so far, an amazing collection of my fantasy cars."

Looking into my eyes, she said, "Conner, there is more here to admire than just a collection of cars. Shall we proceed?"

I wasn't sure what she meant by "shall we proceed?" Looking at classics or something else?

Taking my hand again, she led me further down the line of classic vehicles. One Ferrari, an original Cobra, a Bentley, and two Rolls. The last car was an Aston Martin DB4. Lucky for this classic James Bond vehicle it was covered. Closer examination revealed this car to be quite different from the classic Bond conveyance. No doubt that it was an Aston Martin DB4, but this was a special DB4/GT Zagato. Very rare, designed and built for racing. A book I had on classic and rare race cars contained two photos of a DB4/GT Zagato in racing colors, somewhere on a race circuit in Europe. I had only seen this model in photos.

Until now I had not heard any specific terms of endearment. "Well, Conner, my dear, we could perhaps take this jewel for a spin. I can get either the GT-40 checked out or get this DB4 ready for a joy ride. Now, shall we retreat to the library and search for the material you came her for?"

"Some temptations need not to be resisted. Your offer for taking one of these cars for a spin is very, very tempting. I think the Aston Martin would be less obtrusive on the road and it would be a thrill for me to drive a DB4. Now, on to the business at hand. To the library."

Mandy held my arm as though I was escorting her to a formal ball, and we proceeded to the library. It was much the same as it was when I had last been here. Boxes were still stacked around the perimeter and file folders were lying on the expansive desk. Leather bound books still lined the walnut shelves.

I took a seat in the worn leather chair after removing my jacket and placing it on the back of the chair next to the desk.

Mandy stood in front of the desk and made an observation. "I suspected you were carrying when I felt a bulge under your jacket while we were in the garage. I guess I could have quoted the oft repeated Mae West saying…is that a gun, or are you glad to see me? Since your gun is in a shoulder holster I guess that line wouldn't work. I'm guessing that's a Walther PPK. A very nice and reliable weapon."

"You're quite amazing, Mandy. Not only do you know and appreciate fine automobiles, you seem to also know about guns. I noticed that when you mentioned your father bought an air rifle you specifically stated that it was a German rifle. I have had some experience with those while visiting in Germany, and they are top of the line in air rifles."

"My father had quite a collection of guns. Shotguns, rifles, handguns, as well as swords and knives. All of those are locked in a safe in the basement. I have yet to do a compete inventory on all of that collection."

"You are indeed an amazing woman. Other than my lady, Margo, I don't know very many women that are knowledgeable about cars and guns. Do you also shoot?"

"I do. I have competed in trap and skeet and have done very well. I don't hunt, but I have used the air rifle, on occasion, on the marauding squirrels."

"Very interesting. Now, I'm assuming you have gone through a lot of this material. Perhaps you would know where your grandfather kept a journal of his income? I have found some interesting entries in his personal journal where he kept records of all expenditures, but no record, so far, of what the other side of his finances were."

"I'm sorry, Conner. I have only browsed through most of this paperwork, trying to determine what I can shred. I'm afraid you'll have to search on your own. May I get you a glass of wine, or anything else?"

"Do you happen to have scotch in the house?"

"Yes, I believe we do. I drink scotch occasionally and I think we have some Johnny Walker Black in the cabinet. How would you like that?"

"One ice cube, if that's available. No water. It rusts the pipes."

"Ah, a man after my own heart. Precisely how I like my scotch. Do you mind if I join you?"

"Not at all. Please do, I prefer not to drink alone."

Conner, what are you thinking? You're on the job and you're drinking scotch with a lovely lady that apparently has an interest in you. Get your mind back on the investigation.

Mandy returned with the drinks. She sat my drink in front of me and briefly touched my hand as I reached for the crystal tumbler.

"Conner, I'm glad you're here and I'm very glad that you're okay. You're sure there is no more danger?"

"Well, they have the guys in custody that shot me, but now I'm wondering who was pulling the strings on that hit and why they wanted me out of the picture. There's something that just doesn't seem right about what's going on. I had a meeting with the Senator and he denied having had anything to do with my being shot. I just don't know, Mandy."

"Just be careful, Conner."

She sat in a chair across from the library desk, holding her drink in her right hand. When she crossed her legs, her summer dress exposed a length of lovely skater's leg that was toned, tanned and alluring. She lifted her tumbler in a toast and said, "To you, Conner, and a lot of memories." It seemed to be a casual comment, but I wasn't sure where this was headed. The only thing I could think of in reply was, "To a lovely lady." A beguiling smile from her was her only response.

I continued to search the storage boxes for the journal that I was sure would show me Klienknect's income records. I tried not to look at Mandy as she sat in front of me, watching me search through her father's and grandfather's records. After twenty or thirty minutes of scouring piles of journals and documents I found a journal that, on the surface, was a record of income, for both the senior Klineknect and Mandy's father's income records. I found that to be unusual, as previous journals had been the records compiled only by the senior Klienknect. Apparently, Mandy's father had continued entries in this journal started by his father.

"Mandy, I think I have found what I have been looking for. For now, I believe this will suffice. If I need anything else, I'll let you know. There appears to be a lot more information here that may be relevant to the investigation. If I need more documents, I'll give you a call and set up a time to review other records. I have a sense that information in these journals and records have a bearing on the truth relating to your grandfather's death."

"I'm available at your convenience. In the meantime, I will contact our mechanic and have him check out the Aston Martin. When you come back, she will be ready for a spin in the country, or wherever you would like to take her. Maybe a picnic?"

"That sounds marvelous. I certainly can't pass up an opportunity to drive an Aston Martin DB4, especially a rare Zagato."

I picked up the journal I had found and prepared to leave when Mandy came around the desk, put her arm around my waist, pulled me close and kissed me on the lips. I can't say I resisted as much as I should have. Her lips were full and soft, and her tongue probed in a longing way as she pushed her body against mine.

Leave now, Conner. You're getting way in over your head. The heady intoxication of having a sensual woman at least twenty years younger wanting you can be an overwhelming aphrodisiac. Remember only your mission, to find the truth.

I resisted another temptation, took the journal, then returned to my car. Mandy was again at the front door of the McMansion. Perhaps a figment of my imagination, but as I glanced in my rearview mirror I thought I detected a look of sadness. Surely, I was too far away to discern any distinctive facial expression, so it must have been some sign I picked up from her body language.

I proceeded down the long driveway and out of sight of the estate. My thoughts and emotions were all over the place as I drove back through St. Louis.

Chapter 18

I was sitting in my home office staring at my computer home page, thinking about a lot of things, many of which were not related to my ongoing Barrows investigation. Having just returned from the Klienknect estate and a far too intimate interlude with Mandy, my thoughts included visual images of a sensual lady that seemed to have an interest in me that exceeded a normal client relationship. I needed to clear my mind of thoughts about Mandy. Get back on track.

Still recovering from a temporary debilitating chest wound, my thoughts turned to the potential that whoever sent Curly and Moe from Detroit to take me out of circulation wouldn't stop their mission simply due to the fact that those boys were now in custody. If anything, that situation may foment more exacting diligence to remove me and stop whatever investigation someone perceived to be threatening to their well-being. Hah! Little did that someone know that I had no idea why I had been targeted. FBI agent Gregory 'Twitch' Taylor had given me a file that might have answered some of my questions, but that file had disappeared when I was accosted and shot in the Union Station parking lot. It was also obvious that Twitch would not replicate that file again. He as much as told me that I had been careless with a confidential file that now was undoubtedly in the hands of the very people the FBI had investigated.

My other source of information was right in front of me. My computer. The internet. Okay, I know you can't believe everything you read on the internet, but one source that seemed quite reliable to me was a crime reporter that had gathered endless information on mafia structure and activities. Scott Burnstein.

I had serious doubts that Crazy Joe would share any knowledge he had concerning the family in St. Louis. He would follow in his father's footsteps, maintaining a code of silence. I also doubted that he knew much, if anything, about the Detroit mafia. Turning to the website where Burnstein had reported on the mafia family, I found pages of information about the Detroit family. Glancing through volumes of narrative, I had to smile when I noticed that most of the Italian family members involved in nefarious operations had nicknames. Perhaps that's how Joe Ferranti, Jr. become "Little Joe". It reminded me of my first run-in with a mafia member just north of Kansas City…William "Willie the Rat" Cammisano. I had been riding patrol with a deputy sheriff when we stopped a pickup truck for exceeding the speed limit. Turned out to be none other than "Willie the Rat." By the time Willie took over the Kansas City crime family in 1984 I was a deputy director in the Missouri Department of Public Safety. I knew a lot about Willie.

Allegedly, Cammisano had gotten his nickname from stuffing his victims in sewers, where the rats consumed the evidence. William Dominick Cammisano, Sr. was a feared and ruthless mobster from Kansas City, Missouri. He was the boss of the Kansas City crime family from 1984 until 1988 when he stepped down to become the underboss of Anthony Civella. Other sources claim he remained the boss of the Kansas City family until his death in 1995.

At the young age of 15 he already had an extensive rap sheet. He had been arrested for carrying a concealed weapon, bootlegging, numbers racketeering, extortion, running illegal dice games, pistol whipping a robbery victim, running an alcohol still, being AWOL from the U.S. Army, disturbing the peace, and gambling. He is the father of current Kansas City crime family capo William Cammisano, Jr. Keep it in the family. His brother, Joseph, was also a member of the Kansas City crime family and was his closest associate.

By the 1960s Cammisano had become a high-ranking member of Nick Civella's Mafia organization. He controlled much of the vice rackets in the 12th Street district of Kansas City, which included prostitution, seedy lounges and drug peddling. In 1980 he was called to appear before a U.S. Senate Subcommittee investigating organized crime activity in Kansas City. During the investigation, government witness Fred Harvey Bonadonna described how Cammisano used strong arm tactics in the River Quay neighborhood redevelopment project to turn the area into a red light district with brothels and other vice. Bonadonna stated that Cammisano murdered his father, a business associate of Cammisano's, for refusing to obtain liquor licenses for mob establishments in River Quay. Bonadonna stated, "Willie Commisano told my father that he would kill me. My father told him he would have to kill him first, which he did." Cammisano and his gang essentially destroyed the once bustling town of River Quay by trashing sections of the town and making trouble for anyone who wouldn't allow them to have their way. By 1980, River Quay had become a ghost town. During this investigation, Willie was serving a five-year sentence at the federal prison in Springfield, Missouri for extortion.

In 1983, Willie was released from prison at just the right time to become the new leader of the Kansas City crime family with the 1984 imprisonment of Carl "Tuffy" DeLuna, and Anthony and Carl Civella. Because of the unfavorable publicity of recent criminal trials, the Chicago Outfit officially disowned Kansas City as an affiliate. With the crime family now under his control and now totally independent of The Outfit, this gave Cammisano the opportunity to establish new operations in California, Florida and Washington, D.C. without Outfit approval or interference. This expansion reinvigorated the Kansas City organization. Cammisano also reportedly rejuvenated the crime family's ranks by inducting 10 to 12 new members in 1987. He allegedly stepped down as boss in 1988 when Anthony Civella was released from prison and Willie became his underboss. Still, other sources believe he remained the boss of the Kansas City family until his death in January of 1995. His son, William Cammisano, Jr. is currently a reputed capo and a rising star in the Kansas City family. I also knew that many family members in St. Louis had either died or moved on and the St. Louis family was severely weakened, prompting them to seek alliances with the Kansas City, Chicago and Detroit families. I needed to know the strength of the alliance between St. Louis and Detroit and who the players were.

I knew Scott Burnstein wouldn't provide in his writings about the mob the connection I was looking for, but Burnstein was an unquestioned authority on mob organizations and hierarchy. Let's find out what he knows about the Detroit family.

Underworld sources confirm that an inauguration ceremony for newly appointed Detroit mafia boss Jack (Jackie the Kid) Giacalone, 63, has taken place since the beginning of the year in a Motor City restaurant, similar to the one that was held for his predecessor Giacomo (Black Jack) Tocco, 87, at a posh hunting lodge near Ann Arbor exactly 35 years ago last month.

Veteran Detroit mobster Vito (Billy Jack) Giacalone, Jackie the Kid's dad, ran his crew out of Eastern Market from the 1960s until the 1990s, when he was jailed for the final time in his lengthy underworld career in the expansive Operation Game Tax bust. Jackie the Kid's uncle and Billy Jack's older brother was Anthony (Tony Jack) Giacalone, the syndicate's forceful and fearsome street boss from 1960 until his death in 2001. The pair came up as youngsters in the Market, working for Salvatore (Black Shirt Sam) Ciarmitaro and Joseph (White Shirt Joe) Ciarmitaro.

The recent coronation of Jackie the Kid took place at Vivio's and concluded at the historic Roma Café, Detroit's oldest restaurant, where

Frank Sinatra had dinner every night when he was in town. The festivities were officiated by consigliere Dominic (Uncle Dom) Bommarito and senior capo Antonio (Tony the Exterminator) Ruggirello, Jr. Jack Tocco attended the affair to give his blessing.

Hell, I couldn't even spell all of those names, much less pronounce them, but one name I did recognize. Bommarito. St. Louis area car dealer. Probably not related, but who knows?

Bommarito, at 79, is the Family's most-tenured "made" man currently in active duty, receiving his button in a 1950s ceremony conducted by legendary Motor City mob don Joseph (Joe Uno) Zerilli. He's been Tocco's consigliere for the past six years, replacing Black Jack's brother, Anthony (Tony T), who stepped down from his post in 2008 and died of natural causes in 2011.

The Detroit mob was also involved in Ford Motor Company stock options, with a feud over who controlled what, resulting in the hit on Joseph (Joe the Baron) Tocco. Anthony (Tony Cars) D'Anna was the local mobster that went to Zerilli, who allegedly ordered Tocco gunned down. I discovered that the Detroit mob had been deeply intertwined in the automotive industry since the late thirties. My thoughts concerning that involvement drifted to the dealership of the Senator. Connections, influence, manipulations, and who knew what else?

Perhaps my investigation into the Klienknect deaths is related to activities of the mob and their influences in the auto industry.

Hey, here it is. I know a lot about the law, but I'm not a lawyer. I know most of the content of the constitutions for Missouri and Illinois, as well as the U.S. Constitution. Not because I was simply curious. It was on the detailed test for obtaining my "Private Detective" license in Illinois and my "Private Investigator" license in Missouri. Amazingly enough, there were no questions on those tests concerning my knowledge of the Italian Mafia.

What the hell is their role in all of this?

Part Three

Chapter 19

Margo looks good at any time and fits into any situation. Boot-scooting, Marine Corps Birthday Ball, dining at the governor's mansion, or just out for the evening. Today is June 24 and Little Joe is getting married.

A stunning blonde, Margo looks ravishing in a rose-colored silk dress, with matching jacket. The neckline plunges, but not too much. Just enough to show some cleavage and complement her eighteen-inch necklace of 5 mm Mikimoto cultured pearls. I only knew that much about the pearls because that's what the jeweler told me when I bought them in Japan. A pearl necklace is a staple of any woman's jewelry wardrobe. For formal evening wear or casual every day dress, a cultured pearl necklace is a must have classic jewelry item that can be worn for many years to come. Margo's strand of pearls were of the classic white variety, hand knotted and were very elegant, with matching earrings set in 14k gold. The ready to go package was really quite stunning. As for me, I wore a wool worsted gray suit, with vest. When I looked in the mirror I reminded myself of the stranger in my dreams that picked me up in a Maserati. He had worn a gold chain across the front of his vest, as I did now.

I thought it appropriate to take an Italian car to an Italian wedding. Putting a nicely wrapped wedding gift in the trunk, a set of six Swarovski crystal old-fashioned glasses, I seated my lovely lady in the Italian leather seat and headed for what I thought would be a traditional Italian wedding. Crossing the Poplar Street bridge again I took I-44 across the lower neighborhoods of St. Louis, exiting at Lindbergh Avenue, turning south until I reached Watson Road. Just a short distance on Watson Road, then a quick right onto Rott Road brought us to the Laumeier Sculpture Park, the venue for the wedding. It was 2:10 and we were twenty minutes early. I wanted an opportunity to at least have a few minutes with Crazy Joe and Little Joe. Congratulations, and all that. There were probably twenty vehicles in the parking area and a gathering of what appeared to be mostly Italian families near the gardens.

Judith Shea's "Public Goddess" stands in the center of her "American Heartland Garden" in Laumeier's Museum Circle. Literally heart-shaped, the garden is a popular venue for smaller wedding ceremonies in the spring and summer when the roses are in full bloom, and they were.

Crazy Joe wasn't too difficult to fine. He was holding court in the shadow of the Public Goddess. Wouldn't you know it? Little Joe was close by.

"My friend Joe, what a lovely day and a wonderful occasion to meet by the Goddess." I had been to Italy before they transitioned to the Euro and had kept a souvenir Italian banknote in lire. "As part of my wedding gift, I'm giving you a little change here to help offset your expenses." I handed him a 5,000 lire bank note, which in fact is a "little" gift. Worth about eight American dollars.

"Well, Conner, that's a very generous gift. I'm glad you and Margo could make it and thank you for your generosity. Let me introduce you both to my friends and others that you may not know." He led me around the gardens where we met some of the family. Joe cleans up nicely when he wants to. He actually wore a tux, which I suspected was rented. He was in his element, smoozing with his connections, although I'm not sure Italians called it that. We talked to Little Joe briefly, left our wedding gift on a table placed strategically for that obvious purpose and congratulated him on his choice of brides. She did look the part of an Italian bride today.

Music began playing and that was our clue to take our seats and wait for the bride to march down the aisle to meet Little Joe at the front, where an enormous floral arrangement eclipsed everything. Crazy Joe had some connections somewhere, as a robust Italian lady broke out in song, accompanied by background music that I assumed was taped, with an Italian version of what I thought must be "Here Comes the Bride." And there she came, flowing white wedding dress and all. We all stood and watched her march down the aisle to Little Joe and the priest that would administer the vows.

Unconscious subversive thoughts again. She reminded me of a young lady that was getting an evaluation from her doctor. He says, Well, it looks like you're pregnant. She replies, OMG, I'm pregnant? And he says, No, you aren't. I just said it looks like you're pregnant.

She joined Little Joe and the priest, who said all the right things about devotion and love, through thick and thin, until we die. Yes, it is so.

When the ceremony was over everyone gathered around the table where champagne was being served. A lively group.

"Sir, are you the owner of the red Maserati?"

"Yes, I am. What can I do for you?"

"I'm Sammy Loganno, and you must be Mr. Pennington. You've gotten quite a reputation around the Hill. Can we take a walk?"

I didn't know where this was headed, but I was armed. That got to be my habit since the Union Station ordeal.

I excused myself from Margo and led him to the sculpture part of the park. We stopped at the twelve-foot perfectly round sculpture of an eyeball. Twelve feet in height and starring at you with one big blue eye. On the back side of the eyeball we were out of sight of the wedding attendees.

"So, what can I do for you, Mr. Loganno?"

"Please, call me Sammy. I understand you have been looking into things concerning the Senator. I might have some valuable information for you. First, though, let's move away from the eye. I may be a little superstitious, but I don't want no eyes watching me." We moved to another sculpture in the garden.

"Now, why would you do that, Sammy? You're Italian. As I understand the code, you guys don't talk about family. The Senator is family, right?"

"Well, yes and no. Sure, we're family, but sometimes there are some disagreements that get resolved without everyone's approval. I had a car dealership that was sort of financed by the family, just to get me started. I did well, made a lot of money, and paid my dues to the capo. I didn't own the dealership by myself. There were contributors that acted as sort of a board of directors, overseeing their investments. Giocomelli was on the board. He decided he wanted my dealership. I don't know if he bribed or threatened the other members of the board, but when he wanted to buy my dealership, at a ridiculously low price, all the board members voted to sell out. I believe you would call that a hostile takeover, wouldn't you? He took over my livelihood. I assume you know he has strong connections with the Detroit family. Anyway, you need to be careful in this town. You want to know something about the operations here, you talk to me. I want to see him go down." He handed me a card with his cell phone number on it.

"Thank you, Sammy. I know the code. We never met, and we never talked."

Sammy went back to the wedding gathering, blending in with the other family members. Other than Margo, no one seemed to notice that Sammy had taken a walk with one of the few non-Italians at the wedding.

Crazy Joe had planned a dinner for the wedding attendees at

a nearby Italian restaurant. Little Joe and his new bride departed in a limo, presumably to gather with friends and family for dinner. Wedding presents remained unopened on a table near the entrance to the garden, so Margo and I helped Crazy Joe transport the gifts to the trunk of his Cadillac, probably to be opened at the dinner gathering.

While loading the gifts, Joe pulled me aside and said, "I noticed you took a walk with Sammy. He's been really pissed about losing his dealership and I told him you would be here today, and that he might want to have a conversation with you. So, how did that go?"

"It bears looking into, Joe. It seems, as you warned me, that I may have stepped into a barrel of snakes in this investigation and that the family has some interest in putting the skids on my delving into their business dealings. I'll tread carefully, my friend."

"Thanks for helping with the gifts, Conner. Let's head out for the restaurant and enjoy our dinner. You are coming aren't you, with your lady? The restaurant is the Trattoria Marcella on Watson Road. You know it, right?"

"Sure, Joe. We wouldn't miss it. See you soon."

The drive to Trattoria Marcella was at least fifteen miles from the site of the wedding ceremony, but the restaurant was known in St. Louis and across the country as one of the finest in Italian food and wine pairings. I wouldn't have thought Joe had selected, without outside consultation, such an upscale place. Expensive too. Damn good thing I gave him the 5,000 Italian lire.

Mostly Northern Italian cuisine, the menu was extensive, featuring fare such as lobster risotto and osso bucco. Most of the attendees at the wedding were present at Trattoria Marcella. A long table had been set up in a private dining area, with Chianti wine bottles down the center covered with drippings from red candles. Every other place setting had an open bottle of Lambrusco Italian Red wine.

For a gear head, visiting the Maserati factory in Modina, Italy can only be described as a fantastic voyage. Beyond the factory, and surrounding Modina, are the vineyards of Lambrusco grapes, providing a variety of Lambrusco wines. Not my usual choice for wine, but Lambrusco pairs wonderfully with most Italian foods. So, this evening it will be Lambrusco.

Apparently, Sammy wasn't through talking about the Senator. After a fine Italian meal, Sammy approached me and asked if he could have a few minutes. Of course I was receptive to his conversation. I wanted to know as much as he would divulge.

"Mr. Pennington, let me tell you little more about the Senator. There have been rumors for years that the Senator is gay. Yeah, I know he's married, but it's no great secret among the family that he prefers young men. Okay, here's the deal, some of these boys have put the pressure on the Senator, mainly because he doesn't stick with one of his boys for very long. He bounces around, you know what I mean?"

"Yes, I know what you mean, but what does this have to do with the Senator taking over your dealership?"

"Look, I'm not saying it has anything to do with taking over my dealership, but there are some dark secrets in the Senator's background. You might oughta' look into it."

"Thank you, Sammy. I will indeed be looking into the Senator's background."

The rest of the evening was congenial, and Margo was mingling with the guests, as they prepared to depart the evening festivities.

I approached Joe as Margo and I were ready to depart. "Joe, it's been a lovely evening and a wonderful wedding. I don't see Little Joe around. Has he already left?"

"Yeah, he's not crazy about these group parties. He's a good kid though. This is a good thing, Conner, and thank you for coming. You're okay now, my friend?"

"Yes, I'm good, Joe. Your friend Sammy and I had a nice visit about the Senator."

"Stop right there. We don't talk about what your conversation was. I don't want to know."

"Okay, I get it. You have always told me you don't talk about the family. So, we'll leave it at that. Keep in touch. Margo and I are heading back to Illinois."

It really wasn't like Joe, but he gave me a hug and bid me farewell. Crazy Joe, but a good friend.

Chapter 20

There were a lot of issues that had not been resolved in my mind concerning this investigation. Was it even relevant to anything in this search for the truth that the Senator was allegedly gay?

Back in my office, the day after the wedding, I had an epiphany, of sorts, and a burning question. If Klineknect had driven home shortly after the New Year's Eve celebration and left his Cadillac running, the vehicle would have run out of gas by the time the Senator arrived at the home. According to the personal expenditure records of Gerard, he had filled his Cadillac with gas on the previous Thursday, which was his compulsive habit. Every Thursday. There had been no record of a fill up between that previous Thursday and the time of his death.

Based on my research about this model of Cadillac, the gas guzzling 365 cubic inch, 6.0 liter, massive engine would have drained the gas tank long before Senator Antonio Giacomelli arrived on the scene. Idling in the garage, the Eldorado Brougham would have only achieved the advertised gas mileage for city driving. A mere 6.5 miles per gallon. By my calculations, one hour of city driving would burn approximately ten gallons of gas. This model had a twenty-gallon tank. Two hours of city driving would empty the tank completely. How many gallons had been used since his last fill up? I couldn't be sure of that. My conclusion was that either Gerard rose during the night, and for whatever reason, went to the garage, started the car, leaving the kitchen door open, and went back to bed with his wife. Essentially committing suicide and an intentional murder of his wife. Now why would he do that? Not very logical. Or, someone with a key to his front door came into the home after Gerard and his wife were fast asleep, opened the kitchen door to the garage, started the Cadillac, and left the home, leaving the front door unlocked. The carbon monoxide produced by the Cadillac would undoubtedly result in the deaths of anyone in the home. That would certainly constitute premeditation and intent.

The Senator had indicated that he had a key to the front door, but that he had either lost it or misplaced it. An interesting part of his story was that he usually stayed with the Klienknects when he was in town but opted not to stay with them that fatal night, even though they had arranged for a brunch at the club the next day. Was the Senator implicit in this nefarious deed after all? Considering that the Senator was involved with the mob in St. Louis, then and now, as well as being quite adept at securing bids for selling law enforcement vehicles to the Patrol, I had no doubt that he was very capable of planning borderline illegal activities, as well as covering his tracks along the way. It was quite possible that he had stayed at the Country Club much later than the Klienknects, drove to their home, used his key to enter and started the engine in the garage. But what would have been his motive and what did he have to gain?

There was a possibility that one or more of the neighbors living on Hobbs Lane at the time were still living in that neighborhood. A trip to Jefferson City and a canvass of the area might shed more light on the events of that night. On the other hand, if there were still residents in the neighborhood that were there during this time period, would they even remember anything from 50 years ago?

I was now convinced that Gerard was a compulsive person that locked his doors, religiously. Even with a high alcohol content it would not have been very likely that he would forgo that habit. Again, the incident was either a case of suicide or premeditated murder. I had no idea if Gerard had experienced any level of depression or suicidal thoughts, but then who can predict such things? He was a successful business man, with a lovely home, a devoted wife, a prominent figure in the community, and was looking forward to the new year. Too many unanswered questions. Nothing at this stage of the investigation pointed to an intentional act of suicide, to include murder of the devoted his wife that slept beside Gerard on New Year's Eve. Was Mandy correct in her thinking these were not accidental deaths?

Another visit with Mandy may yield some answers to some of those questions, but she was also very young when her grandparents died. She may not know anything about the incident other than what she has since read in newspaper articles, or what her father may have related to her about that night, or whatever she has gleaned from the records and other documents. Given Mandy's apparent attraction to me I wasn't sure I should spend time with her alone at the estate. But, I'm a big boy. I can handle that. Besides, being in the company of a sensual lady doesn't mean yielding to temptations. Right?

For whatever reasons, recently I was in the habit of leaving my cell phone off. So, I was startled by the ring tone, because today was one of those days when the damn thing was actually on.

"Mr. Pennington, this is Detective Tanner. The two guys you and Mr. Meza trussed up have been identified as Frank Cusumono and Marcus Bommarito. Both of these guys have old family connections here in St. Louis but are now associated with the mob in Detroit. The Eastern District U. S. Attorney and the FBI are now involved in this case. The local Agent in Charge, Gregory Taylor has indicated that in all likelihood Cusumono will eventually be put in a witness protection program. It seems he has a propensity to talk. The other guy, Bommarito, left his fingerprints on the .380 and the ballistics from his gun match the bullet taken from you, as well as the two murders that I mentioned before. So, in that respect, I'll thank you for clearing up those cases for me. Just remember though, this is still my town." My phone went silent as the connection ended.

Very interesting. I had been to the old Cusumono restaurant on Manchester Road and wondered if there was a family connection there. As Hillary Clinton said in her testimony about the Benghazi situation, "What difference does it make?"

Although my phone was still on, I wasn't quite ready to call Mandy to ask her about her grandfather's state of mind, doubting that she would remember such things, given her age at the time. Still, I would like to know what her father's relationship was with Gerard as well as with Mandy's mother. What appeared to be a relatively simple investigation was now turning over crusted, moss covered stones that had been long buried. Now I had serious concerns about not only my own safety, but also the safety of people I cared about.

The income journal begun by Gerard Klienknect and continued by Alfred Klienknect was as detailed as the expense journal. I noted that there had been no entries made by Gerard indicating that his son had ever repaid any of the "loans" his father had provided to him. Many of the loans were quite substantial and over a five-year period had totaled slightly more than $245,000. Was that even significant? Perhaps more relevant, and interesting, were the account interests and dividends received from an offshore bank account in the Bahamas. Were there perhaps copies of income tax returns among those boxes of files at the estate? Based on my calculations, Gerard had deposited close to ten million dollars in offshore accounts. Surely it wasn't still there, after all these years. Mandy didn't mention anything of that nature, but then I hadn't pursued that line of questioning either. Had Mandy hired me to simply find the truth about the deaths of her grandparents, or was there a monetary motive?

My mind was in a whirl. If the Klienknect deaths were not accidental and not a murder/ suicide, there were a number of individuals to consider as being complicit in that event. Certainly not Mandy, as she was too young to even consider such a thing. I knew her to be a courteous ice skating student, intelligent and affectionate. Why did I think 'affectionate'? She had not exhibited that trait during the time I knew her as a student, as least not in my observation. Other considerations were the Senator, the mob, maybe even the son. I couldn't really grasp the concept of the son committing patricide. It happens, but perhaps not likely in this case. The Senator had mentioned in the sit-down that at some point in time he had a key to the Klienknect home but had lost it or misplaced it. Had someone else taken the key and used it to enter the home on New Year's Eve? If so, who could that have been? And where exactly was the Senator that early morning after celebrating with his associate at the Country Club the night before? He had chosen not to answer that question when I posed it during our meeting at Giovanni's by saying, "Next question." There was just too much I didn't know at this juncture of the investigation. More questions than answers.

Against my better judgement I called Mandy. She picked up my call almost immediately.

"Mandy, this is Conner. I still have a lot of questions about this investigation. If it's convenient for you I would like to take a look at more of the documents stored at the estate, particularly any copies of income tax returns. Can we do that?"

"Well, Conner, it's always good to hear from you. Give me a day or two and I will search through some of those boxes and locate the tax forms. I'm sure they are all there. I'm not sure why you need them, but if I can't locate them I will let you know."

"That's great, Mandy. You've been a big help in this investigation. I look forward to hearing from you about those returns."

"Thank you, Conner, you are always so gracious. By the way, I've had our mechanic check out the Aston Martin DB4 and she's ready for the road. When you come by to pick up those returns we can take her for a spin, so plan some time to do that. You aren't going to charge me for that time, are you?"

"No, absolutely not. It would simply be a thrill to drive the DB4. By the way, I was so overwhelmed with your father's collection of automobiles that I didn't notice the particular model of his DB4. I thought maybe it was the Zagato."

"Yes, it is a Zagato. It wouldn't have been in the collection otherwise. This is the one with the aluminum engine, aluminum body, and the straight six-cylinder engine, with double over head cams. It has a top speed of 154 miles per hour and there were only 25 of this model produced."

"I'm impressed with your knowledge and description of the DB4. I don't know too many people that have that level of interest and understanding of finely engineered automobiles. Are you sure you don't have a problem with me driving what must be a very valuable Aston Martin?"

"Look, Conner, you drive a Maserati and I certainly trust you behind the wheel of my Aston Martin. If I didn't trust you in all things, I wouldn't have hired you as my private investigator. You were my idol from years ago, and you still are."

"I'm no idol on anyone's list. That's not who I am."

"Okay, maybe I used the wrong word to describe what I think of you. Hero, idol, mentor, teacher. I know you were a combat Marine, you were always patient with me as an instructor, you are a gentle person, but not someone to be trifled with. You're a handsome man, and your blue eyes penetrate and melt me. Okay, I know I went too far with that. I'll give you a call when I find the tax returns."

Conner, you need to limit your exposure to Mandy. Temptations are one thing and yielding to those temptations is quite another. Be careful.

Mandy had mentioned in one of our earlier meetings that her

husband spent a lot of time away from home. Either at the hospital or perhaps with another woman. Was she simply looking for payback or something else? This certainly adds another complication to the investigation.

Two days later Mandy called and told me she had located her grandfather's tax returns. I was surprised that the returns had been kept for so many years, but then all of the storage boxes I saw at the estate must have contained records from the days when Gerard was operating his dealerships. Mandy's father, Alfred, apparently had no compulsion to destroy records, or perhaps even review his father's records.

We arranged to meet 10:00 on that Thursday morning.

I arrived at the estate precisely at 10:00, as I'm sure Mandy expected. If I had any doubts about actually driving the Aston Martin, they were quickly removed when I saw praked the car in the circular drive. For prior visits Mandy had been standing on the top step in front of the massive front door, as she was now. I didn't remember her having such a tan the last time we met, but the short white tennis skirt she was now wearing accentuated her long tan legs. Just returned from the tennis courts, I'm sure. The clinging white top was a striking contrast to her tanned arms and her cleavage was exposed more than would be expected for someone who actually played tennis. A very alluring package. She held a briefcase in her left hand and turned to close the front door as I left my car and climbed the stone steps.

"Conner, it is so very nice to see you. I thought this might be a good day to take the DB4 for a spin. My mechanic has done a complete inspection and assures me she is road ready. I must apologize for my attire. I had an early game of tennis with a friend and didn't have time to change. I hope you don't mind." I saw no evidence that she had played tennis that morning, other than her attire. From her white tennis shoes to her sparkling white top I saw nothing that indicated any level of physical exercise. She was a competitive woman that would have run an opponent ragged. She had taken the time and the thought as to how she would dress to get my attention.

She descended two steps as I came up to her. "Mrs. Barrows, I am very much looking forward to driving the DB4 and I must say you look quite nice today. I have been accused of fancying myself as the fictional British legend...James Bond. It isn't true, but his alleged choice of a DB4 is an iconic characteristic of 007 and I have fantasized about driving one since I saw the first Bond movie." Still on a step above me she wrapped her arms around me, pressing her breasts close to my face, then whispered in my ear, "Please don't call me Mrs. Barrows. It's Mandy."

She picked up the briefcase, took my arm and led me toward the Aston Martin. "This is going to be a fun day. It has been a long time since I have been up the Great River Road, so I'm thinking that would be a wonderful drive in the Aston Martin." She handed me the key and I followed her to the passenger door, taking the briefcase from her, then opening the door and assisting her as she leaned seductively toward me, sitting down on the green leather seat, pulling her tanned legs in last. "You are such a gentleman, Conner. I can't remember the last time a man opened a car door for me." Her smile was beguiling, and her eyes seemed to have an extra sparkle, a shade of blue green and flecks of gold...or so it seemed.

The leather seat was not quite as comfortable as those in my Maserati, and the wood trimmed steering wheel was larger than I expected. The shift lever rested below my right hand and I noted that the gear had been placed in first . The shift pattern had been engraved on the top of the knob. I placed the briefcase on a ledge behind the passenger seat. Depressing the clutch, I found it to be quite firm, allowing me to easily move the shift lever to a neutral position. A turn of the key brought the engine to life, with a smooth purr, rather than the throaty rumble of a V-8. With the clutch depressed,

I shifted into first gear, released the hand brake and moved around my Maserati, then down the curving, overgrown driveway.

We picked up Highway 67, in a northly direction, crossing the Mississippi River into the town of Alton, Illinois where we turned north on Highway 100, also known as the Great River Road. To a great extent, the Great River Road follows the Mississippi River and is a great bald eagle observation point in the fall. Giant eagle nests were lodged in huge trees along the highway. It was invigorating to feel the suspension grasp the roadway and hold the curves. Traffic was light, and I occasionally pushed the DB4 to 110 miles per hour. A little more at times. Glancing at Mandy, I observed that she was watching me intently. The smile and sparkling eyes were a buoyancy that prompted me to speed through curves that were posted at limits far below my current speed, reminding me of the drive to the Montelle Winery. No recriminations or instructions from the enchanting lady sitting next to me, even though the machine I was piloting was worth at least four million dollars.

"And what is our destination, Mandy? If you don't watch me closely, I'll have us in Wisconsin before you know it."

"It's been said that the largest and most beautiful park in Illinois is Pere Marquette, which is just north of Grafton. They have a lovely lodge there and a comfortable restaurant. Perhaps we can stop for lunch, stretch our legs and have a glass of wine?"

"Why do I get the feeling you had all of this planned? You dazzle me with your tennis togs and the opportunity to drive a vintage Aston Martin, and now lunch and wine at a romantic lodge."

"You deserve it, Conner. I'll show you where to turn into the park and lodge. Just enjoy the scenery."

"I am, Mandy. I am."

Chapter 21

The lodge was huge, made of logs, and very rustic. As I parked the DB4 and left the driver's seat I walked in front of the car and around to the passenger side, opening the door for Mandy. The subtle scent of gardenias wafted from the cockpit. Her tan legs swung out first, and I held out my hand to assist her in rising from the low-slung frame while I stood admiring the sensual curves of the Zagato, as well as the curves standing before me. I could still sense the warmness of the thin wood rimmed steering wheel and the excitement of driving such an exalted rare automobile, all the while in the presence of a captivating socialite.

"Mandy, I'm guessing this Zagato is worth at least four million dollars. I'm impressed you let me drive it without making some comment about me pushing it through the curves and on the straightaways. Thank you for that experience."

"It's just a car, Conner. I know you love fine cars and are quite versed in their ancestry and heritage, but you are off just a bit on the value of the Zagato. A 1963 model recently sold at auction for slightly more than fourteen million dollars."

"Oh my God! And you have kept this vehicle at the estate all these years, without 24-hour security surrounding the property?"

"I didn't point it out to you when we were at the stables, but there is more than adequate security. I turned the system off before you arrived that day. By the way, I noticed you didn't retrieve the brief-case from the ledge behind the seats, and that's good. Let's have a leisurely lunch and you can review those old tax returns back at your office." Taking my hand, she led me to the lodge and the restaurant.

The interior of the lodge was as rustic as the exterior promised. A huge stone fireplace that could accommodate six-foot logs in its firebox dominated the reception area. There were oversize leather couches facing the now empty cavern of the well-used pit which would create enough heat to warm the room. The mantle and stones surrounding the open fireplace were darkened from years of roaring fires, now silent and empty in the warmth of early summer.

It was obvious Mandy had been here before, as she led me to the cozy restaurant on the far side of the vaulted log ceiling that rose thirty feet above our heads. It was now early afternoon and I observed only two other patrons seated at a heavy wooden table.

The person I assumed would be our waiter approached and ad-dressed us as we came through the entryway. "Good afternoon. Do you have a preference for seating?"

I didn't, but apparently Mandy did. "Yes. We would like a table by the window. Perhaps a little privacy with that." We were led to a far corner of the restaurant where a table for two was set near a win-dow that overlooked the rolling hills and forest. A partial partition gave the feeling of privacy, separating this table from the remainder of the open seating. Cozy and intimate. I had the recurring feeling that Mandy had planned this also.

Hovering nearby, our waiter asked, "May I take your drink orders?"

Not sure what fare might be on the lunch menu, I demurred on the request and indicated I would pair my choice of wine with my selection from the menu, which I had yet to review. Mandy was ahead of me, glancing briefly at the wine selections, she requested the Benovia 2015 Three Sisters Chardonnay. I found her selection twenty items down the list of white wines and silently nodded my approval of her choice as I read the brief description. *With a persistence of lightly-toasted oak, this youthful wine offers intense luxury.* It somehow seemed to fit the description of the sensual lady sitting on the other side of a well-worn oak table. Turning to our waiter I indicated I would have the same.

Although the large wooden sign on the Great River Road proclaimed this to be the Pere Marquette Lodge and Conference Center, I was impressed by the large variety of wine selections. Rooms were available at the lodge, as well as cabins that were scattered around the property, giving the conference attendees a sense of seclusion while also providing interesting meals and wine choices.

The menu was also fairly extensive, with a wide selection of appetizers, soups, salads, sandwiches and more substantial fare. The *Hickory Trail North* appealed to my increasing appetite. Simply a traditional Reuben on marbled rye. Typically, my selection when I traveled to New York City, but usually with the resulting heartburn that required a generous handful of Tums. I had no Tums with me, so I settled for the *Fern Hollow Salad*, described on the menu as tossed lettuce topped with assorted meats, cheeses, tomato, egg, red onion and croutons. I asked the waiter to leave the red onions off the salad. No Tums, no onions. Mandy ordered the *Grilled Chicken Ceasar Salad*, without even a glance at the menu selections.

Our glasses of chardonnay arrived, and Mandy raised her glass in a salute. "To you, Conner, and what promises to be an interesting future." This toast was presented with a seductive smile. I wasn't sure of the direction this was taking, but I touched my glass to hers and added my own toast. "To unearthing of the truth. May we accept it as it is revealed."

"I will certainly embrace revealing the truth. I asked you earlier in our meetings if you would take a side step in your investigation and check out Dr. Barrows." This was said with more than a subtle note of disdain when referring to her husband as Dr. Barrows. "You indicated you wouldn't do that. I'm okay with that, but would it be possible for you to perhaps contact one of your associates to investigate what my dear husband is doing with all of his time he spends away from the hospital?"

"Mandy, your husband is a good surgeon. He saved my life after I was shot. I'm sure he is quite busy at the hospital and perhaps takes some time to relax."

"Right. That's his story anyway. I've called him at the hospital when he was supposed to be there, and he wasn't. When I asked him about his absence he simply tells me he went out to play a round of golf."

"Well, isn't that possible?"

"Possible, yes, but not likely. He does keep a set of clubs in his trunk, but I doubt that he uses them. I'm not a private investigator, but either he is very good at playing golf, or he buys new golf balls after he plays. I play golf myself, but not often. When I play I usually lose a ball or two, or three. I have counted the golf balls in his bag and there is always the same number before and after he allegedly plays. Okay, that doesn't confirm that he hasn't played golf with his buddies, but it certainly raises some doubts in my mind. Conner, he's changed over the past couple of years. He really doesn't pay much attention to me and although he has a very comfortable income as a surgeon he has been pressuring me to sell the stable of cars at the estate, including the Aston Martin. In fact, specifically the Aston Martin. I simply don't trust him any more and I question his motives for wanting a huge amount of assets to add to his burgeoning bank account. Damn it, if he wants a divorce he can certainly have it, but he's not getting a pile of money to start a new life with some bimbo."

"I understand your concern. I do have an associate that I will contact to investigate the activities of Dr. Barrows. I can tell you from experience that things don't always work out the way we originally envision them, or the way we expect our lives to be. It's difficult for me to understand a man that would not devote his time and attention to a lovely lady like yourself."

"Thank you, Conner. So, let's change the subject. I really don't want to think about Dr. Nathan Barrows right now. Let's enjoy our lunch and our time together." Taking a sip of her chardonnay, she reached across the table with her left hand and covered my right hand as I rested my fork on the side of my plate. Her touch was warm, with a sensual energy that was more of a caress than a simple touch. "You have been very attentive and professional and I'm sorry this investigation put you in danger. I am grateful to my dear husband for one thing, and one thing only. He took care of you when they brought you to the hospital. I've become quite attracted to you. Part of that feeling is a carry-over from our connection years ago, I'm sure. I'm just very glad that you're here now." Her eyes absorbed me with a consuming desire and her subtle smile betrayed the depth of feelings she was not ready to reveal. *Come on, Conner. Why are you even thinking this young, voluptuous, sensual lady would want anything more than a conclusion to the investigation, which is why she hired you to answer the ultimate question she had about her grandparent's deaths? Don't flatter yourself, son!*

Noticing that our wine glasses were nearing the bottom, our waiter returned to the table and asked if we would like another round. Mandy simply responded with an affirmative confirmation that a refill would be nice. In my mind I'm wondering if another glass of wine is really a wise decision when driving a multi-million-dollar vehicle back to the estate. It's well known that one of the first things alcohol effects is the decision-making process. Maybe it was already too late. Intoxication can be induced in many ways, and in this case, Mandy was certainly a contributing factor for a level of intoxication that couldn't be measured on a breathalyzer. Still, I decided to risk it.

The wine was a nice complement to our salads, which were almost entirely consumed. Mandy pushed her plate to the side and moved her chair closer to mine, her bare leg pressing against mine under the table. Her left hand rested briefly on my right thigh.

"It is so nice not to be in a hurry, rushing here and there in an effort to appease other people's wishes. We're not in a hurry, are we?"

"I suppose not, Mandy. But tell me, what have you done since you left Jefferson City? Many years have gone by and I have no idea where you've been between then and your contacting me about this case."

"Well, I finished high school in Jefferson City before we moved to St. Louis. My father took over all the dealerships that my grandfather had started, then expanded with other dealerships. Three of the original dealerships were turned over to Senator Giocomelli, as was the agreement in the partnership. I went to Washington University and after three years of undergraduate work I entered law school and graduated with my J.D. degree. I never took the bar exam. I met Nathan shortly after graduating from Wash U and we were married three months later. Twelve years later, no children and no pets. I have had a comfortable, if not troubling, life. Losing my parents was a tragedy and I can't say I'm really over that yet. I still struggle with that and now the distance that has grown between Nathan and I compounds spells of depression. I know you're a private investigator, not a psychologist, so I'll stop there."

"That's okay, Mandy. Actually, one of my undergraduate degrees is in psychology, but you're right, I'm not a psychologist. You have certainly experienced some trauma in your life. Sharing those experiences with someone that cares can be a part of the healing process. I'm a pretty good listener and I do care. Anything you share with me is strictly confidential."

"Thank you. I feel very comfortable discussing some of my dark secrets with you, like my depression. It isn't often, but being lonely probably contributes to a sense of loss of self- worth and not know-ing which way to turn. I try to keep myself busy by working on all the issues surrounding the sale of the estate. It's so refreshing to have you around, even though it is only occasionally. It's really funny, Nathan has no interest in the vehicles at the estate, except for their monetary value, whereas you are genuinely interested in the cars as works of fine engineering, design, and essentially exquisite art. We are on the same level with that. You have been an uplifting influence and my depression seems to be fading with each visit we have. You are such a gentleman and treat me like a lady, with respect and at-tention. I keep thanking you for so many things and I'm adding your understanding and compassion to your many fine qualities."

"You are far too generous with your compliments. I am curious about one thing. Did you actually play tennis this morning?"

"Now why do you ask that?"

"I saw no physical evidence that you had played a competitive game of tennis, and I know from ice skating experience that you are quite competitive. I'm also sure that you are aware of how striking your tennis outfit is and the impact you have on me."

"Really? To be honest, I did not play tennis. So, what impact do I have on you?"

"My dear Mandy. I suspect you are being coy with me. You arouse me with your intellect, your appreciation of art and fine cars, your physical beauty and your aura of sensuality. You're very charming. I could say more, but I dare not."

Her left hand again rested on my thigh as she replied, "You're a very charming man and those blue eyes still melt my resolve to ignore your charismatic presence. I propose we have an after-lunch drink for dessert. Perhaps a martini, or something a little more exotic. Having experienced two of their more exotic specialties here at the lodge I would recommend either the Glaya, which is scotch, Seville oranges, spices, herbs and honey, or Lochan Ora, which consists of

Chivas, honey, herbs and spices. I know you like scotch, as do I, which is why I recommended those liqueurs."

"Select your personal preference and I will have the same. I trust your judgement."

Our waiter returned, whereupon Mandy ordered two double shots of the Glayva. I had never heard of it, but then I hadn't traveled in the same circles Mandy had.

Crystal tumblers reflected the ambient light streaming through the nearby window into the golden concoction of liquid danger. Nighty-eight proof, as I later discovered. Another seductive smile and Mandy deftly touched her glass to mine, "To the future and to you, my gentleman friend."

Three sips had been enough to tell me I wouldn't be driving the DB4 for some time. For now, who cares? "To a very sensual, sexy and beautiful lady." Did I really say that?

Glayva will warm parts of you that you never knew existed. In the presence of Mandy there were already parts that were reaching the higher limits of my personal thermometer. The liqueur was smooth and erased any concerns that may be lingering in the ambiance of such alluring company. Our conversation continued with an easy flow, touching often and with more seeming intimacy and desire. With our tumblers almost empty Mandy rose from her chair and asked to be excused, promising she would return in a flash.

I had no doubt she would. I watched as her shapely legs moved her across the restaurant toward the lobby. Focusing on the forest outside the window it seemed as though a light fog had moved into the area. Or perhaps the only fog was in my brain.

I couldn't be certain how long Mandy had been gone, but as she returned she exhibited a projection of confidence and accomplishment. At least that was my take on her tennis clad image.

Taking my hand, she pulled me away from the table. "Conner, my dear, let's take a walk."

Chapter 22

With her arm looped through mine she pressed her body close and walked with me through the massive lobby to the exit doors leading to the parking lot and the lone vehicle sitting majestically on display. The DB4.

"Mandy, I don't think I'm in any condition to drive your Aston Martin."

"Not to worry. I've arranged for us to spend some time together and recover from a bit too much libation."

She led me past the DB4 and walked toward a cabin just north of the prized vehicle. Taking a key from a pocket that must have been reserved for tennis balls in her pristine, very short tennis skirt, she opened the door to a cozy room with Indian area rugs and a dark brown leather sofa and love seat. A counter separated the small living area from a kitchenette, with a coffee machine perched on the corner by an apartment size refrigerator.

"Some coffee, perhaps?"

"Wonderful. It won't sober me up, but if you make it, I'll drink it." *Don't start being a smart-ass at this point, Conner.*

"Make yourself comfortable on the sofa and I'll make us some coffee. We'll have some time to discuss whatever you want to talk about. Then we'll drive back to the estate." Mandy busied herself with the coffee machine, as though she were comfortable with the surroundings of the cabin. When the coffee began perking she came to the sofa, placed both hands on my thighs, leaned forward and exposed quite a view of her full breasts as she kissed me on the mouth, her tongue parting my lips as her hands moved slowly to my inner thighs. Resistance was nil. My arousal was evident to Mandy when she moved her right hand to my crotch and grasped my throbbing hardness.

"Don't move, Conner. I'll be right back." In my fuzzy state of being I was sure she would be.

Moments later she reappeared, sans the white tennis shoes, the white, short skirt and the tight, clinging top. She stood before me in her very brief frilly white bra and panties. Bending over again, she removed my shoes, then leaned closer and whispered in my ear, "Conner, I've dreamed of this for a long time. You won't be disappointed. She removed her bra and exposed erect nipples at the crest of firm, full breasts. My shirt was quickly disposed of as she unbuttoned each button with slow deliberate movements. The remainder of my clothes soon followed. Pushing me into a reclining position, she straddled my torso, then lay her breasts against my chest as she smothered me with kisses, reaching again to my now exposed erection.

I was overcome with desire as she caressed me and rose slightly, one of her breasts and an inviting nipple now at my hungry mouth. Deep guttural moans of pleasure erupted from Mandy as my tongue circled and licked the hardening nipple, eventually consuming the fullness of her breast as I took it in my mouth.

"I want you, Conner." With one hand she slipped her tiny panties off, with the final comment, "I want you inside me. Now." My decision-making and judgement had long since left my alcohol soaked brain. The view from where I lay was tantalizing and irresistible. Her smile was conquering, beguiling and totally unabashed. I felt her fingers close around me as she rose slightly then directed me to her now very wet vagina. Lowering herself onto my stiff shaft, she moaned again with pleasure. A state of euphoria swept over me as Mandy slowly lowered herself, taking me deeper and deeper. Her rhythm matched my thrusts, until it reached a crescendo that resulted in a unified orgasmic release of monumental pleasure. She collapsed on my chest and I held her tightly in my arms. The world had ceased to exist.

"My God, Mandy, I am so sorry..."

"Stop, Conner. No apologies, please. I intentionally seduced you. I admit it. I wanted you and I have no regrets. I planned this, and I hope you have no regrets about our love-making. It will never happen again, and I hope we are still friends."

It reminded me of a Willie Nelson song..."We were always more than lovers, and I'm still your friend, if I had the chance I'd do it all again."

The next hour and a half was spent holding each other on the leather sofa in the cozy cabin.

"Conner, I almost lost you when you were accosted and shot in the parking lot at Union Station. I couldn't take the chance that it would happen again, and I would lose you forever. I realize I don't have you even now, but for a while I did. I will cherish this wonderful memory. You have brought me a level of happiness that I have not experienced in a very long time, so don't punish yourself over recriminations of a trip into a mutual desire of passion and, yes, friendship. You have fulfilled my fantasies and I am indebted to you for being a thoughtful and passionate lover, even though this was the first and last."

"Mandy, Mandy. I don't know what to say. You are a very desirable lady, but you are right, this cannot happen again. Yes, I enjoyed every moment with you and I enjoy your company. How can I continue being your hired private investigator? I have overstepped every boundary that is set for a professional."

A smile crossed her radiant face and she simply replied, "We will survive, Conner. We will survive. This afternoon at Pere Marquette will not be mentioned again, but it will be in my memory. In my own way, Conner, I do love you, and have loved and respected you for many years. Please don't work to destroy that memory."

Two hours later we began drive back to the estate in Creve Coeur. It was more subdued than the drive up the Great River Road. I was mulling over my indiscretion and I'm sure Mandy had her own thoughts about what had happened. When I glanced in her direction as we drove down the Great River Road she appeared not to be distraught or in any way worried about our making love in the cabin at Pere Marquette. She smiled often and at times placed her left hand over my right hand as I shifted the DB4 up or down the gears, depending on the curves or hills.

"You seem very comfortable driving this vehicle. I can tell you really love this DB4, don't you?"

"It's a rare and beautiful classic. What's not to love about this work of art? I could certainly never afford such an exotic machine, so I appreciate even more the opportunity to drive one of the very few remaining DB4/GT Zagatos."

"Never give up your dreams, Conner. Unless you have a crystal ball we simply don't know what the future holds. I know we said we would not discuss what happened today, but I will tell you now I have no regrets about intentionally seducing you. I will cherish that memory and I don't want you to beat yourself up over that special time. I'm not much on philosophy, so I won't go too deeply into what I feel about my role in that seduction. As we drove up the Great River Road in this beautiful Zagato I reflected on life and how it isn't always the destination that is important, it is more about the trip and eventually arriving at your destination. The experiences we have, the love we share and the moments of ecstasy that brighten and fulfill our dreams of a meaningful journey are an important and significant part of the passage through our struggles in the face of trauma and adversity. You have provided for me that fulfillment. I know it won't happen again, nor do I hold you to any obligations, other than to continue to try to find the truth about my grandparent's deaths. I only hope that today doesn't impact negatively on your relationship with your lady, Margo. I wouldn't want that. I accept whatever blame you wish to attribute to me for seducing you, just don't think too badly of me in the process."

"You wax eloquently with your philosophies on life. I was certainly complicit in the events of today. I don't attribute any blame for your successful seduction. Remember, I was there too. With or without the events of today you are already a part of my journey."

We rode in silence for the next twenty-five or thirty miles. The hum of the engine seemed to accept and absorb the feelings of the cockpit occupants. We were one with the machine that propelled us south on the Great River Road. My mind wandered briefly to the old cliché about if these walls could talk what would they say? The current question being, what tales would this vehicle tell about past occupants or events? Certainly something interesting, or even profound. No computers on board this machine, so there won't be stories told about the past, present, or future.

Arriving back at the estate Mandy reminded me to retrieve from the rear shelf behind the passenger seat of the DB4 the folder containing the tax records she had found. We embraced when I left the car and she exited the passenger side, but no passionate kisses. I watched her as she stood on the steps to her inherited estate and I drove away in my Maserati. A hesitant wave and the image in my rearview mirror was gone.

As I approached Green Mount Road I was prepared to call Margo and let her know I was on my way, until I remembered she had left to visit her son and daughter in Texas two day earlier. Perhaps for the best.

Pulling into the garage I picked up the folder containing the tax returns and went directly to my office. Trying to suppress the events of the day, I delved into the returns that had been filed by both the senior Klienknect and the son. I wasn't an accountant, but I didn't need to be one to see what was revealed in those documents.

Chapter 23

The income that was reported to the IRS was far beyond anything I had ever reported as income, but there appeared to be nothing relevant to my investigation. IRS audits can go back ten years and I personally didn't know anyone that kept those records beyond that time frame. Stacked before me were over forty years of returns, with the exception of 1992, which was not among the files. Most likely not relevant anyway. There was a remote possibility that the mob, and the Senator in particular, had been using the dealerships to launder money. But, that wouldn't be reflected in the Klienknect tax filings. The high-dollar dealership owned by the Senator evidently had huge pass-through assets. Having no access to the Senator's tax filing reports I couldn't be certain that sales and profits from his collection of exotic vehicles was properly reported. If there was a mob connection there, it might not be a good idea to even consider pursuing any investigation into his operations. One run-in with mob connected goons is quite enough.

I wasn't sure what I expected to find in these documents, but maybe I just didn't know where to look. There was another file that reflected huge amounts of money deposited in an off-shore bank account. Whether it was still there or not, I had no idea.

I was about to give up on going any further in examining years of tax forms, when I noticed that Alfred Klienknect repeatedly claimed losses equal to winnings, no doubt related to gambling. Had this been an ongoing addiction of young Al? It could explain the large sums of money that his father had 'loaned' him, which apparently had never been repaid, according to account ledgers compiled by his father, Gerard.

I had the sense that unless you were a tax accountant few things could be more boring than reviewing tax forms. Concentrating on finding any anomalies in the stack of forms before me became even more difficult when my olfactory senses caught the subtle hint of gardenia. Perhaps Mandy had touched these documents and hence transferred some of her cologne. Or was my mind simply playing tricks, harboring a level of guilt related to my actions with Mandy? My thoughts then drifted back to the cabin at Pere Marquette. That moment of indiscretion also brought an 'aha' moment. When questioning the Senator about his absence from the Klienknect residence the night of their deaths, where exactly had he been? Had the Senator been involved in a similar moment of indiscretion, which kept him from staying with the Klienknects on New Year's Eve? At Little Joe's wedding Sammy had somewhat confidentially confided in me that Senator Antonio Giocomelli was rumored to be gay. So what? Sammy had an axe to grind with the Senator and was determined to take him down, any way he could.

Still, perhaps the Senator had made a connection with a friend that night and didn't want to bring a 'friend' with him to the Klienknect home. Researching and discovering a liaison from that many years ago seemed unlikely, if not impossible. I had a lot of questions about the Senator, about the accumulated debts of the son, Alfred, about the possible involvement of the St. Louis mafia during those affluent years during the burgeoning expansion of the automobile dealerships, which was apparently enhanced by the influences of a connected State Senator.

It was now apparent to me that the senior Klienknect did not drive home from the country club on New Year's Eve and leave his car running, with the garage door open into the kitchen. Given the time he would have arrived at home, the Cadillac would have simply run out of gas before the arrival of Senator Giocomelli the next morning. Still, I had no way of knowing if the statement given by the Senator was in fact the truth, that the engine was running when he entered the home around 10:30 in the morning.

Conner, get your head and ass wired together. You've been skipping around all over the place and headed nowhere. Follow a theory to the end and see where it leads. Exhaust that avenue until you reach a dead end, then retrace your steps until you find your way out of this maze. There is an answer. Find it! Go back to the beginning of this incident and discover the cause of death and the events leading up to those fatal hours.

Is my conclusion of homicide by carbon monoxide poisoning correct? Based on my assessment of the consumption of fuel by the Cadillac Brougham, I have to assume my calculations are correct. Someone arrived after the Klienknects were asleep and started the vehicle, leaving the kitchen door open, and intentionally asphyxiating the couple as they lay sleeping in their home. Who would have the opportunity and the motive?

Back to the basics, Conner, or you will never unravel all of this shit. Motive and opportunity.

Given the mafia connections, the Senator may have had the motive, but did he have the opportunity? Considering that the Senator was benefitting financially from his liaison with Gerard, was there a bonafide reason for him to eliminate Gerard? Not too likely at that point in their relationship. The Senator benefitted and presumably, the mafia benefitted.

Mulling over the events of the evening, as best I knew from accounts in the newspaper and the police reports, I found that the Senator's statements were at least consistent. My friend and mentor, First Sergeant Ron Meza, had believed the Senator when he told us that the Kleinknects had left the country club before he did on New Year's Eve, that they had an arrangement to meet the next day at the club for a New Year's Day brunch and that his partner and friend, who was always on time, did not arrive at the appointed hour of 10:00 in the morning. The question in my mind was how late did the Senator stay at the club after the departure of the Klienknects? The Senator was not only vague on that issue, he simply would not provide any additional information along those lines.

I had a plan. Maybe not a good plan, but a plan. I called Twitch Taylor with the FBI. I left a voice mail on his private phone at his downtown office. Forty-five minutes later he returned my call.

"Special Agent Gregory Taylor, thank you for returning my call."

"Conner, I didn't expect to hear from you again so soon. We've been gathering information from this Frank Cusumono fellow that was apprehended, but I can't go into that. It's an ongoing investigation. So, what's this call about?"

"I'm sure you recall that my friend Ron Meza and I met with your undercover guy, Sal Moretti, and had a discussion about the activities of the St. Louis mafia. He shared a lot of history about the various connections between St. Louis, Chicago, Detroit and Kansas City. When we met with him I recognized him from my meeting with Antonio Giocomelli. One of the guys that's on the inside of the Senator's circle. I don't want to compromise his undercover position, but I would like to use his connection to the Senator to get another sit-down with Giocomelli. A confidential, one-on-one sit-down. Maybe he could just tell Giocomelli that he heard word on the street that Pennington would like another meeting. What do you think?"

"It's possible, but not very likely. There can't be any discernable connection between Sal and this office, or with you, for that matter. Moretti has been undercover for over five years now and I don't want to do anything to blow his cover."

"I understand, my friend. I won't be asking the Senator anything that would incriminate him concerning the death of his associate, Gerard Klienknect. I'm not sure how I would get word to him that anything we discuss would be completely confidential. There are just some unexplained issues based on my last conversation with him. I'd like to give him a chance to clear up some of those issues."

"Okay, Conner. I'll talk to Moretti, but I'm leaving it up to him whether he wants to approach the Senator about a meeting with you, or if he may think it's too risky for him to even broach the subject. I don't second guess my people and I trust their judgement. I'll let you know."

Twitch Taylor called at 9:30 the next morning.

"Listen, it's against my better judgement, but I talked to Moretti and he can meet you at 3:15 this afternoon at the same bar where you met him before. I don't know if he will be able to set up a meeting with Giocomelli, but he wants to talk to you first."

"That's great. Let him know I'll be there." End of conversation.

At 3:15 I walked into the bar on Washington Avenue. Same routine, same bartender. He led me back to the same room where Moretti and I had met before. The only difference was that now the tavern was open and there were three or four customers sitting at the bar, nursing suds and watching a big screen TV hanging above the bar. The door to the little meeting room was closed, but when the beefy bartender opened the door, there sat Moretti.

"Have a seat. A beer before we get started?"

"Sure." As test of the bartender's memory I asked for the usual. Years ago, I had breakfast with a group of guys in Jefferson City every Friday morning for forty years. Same place, same waitress. I also ordered the same breakfast every Friday. Two eggs over easy, hash browns, sausage, wheat toast and coffee. It wasn't too long before the waitress simply asked if I wanted 'the usual.' I always did. Fifteen years of this and I left for adventures in San Antonio and was gone for three years. When I came back and had breakfast with the boys,

I asked the same waitress for 'the usual.' She remembered. The bartender here didn't disappoint me. He brought the same beer I had ordered the last time I met with Moretti.

"I did some checking on you," Moretti said. "You were a Marine officer with a top- secret clearance. I hope that means you know how to keep your mouth shut. So long as you understand what is said here today doesn't go beyond this room. I mean to no one. Not even Twitch. Understood?"

I couldn't help it. A smile crossed my face when I replied, "I didn't know Taylor's nickname had followed him here to St. Louis. Anyway, yes I understand the rules."

"Okay. I can set up a meeting with the Senator. I told you when we last met that the Senator is the St. Louis mob capo. That's true to a certain extent. He fills that role and the associated families in Kansas City, Chicago and Detroit accept that. He is actually my CI. My confidential informant. I had some incriminating evidence against him about ten years ago, but not really enough evidence to bring to a grand jury. He didn't know that. He thought he was washed up, so he took my suggestion to be my informer rather than do time and lose everything he had worked for. He keeps me advised about family activities and I pass on to Twitch information, but I have never revealed to him who my informant is. And neither will you. I wanted to make sure you understood the rules before I talked to the Senator. You asked that the meeting be strictly confidential. One-on-one. Giocomelli won't be comfortable with that, but I'll let him know you can be trusted. I presume a meeting at Giovanni's on the Hill will be a satisfactory meeting place."

"If that's a comfortable place for the Senator, then sure, that works for me."

"Give me your phone number and I'll contact you when the meeting is set up."

Moretti wasn't as long winded as he was during our last meeting.

No history this time. Down to business and move on. I liked that. With his last comment, Moretti lifted his beer mug in a sort of salute, indicating the meeting was over.

Hopefully that was a level of progress, depending on the outcome of another sit-down with the Senator. I wasn't going to hold my breath waiting for word from Moretti about a scheduled meeting with Giocomelli. It may not even happen.

Chapter 24

If you can't trust a fellow Marine, who the hell can you trust? Moretti would make good on his promise to contact the Senator for a sit-down.

Patience is a virtue, they say. Waiting, on the other hand, is a bitch. So, when my phone chimed three days after talking to Moretti I had high hopes. I didn't recognize the number on my screen, although it was an area code from St. Louis.

"Hello, this is Conner Pennington."

"Right you are. This is Moretti. The Senator will meet with you. Apparently he has a busy schedule with his auto dealerships, but we'll meet with you on July 18th at 1:30 in the afternoon. Giovanni's, where you met with him the last time. That's the best I can do."

"That works for me, Mr. Moretti. I appreciate your arranging this meeting. What are my parameters for this meeting?"

"He now knows that you know he is my confidential informant, but don't address that issue. He's very sensitive about that and doesn't want any leaks. Don't push him on any mob activities. If he feels comfortable with you, he may bring up some of those things himself. As for your conversation with him, that's up to you as to how far you venture. If he doesn't want to answer your questions, he won't. I would suggest you make this meeting a lunch. The Senator likes Italian food and is more comfortable discussing issues while sharing the table with whomever he is holding a meeting with. That's the way these guys do business."

"Thanks for the advice. Do I pick up the tab for the meal with the Senator?"

"Hell no. I've been with the Senator many times for meals and meetings, and the Senator has never paid for a meal at Giovanni's. Don't even offer to pay for the meal. It would be an insult to the Senator. Have a good day." Typical of Moretti, that ended the call.

Driving in from Fort Worth, Texas, Margo arrived home late Thursday evening. After a 750-mile road trip it's good to take a day off to recuperate. We took that time on Friday. It was good to have my lady back. My inebriated seduction by Mandy weighed on my conscience, but I realized how deeply I loved Margo and knew this was the lady I wanted to spend my life with.

Saturday promised to be a nice day for riding our motorcycles, so we planned a trip up to Alton, Illinois and a visit to the joint where we first met. Fast Eddie's. It's a bar, a restaurant, a dance hall and a biker hangout. Live music and three ATMs scattered throughout the interior of the building. Why? Because Fast Eddie's takes cash only. No credit cards, no coupons. The fare is simple and always the same. Peel and eat shrimp, hamburgers, pitchers of beer and pretty damn good margaritas. One of our favorite places to dance. Fast and slow belly rubbing dances, depending on the band scheduled for that day. Not too much into blues or jazz, but then we preferred the Soulard Blues Band for that type of music, usually at the Boat House in Forest Park. That was an interesting place also, constructed for the 1904 World's Fair in St. Louis, but that's another story.

Following motorcycle protocol, I rode in front on my chopper, taking the left side of the lane, while Margo rode her Harley Fat Boy in the right side of the lane, twenty to thirty feet behind me. The formation keeps errant drivers from horning into our procession. At least that's the goal. We tried to stay off the interstate highways, where tractor trailer operators seemed to have little regard for motorcyclists. We called our bikes the ultimate convertibles. Riding in the wind, surrounded by nature and blue sky. The rumble of a powerful engine between your legs, a twist of the throttle with your right hand and an immediate reaction of rapid acceleration. Living is more fully appreciated when you take a few risks and live a bit on the edge. Perhaps that's why I became a Marine and am now a private investigator. Boring is not among my lexicon of words I care to include in my vocabulary, or in my life.

On the north side of Fast Eddie's is a large parking lot with barriers that narrows the restricted entrance, allowing only motorcycles to park there. Spaces are marked off for the size of a bike and we were lucky enough to find two spaces together. Many bikers in Illinois don't wear helmets. It's not required by law, so when we left our helmets with the bikes we really didn't have any concerns that they would not be there when we returned. Some bikers may beat the crap out of you, but they typically don't steal from another biker. Most are also patriotic and won't mess with a biker, or the rider, wearing Marine emblems on his helmet and bike. It's worked so far. We dismounted and headed for the outdoor bar area where the music was in full swing. Most tables and seats were taken, even though it was only 1:30 in the afternoon. We found a sociable looking couple sitting at a table for four and asked if we could join them. They were probably pretty well into their cups and they graciously invited us sit at their table. We discovered they were there on their first date and we shared with them that our first date had also been right here at Fast Eddie's.

I've always been amazed that on any given dance floor there are more women dancing than there are men. What's that about? I'm not one to sit on the sidelines, regardless of the venue. I'm a participant. Margo was the same and I realized the time was now as she stood and took my hand, indicating she was ready to dance. Before we made our way to the dance floor I took two cards from my wallet that I carry for such occasions. I placed one top of each of our drink glasses and followed my lady to the center of the dance floor. The card simply said, "I've gone pee…don't touch my drink."

It was a slow country song, to which Margo tends to make some pretty seductive moves. What the hell, I go along with her and enjoy the sensations of her curves as they rub against various parts of my body. Almost anything goes at Fast Eddie's. We stayed on the floor for three more songs, then the band took a break, providing an opportunity for me to get in line for some shrimp and sauce. When I returned to the table with the shrimp there was an obviously intoxicated guy hitting on my lady. As I stood behind him I heard Margo tell him she was with her guy and he was returning shortly. He wasn't taking the hint to move on.

"I think I heard the lady tell you she was already with her man." I wasn't ready for an encounter with an inebriated, obnoxious and overbearing country boy, but sometimes it can't be avoided. "I suggest, my friend, that you return to wherever you came from."

Without even turning to face me he replied, "I don't think I was talking to you. I spotted this fine-looking lady sitting by herself and she looked like she needed company, so here I am."

"Well, my friend, she's not by herself anymore. I brought her here and when it's time to leave, she'll be leaving with me. I think perhaps you may have had a few too many drinks that have clouded your judgement. No harm done. Yet."

Finally turning to face me, his next remark put me in a wary situation. "Buddy, I ain't your friend and you don't tell me what to do." I made the observation that he couldn't have been much into maintaining any level of muscle tone, although he did have a good sixty pounds on me.

I used my tried and true comment that has warded off many offensive men crossing my path in the past. Looking him straight in the eye, I simply said, "Mister, you really don't want to fuck with me." That usually worked, and it did this time. It took a moment to register, or maybe he was simply sizing me up. A light finally came on somewhere in his alcohol addled brain. He stepped around me and moved through the crowd to a distant table. What he didn't know, or maybe it finally permeated his clouded brain, is the fact that it would not have been in his best interest or continuing good health to challenge my confrontation. I'm not a muscle-bound weight lifter, but I run daily and continue my regimen of intense workouts, starting with 100 pushups. I haven't actually used any of the hand-to-hand combat skills since I left the Marine Corps, but I'm confident that muscle memory would return when called upon.

Another twenty-one-year-old celebrating his birthday. Way too much alcohol. Just short of unconscious, as two burly companions walked on either side of him, carrying him out of Fast Eddie's. Never short on action, between the bikers and the newly arrived youngsters reaching drinking age. Margo and I had three more dances after consuming the shrimp, skipped any further drinking and returned to our bikes. Another hour on the road without confrontations would be nice. It was.

Our return ride was somewhat uneventful. No wind to blow us around and only one situation of slow traffic. On a four-lane divided highway a tractor/trailer unit was traveling at an unusual speed. Fifteen miles per hour under the speed limit. I was riding in the lead, toward the left of the lane, while Margo followed, taking the right portion of the same lane. Bikers accepted this riding position as being the safest and I kept a watch on Margo in my rearview mirror. Approaching the slow- moving semi, I pumped my left arm in the air, giving her the signal that I was going to give my Honda Fury a twist on the throttle and accelerate around the behemoth in front of us. Ironically, this was the same signal we gave Marines to tell them to double-time...RUN. This model Honda has a big V twin engine, extended forks and a computer package that boosts horse-power. Putting on my left turn signal I twisted the throttle, glanced back to see Margo with her left turn signal also activated and shot into the passing lane.

It seemed a bit longer, but it was only seconds before I had passed the semi and pulled into the driving lane, well ahead of the truck. Margo loves speed, so I was not surprised when I heard her Harley Fat Boy under full throttle as she sped past me and took the lead. Big bikes have a power-to-weight ratio often exceeding that of race cars. A flash of gleaming purple and shiny chrome, with the signature rumble of a Harley, brought back thoughts of an old classic song by the Eagles.

He was a hard-headed man he was brutally handsome
And she was terminally pretty
She held him up and he held her for ransom
In the heart of the cold, cold city
He had a nasty reputation as a cruel dude
They said he was ruthless said he was crude
They had one thing in common: they were good in bed
She'd say, "Faster, faster. The lights are turning red."
Life in the fast lane, surely make you lose your mind
Life in the fast lane.

Exhilarating. Yeah, that's right. Life in the fast lane.

Arriving back at our home, we parked our bikes in the "Toy Box", a motorcycle garage I had specifically constructed to house our machines. Piles of documents and paperwork awaited me in my office, but priorities beckoned. There is just something arousing about riding with Margo that can't be totally explained. Her physical presence reflects an aura of sexuality, permeating my thoughts and desires. Forget the paperwork. Some private time with Margo is in order.

R.N. ECHOLS

Later, back in my office, there was no surprise. Everything was just as I had left it. The Barrows investigation was temporarily on hold until I had my meeting with the Senator. Matt, the attorney I worked for in Belleville, had asked that I investigate a traffic accident on behalf of one of his clients.

While traveling south on a state numbered highway his client was attempting to pass a tractor trailer unit that was hauling a large load of farm equipment, when the driver of the rig decided to make a left turn, pushing Matt's client into a telephone pole, causing serious damage to not only the vehicle, but also the client. I knew that road fairly well, as Margo and I had ridden it on our motorcycles. It was still early afternoon, so I reviewed the pertinent data from the accident report that Matt had given me. The traffic crash had happened a year earlier, almost to the day, with the recorded time of the crash being almost an hour from the current hour.

Examining the scene of a crash one year later has obvious inherent issues, namely the total loss of evidence related to the occurrence. The best I could do would be to examine the site as close to the time of day when the two vehicles collided, taking into consideration the angle of light and perhaps even the flow of traffic. I gathered the necessary investigation tools I used for investigating traffic crashes and placed them in my saddle bags on my motorcycle. A collapsible measuring wheel, some chalk, a camera and a thirty-five-foot measuring tape. A hammer, three or four ten penny spikes, a roll of orange tape and a range finder also went in with my other tools.

Five minutes later I was on my bike again and riding to my destination, only seven miles from home. I rode my motorcycle to do this investigation as I knew there was a very narrow shoulder on this highway and there would be no safe place to park a motor vehicle. I rode about five hundred yards north of the intersection where the collision happened, parked on the west side of the highway and used my range finder to establish the distance to the intersection. I was correct in my estimate of distance, as I only had to walk ten or fifteen feet to a point where my range finder indicated I was five hundred yards from the intersection. I cut a four-inch section of the orange tape, removed the hammer and one nail from my saddlebag, watched for oncoming traffic and when all was clear I moved to the center of the highway, pushed the nail through the plastic construction tape and drove the spike through the asphalt so it was flush with the center line. That would be one of my reference points for the investigation. I then moved back to the narrow shoulder, replaced the hammer and removed my camera. I took a dozen photos at that location, from the shoulder and the center of the road where I had marked the five- hundred-yard point.

I noted that there were no signs on either side of the highway indicating an upcoming intersection. It was a 'T' intersection for a county road leading to the left. The sightline to the right was unobscured. Simply an open farm field, but to the left, where the county road met the highway, a view of that road was obscured by a growth of trees. No yellow line defining a no-passing zone was evident from the five-hundred-yard mark to well past the intersection. Using my tape measure, I found the distance from the center line of the highway to the edge of the asphalt to be twelve feet. Placing my gear back in my saddlebags I rode to the spot of the collision. Parking my bike as far off the road as I could on the narrow shoulder of gravel, I took another dozen photos in all directions. Another nail and strips of orange tape were used to locate the center of the intersection and the reported location of initial contact between the client's vehicle and the tractor trailer unit. There wasn't much else I could do at the scene.

Back in my office I again reviewed the accident report. It was quite thorough, giving the serial number on the combine that was being transported on the flat-bed trailer, the license plate number on the trailer, registration for the tractor unit that pulled the trailer, the driver's name of that unit, as well as his license information. All relevant information pertaining to the client and his vehicle was also contained in the report. Included with the report were photos taken by the investigating state trooper. A series of six black and white photos showed the rear of the trailer, with the combine chained to the bed, a side view of the rig, a front view, and a shot of the client's vehicle. Back, front, and side. All of which were taken to show that the front of the vehicle encircled a telephone pole just to the south east of the intersection.

I researched federal regulations relating to the transportation of oversize loads and found the hauler to be in violation of at least five of those regulations. No flags were mounted on the large piece of equipment, nor were there any flashing lights or a sign indicating an oversize load. Furthermore, even if the driver of the rig had indeed used a turn signal to indicate his intention to turn left it would have been visually blocked by the farm equipment.

Matt was suing the transportation company that was hired to move the combine, seeking real and punitive damages on behalf of his client. To complete my investigation, I used my measurements of the highway and the photos to build a diorama of the actual scene of the accident. I searched a number of hobby stores, toy stores, and model railroad shops to gather the right materials to depict the model of truck, trailer, combine and specific model of vehicle driven by the client. It was built to scale, and I included seven miniature plastic trees to recreate the blocked view of the intersection while driving south. Four days to complete my report and the detailed diorama. Matt was quite impressed.

He asked me to attend a meeting in his conference room when he called in the transportation company attorney to discuss an out of court settlement. Very little argument was presented by the opposing attorney when he was shown my report and the diorama. A settlement was quickly reached. Three days later I was presented with a $3,500 check for my work on this investigation.

Time was now drawing nigh for my meeting with the Senator.

Chapter 25

I had a good idea where I wanted to take the conversation and had a list of questions concerning what I wanted to learn from the Senator. Beyond that, I had no idea how the meeting would progress.

Pretty much the same routine as the last sit-down with the Senator. Drive to Little Italy, a.k.a., the Hill, park close to Giovanni's, get myself escorted to the meeting room where, no doubt, the Senator would be waiting. And so it was.

Regal and confident, the Senator sat on the far side of the round table, smaller than the one that had been in this room when I met with him the last time. A crème colored silk suit, dark silk shirt, open at the color, and impressive diamond rings on damn near every finger. He didn't rise when the waiter ushered me into the room.

"Mr. Pennington, have a seat. I know a little more about you than I did when we first met, and perhaps you know a little more about me. It is understood between both parties that whatever we discuss here will remain here. Capisce?"

"Yes, sir, I understand."

"A formality, Mr. Pennington. You're not wearing a wire, right? Just a brief examination." An associate of the Senator's that I hadn't seen before was standing in the corner of the room. Apparently, the Senator had anticipated a search and had given instructions to his guy that now came forward and performed a thorough search for any recording or transmitting device. Having completed his task, he nodded to the Senator and left the room, closing the door as he departed. The Senator continued, "I've worked with the FBI for years now and I've learned a few things, like being careful. Okay, Mr. Pennington. A glass of wine perhaps? I would suggest the Antinori Marchese Chianti Riserva 2014." I glanced at the wine list provided by our waiter and found the Antinori under the list of red wines from Italy. It was described as: "An intense ruby red in color, the 2014 Marchese Antinori reveals a floral nose with notes of ripe cherries, spices and toasted oak. On the palate, the wine is supple and balanced with red fruit notes that linger on the finish". I'm not sure which wine connoisseur sampled this wine and then wrote such a flowery description, but who was I to negate the suggested preference of a mafia boss?

"Senator Giocomelli, that appears to be a delightful wine. I concur with your selection and would love to try the Antinori."

"Wonderful, Mr. Pennington. Now, before we proceed further, all my friends call me Tony. I have no misconceptions that we will be friends, but for the sake of this meeting and sharing a meal, please call me Tony. In turn I will call you Conner. So, look at the menu, we will order, and we will talk like gentlemen over a delightful meal. Capisce?"

"I understand, Tony. You know I only want to find out what happened to your associate and partner that New Year's Eve. I'm looking for exculpatory evidence, meaning evidence that excludes you from any action in the demise of your partner. I don't think you were involved, but you may know something that leads me in the direction of who may have been involved. I've come to the conclusion that it was not an accidental death."

"Ah, I see, Conner. And what is it you would like to know?"

The waiter returned with our wine, then asked if we would like to order a late lunch.

"Gino, we will start with an appetizer of insalata di polpo." Antonio was quite used to giving orders, it seemed. "Close the door when you leave and please knock before you reenter."

"Yes sir. I will prepare your appetizer."

"Now, Conner, shall we?"

"During our last conversation I asked if you had a key to the front door to the Klienknect home. You replied that you did at one time, but that you had either misplaced it or lost it. Is that correct?"

"Yes, that is correct. I'm not sure of the relevance of that issue."

After a sip of the full-bodied wine, I ventured further. "I've heard a rumor that you are gay. Is that correct?"

"Well now, Mr. Pennington, you do have some balls asking me a question like that. Okay, I know you were a Marine officer, so I shouldn't be surprised that you got a pair." I quickly noticed that he had moved from calling me Conner to a more formal address as Mr. Pennington. Had I pushed the conversation too far, too fast?

"Tony, I make no judgement about that issue. I've been around the block a few times and it makes no difference to me whether you are or not, but it may have some bearing on this investigation."

A long pause and a bit more than a sip from the wine glass before Giocomelli responded. "I like that, Conner. You got some balls. I don't know where you heard that rumor, but yes, it's true. Never been married, no kids. So, where are we headed with this?"

"I have a theory that you didn't go to the Klienknect home on New Year's Eve not simply because you didn't want to disturb them. Perhaps you had someone you wanted to spend some private time with that evening. Is that a correct assumption?"

"I hope you're being paid well to investigate the deaths of the Klienknects. You're persistent as hell and dig into things most people would be very hesitant to even question. But yes, you are correct in that assumption. When I was in Jefferson City I would meet my lover, who was young, immature, and very fickle. I discovered three months before that fateful evening that Josh had been seeing other men, all while he lived in the apartment I provided for him. Oh, I took very good care of Josh. No loyalty from him, though. I cut off his support and told him to move on. I had always paid his bills, but when it became evident he was exploiting my largess and financing his lover on the side that was the end of it. I met another person that was more mature, considerate and not dependent on my support. That was the person I left the club with on New Year's Eve. Steve was just so much more than Josh. Now, I have suspected over the years that Josh took my key to the Klienknect home. He knew I stayed there quite often when I was in town for legislative sessions. He may have discovered that I was with Steve that night and was seeking revenge, perhaps with the thought of getting back at me for leaving him. I've thought about that many times. I believe what you're telling me is that you think someone came into the Klienknect home and started Gerard's vehicle with the intent of killing everyone in the home. Including me. Is that correct?"

"That thought has been part of the basis of my investigation. I have done some research on the vehicle that Gerard had at the time. Had he left the car running in the garage after driving home that night it would have run out of gas before you arrived the next morning. You have been consistent in your statements that the engine was running when you arrived at the Klienknects around 10:30 on New Year's Day. You have also repeatedly stated that the front door was unlocked and the kitchen door to the garage was open. It seems you also know that Gerard was obsessed with locking doors." Before the Senator could respond there was a knock on the door, eliciting a brief order from the Senator. "Enter."

Our waiter opened the door, pushing a cart with our appetizers arranged on top of an ornate carved wood serving tray. He placed the dishes on our table and filled our wine glasses from the bottle next to the serving tray. Preparing to leave, he asked with what seemed a level of reverence, "Will there be anything else, sir?"

"We will order our main meals later, after the panzanella salad, which you can bring in twenty minutes." I wondered at this point if the Senator may also have some level of OCD, or if he was simply following a routine he had developed over the years while dining at Giovanni's.

The appetizer dishes were small, reminding me of the Spanish tapas, or even the Greek mezedes. It appeared to me to be more of a salad than an appetizer, with boiled baby octopus predominate in the dish. Having spent weeks in Greece I remembered that these dishes stemmed from an old tradition there of offering quick bites while imbibing or doing business. To the credit of the Senator I assumed he selected this small dish as a sign of the two of us doing business. A nice gesture.

"Ah, one of my favorites, Conner. You have traveled to the continent, yes?"

"Yes, I have. I must say, you have made an excellent choice. I have had similar appetizers while in Greece and enjoy the dish very much."

Between bites of the savory appetizer I continued the conversation. "You have been very successful in the motor vehicle industry, beginning with your partnership with Gerard. My research reveals that you possibly took advantage of your position as a state senator on the budget committee to direct and control bids for the Highway Patrol to dealerships owned by you and Gerard. Even now you have a very well-placed store for the sale of rare and collectable vehicles."

"You're a thorough investigator man, Conner. I know you have visited my store on Manchester Road. I can assure you, there is nothing illegal with my operation there, nor was there anything illegal about influencing the outcome of state bids when Gerard and I were partners. It was politics then, just as it is now. I also know that you are a car guy. You drive a Maserati and appreciate fine motor cars. You might say that I am also a connoisseur of exotic and beautifully engineered machines. Still, I see no connection or relevance to the issue you are investigating."

"It's a murky cloud that has covered the purportedly accidental deaths of the Klienknects. There are so many avenues to travel. After the deaths of Gerard and his wife what was your relationship with Gerard's son, Alfred?"

"Alfred inherited the majority of his father's dealerships and initially didn't do too well in his operations. As stipulated in Gerard's will, I continued a partnership with his son. Alfred was a troubled young man at the time. He drank a lot and gambled even more. He was deep in debt to the Detroit family. I know that Gerard had loaned Alfred fairly large sums of money to pay off those debts, but it didn't seem to slow down his addictive gambling behavior. I attempted, sometimes successfully, to intervene and sooth some aggressive actions contemplated by the Detroit family. I still had a fairly large stake in those dealerships and had even thought about forcing Alfred to relinquish control and turn over the finances and operations to me. A change in several general managers, forced by me, promoted better overall operational control, especially when I made it clear to Alfred that he would no longer have my influence with the Detroit family if he didn't follow directions from the new general managers. It was more the result of a change in managers that dealerships were expanded. After the deaths of Alfred and his wife in a traffic crash I sold out most of my holdings in those dealerships. His daughter now has control of those operations. I understand she doesn't personally supervise the operations on a regular basis, but does have oversight on hiring, promotions, expansions, and finances.

"Look, Conner, I served for twenty-seven years in the state legislature. Very little opposition when it was election time, mainly because

I looked after the interests of my constituents. Sure, I took political advantage of my position, but again, nothing illegal. Furthermore, I had no reason to facilitate the deaths of the Klienknects. They were friends and it was a mutually beneficial arrangement. In a more direct answer to your question about my relationship with Alfred, I can't say it was anything near the trust Gerard and I shared. He was a negative person with little ambition. Somehow, he was able to succeed in a very competitive business and expand operations, but I never really respected him. Based on my connections at the time to the Detroit family I understood that he not only had sizeable outstanding gambling debts, but he also was into cocaine. To what extent I can't honestly say."

"That's quite enlightening, Tony. Thank you for sharing that information. I have seen some indications while reading through documents left by Gerard and Alfred that there had been some money issues between father and son."

Before I could continue my line of thought there was another knock on the door, with the expected response from the Senator. "Enter." I noticed the timing of our server coincided with the needs of the Senator. Just prior to each entry the Senator moved his hand from the top of the table, reaching underneath for what I presumed to be a call button connected to the kitchen. How clever.

Gino wheeled in the serving cart with our salads. He removed our appetizer plates and placed them on the lower level of the cart, then removed the salad plates and put them before us. The panzanella salad appeared to be a meal in itself. It was a Tuscan salad which included chunks of soaked stale bread, red onions, cucumbers, red pepper, yellow pepper, capers, and mozzarella, seasoned with olive oil and vinegar. Dining with the Senator was a local trip through the culinary delights of old Italy. We had not consumed much of the hearty red wine, but our waiter left the bottle in the center of the table and departed, closing the door after he pushed the serving cart into the hallway. Fortunately, the salad portions were not too oversized.

"A delightful summer salad, Conner. Enjoy."

"I can understand why you would frequent Giovanni's restaurant. Such delicious Italian fare." More sips of wine and we began on our salads. Not wanting to drift too far from our conversation, I interjected, "Taking a trip back in time, do you recall the weather conditions on the morning you went to the Klinknect home?"

"Now that you mention it, yes I do. I haven't thought about that for a long time now, but as I recall, it was quite cold and there was an inch or two of snow on the ground. One of the reasons I remember that now is when I arrived at their home I noticed tire tracks in the driveway and a set of footprints from the driveway to the front door and back to the driveway. I assumed someone had come to visit the Klienknects but found them unavailable. The front porch overhang prevented snow from collecting near the front door, so I couldn't tell if the footprints in the snow actually reached the front door. Your mention of the weather conditions must have prompted a recall of what I saw that morning. I thought nothing of it at the time. And what do you make of that, Conner?"

Between sips of wine and enjoying the Tuscan salad I paused and reflected on the Senator's observations of the cold morning.

"I'm not sure what to make of that, but it is interesting and perhaps quite relevant to what may have happened in those early morning hours. Do you recall when the snow started that evening?"

"No, Conner, I don't. I must admit I had other things on my mind that evening. Snow wasn't one of them."

"I understand. Perhaps I can research the archives of the weather gurus and discover when the snow started accumulating. Maybe. Given the passage of years since that incident there might not even be a record. If there is some indication of a record, it's unlikely it would have been precise in recording when the snowfall began. It's worth a try, though."

"Apparently I don't think along the lines you do, so tell me why it's important for you to know when the snow began accumulating."

"If you observed only one set of tire tracks in the driveway, that would indicate to me that the snow began accumulating sometime after Gerard arrived home and parked his car in the garage. It would be interesting to know, then, when that snowfall began, which would pinpoint a time for the arrival of another vehicle."

"Well, Conner, that was a long time ago. I can't say with any degree of certainty that there was not another set of tire tracks in the driveway. I don't believe there was, but I just don't remember. Maybe I'm not quite as observant as you may have been in that situation."

"Oh, you have been quite helpful. Can I assume your former friend in Jefferson City owned a car?"

"He certainly did. One I bought for him. When we parted ways, I did not request a return of that vehicle. I just wanted to remove myself from that relationship."

"I've been through a couple of divorces, so I know what you mean."

Throughout our conversations we had devoured most of the delicious salad. As if on cue, there was another knock on the door, with the same response from the Senator. "Enter."

I again assumed our waiter had some level of communication with my host. When he entered he asked, "Would the gentlemen wish to order your main course now?" This was questioned as he proficiently removed our salad plates.

The Senator responded first, obviously familiar with the menu. "I'll have the Ossobuco alla Milanese."

Glancing down the menu entrees I found the Senator's selection. It was described as an incredibly tender veal shank that has been cross cut, braised with white wine, vegetables and broth, creating a rich and delicious sauce for the meat. Hell, everything had been delicious so far. "I'll have the ossobuco also." How could I go wrong?

Without recording our orders our waiter simply said, "Very good, gentlemen." Retreating and closing the door as he left we were again alone in our comfortable and very private meeting room.

"What other questions might you have, Conner?"

"I believe you have answered the questions I came here to present. I appreciate your forthright answers and for being candid. I will assure you again that what we have discussed here will remain here. Your responses have given me some things to think about and consider in my overall investigation. I'm sure you know who hired me to find the truth about the deaths of Gerard and his wife?"

"Yes, I do. Be careful there, Conner. My sources of information are fairly extensive. I know you drove one of Mandy's vehicles up the Great River Road. An Aston Martin DB4/GT Zagato, if I'm not mistaken. She's a lovely lady, but also cunning and manipulative. She's used to getting her way."

The wait staff must have known the Senator's preference for food, as it was only a few minutes before there was another knock on the closed door. Again, the requisite, "Enter." Our ossobuco was presented with a flair. Presentation being the operative word. Once the waiter left the room, the Senator continued with his conversation.

"So now, Conner, enjoy a real treat." Raising his glass in a salute, he simply said, "To finding the truth, my new friend. Gerard was a good and a trusted friend of mine. I wish you success in your search for the truth."

"I'll drink to that, Tony." The ossobuco was tender and delicious, as promised, and

the selection of wine paired well with the veal shank. We relaxed and enjoyed an Italian dish, which originated from the central region of Italy, near Milano. Great choice.

"I like your style, Conner. Perhaps you should consider coming to work for me?"

"I am honored that you would ask, but I sorta' like the challenges of what I do, and besides, it amuses me. Risk now and then heightens the experiences of life, don't you think?"

"I do, Conner. I do. If you change your mind, you know where to find me."

No discussion was made about the bill. We concluded our meal, with causal conversation, rose, shook hands and I left the Senator in the Giovanni meeting room.

I didn't know yet what revelations would come from this meeting.

Chapter 26

Three days after my meeting with the Senator I was reviewing the notes I had made after the meeting when my phone rang. I had not talked to Mandy since our drive up the Great River Road, so I was somewhat surprised that her name showed up on my cell screen. What could I do? I took the call.

"Hello, Mandy. How are you?"

"I am doing quite well, thank you. The reason I'm calling is to ask if you have found another investigator to do some checking on my husband. I know you told me you didn't want to do that yourself, maybe a conflict of interest."

"Yes, I found someone to take the case. A friend of mine has been a private investigator at least ten years longer than I have, and he has been on the job for you now for about two weeks. He has indicated he will have a report ready for me next week. When he completes this job, I can mail the report to you."

"And where would you send that report, Conner? Certainly you won't send it to my home address and mail delivery to the estate was stopped years ago. I can perhaps understand your reluctance to meet with me and deliver the report in person. Still, I believe we agreed that Pere Marquette would not be discussed again, and that we would continue as friends. Am I right?"

"Yes, you are correct."

"I'm a bit surprised you didn't tell me that you had someone investigating my husband. Why didn't you?"

"Mostly for psychological reasons, Mandy. I didn't want you to know that an investigation was in progress simply due to the fact that it may reflect in your behavior around Dr. Barrows, giving him a clue that something was different on the home front. You wanted to find the truth about your husband, which is always my goal. It's also been my experience that when a person knows, or suspects, they are being investigated their behavior adjusts accordingly. I wanted Dr. Barrows to continue whatever activities or routines he currently has without a conscious or unconscious level of interference from you. Does that make sense to you?"

"Yes, it does, Conner. And how is your investigation going? Have you made progress concerning the deaths of my grandparents?"

"I believe so, but there are still avenues I need to explore, which will include another interview with you and more searching of records you may have at the estate."

"Please keep me informed, Conner. Let me know when your friend has completed his report on Nathan and we will set up a time to meet at the estate, where you can go over whatever records you think may be relevant to providing you more information."

"We will move forward on this and I'll contact you as soon as I get the report on your husband."

"Thank you, Conner. Have a great day and I'll see you soon. Bye for now." My cell screen went dark, ending the unexpected conversation with Mandy.

A week later my own investigator, David Roberts, called me to let me know he had completed his report on Dr. Nathan Barrows.

"An interesting case, Conner. It was fun." David always had a weird sense of what was fun. I knew he kept poisonous snakes and spiders in glass cases at home and had been bitten once by one of his rattlesnakes. An almost disastrous situation for him. An antidote had to be flown in by a military fighter jet from Atlanta to save his life. Some people really live on the edge and David was one of those, for sure.

"Well, I'm glad you enjoyed this foray into what you really like to do. As I recall, you specialized in these types of cases. So, we can either meet someplace or you can bring the report to me at my home. Also bring me your bill for your time and efforts in this case and I'll write you a check."

"Oh no, Conner. No check on this one. I much prefer cash."

"Okay, my friend. And how much cash would that be?"

"Let's make it an even $4,000. Twenties or fifties would be nice. Nothing smaller and nothing bigger."

"Flying under the radar, are you? No problem. When can I expect you?"

"In about two hours, if you have the cash by then."

"I'll have it. See you soon." I wasn't concerned about the cash outlay. I was sure Mandy could well afford to reimburse me for the investigation. I wasn't sure what the report would reveal, but either way I knew David would provide a very complete packet, most likely with color photos and anything else pertaining to Dr. Barrows. I need to remember to get some sort of receipt for the cash payment when I present my bill to Mandy

I went to my wall safe and removed, in cash, the required fee for Mr. Roberts, most of it in fifty-dollar bills, with the remainder in twenty-dollar denominations. A passing curiosity had me examining some of those bills, simply due to the fact that I knew Margo had taken her two grandsons to the Bureau of Engraving in Fort Worth when she visited them a few weeks ago. No surprise to me, most, if not all of the bills, had been printed in Fort Worth.

Mr. Roberts arrived precisely two hours later, pulling into my driveway in a late model, nondescript Chevy Malibu. My connection with him over the past four years had been by phone only and I noticed he had added a few pounds to his six-foot frame since I last saw him, and he now sported a trimmed beard and gray streaks had appeared in his full head of dark hair. Subtle changes, but I easily recognized him.

"David, I can assume that your thoroughness in this investigation has yielded some interesting information. It's good to see you, my friend."

"As I told you on the phone, it's been fun. Glad to be of service. I have another appointment, so let's exchange packages and I'll be on my way." I knew what he meant. I handed him a bulging envelope containing $4,000 in cash and he handed me an even larger bulging manila envelope containing the investigation packet and a hand-written receipt for the cash. We shook hands and he returned to his ride, not even bothering to count his proceeds. It's nice to be trusted by friends.

I returned to my office and removed the receipt, but nothing else. I would leave that to Mandy. Maybe I just didn't want to know what the contents revealed. I then called Mandy to let her know I had received the final report on Dr. Nathan Barrows. I detected what I thought to be an excited response.

"Thank you, Conner. When can I expect delivery of the report?"

"I can meet you at the estate tomorrow afternoon. Say 1:30?"

"That would be great. I have continued going through paper-work at the estate and I have discovered more information that I think you might find interesting. I'll see you tomorrow. Be careful, Conner." I wasn't sure why she added to last comment. Be careful? About what?

With the exception of the absence of an Aston Martin DB4 sitting in the driveway, the estate looked pretty much the same as it did upon my last arrival here. On time and, as expected, Mandy was standing on the steps. As I drove closer to the front entryway, Mandy descended the steps and I noticed a broad smile on her freshly painted lips. She wore a floor length, sheer summer dress, with colorful embroidered flowers. Painted toe nails were exposed through her leather sandals. A light breeze blew across the vast expanse of the property, seductively pressing the dress against her shapely body. *Conner, you are here on business, and business only. Your indiscretions will haunt you. Don't go there.*

As I closed the door to my car she approached, touching my arm as she closed the distance between us. "Just a friendly hug, Conner. Nothing more." The hug was nice, but the scent of gardenias brought back memories of our time together in the cabin at Pere Marquette. I was aroused by the press of her body against mine and the touch of her lips on my cheek. I broke the embrace before the entanglement progressed into a situation I wasn't sure I could handle.

"I'm glad you're here, Conner. It's always good to see you. I see you have a packet for me. Let's go to the library and I'll show you what I have found." She took my hand and led me up the steps, through the grand entry and down the hall to my dream library. When she seated me in the worn leather chair behind the mahogany desk I handed her the stuffed envelope I had received from David. It was intact, save the extracted receipt. The envelope was laid on the coffee table in front of the overstuffed chair cradling the voluptuous form of my smiling hostess, currently my present employer.

Even though it was a warm day, I had worn a summer sport coat, adequately covering my shoulder holster. I didn't need the Walther to protect myself against Mandy. It was simply a habit. Like my American Express card, I don't leave home without it.

"May I take your jacket? You might be more comfortable, and we could be here for a while." I removed my jacket and handed it to her. "I'm not surprised you are carrying a weapon. Is that to protect me, or to protect yourself from me? I'm just kidding, Conner. I'll behave myself." Crossing her tanned legs at the knee and exposing a length of shapely gams, as I had heard legs referred to in the old days, I wondered just how much she would behave herself.

"It's past noon and you might want to fix yourself a drink. I have some questions that might be stressful for you. If you decide on a drink, I'll have one too…if it's scotch. But only one."

While rising from her chair she said, "I know how you like your drink. One ice cube only, with two shots of scotch. I'll have the same and I'll be right back."

Returning with the drinks in crystal tumblers she placed one in front of me on the leather blotter centered on the vast desk top, then seated herself in the chair facing me.

"So, what might be the difficult questions you want to ask me? It isn't about us, is it?"

"No, it isn't. I would like to know more about your father. I had a meeting with Senator Giacomelli. He informed me that while working with your father after your grandfather died he discovered Alfred was in debt due to gambling. He also had the opinion that your father was using cocaine. All of this was connected to the Detroit mob. Give me a history of what you remember about your father in the early days after the deaths of your grandparents. I want to know your perceptions of the man you think your father was before and after your family moved to St. Louis."

Lifting her glass from the coffee table, Mandy took a long swallow on her drink and with a deep sigh, responded, "It's interesting that you would bring up questions about my father. I found the will that my grandfather had written, but we'll get to that later. It's what I thought you might find interesting. Anyway, addressing your questions, I'll tell you what I remember and what I think I know.

"Going back to the time when I was your ice skating student, my father was gone a lot. He often made to trips to St. Louis to take care of business there, even though there was only one dealership in St. Louis at that time. We lived in Jefferson City until about six or seven months after my grandparents died, then we moved to this home in Creve Coeur. I was overwhelmed with the grandeur of this place, as our home in Jeff City had been so much smaller. My father bought out three other dealerships within six months of moving here. My recollection of those days was that he drank a lot. Perhaps it was more than that, as you suggested. I hadn't been exposed to people that used drugs, but that may have influenced his behavior and the way he treated my mother and myself."

"And how was that, Mandy?"

"It was as though he showed very little interest in my mother, or in anything I might have been involved with. There were a lot of arguments at home. I was usually in my room and didn't hear what the arguments were about, but I could hear their raised voices. My mother was a strong-willed woman. Not someone to be pushed around. I thought for a long time that they would divorce, and in a way, I had secretly wished they would. In my mind, a divorce would end the fighting, but I also understood that our newfound social and financial privileges would most likely come to a screeching halt. Maybe I got that impression from my mother when I asked her about the fighting between her and my father."

Another pause, followed by a gulp of scotch, the tumbler shaking slightly in her hand as she returned it to the table. "I've never said this to anyone before, Conner. I didn't much like my father. When I was competing in figure skating, although not being entirely successful, my father was never there. I was even jealous of other girls when both of their parents were there to support them."

"I'm sorry, Mandy. I never met your father, but I suppose I didn't think too much of it back then."

"I guess everyone has family issues sooner or later. Mine just seemed to be more often than it should have been. I actually began to despise my father. By the time we moved to St. Louis and into this big house, I had begun to accept that my father was not like other fathers. Mother and I were close and mostly distanced ourselves from Alfred. Now that's funny that I would refer to him by his first name after all these years, but somehow it seems appropriate. He just seemed to be a distant entity from the little family that consisted of my mother and me. This estate already had the ten-car garage, or stables, when we moved here. I'm not sure if my father selected this place because of that, but it seemed that every three or four weeks he would purchase cars in an effort to fill the entire garage. I don't know what negotiations he went through to purchase some of those cars. I wasn't privy to that, but I did notice that his collection changed over the years. New cars were added, and others went away. I found a document on the purchase of the Aston Martin." A throaty chuckle, then she added. "Either he had some connections somewhere, or he was very astute in his purchase of collectible cars. He paid $725,000 for the Aston Martin in 1987. A very rare find, especially in a left-hand drive model. At the time I knew nothing about the value of the cars he collected, so I never questioned how the hell he was able to purchase them. Being around cars all of my life, I took an interest in the engineering and design of what I thought to be a fascinating history in the love affair people had with motorized transportation. It was fascinating to think about. The evolution of engines, suspensions, aerodynamic designs, the hunger car companies had for faster and faster cars and the advancing technology. I spent a lot of time in my father's garage. Thinking back on those days, it may have been a subconscious need or desire to connect with my father. A girl needs her father, you know?"

"I understand, Mandy. What else would you like to share with me about those days?" I almost felt like I should have a note pad and Mandy should be lying on my couch in a psychologist office.

"When my parents died in that traffic crash I was devastated. I was close to my mother and I had never connected with my father. It was such a loss. I was in counselling for two years. I was married by then and maybe my psychological state had some impact on my marriage to Nathan. He became more distant and less attentive. Anyway, I'd like to know now what your investigator has documented in his report of Nathan's activities. May I open the mystery envelope now?"

"Of course, Mandy. As you can see, I have not examined the contents, and I wasn't sure you wanted me to know what was in the report."

"Conner, I trust you explicitly. I have already shared with you more than I have anyone else. This is the next step." Another sip from her tumbler of scotch, she picked up the envelope and removed the contents. Pulling color photos and printed documents from the envelope she exhibited no immediate response.

"Just as I suspected, but I didn't know who she was. I've actually met this woman at events hosted by the Hospital Association. Isn't that ironic? I think my decision was made even before I asked you to investigate Dr. Barrows. There will be a divorce in the future. If he thinks he will be grabbing assets from this estate, he is sorely mistaken. I'll be talking to my attorney and will preserve what is mine." I thought then of the warning from the Senator. "Careful Conner, Mandy is a cunning and manipulative woman."

"I hope that decision has in no way been influenced by our trip up the Great River Road. I think a lot of you Mandy, but I don't want you to make a rash decision that will potentially have a negative effect on the rest of your life."

"Oh no, Conner. I have thought about this for some time. I'll be quite alright. While we are on the subject, though, there is a bit of other news, before you depart with the newly found documents."

Chapter 27

Taking another sip of her scotch, Mandy leaned forward in her chair and with a conspiratorial, satisfied smile gave me her news. "I'm pregnant."

Not quite sure of my resistance to the many charms of Mandy, I had not consumed much of my scotch. Now I did. I know the stunned look on my face spoke volumes.

Noting my shocked expression, Mandy responded, "Conner, I'm not holding you to anything. I have wanted a child for a very long time and I have been going to a fertility clinic for two years. The doctors have indicated that I am fertile, but apparently Nathan is sterile. I didn't want to go the way of impregnation through a sperm bank, where I wouldn't know the donor. I admitted to you that I had intentionally seduced you when we went to Pere Marquette. I don't apologize for that. I want a child that is a product of a man I know, respect, who is intelligent, has character, is athletic and has blue eyes. So, I decided I wanted you to be the father of my child. The specific date of our trip was based on my biological rhythms as defined by my doctor. Body temperature, ovulation period and everything that could be medically calculated. I'm hoping it will be a boy, but I don't know yet."

"Oh, Mandy, what can I say?"

"You don't have to say anything. My son, if it is a son, will never know. My child will carry the name of Barrows and my divorce from Nathan will happen after the birth of my child. I haven't decided yet, but I may keep this estate and raise my child here. I have no regrets about seducing you and I am grateful to you for being a passionate lover, even though it will never happen again, and our liaison was so brief. Thank you, Conner."

I was somewhat overwhelmed by the enormity of the situation. Another gulp of my scotch didn't seem to help me absorb this unexpected news. Hell, I was already a grandfather and certainly hadn't anticipated being a father again.

"Conner, I understand your concern about my pregnancy, but you need not be. It was what I wanted, and you have just inadvertently become my sperm donor, in a very delightful way. You're only human and I respect you in many ways. Please have no regrets. You have done me a great favor and I will forever be indebted to you. More than that, Conner, I will always love you in a very special way. When I look into the eyes of my child I will see you. You have been a strength in my life for many years and I will always cherish that feeling. Again, don't beat yourself up over something that was of my doing. Call it serendipity, karma, or whatever you want, but I am happy again after many years of unhappiness. Would you deny me the pleasure of knowing that my child is the result of a moment of passion between the two of us?"

"No, Mandy. I can't deny that our lovemaking in the cabin at Pere Marquette was more than a casual moment of lust. You are a very beautiful woman, and very desirable. My one regret is that I succumbed to my desires to make love to you when I am already committed to another woman. For that I can't really forgive myself. Hell, I can't even put the blame on your elegant seduction techniques. When you hugged me upon my arrival today I will admit that the feel of your body against mine aroused me and reminded me of the warm, smooth flesh against mine when we held each other and made love on a day I will never forget. In a way, I am honored that you chose me to be the father of your child. There is no doubt that such a lovely lady could have had her choice of any number of sperm donors. I suppose I shouldn't put it that way. Given what you have told me, I wasn't just a sperm donor. Your mere presence still elevates my hunger for you, but we need to both understand that it won't reach that level again. I'm not sure it's possible to love two women at the same time, or at least with the same intensity. I do love Margo and I never want anything to interfere with that."

"I respect that, Conner. Between my pre-law classes in undergraduate school I took a number of courses in psychology, perhaps in an effort to better understand myself, and my father. It really didn't help in understanding my father, but I did gain a better understanding of myself. I learned that many young girls adored their fathers and even set them up as a measurement for future relationships with men, including a husband. Divorces often resulted when a husband didn't measure up to the standards that the girls perceived about their fathers. I didn't have that problem. I didn't adore my father. Looking back, though, I did understand that there was a substitute for the role model my father didn't fulfill. Although not old enough to be my father, that person was you. You were attentive, understanding, and you were there in my life. I hope that gives you more of an understanding why I wanted you to be the father of my child."

Choosing my words carefully, I replied, "Am I to believe, then, that you simply hired me not so much to investigate the deaths of your grandparents as it was to reconnect and create a situation that would lead to conceiving a child that you had wanted for some time?"

"No, Conner. I am not that conniving. Well, not entirely. I do want to know the truth about my grandparents, so when I saw your name in the paper about your having solved another cold case I felt that you would be the ideal candidate for investigating this case. I was confident that your investigative skills would lead to the truth, but I didn't know in the beginning if you had changed from the person I knew as my skating instructor and my surrogate father. When I first met you at the estate, after all those years, I noticed something different. There was a hardness in your eyes that had not been there before, but I discovered that you were still the man I knew as being understanding and compassionate. The hardness perhaps comes from your time in the Marine Corps and your experiences in combat. Of course, you're older than when you taught ice skating, but then I am too. You're still a very handsome man and have all the attributes I want to see in my child."

"So, your recent impressions of me led you to conclude that I should become your sperm donor?"

"I wish you wouldn't put it that way, Conner. You are more than a sperm donor. How can I explain more than I have that my feelings for you are more than a one-time romp in bed? I know you have a lady in your life that you dearly love, and I won't attempt to interfere in that relationship. Would I want you in my life if you weren't involved? Yes, I would. I know that won't happen, but I am grateful to you that you are the father of my child. I hope you understand what this means to me and that there will always be a part of me that loves you."

"I accept that Mandy, and you need to know that there is a part of me that will always cherish memories of you. Having another child is, of course, a bit of a shock to me at my age. Your explanations help me to understand your motivation and I know you will be a wonderful mother.

"Perhaps it's time to move onto the subject of your grandfather's will. I assume you have read the will and understand the contents, having a jurisprudence degree. If you would, give me your take on what in the will is relevant to this case."

"One of the more interesting parts is that my grandfather bequeathed to my father an off-shore bank account. Actually, although it was called an offshore account, it was a numbered Swiss account. It seems the original amount in that account was close to ten million dollars, but by the time my father collected and closed the account, it amounted to slightly more than twelve million. Based on the timing and the amount, that explains a lot about the move to Creve Coeur, the purchase of this home, the expansion of dealerships, the purchase of expensive vehicles, and a lot more. What isn't explained is how and why my grandfather set up that account. Where in hell did he get that amount of money? Off-shore accounts during that time would have been very unusual, but I understand the reasons for doing that. In obtaining my law degree we touched on money laundering and avoiding taxes through the transfer of funds to those types of secret accounts in the Cayman Islands and other locations. I'm not even sure those offshore accounts were available, so most transfers of money in the 60's and 70's were to secret numbered Swiss accounts. Even the Nazis took advantage of that before and during World War II. So, was my grandfather involved in illegal activities? I don't know. If he was, did that lead to the deaths of he and my grandmother? It's all very complicated and that's why I need you. So, you see, it wasn't all just so you would be my sperm donor, as you call it."

"I'm sorry, Mandy. I won't call myself a sperm donor again. I realize now that it was much more than that. I am flattered that you selected me to be the father of your child. Let's move back to the investigation."

Draining the last of the liquid in her tumbler, which was by now half water from the melted ice, and half Johnny Walker, she continued, but not in the vein I would have thought. "I'm ready for a refill. How about you, Conner?"

"One more round, but only one shot this time, no ice. It isn't that I don't trust you. I'm just not sure I trust myself."

"You can trust me, my dear Conner," she said with a smile.

Uncrossing her tanned, shapely legs, she rose, gathered my tumbler, then picked up her empty glass and moved seductively to the bar just off the kitchen. I sat in the comfortable worn leather chair, contemplating my wisdom in even considering another libation in the presence of this woman that had intentionally seduced me only a month earlier. Trust me, she said.

Returning with the drinks, she set them down and continued the conversation. "I know you aren't my financial advisor, that's not why I hired you, but you're a car guy and I would like your advice on some issues I need to consider. Before I file for divorce I would like to shorten my list of assets. If I don't, Dr. Barrow will clean me out in a divorce settlement. My father's collection of cars is quite valuable, and I don't want that son of a bitch to get any of those cars. He only cares about the value, not the actual vehicles. I would like to keep some of that collection, as I plan to stay here in this home when it's all over, but probably shelter some of the more expensive cars so I won't have to claim them as assets and he won't get his grubby hands on them. I don't need an answer right now, but please think about it."

"I will think about it. My immediate thought is to place them in the facility that is owned by the Senator. He can probably figure out a way to house your vehicles and not have them on his inventory. Most of his operation includes vehicles that are on consignment. I don't want to get involved in anything that is illegal and Dr. Barrows may even hire an investigator to chase down what he may perceive to be hidden assets. My interest in your future welfare and finances now reaches beyond simply ensuring a comfortable level of living for you because I am influenced in those decisions by the fact that I wish for our child a comfortable future."

"That's very considerate of you, Conner. I knew I had made the right decision to bring you back into my life. An unexpected turn of events for you, but I'm happy with the results."

"Give me some time to think about all of this. Now, I assume the will you have shown me is a copy that I can take with me."

"Yes, it is. If there is anything else you might need, it is probably right here in one of these boxes. From the tone of your conversation it feels as though you are preparing to leave for today."

"You're right. I think I should also pass on the drink you brought for me. One double scotch is quite enough. I don't want to have any level of impairment when I drive back through the St. Louis traffic. I have a lot to think about, but I will be in contact with you. In the meantime, if you find anything that would contribute to finding the truth about your grandparents, please call me."

"I will, Conner. Thank you for your understanding, and for forgiving me for my actions at Pere Marquette."

Walking me to my car, she hugged me again and returned to the front steps of the estate. As I drove away and glanced in my rearview mirror I saw Mandy standing to the side of the Neptune fountain, and I was positive this time that she had thrown an air kiss and a wave.

Chapter 28

The drive down the winding cracked driveway seemed to be a greater distance than when I had arrived. It also seemed ages ago that I had driven this route earlier today, when in reality it was just hours earlier. So much more to think about.

As I passed between the two lions at the entrance to the Barrows estate and drove east on Ladue toward Lindbergh Boulevard one word came to mind. Lamentations. A book in the Old Testament of the Bible describes the desolation of Judah after the fall of Jerusalem in 586 BC. It was also a word used in old English that defined a sense of regret or sorrow, often as a passionate expression of grief. Was I now experiencing a feeling of regret about having made love to Mandy and not wearing protection and as a result, becoming the father of a child that I would most likely never know? I couldn't change the outcome, and Mandy had made the argument that our liaison had made her fulfilled and happy. If in your lifetime you make a person happy, how can that be so wrong? A twist of fate, for sure.

When I arrived home, I found a note from Margo telling me she was going shopping. It was now 2:30 in the afternoon and Margo had indicated she left at 2:00. I knew from past experience she would be away for another two or three hours.

My thoughts were all over the place and I couldn't even recall how I had arrived at home and now sat in my office examining the will that Mandy had given me.

A codicil had been added to the first writing of the will. Contained within that codicil was the legal term of *Fideism commissar,* assigning all assets not previously awarded to Anthony Giocomelli to be immediately provided to Alfred Klienknect. It was specified that the offshore account in Switzerland would be the sole property of Alfred. The number for the account was provided in the codicil. My immediate thought was, when did Alfred know about this account, if he knew at all?

Researching the current Swiss and offshore regulations pertaining to depositing assets in a foreign country, I found that a law enacted on March 18, 2010 had an impact on reporting assets to the taxing entity of your home country. The Foreign Account Tax Compliance Act (FATCA) was not in effect when Gerard Klienknect deposited his liquid assets in Switzerland. I also noted in my research that such accounts were often opened as a protection from a litigious former spouse. That prompted another thought. Perhaps it would be advantageous for Mandy to dissolve some of her material assets and place them in a numbered account in a Swiss bank. My ex was from Switzerland and I knew the supreme trust the Swiss citizens placed in their banks. Confidentiality and secrecy was top priority on which the Swiss banks built their exceptional reputation.

I then thought back to the information the Senator had provided during our last sit-down. Something he had said kept nagging my subconscious. Than it came to me. The weather on that fateful night. I began a search of records kept at the weather station near Columbia, Missouri. Those records, although not as definitive as I would have liked, indicated that on that New Year's Eve, December 1957, the temperature had been 28 degrees fahrenheit. There had also been a prediction of snow, with measurable accumulation. There was no indication from those records when the snow was expected to begin. Who the hell would even remember that?

The Senator had recalled in our conversation that when he arrived on New Year's Day to check on the Klienknects he noticed tire tracks in the snow on their driveway. Unfortunately, he did not recall if those tracks led into the garage, or if there were more than one set of tracks. Of some significance, perhaps, was the fact that he had seen footprints in the snow that led to the front door, then the same prints leading back to the driveway. It was still of importance to me in my investigation to ascertain when the snow began accumulating that evening. My guess was that I would never know.

Back to the will, the ledgers, the photo album and other documents kept for decades. It seemed to me that Alfred may have either inherited the genes for OCD from his father. On the other hand, if it's not an inherited gene, he may have picked up some of his father's habits. Alfred's compulsive gambling, a possible addiction to cocaine, and his continued recording of minute expenses all indicted some level of OCD.

I also understood from my conversation with the Senator that Alfred was not a good manager of his expanded holdings in dealerships until he was forced by the Senator to hire general managers, probably vetted and selected by the Senator, to take over operations. An influx of over twelve million dollars would certainly go a long way in influencing the success of properly managed dealerships. I wondered if Alfred also used some of that money to pay off his gambling debts that were allegedly owed to the Detroit family.

I was searching for answers that weren't easily answered, especially since it had been so many years since the deaths of the elder Klienknects. Tragically, the reported accidental deaths of the next generation, Alfred and his wife, had an impact on the Klienknect motor dynasty. Creating a planned traffic crash would be almost unimaginable. Was it even a remote possibility? I knew little about that crash. According to Mandy, it had occurred on Lindbergh Boulevard when a vehicle being pursued by the St. Louis County Police passed through a turn-around opening in the center barrier and crashed head-on into the Klienknect vehicle. That would be very difficult to plan, wouldn't it? My next thought was, would the St. Louis County Police Department even have a record of the investigation after all these years. Even if they did, would I be able to obtain a copy of that investigation? What the hell would that report tell my, anyway?

As I sat pondering all the possibilities my mind drifted. Old songs, old memories. This one going far back in years to Barry Manilow.

I remember all my life
Raining down as cold as ice
Shadows of a man
A face through a window cryin' in the night
The night goes into
Morning just another day
Happy people pass my way
Looking in their eyes
I see a memory
I never realized
How happy you made me
Oh Mandy well
You came and you gave without taking
But I sent you away
Oh, Mandy
Well, you kissed me and stopped me from shaking
And I need you today
Oh, Mandy

Out of the blue. Sure, I remembered the song and the name Mandy was floating through my head. Considering the revelations of today, I shouldn't be surprised.

Stress and frustration can be a distraction. I moved from behind my desk, dropped to the floor and pumped out 100 pushups. I wasn't breathing hard, but the expended energy helped me refocus.

Reviewing in my mind the comments the Senator had made when I asked him if he was gay, and the explanations about his partner, I wondered if the person I saw with him in the photo album was the lover he had broken up with, or if that was his lover that he had spent the night with on New Year's Eve. What were their names again? I had made notes after the fact but had not bothered to remember their names. The one I would be interested in was the lover that had been shunned. The most recent lover of Giocomelli had an alibi for that night, if what the Senator told me was true. He was with the Senator New Year's Eve. The missing key, the tire tracks in the driveway and the footprints in the snow leading to the front door gave me pause. It was evident, based on the Senator's recollections, that someone had been at the Klienknects before the Senator arrived on New Year's Day. Could this have been the person that arrived after the Klienknects were asleep, opened the front door, started Gerard's car, leaving the kitchen door open, then leaving without locking the front door? According to the police report there was no forced entry to the home. The conclusion would be that entry was made by someone with a key, unless the front door had been left unlocked by Gerard. But, Gerard's condition of OCD made it unlikely that the front door had been left unlocked. Arriving through the garage after driving home from the country club, Gerard would not even have used the front door, which most certainly would have been locked before he and his wife left for the club for an evening of celebration. Locked doors were an obsessive compulsion with Gerard, as confirmed by Mandy and the Senator.

My concern at the moment was not who inherited what, or how much from Gerard, but who had a motive to eliminate the couple, and who may have had the opportunity? On the other hand, money and greed can be a great motivator. It was evident that the Senator would benefit to a certain extent, but their partnership may have been more financially rewarding than the few dealerships he assumed ownership of when Gerard died. Mandy could have reaped some benefits, still unknown to me, but she was too young to be a viable suspect. Certainly Alfred Klienknect benefitted financially. In fact, the influx of more than 12 million dollars seemed to have solved a number of his problems. A case of patricide? Surely not. Gerards accounting ledgers indicated he had taken care of Alfred's financial problems on a regular basis, but the Senator indicated he had stepped into a deal with the Detroit family when Alfred was knee deep in the swamp and up to his ass in alligators. That brought up another thought from the past, one of the sayings passed on to me by an old friend, a judge from southeast Missouri. He told me it was difficult to remember your original mission was to drain the swamp when you're up to your ass in alligators. Was that my current status? Say it ain't so!

Contacting the capo of the Detroit family to perhaps discover how much was owed in gambling debts by Alfred Klienknect was not an option I wanted to pursue. Thirteen months in Vietnam, where the Viet Cong were desperately trying to remove me, and not even a hint of a purple heart. Well, maybe a hint. Then in a parking lot at Union Station in downtown St. Louis I not only get shot, but I also get no medal for my almost fatal wound. Learning from "Moe and Larry" that the hit order had come from the Detroit capo didn't endear me to seeking a sit-down with the high-mahoof of Motor City.

Sorting through all the possibilities of who was responsible for the demise of the Klienknects that early morning years ago was frustrating. I'm still missing some clues. At times like this I take a drive in my Maserati, while listening to a CD and letting my mind randomly search through the tabs I have left open. Maybe too many tabs.

Some back roads, curves, and some straight sections of road where no local police or sheriff's deputies patrol. I put in one of my favorite CDs by Joe Walsh. "Life's Been Good."

> *I have a mansion, forget the price*
> *Ain't never been there, they tell me it's nice*
> *I live in hotels, tear out the walls*
> *I have accountants pay for it all*
> *They say I'm crazy but I have a good time*
> *I'm just looking for clues at the scene of the crime*
> *Life's been good to me so far*
> *My Maserati does one-eighty-five*
> *I lost my license, now I don't drive*
> *I have a limo, ride in the back*
> *I lock the doors in case I'm attacked*
> *Lucky I'm sane after all I been through*
> *I can't complain but sometimes I still do*
> *Life's been good to me so far.*

Some of those words are starting to sink in. Yeah, my Maserati does one-eighty-five, but I'm not close to that. One-sixty-five, then I back off. Other words in the song resonate in my head, "I'm just looking for clues at the scene of the crime." That's one thing I haven't done yet but should. Canvass the residential area where the crime was originally committed in the hopes that a neighbor that lived there at the time still lives there and remembers the incident. Small chance, but what options do I have? I had to chuckle at another line in the song. "I have a limo, ride in the back, I lock the doors in case I'm attacked." Well now, I can relate to the part about being attacked. Already been there. Okay, life's been good to me so far.

The Maserati sky hook suspension makes the computerized adjustments as I negotiate the upcoming curves. Corners like a scared cat and holds the road with very fat low-profile tires. Now I'm concentrating on my trajectory and staying on the road, taking multiple curves at least twenty-five miles per hour above the posted recommended speed. Using the paddle shifter, I downshift going into the sharp curves, using the engine for braking, then power through and out of the curve. I feel that I am in control of my machine and have a sense that I am getting control of the investigation. Life's been good to me so far.

Chapter 29

Another trip to Jefferson City. When it's all said and done the bill goes to Mandy. I don't think she'll have to sell the Aston Martin to pay my fee and accumulated expenses, but it's starting to add up.

I have driven from St. Louis to Jefferson City so many times over the years that I could have put my vehicle on automatic pilot, if it had one. When I worked for Public Safety I covered the entire state and often traveled to St. Louis for events and state business. Two and a half hours later I arrived in Jefferson City and I checked into the Hampton Inn, which was about one and a half miles from the scene of the crime. It was still early afternoon, so I drove to Hobbs Lane, where the Klienknects had lived. I'm looking for someone of retirement age who lived there on that fateful evening and still does.

The home just south of the residence of Gerard and his wife was well maintained. No vehicles were evident at the residence. It was a two-story brick home and with the growth of trees didn't really have a view of the Klienknect home. Almost fifty years ago these trees would have been much shorter, and the view would not have been as obstructed as it was now. I rang the door and got no response. I waited a few minutes and rang again. Still no response. The next house to the south yielded the same results.

Moving to the north side, I rang the doorbell and still had no response. There was a car in the driveway, so I made the assumption that there may be someone at home. I heard what I thought was a ballgame on the radio coming from the back of the home. Stepping stones led to the backyard and a wooden gate was set into a fence that was close to need of replacement.

"Hello, anyone home?" Yelling from the diaphragm, as I had been taught in the Marines, I hoped I had sounded off above the noise of the radio. They always told us, sound off like you've got a pair. After a couple of attempts I did get an answer.

"Yeah, who the hell's there?" The voice was gravely and punctuated with a lingering cough.

"Sir, I'm investigating an incident that happened next door to you many years ago and I'm trying to find a neighbor that may have lived here at that time. If you've got some time I would like to talk to you." After a few minutes an older fellow appeared at the gate, opened it slowly, and presented himself.

"I'm Jack McKenna and I've been here a long time. Now, what is it you want?"

Jack was straight backed, used a cane, wore a light cardigan sweater, although it was reasonably warm, and had a beer in his hand. I guessed his age at close to ninety. He had penetrating blue eyes that were only lightly starting to cloud over with possible cataracts. At close to six three and slender, he had no evidence of a beer gut or major infirmities. Just the cane, which didn't appear that he really needed all that much. Maybe it was for self-defense.

"Sir, my name is Conner Pennington. I'm a private investigator."

"Really? A bit like Tom Selleck in Magnum, P.I.?" Here we go again. I've heard that too many times now, as well as the Colombo comparison.

"Well, sir, I'm looking for someone that lived in this neighborhood in 1957 and 1958. Sometime during that era. Is it possible you lived here then?"

"Son, I don't get many visitors these days. Betty, my wife, died five years ago, my kids and grandkids have all moved away and they just can't seem to find the time to visit. Come on back here. I'll tell you what, son, I lived in this very house during those years. Let me turn the radio off and get you a beer. I wouldn't normally do that, but I saw a Marine Corps pin on your lapel. Sit your ass down, young fella'."

"Sir, did you know the Klienkects when they lived here?"

"Before we get into any of that, tell me about yourself. So, young fella', were you a combat Marine?"

"Yes, sir, I was. I was the commanding officer of a tank company in Vietnam."

"Conner, wasn't it? Conner, you can drop the sir. We were both officers. I was a Marine pilot in the big one, World War II and also flew in the Korean War. You're probably old enough to remember a TV show in the 70's about a Marine fighter squadron, VMF-214, known as the Black Sheep Squadron. The show was called Baa Baa Black Sheep."

"Sure, I remember that show. It was one of my favorites. I believe it starred Robert Conrad playing Major Greg "Pappy" Boyington."

"That's right. I watched it some, but the show wasn't close to anything resembling reality. I flew an F4U-1 Corsair in the Black Sheep Squadron, with Pappy Boyington. He was an unconventional officer and never got along with the higher ups. Hell, I was young and invincible back then. We flew off the island of Vella Lavella, attacking the Japanese every chance we got. Pappy shot down 26 Japanese planes and I shot down 13 myself. He got himself a Medal of Honor, but only received it after he was released from a prison camp near Tokyo. He was awarded the medal while in a prison camp, but they held it for him until he got home. He was also awarded the Navy Cross, as were six others of us in VMF-214. Boyington was a heavy drinker and a womanizer. I understand he died in 1988 in

Fresno, California, where he lived with his fourth wife. He's buried at the Arlington National Cemetery. There were nine pilots from the squadron that flew up there for his burial ceremony. Sorry, I don't often get a chance to talk about those days, but sharing those times with another Marine means a lot. Fellow Marines understand.

"Anyway, I retired as a colonel in late 1956. I moved here after I retired from the Corps and have been here ever since. Shortly after arriving here I went to work for the Central Bank and Trust Company. Now it's just called Central Bank. I know I'm bouncing all over the place. I tend to just spit it out when a memory or thought enters my head. Conner, my friends call me Jack. Another old Marine friend told me years ago that when they put me in my coffin they're just going to refer to me as "Jack in the Box." I didn't think it was too funny at the time, but it has a sort of a ring to it. Now what are you investigating that has any relevance to me?"

"First of all, I enjoy hearing about your time in the Corps. That's a big part of what the Corps is all about...the legacy. To answer your question, this is probably a very long shot, Colonel, but I'm investigating the accidental deaths of the Klinknects that happened sometime after midnight on New Year's Eve. The date was January 1, 1958. I'm really reaching here, but do you recall that date, or anything about the deaths of the Klienknects?"

"I knew the Klienknects, but not all that well. I think his name was Gerard, and I don't remember his wife's name. Anyway, I do remember some of the events about the deaths. I remember the police being there, as well as an ambulance and a bunch of other cars. I didn't find out until later that they had been poisoned by fumes from a car that was left running in the garage. Gerard must have been out celebrating too much that evening and just didn't turn off his car when he got home. Damn shame."

"That was the conclusion of the police investigation. They didn't think it was a suicide. Just tragic accidental deaths. I have been hired by the granddaughter of Gerard to investigate the circumstances of her grandparent's deaths. Documents kept by Gerard and research I have conducted has led me to the conclusion that the deaths of Gerard and his wife were not accidental."

"Really? And what led you to that conclusion, my young friend?"

"One of the first things that popped up was that Gerard had a compulsive habit of filling up his Cadillac's gas tank every Thursday. Only on Thursdays, unless he was traveling. He kept minute and accurate records of every dime he spent. Considering the vehicle he had at the time, if he had left the country club around 12:30 to 12:45, after celebrating New Year's Eve, and parked his car in the garage after arriving home, his car would have run out of gas before he was discovered the next morning. The car was found still running the next day. So, my initial thought was that he was not the person who left the car running."

"Interesting. So, what is your conclusion about all of that?"

"I know you told me to call you Jack. I left the Marine Corps on an early out and had just picked up the rank of captain, so you'll have to excuse me for continuing to call you sir or Colonel. It's a long story and I don't want to bore you with all the details of what I have found, but I believe someone came to the home and started the car after the Klienknects were asleep, with the intent of poisoning them. Premeditated murder."

"Conner, I'm an old man now and I have nothing to do and all day to do it. Bore me. I'm in for a dollar. It sounds like you have a difficult problem to solve, especially since it happened so many years ago. How can I help you?"

"You indicated you remembered that night, or at least the next morning when the police and ambulance were next door. What can you tell me about your recollection of anything out of the ordinary that went on New Year's Eve, or the next morning."

"The first thing that was unusual about that New Year's Eve

was that Betty and I hosted a celebration party. We hadn't done that since we left the Corps. You know how that goes. When your commanding officer announces he's having a party and that you will attend, you will have a good time. You go. Well, we had that kind of party, even though some of the bank officials came just to keep an eye on me, I think. Hell, old man Cook was there, as was his young son Sam. Sam only lived about a half a mile from our home, so I doubt that he was overly concerned about driving home after a lot of celebrating, even though I don't think he was much of a drinker. I know, I'm getting off track again. I tend to ramble on sometimes, but it's good to have a younger Marine sit here and listen to my ramblings."

"I'm in no hurry, Jack. Before we go too much further, though, I'll have another beer, if you don't mind."

"Hell, no, I don't mind. Keep your seat, I'll be right back." The Colonel ambled into what I presumed was his kitchen and returned shortly with two cold beers.

"You probably know this, Conner, but banks are notoriously stingy. They don't pay a big salary, except for the very top guys, so they give you an impressive title instead. Within a short time, I was the assistant to the vice president of the loan department. The bank used photos of me standing by a Corsair, and touted me as a war hero in their promotional material. Maybe it helped their business, I don't know, but quite often customers would come into the bank and ask specifically for me, by name. I retired as one of their vice presidents in 1987. I did some consulting work for them on the side, until Betty passed away. I just couldn't find the energy or drive to continue on after that. I miss her terribly. She was the only woman I ever loved, and we had a great life together." Jack's head dropped a little and I thought I saw tears forming in his eyes. He was silent for a moment, then continued speaking.

"I'm getting off the subject again."

"I understand, Colonel. As I said, I'm in no hurry." The afternoon sun was dropping into the tree line, just west of Jack's home. I glanced in that direction and could see the garage doors to the home where the Klienknects had lived, and died, on that early morning of January 1, 1958. Giving Jack a moment to recover, I said, "Tell me about your party that evening."

With a slight smile he replied, "It was a damn good party, if I say so myself. We had around thirty people here, drinking my champagne and a bucket load of h' ordeuvres and appetizers Betty had prepared. She was a wonderful cook and hostess. Anyway, the party went on until 2:30 or 3:00. Of course, half of the group had left long before that time, but once the champagne was consumed the party was pretty much over. I walked some of them to their cars, just to make sure they were okay to drive. For the ones that left early I noticed the street was almost impassable. You may have noticed, this is not a very wide street. I believe I was told it was built as a private drive and wasn't legally opened to the public until 1955. This used to be the upscale neighborhood in Jefferson City. Not so much anymore, but I'm comfortable. Where was I?"

"You were telling me about your New Year's Eve party. A lot of guests and a bit of the bubbly."

"Ah, yes." Looking at his watch, Jack glanced up and said, "I prefer to eat earlier these days and I think the country club is open for dinner. I'm still a member there and I'm hoping you will join me for dinner. Do you have anyplace you have to be for a while?"

"No, sir, I don't. I'm staying at the Hampton Inn just down the road and I've already checked in. I would love to join you for dinner."

"Give me a few minutes and I'll be ready. I would say you are appropriately dressed for the club. Not too many guys wear sport coats these days, so I'm guessing you have something under that jacket that you don't want exposed to the public. Am I right?"

"Yes, you are right. Not too long ago I was shot as a result of this investigation. Still, even before that incident I usually carry a weapon. At the moment, I'm carrying a Walther PPK in a shoulder holster. I hope you don't mind."

"Good for you, son. Hell, you're a Marine. If you can't rust a Marine with a concealed and loaded weapon, who the hell can you trust? We'll go over to the club, have a nice dinner, a few drinks and continue this conversation. You good with that?"

"Yes, sir. Sounds like a plan."

Colonel McKenna opened the door to the kitchen, returning a few minutes later, wearing a light cashmere sport coat and a pair of gray slacks. A striking figure that had not lost his military bearing.

"Do you mind if we take your vehicle over to the club?"

"Not at all, Colonel."

The drive to the club was very short, as I expect it had been when the Klienknects drove the same route so many years ago. Jack was silent during the trip. The parking lot wasn't crowded, so we found a spot reasonably close to the club house. When we entered, the maître de immediately recognized the Colonel and welcomed us to the club.

"Seating for two for dinner, sir?"

"Yes, Stephan. Contact the bar and have them bring my Macallan 25-year-old scotch to the table. My locker number is 2475." When Stephan had left the table where we were seated, the Colonel asked, "Being a Marine officer I assume you do drink scotch."

"Yes, sir, I do, and that's a long story too."

"I'd love to hear it. I've got the time and it seems you do also."

"When I arrived in Viet Nam in 1958 I took over a tank company as the commanding officer. A billet I wasn't supposed to have. It should have been designated for a captain, but I was still a first lieutenant. My company first sergeant took me aside and told me we needed to have a Come-to-Jesus meeting. And we did. He explained to me that he had a lot of combat experience, so we should go with my education and his experience. I agreed and told him I was there to learn from him. We got along great and every three or four weeks he would show up with a bottle of scotch, which we would proceed to consume in the shade of one of our tanks and solve all the world problems. I've been drinking scotch ever since."

The bottle from the Colonel's locker arrived and the Colonel poured a healthy portion, with the comment, "Conner, I don't know what brand of scotch you had in Viet Nam, but I'll be willing to bet this will be the best scotch you've ever had."

I took a sip and had to conclude he was absolutely correct. It was mellow, smooth and could only be defined as a top-notch sipping whiskey.

A waiter arrived and presented two dark blue leather-bound menus, emblazoned with the gold emblem of the Jefferson City Country Club.

"Conner, order whatever you would like. I'm treating tonight, but maybe not next time. So, enjoy. I don't get out often, so tonight is special to me." He lifted his tumbler of liquid gold and made a toast, "To comrade in arms, and to the Corps."

"I'll drink to that, sir." Jack's eyes gleamed with a level of enthusiasm that I hadn't noticed when I first met him in his back yard. I believe he was enjoying my company. I also found him to be a very interesting man, one that had flown with none other than Pappy Boyington and had been in the Pacific campaign during World War II. I felt honored to be in his presence.

It had been years since I had dinner at the JC Country Club and I was delighted that they still had on the menu the filet plus. It was an 8-ounce filet stuffed with crab meat and doused with hollandaise sauce. A baked, stuffed potato on the side, green beans amandine and a house salad. With this delightful scotch, what could go wrong? I ordered the filet plus, medium rare. Mc Kenna ordered the grilled Atlanta salmon, with a house salad.

While waiting for the dinner entrees, I asked Jack, "You mentioned there were a lot of cars that your guests had parked near your home. Did you notice anything unusual when you escorted your guests to their cars?"

"Now that you mention it, I did. Probably one of the last guests to leave was pretty well oiled so I walked them to their car. It was late, or early, however you define that hour. It had just started snowing and was starting to accumulate on the ground. I thought one of my guests had parked in the Klineknect's driveway. I noticed a person getting into the car and didn't recognize him as a guest at my party. I thought I did recognize him, but I wasn't sure. It was cold that night and I wasn't bundled up and didn't want to be outside very long. Anyway, I had only met Gerard's son two or three times, but that's who it reminded me of. I know Gerard had just purchased a new Cadillac a few weeks before, which he was very proud of. Maybe I misspoke. I doubt that he purchased it, because I knew he was a car dealer. He was probably driving it as a demonstrator. I'm not sure what you call those vehicles. Anyway, the car I saw in the driveway was not a Cadillac and the person getting into the car was not Gerard. Does that help you any at all?"

"More than you know, Colonel. More than you know."

"A delightful evening Captain Pennington. I hope you will let me know how this investigation turns out."

"I will indeed, sir. Thank you for a wonderful evening. I'll keep you posted."

We finished our drinks, returned to the parking lot and I drove the Colonel home. He offered me a drink, which I refused on the excuse that I was tired and would like to hit the rack. We shook hands, exchanged pleasantries and departed. I liked him from the beginning and respected his time in the Corps and his heroic efforts in fighting the Japanese in World War II.

Returning to the Hampton Inn, I had a lot to think about. Who was the person in the Klienknect driveway on that fateful evening?

Chapter 30

I had thought of the possibility of patricide before now. Who would have the most to gain from the death of Gerard? His son, Alfred.

After dinner with the Colonel, I returned to the Hampton Inn, took a hot shower, pulled back the sheets on the king size bed, fluffed up the pillows and lay back. Thinking. Jack's recollection of the early morning hours in 1958 provided some potentially important information. As best he could recall, the snow had not begun to accumulate until well after midnight, possibly even 2:00 or 2:30. He had noticed a car in the driveway of his neighbor's home, as well as a man getting into the car. He noticed that the vehicle was not the Cadillac that Gerard had just acquired. Is it possible that he would remember what make of car it was that was parked there in the snow-covered driveway? Not likely. Thoughts of questions I should have asked plagued me, but then there are a lot of Monday morning quarterbacks. I could always return and have a chat with a World War II Marine veteran. I was sure he wouldn't mind.

I had discovered while searching through volumes of information and data recorded by both Gerard and his son, Alfred, that there was a shared tendency to record minute financial details. More searching of those records may yield additional information that could be relevant, but those records were at my office in Illinois, as well as boxes of paperwork housed at the estate in Creve Coeur. If I can get some sleep I might get lucky and have an epiphany in the middle of the night that will solve the whole mystery. A fantasy, but who knows?

A restless night to be sure. No great revelations came to me during those hours, so at 5:30 the next morning I used the in-room coffee maker to fix a small cup of coffee that wouldn't satisfy the longings of any self-proclaimed caffeine addict. It was hot, and it was black. That works for me. Downstairs in the lobby I picked up a copy of the latest edition of USA Today, compliments of the hotel. The news seemed to be a rehash of yesterday's news, but at least it helped pass the time until the hotel began serving a hot buffet breakfast. Scrambled eggs, sausage, biscuits and sausage gravy, with fresh fruit on the side. Filling my plate, I settled at a vacant table and considered my plans for the day. A vacant table? Hell, they were all vacant at this hour.

Thirty minutes later business types began to drift into the dining area, as well as what appeared to be a few construction workers. Although I had lived in Jefferson City for forty years I didn't recognize anyone and didn't really expect to. It was unlikely that people I knew over the years would be lodging at the Hampton Inn. Then I saw a gentleman that looked familiar. He sat at the table next to mine, reading the USA Today paper, not having partaken of the breakfast buffet yet.

"Good morning, sir. You look familiar. Are you originally from Jefferson City?"

"Good morning. Yes, I am from Jefferson City, but that was many years ago. I live in Kansas City now. I'm here visiting family. I'm Jack Garvin. And what is your name?"

"I'm Conner Pennington. I graduated from high school here in 1961."

"I can't say I remember the name. Did you graduate from Helias or Jefferson City High School?"

"Jefferson City High School. Well, I remember your name. I think you were one year behind me. You must have graduated with my ex, Elaine Newsome."

"Sure, I remember her. We went to grade school together."

I was mostly killing time until I thought the appropriate hour had arrived to call on the Colonel. I learned from Jack that he had left Jefferson City shortly after graduating from high school, moved to Kansas City, taught school for 25 years, and had authored a couple of books. An interesting fellow. Glancing at my watch I saw that it was now 7:30 a.m. I thanked Jack for the friendly conversation and indicated I had an appointment before leaving town.

Returning to my room, I shaved, packed my travel bag and checked out at the front desk. I noted that Jack was no longer in the dining area and thought of the irony of that short meeting with Jack, when I was on my way to meet another Jack. Placing my small leather travel bag in the minimal trunk of the Maserati I reached up to close the trunk lid and thought of the open trunk in the parking lot at Union Station. I had no reason to believe my situation here would have the same outcome as that almost fatal encounter. Before closing the lid, I again admired the tan leather bag that matched the Italian tan leather of the Maserati cockpit. To ensure there was no mistake as to where the luggage belonged, there was a Maserati emblem stitched to the front of the soft leather. No one is shooting at you now, Conner, so close the trunk lid and carry on. Which is what I did.

I decided to take my time getting to the residence of Jack McKenna, so I took a short detour to a gas station to fill the gas tank with premium fuel. Unfortunately, this station only had fuel that was not rated at the level required by the hungry V-8. Two gas stations later I found what I needed to keep Mr. Maserati happy. More expensive, of course, but at least the 93 octane would propel me down the road without complaints from the sometime sensitive engine. Depending on my speed, the 24-gallon tank can empty fairly quickly. It's always best to fill up before undertaking any journey. Be prepared.

I arrived at the McKenna residence at 8:20, rang the doorbell and waited for what had most likely been two minutes, but seemed longer. I heard the dead bolt slide open and presumed that Jack had taken a peek through the security hole in the middle of the door before swinging it open.

"What a surprise, Conner. Good morning to you. I'm not sure what brought you here, but come on in. I just put on a pot of coffee. Please join me."

Taking words literally and being a bit of a smartass, my reply was, "What brought me here was a Maserati. Sorry, Colonel, I couldn't resist that comeback. And, yes, I would love a cup of coffee."

I followed him into the kitchen, which had not been upgraded probably since the home had been built over fifty years ago, Jack brought out two sizeable mugs.

"Do you take crème or sugar with your coffee?"

"No, sir. Hot and black, the only way it should be."

"Good man," he said, as he poured the steaming java into both mugs. "Now, to what do I owe this early morning visit?"

"First, I wanted to thank you for a very pleasant evening, and before I leave for Illinois I wanted to ask if you recalled anything else about the incident next door in 1958."

"Beyond what I've already told you, what specifically do you want to know?"

"The vehicle you noticed in the driveway next door, and the person you saw getting into that vehicle might have some importance to my investigation. You mentioned that the car wasn't the Cadillac that Gerard had recently acquired, but can you give me any more details about that vehicle?"

"Conner, I'm not a car guy. If it had been a fighter plane I could have told you the manufacturer, the make and model, and probably even the horsepower and top speed. I just remember it wasn't a big car, like the Cadillac. I can't tell you much more than that."

"Do you have an impression about the color, whether it was a newer car, if it was a two door or a four door, or if it had snow accumulated on it like the driveway?"

"I wish I could tell you more about what I saw, but it was so long ago, and I really didn't think too much about what I saw. As I mentioned earlier, I first assumed that it was one of my guests leaving. I do recall that it was a man, by himself, which did strike me as a bit odd, as all of my guests were couples. The impression I had was that he resembled Gerard's son, even though I had never actually met the son. I had only seen him at a distance and it didn't seem that he visited his father very often. Hell, I didn't even know that it was Gerard's son until he told me one day that his son had dropped off his granddaughter for the weekend. I did meet the granddaughter though. She was a sweet thing and quite attractive. Don't remember her name either, though."

"That would be Mandy. She is the person that hired me to investigate the deaths of her grandparents. I can confirm that she has grown into quite an attractive lady. She and her husband now live in St. Louis. Both of her parents were killed in a traffic crash about eight years ago, so she inherited most of what her father had built up over the years. Mostly auto dealerships."

"My, my. That girl has had some tragedy during her life. I'm sure she doesn't remember me, but I do hope she is doing well."

"She'll be okay, I think." I sure wasn't going to divulge that she was pregnant with my child. "She's been trying to put all of that behind her and she's looking toward a brighter future. Can I get a contact number from you, in case I think of anything else, but also to keep you up to date with the investigation?"

"Sure. I'd love to hear from you and when you're back in town, please come to visit." He gave me his cell phone number, we exchanged pleasantries, I gave him my business card with phone number and e-mail address, then the Colonel walked me to the door. I wasn't sure how many years Colonel Jack McKenna had left, but then none of us do. I hoped I would see him again.

The neighborhood was quiet as I drove slowly through the narrow street of Hobbs Lane. There was no reflection of the tragic event that had left its mark on the families living on Hobbs Lane in 1958.

The drive back to Illinois was uneventful, giving me time to think about what I had learned and what was still missing in my investigation.

Chapter 31

Back in my office I again scanned through the detailed ledgers kept by Gerard and Alfred, looking for any anomaly or indication of who may have been involved in the deaths of both generations of Klienknects.

Gerard's ledger was more detailed than was the ledger kept by Alfred. It wasn't difficult to track the activities of Gerard prior to his death, as it was all recorded penny by penny. Gerard's last entry was the Thursday before his death, when he filled up with gas. Prior entries indicated he had purchased Christmas gifts for his wife, a doll and doll house for his granddaughter, Mandy, and miscellaneous gifts for Alfred and his wife. I wasn't sure what sort of doll would cost $32.00 in 1957. Based on my research of 1957 prices, this must have been a very lovely doll. The average income in the U. S. was $4,650 and tuition at Harvard was $1,250 a year. His ledger did not reveal anything more of particular interest. Nothing out of the ordinary.

Turning to the ledger kept by Alfred, I began to search entries made prior to and after New Year's Eve. As expected, I found hand written details of purchases for the coming Christmas. Unlike the promotion of Christmas in retail stores today, which often begins long before Thanksgiving, Christmas shopping in 1957 didn't get very serious until the early days of December. Numerous entries were made that reflected gifts purchased for Alfred's wife, Mandy, his mother and father, as well as what I assumed were close friends. His generosity was only exceeded by his father. Still, I knew he had been receiving sizeable financial "gifts" from his father, with no indication of repayment.

Apparently, Alfred took his ledger with him when he traveled. On December 30, 1957 there was an entry for purchase of gasoline in Jefferson City. Later, on that same day, there was another entry for lunch in Jonesburg, Missouri, then a much later entry for more gasoline in St. Louis. I had driven from Jefferson City to St. Louis in the early sixties and knew it took almost all day to reach your destination. This was prior to the construction of Interstate 70, when U.S. 40 was a two-lane highway that stretched from Kansas City to St. Louis. Hills and curves along that route often prevented passing the many trucks and slower vehicles. Dinner at the Mayfair Hotel warranted another entry for $28.00. On one of those early trips to St. Louis I had stayed overnight at the Mayfair Hotel. Very elegant, with a lot of dark wood in the lounge located in the mezzanine off the lobby.

Curiosity led me to research information on the Mayfair. It was an eighteen-story building that was built in 1924 and 1925, during the boom of big hotel construction in St. Louis. The only competition for the Mayfair Hotel was the Lennox Hotel, where I had also spent an evening as a guest. The Lennox was a 25-story hotel that opened in 1929 and was at the time the tallest hotel in the city. The Mayfair and the Lennox were within a few blocks of each other in the downtown district. Further research led me to believe that the Detroit mafia had financed the construction and operation of the Mayfair Hotel. It wasn't unusual for the mafia to branch out into legitimate businesses during those years.

The next entry by Alfred was dated December 31, 1957, specifying an amount of $8.00 for a babysitter in the hotel. Following that entry, for the same day, was an amount of $10.00 for tickets at the Fox Theatre. Time for more research. I wanted to know the activities were scheduled at the "Fabulous Fox" on that day.

The renovated Fox Theatre is a venue that now presents traveling stage shows from Broadway, which I have attended a number of times. In 1957 it was touted as the premier movie theater in St. Louis, with the largest movie screen in the city. The Fox was built in 1929 by movie pioneer William Fox as a showcase for the films of the Fox Film Corporation and elaborate stage shows, which it still continues to this day. It was one of a group of six spectacular Fox Theatres built by Fox in the late 1920s. The others were the Fox Theatres in Brooklyn, Atlanta, Detroit, San Francisco and Chicago. When the theater opened on January 31, 1929, it was reportedly the second-largest theater in the United States, with 5,060 seats. It was one of St. Louis's leading movie theaters through the 1960s and has survived to become a versatile preforming arts venue.

The Fox was designed by an architect specializing in theaters, C. Howard Crane, in an eclectic blend of Asian decorative motifs sometimes called Siamese Byzantine. The interior is the architectural twin of another Fox Theatre built in Detroit in 1928. Another connection to the Detroit money, maybe even more mafia connections from the family operating strong in that city and expanding into other cities. Reporters in 1929 described the Fox Theatres in St. Louis and Detroit as "awe-inspiringly fashioned after Hindoo (sic) Mosques of Old India, bewildering in their richness and dazzling in their appointments...striking a note that reverberates around the architectural and theatrical worlds." William Fox nicknamed the style "the Eve Leo Style", in tribute to his wife, who decorated the interior with furnishings, paintings and sculpture she had bought on her trips overseas.

The Fox was completely restored in 1982, with premier club seating that reduced the maximum seating to 4,500. On the last day of December 1957 the movie being shown was "The Enemy Below", starring Robert Mitchum. It was a movie about submarine warfare in World War II, and apparently Alfred thought it might not be an appropriate movie for young Mandy, thus the babysitter. I'll give Alfred credit for that decision, even though it may have been his wife that made that call. I saw that movie years ago and would agree that it wouldn't be proper viewing for a young girl. Having been in combat, the movie depicted scenes that had me gripping the arms on the theater chairs.

Following the entries in the Alfred ledger, I found evidence that Alfred and his wife had celebrated New Year's Eve at the Mayfair Hotel. The babysitting charges showed Alfred Klienknect paid the babysitter for seven hours, from six in the evening until one in the morning.

The last ledger entry for the St. Louis trip was on January 1, 1958. A ten-dollar tip was recorded as paid to the bellman and it was noted that the room was complimentary. No charge. Well, wasn't that interesting. Mafia connection?

To verify Gerard's alibi for the night of his father's death I made another trip to St. Louis. The old Mayfair Hotel is located at 806 Charles Street. In 1977 the hotel was renovated. Some 85 rooms were removed and the interior redecorated, but original features were kept when possible, maintaining the building's historic value. The hotel was added to the National Register of Historic Places on September 17, 1979. Then, the hotel was sold in 2003 to local businessmen Michael and Steven Roberts, who renamed it the Roberts Mayfair Hotel. The hotel was managed by Wyndham Hotels for a time during this period. The brothers built a condominium tower next to the hotel, which proved unsuccessful, forcing them to sell the hotel to UrbanStreet Group in 2012, who then resold it for $4 million to Magnolia Hotels in 2013. Magnolia renovated the hotel and reopened it in 2014 as the Magnolia Hotel St. Louis. My suspicions were confirmed. There were no hotel guest records that dated back to 1957 or 1958. Long gone.

No cell phones during that time, so it must have been quite a shock when Gerard and his wife and daughter returned to Jefferson City on New Year's Day and learned of his parent's deaths.

Unless Alfred had hired someone to kill his mother and father, it appeared that he had a solid alibi. If not Alfred, then who had the most to gain?

Chapter 32

Exculpatory evidence appears to have eliminated Alfred as a suspect in the deaths of his parents. He had an alibi. Wasn't even in Jefferson City on the early morning event of the new year in 1958.

When Sal Moretti called me earlier to let me know he had arranged a sit-down with the Senator my phone captured his number and I later added "Moretti" to that number and saved it in my phone data bank. I needed to ask the Senator some questions and I had no contact information for him. Moretti was my go-between. Bringing up his saved number, I pushed the magic button and called Moretti.

"This is Moretti."

"Conner Pennington here. I would like to contact the Senator again. Can you arrange that?"

"Conner, this is not a good time to talk."

"When is a good time, Mr. Moretti?"

"I assume you think this conversation is important, or you wouldn't be calling me, is that right?"

"That's correct. I only need to talk to the Senator for a few minutes. This doesn't need to be a sit-down. I think it can be done over the phone."

"Alright, Conner. As it so happens, I'm with the Senator right now. We're in his car, headed to a meeting. I'll see if he will talk to you on the phone."

"So, you're talking on the phone while you're driving?"

"No. This is a hands-free setup. I'm pulling into a parking spot near the Hill area. Give me a minute to talk to the Senator and if he wants to talk to you I'll call you back at the number I have on my phone for you. You can live with that? If I don't call you back within five minutes, you'll know a conversation with the Senator isn't going to happen today." Typical of Moretti, my phone screen indicated the call had been terminated.

Four minutes later my phone buzzed, signaling an incoming call. It was the Senator.

"Mr. Pennington, you've got maybe ten minutes to tell me what's going on. Is this about your investigation, or have you decided you're going to come work for me?"

"It's about the investigation. Again, I'm flattered that you would ask me to work for you, but my answer to that is the same as it was the last time you asked. You mentioned a connection to a person named Josh the last time we talked. Do you happen to remember his last name?"

"I'm not sure why you want to know, but yes, I do. It was an uncommon name, which is why I remember. His full name was Joshua Stonewall Jackson."

"Thank you. I may be asking too much, but how did you meet Mr. Jackson?"

"This line of questioning is starting to get beyond what I'll talk to you about on the phone. I'll sum it up for you and it goes no further. Capisce?"

"Yes, sir, I understand."

"Josh was a mechanic at one of Gerard's dealerships. We just sort of hit it off, until his philandering got out of hand, especially when he began charging his flings to my account. We didn't part on good terms."

"Two more questions. Did you ever play golf with Josh or Steve? I came across an old photo of you with a young man, and it appears that the two of you were either going to play golf or had just finished. My other question relates to your comment that you purchased a car for Josh. Do you remember the make of that car?"

"I never played golf with Steve, but I provided golf lessons for Josh and we played at the club when I was in town. The car I gave him was provided from Gerard's dealership. Probably a Ford. Now, is that all?"

"One last question. Did Josh ever accompany you to the home of Gerard and his wife?"

"Yes, he did. Quite often, after a round of golf with Josh and Gerard we would have a bar-b-que in Gerard's back yard. A few drinks and hamburgers. No more questions. I've gotta' go." I didn't know if the Senator had picked up the brusque habit of Moretti's, or if Moretti had picked up the habit of ending a call from the Senator. No goodbye, kiss my ass, or any courteous method of signing off. Either way, the call ended. That's okay. I had more information than I did before my impromptu call to Sal Moretti, Twitch Taylor's undercover FBI agent.

Not everyone has it, but perhaps more people should. Friends in low places. I do, or at least friends that can do things under the radar and have little compulsion to reveal their methods or activities. Okay, my friend is not really in low places, but he comes into contact with a lot of people that are in low places. He's well educated and well-traveled. A lot of his education (and training) is in martial arts, hand-to-hand combat and a variety of weapons training. He's a bounty hunter by trade and a lifelong friend of my oldest son. He still calls me Pops and vows he would do anything for me. Well, maybe not take a bullet for me. He goes by Gunner, not his real name, but that fits him quite well. He reminds me a lot of Steven Seagal. Gunner is big, and I don't mean just tall, although he is almost 6'5" and weighs at least 240 pounds, which is all toned muscle. He keeps a trimmed beard and a long dark pony tail. He has scars from four knife wounds and puckered evidence of three gunshot wounds. He lives on the edge and I knew he had been in a body cast nine months ago after losing a wrestling match with a brahma bull. I had only four or five numbers on my speed dial for my cell phone. Gunner was one of those.

"Gunner, this is Conner Pennington. Are you over your trauma from the brahma bull?"

"Yeah, Pop, I am. I saw your name on my cell screen. I haven't heard from you in a while. How've you been?"

"I haven't caught up with you yet, but I did take a bullet about three months ago. Touch and go for a while, but I'm good. I need your expertise in an investigation I'm involved with. You have some time on your hands?"

"For you, Pop, I do. What do you need?" Gunner was always eager for some sort of action. I could hear it in his voice.

"I want to locate a guy that lived in Jeff City in 1957 and 1958, and maybe still does. The last I knew of his whereabouts was 1957."

"That's gonna' be fun, Pop. Hell, that was a year before I was born. You got a name for this guy?"

"Yeah, Gunner, I know when you were born…three months after Christopher was born. You might choke on this name. Joshua Stonewall Jackson. His parents must have had a sense of humor, but no more than the Popp family naming their son Soda and a daughter named Lolly Popp."

"Don't knock that name, Pop. My gym teacher all through grade school was Soda Popp. He's a good man. So, you just want me to locate this guy, or do you also want me to do a Come-to-Jesus meeting?"

"Just locate him. My client will pay you well, but no Come-to-Jesus meeting on this one. Maybe later, depending on how things go.

I'll send you an e-mail with a photo of Joshua from 1957. I believe he would be around 78 to 80 years old now."

"With a name like that he shouldn't be too hard to find. I've found other guys with less information. Give me three or four days and I'll have him on your porch, if that's where you want 'em."

"Gunner, my friend, just find him and let me know where he is. Don't rough him up, okay?"

"I'll do it, Pop. Take care. Bye." At least Gunner gave some sort of salutation before he disconnected.

Two days later I got a call from Gunner with a full report on Joshua. He moved from Jefferson City in January of 1958 and relocated in Springfield, Missouri. Having had training as a Ford mechanic, he soon found a job working for a Ford Dealer in Springfield. In the evenings he attended a community college for two years, then transferred to Southwest Missouri State University, where he earned a degree in business. He became involved in city government and was elected a city councilman in 1967. He was also by that time an owner of a car dealership in Greene County, just outside of Springfield. In 1978 he ran for the state legislature and was elected as one of eight state representatives for district 130. He was currently serving in the state legislature as a representative from that district.

He was a conservative democrat among eight representatives from that district that were all republicans. Not that it mattered in my investigation. Gunner gave me his contact information, including his home address, his dealer address, his e-mail and his cell phone number, all of which was posted on his legislative web site on the internet. I immediately contacted my bank and had them send Gunner a cashier's check for $1,000.00. When Gunner goes after someone, they can't hide. His reputation for finding people was as good as gold.

My first thought was to travel to Springfield and contact Joshua in person. I discussed this with Margo, who had been involved in this investigation from the beginning, except for the momentary indiscretion with Mandy. I called it momentary, but I didn't think Margo would. She declined to make this trip because of a scheduled dental appointment.

On a Thursday morning I packed and drove my Maserati down Interstate 44 to Springfield. Almost 200 miles later I checked into the Drury Inn & Suites at 2715 Glenstone Avenue, one of the main drags in Springfield. When working for the Missouri Department of Public Safety I had often stayed in this area. The Highway Patrol Headquarters was one half mile from the Drury and the Springfield Police Headquarters is only four miles distance. My plan was to take advantage of the social hour at the Drury, have dinner and get a good night's rest before paying a visit to Joshua Stonewall Jackson at his dealership the next morning, if in fact he would be there. If not, I had his cell phone number, his home address, and the number for his legislative office in Jefferson City, although I knew the legislature was not in session during the summer recess.

When in Springfield I often ate at the Steak & Ale restaurant on South Glenstone. Why not tonight? I found the restaurant, but it had a different name. Jimm's Steakhouse & Pub. My waitress was Amber, who recommended the prime rib, which I love when prepared well. Hard to forget the name Amber. That was the name of my brother's daughter. An appetizer of escargot and a Manhattan Up while I waited for my main meal. An excellent choice. Returning to the Drury Inn I planned my "assault" for the next day, took a hot shower, fluffed up the pillows and went to bed.

I was taking a chance that Representative Jackson would be at the Ford dealership in the morning. I had known other legislators who had owned auto dealership while serving in the state legislature. Along the way there had also been doctors, lawyers, merchants and thieves. All with their own ideology and some with do good intentions.

I drove south on Glenstone, then east on Sunshine to the interchange of U.S. 65. This highway had been expanded from two lanes to a divided four lane some years ago, mostly to accommodate the flow of traffic going to Branson, Missouri.

The Ford dealership wasn't difficult to find, as there were billboards along the highway advertising the location and touting it as the premier dealership in Springfield. Stonewall Ford. Legislators and car dealers apparently have huge egos and love seeing their names on posters, billboards and flyers. Name recognition helps in getting votes as well as selling cars. Since I had worked for the Missouri Auto Dealers Association for seven years I knew that a number of legislator/dealer owners kept an office at the dealership, serving a dual purpose as a contact point for not only customers, but also showing a presence and conducting business for their position in either the state senate or house of representatives. As I drove into the lot of Stonewall Ford, I was hoping this was the case with Joshua Stonewall Jackson. As I entered the large glassed showroom, I was immediately greeted by a salesman.

"Good morning, sir. I see you like nice cars. That's a Maserati, isn't it? Are you looking for a trade today, maybe a new Mustang GT with all the extras? Today could be your lucky day. We can make you a great deal."

"Good morning. Yes, that's a Maserati, but I'm not looking to trade it in for a Mustang. I'm here to talk to Joshua Jackson."

The salesman was a bit crestfallen as he replied, "Honestly, we can make you a very nice deal today." A long pause, then he continued, "Mr. Jackson is not here at the moment, but he should be arriving in the next half hour. He usually comes in around 9:30 or 10:00 in the morning. Is this related to his position as a state legislator?"

Not wanting to divulge my true mission, I simply replied, "Yes, it is." I wasn't above delivering a little white lie now and then.

"May I tell Mr. Jackson who is calling when he comes in?" I gave him my card, which only listed me as a principal associate in the Condor Consulting Group. Could be anything, right?

"Well, sir, would you like a cup of coffee while you wait?"

"That would be great. Thank you. Just black, please."

As I waited for the arrival of Mr. Jackson I pondered my plan of action. I wore a wrist watch that recorded audio, video and took photos. I wasn't sure where my conversation with Jackson would take me, but my intention was to surreptitiously record the entire conversation on my wrist mounted device. Having studied Missouri law, I knew my parameters for eavesdropping. The statute in Missouri relating to recording a conversation or a phone call only requires that one person is aware that they are being recorded. I also knew the word eavesdropper originally meant one who stands in the eavesdrop of a building and listens to conversations inside. So, now I'm officially an eavesdropper, of sorts.

Time seemed to pass slowly as I waited for Jackson. From my seat next to the back wall of the show room I noticed a new Ford entering the parking lot, then proceeding to what I presumed was a reserved spot in front of the dealership. The man that entered the show room was the right age and appeared as though he was in charge of his surroundings. If this was Jackson, he had not aged well, even though he would now be approximately 78 years old. I watched him as he crossed the open area and went directly to a door with a sign reading EMPLOYEES ONLY. From the red veins in his cheeks and covering most of his nose it was evident to me that Joshua was a frequent and heavy drinker. Casual attire must have been his uniform of the day. A Hawaiian shirt was draped loosely over a fleshy body that had not seen any exercise in years, his silk slacks were a bright yellow and his leather shoes were white and bright enough to reflect the color of his slacks. This really wasn't what I expected. He did not look like a healthy, happy entrepreneur or state legislator.

Before reaching the entrance to the back offices he was approached by the salesman who had taken my card.

Handing Jackson my business card, the salesman said, "Sir, there's a gentleman here to see you."

"Okay. Bring me a cup of coffee and send him in."

Three minutes later the salesman returned with Jackson's coffee and ushered me into the inner sanctorum.

The boss's office was large, with a large glass desk and a comfortable leather chair, in which was seated Representative Jackson. The walls were covered with photos of Jackson with four different Missouri governors, various other celebrities and politicians, as well as certificates awarded for his community work. The salesman left the coffee on a coaster near the one thing on the glass top…a laptop computer.

Glancing again at my business card, Jackson started the conversation. "Mr. Pennington, are you a lobbyist?" He was getting directly to the point, which gave me permission to do the same.

"No, I am not a lobbyist. I'm a private investigator. I've been hired to investigate the deaths of Mr. and Mrs. Gerard Klienknect. You worked as a mechanic for Gerard at his Ford dealership in Jefferson City from 1956 to 1958. You also had a relationship with Senator Antonio Giocomelli that ended in 1957." Jackson sat up straighter in his chair and his eyes became almost glassy.

"I should ask you to leave right now, but I know your type and you won't stop, will you?"

"No, I won't. Tell me about the early morning hours of January 1, 1958."

"Listen, I was young, impetuous and drunk. I wanted to hurt the Senator. He dumped me and took up with someone else. I've made amends for what I did that night. I've served the people of Missouri for over 35 years now. I was on the city council here in Springfield, I've done charity work and donated huge sums to various organizations. What happened that night was a long, long time ago. I know the neighbor saw me that night, but no one has connected me to that night. Why now?"

"Tell me, Mr. Jackson, how did you get into the Klienknect home? Wasn't the front door locked?"

"Of course it was. I had a door key that I had taken from the Senator when I got the feeling he was going to dump me. I wasn't sure what I was going to do with the key, but I knew he usually stayed with Gerard when he was in town. Looking back on the situation I guess I thought I could go over to the Klienknect's home and use the key to get inside and confront Tony. It never worked out that way."

"Okay, so your motive was revenge against the Senator. You know now that the Senator wasn't there that night. As a mechanic you were aware of the dangers of carbon monoxide poisoning. You killed two innocent people that night."

"There isn't a day goes by that I don't think about that. I've tried to make amends for my actions. What are you going to do now, Mr. Pennington?"

"I've found what I came looking for. I believe it would be in your best interest to turn yourself over to the authorities. I can't promise any leniency after all these years, but for now I'm going to leave it up to you to do the right thing, but I'll be watching you." As I rose to leave, I turned and saw that Jackson was crestfallen. Defeated, but seemed to be at peace, having acknowledged his guilt and released the burden he had carried for years.

I returned to the Drury Inn, downloaded my audio recording from my "spy" recording watch, shut down my laptop, checked out of the inn and drove north on Glenstone Avenue to Interstate 44, which would take me back through the wooded hills of Missouri to St. Louis.

Epilogue

Four days after my conversation with Joshua Stonewall Jackson I called the Stonewall Ford dealership in Springfield. I wanted to ask Jackson if he had done what was right by turning himself in to the authorities.

"Hello, the is Stonewall Ford. How may I help you?"

"This is Conner Pennington and I would like to speak to Mr. Jackson." It was late morning. I felt I had allowed Jackson enough time to follow his habit of arriving late at the dealership.

"I'm sorry, Mr. Pennington. Mr. Jackson died of a heart attack two days ago."

"My condolences."

"Were you a friend of Mr. Jackson's? I understand funeral arrangements have not yet been made. I'm sure there will be a notice in the paper about visitation and the funeral. He was a noted figure in Springfield."

"I'll check the paper for that information. Thank you. Goodbye." My next step was just that. Check the Springfield News Leader, the prominent paper in that area.

Springfield News Leader
July 31, 2014
LOCAL LEGISLATOR DIES

Representative Joshua Stonewall Jackson, of Springfield, Missouri passed away on Wednesday. He was a state representative for district 130, as well as the owner of Stonewall Ford. Friends indicated Mr. Jackson had a history of heart problems and the county medical examiner confirmed that Jackson had succumbed to a fatal heart attack.

Jackson had been a city councilman for seven years and served in the Missouri legislature for 38 years. He was involved in many charities in Greene County and donated generously to many organizations.

A full obituary will follow in the evening news.

An outdated photo of Joshua Jackson was included with the brief announcement.

I had not contacted Mandy yet about my conversation with Jackson, but it was time to let her know my investigation was complete.

"Mandy, this is Conner. I have completed my investigation and would like to meet with you, give you my report and return your family files."

"Oh, Conner, you found the person that murdered my grandparents? Are they going to be punished?"

"Mandy, I would rather explain in person. When can we meet?"

"Tomorrow morning at the estate at 10. I want to hear all about it. Bring your bill and I will settle that too. Will a check be okay?"

"Yes, a check will be fine. I'll see you in the morning. Bye for now."

The next morning, I loaded all the files I had gotten from Mandy. The Jaguar trunk was almost large enough to accommodate all the material, but two boxes sat in the back seat as I drove through downtown St. Louis to the estate in Creve Coeur.

It wasn't a surprise that Mandy was again standing at the front door, waiting for me, but it was a surprise to see the elegant Aston Martin DB4/GT Zagato sitting in the curved driveway behind the Neptune fountain. Admiring the curves of the Aston Martin, I was temporarily distracted, until Mandy touched my arm.

"Conner, come inside, tell me all about it and let's celebrate. I have champagne cooling. Is that okay?"

"That works for me, Mandy." A hug, a kiss on the cheek, then she led me inside to the library.

While pouring the champagne into two flutes she said, "I have some news for you. I'm in the process of filing for divorce. I also had a recent sonogram and the doctor has confirmed that it's a boy. His middle name will be Conner, if that's okay with you."

"Well, I know you said you were hoping for a son, so, congratulations. As for giving him the middle name of Conner, that's entirely up to you. Our liaison at Pere Marquette was not something I had planned, but in a way, I am honored you chose me to be the father of your child. I am certainly not a marital counselor, but you might want to reconsider your divorce and perhaps work on rebuilding a relationship with Nathan to give this baby boy a father figure in his life."

"No, Conner, that isn't going to happen. My dear Dr. Barrows has shown me how little he cares. I see no reason to try reconciliation. I did take your advice though, and I moved most of my father's collection of automobiles to the facility owned by Giocomelli. I have also opened a numbered account in Switzerland. Now, tell me about the person that killed my grandparents."

"With the help of a friend I located the person that murdered your grandparents. Then I met with him. I have a recording of that meeting. No one else has heard this recording and after I play it, no one else will hear it again." Mandy sat silently, listening to the recording.

When the conversation with Jackson was completed, she sighed deeply and said, "Has he turned himself in to the authorities? He should be in jail right now."

"Justice is a fickled mistress. I checked on him four days after our meeting, and he did not turn himself in. Perhaps due to the stress caused by knowing that his secret had been uncovered, he had a fatal heart attack, two days after our meeting. I see no reason now to divulge his past."

"Okay, Conner, perhaps there is justice in that outcome. At least now I know what really happened. Thank you for digging through that mess and discovering the truth about the deaths of my grandparents. Have you prepared a statement of your time and expenses for your work?"

"Yes, I have." I gave her three sheets of printed documents, which reflected my expenses and time. The total amount was $42, 459. There was no hesitation as she removed her checkbook from her purse and wrote out a check. When she handed me the check I noted that she had rounded it up to $45,000.

"Mandy, you don't need to increase the amount. We agreed in the beginning what my fee would be, plus expenses."

"My dear Conner, you have brought me an inner peace in so many ways. Solving the mystery of my grandparent's deaths and providing me with a son that will be an important part of my life. I want you to know how grateful I am. There is a reason the Aston Martin is parked in the driveway. There is no way in hell that my soon to be ex will get his hands on that car. I know you love that car and I hope it will have some special memories for you." She handed me the keys to the Aston Martin. "It's yours, Conner."

"Mandy, Mandy. I don't know what to say. Your generosity is overwhelming, but I can't accept such a valuable gift."

"You must, Conner. It has already been taken off my asset list. I know you can't take it with you today, so make arrangements to bring a driver when you return. I want it out of here soon and I want you to enjoy a motor car that you richly deserve. I'll think of you often and will remember our special interlude at Pere Marquette, resulting in a gift that is more precious to me than the DB4 Zagato."

Still stunned by the thought of owning this very special motor car, I put the keys back on the desk and tore up the check Mandy had written. "I can't accept the check and the car too. Take the keys, put the car back in the garage, and I will contact you when I have a driver with me." I raised my champagne flute and we gently touched the rims in a tinkle of fine crystal. Mandy seemed very pleased with herself. She was, quite simply, radiant.

For the next thirty minutes Mandy and I carried boxes and files from the Jaguar to the library. With the transfer completed, Mandy gave me another hug, lasting longer than I was comfortable with, then said, "Don't wait too long to pick up your DB4."

"Does tomorrow at this time work for you? If so, I will find a driver to facilitate transporting the DB4 to its new home."

"Until tomorrow, then. Thank you, Conner. Thank you."

I arrived at the Barrow estate the next morning at the appointed hour, with my driver, Margo. The Aston Martin was parked again in front of the imposing home, behind the Neptune fountain. That was no surprise, but the surprise was yet to come. Typically, Mandy would be waiting on the front steps. She was not. An older black gentleman was now standing where Mandy normally waited. I parked the Maserati, walked around the front of the car, and opened the door for Margo. As I approached the gentleman on the steps, he extended his hand and introduced himself.

"Mr. Pennington, I presume. I'm Gordon Wheeler. Miss Barrow asked me to meet you here and to give you this envelope, as well as the keys to the DB4. I see you are driving a very nice 90th Anniversary edition of the Maserati Gran Sport Coupe and have every confidence that you will take care of and cherish the DB4. I have taken care of Mr. Barrows motor cars for years, but I understand that will no longer be necessary. Miss Barrows has provided a very nice retirement plan for me, and I'm ready. My ancestors are from England, where they have all been involved in carriages and motor cars. Perhaps that's where the name Wheeler comes from. Miss Barrows speaks highly of you and has every confidence that you will enjoy this motor car, just as it should be." Mr. Wheeler handed me the envelope and walked to a red 911 Porsche, opened the door, got in, and drove away. Perhaps his retirement gift from Mandy.

I opened the envelope. A hand-written note was inside.

Dear Conner:

I'm sorry, but I just couldn't bear to say goodbye to you again. By now Mr. Wheeler will have given you this note and the keys to an awesome vehicle. I know you will enjoy it and cherish it for years to come.

In the front passenger seat, you will find the title that has been signed over to you, as well as all the maintenance records and manuals.

I can never thank you enough for EVERYTHING, but I hope this motor car indicates my eternal gratitude.

Always,
Mandy

Two months after the conclusion of the Barrows investigation Margo and I purchased a property in Fort Worth, Texas. My only requirement was that the home have a three-car garage. Margo's requirements went beyond that, but we reached an agreement and prepared to move to Texas. No more long drives at Thanksgiving and Christmas to visit her family in Texas. No more southern Illinois freezing winters.

In addition to the traditional movers, I called a company that provided enclosed auto transport. They picked up my Maserati, two motorcycles, and a very rare and exquisitely beautiful and awesome Aston Martin DB4/GT Zagato.

What adventures might arise in Texas I didn't yet know. It's a big state. Anything can happen.

CPSIA information can be obtained
at www.ICGtesting.com
Printed in the USA
FFOW03n1705110418
46228930-47594FF

9 781478 797630